D0827986

i'm not her

i'm not her

cara sue achterberg

SOMERSET CO. LIBRARY
BRIDGEWATER, N.J. 08807

This is a work of fiction. Names, characters, places, and incidents are either products of the author's imagination or are used fictitiously. Any resemblance to actual events, locales, organizations, or persons living or dead, is entirely coincidental and beyond the intent of either the author or the publisher.

Studio Digital CT, LLC
P.O. Box 4331
Stamford, CT 06907

Copyright © 2015 by Cara Sue Achterberg
Cover design by Barbara Aronica-Buck

Story Plant Paperback ISBN: 978-1-61188-215-5
Fiction Studio Books E-book ISBN: 978-1-936558-67-4

Visit our website at www.TheStoryPlant.com

All rights reserved, which includes the right to reproduce this book or portions thereof in any form whatsoever except as provided by US Copyright Law. For information, address The Story Plant.

First Story Plant Printing: August 2015
Printed in the United States of America

0 9 8 7 6 5 4 3 2 1

For my mother, who taught me that everyone's got a story.

I wish that for just one time you could stand inside my shoes
And just for that one moment, I could be you
—Bob Dylan

chapter 1

~ ~

It's a Tuesday like any other when I stop in the Shop N Save to grab the weekly donuts for the staff meeting. I'm not invited to the staff meeting, but that's not the point. I'm only an assistant claims adjuster. Truth be told, I don't really adjust anything, except everyone else's paperwork. I don't eat donuts either, too much sugar, white flour, and fat.

Waiting in line, I study Leann, like I always do. I don't know why I'm so fascinated by her. Sometimes you can't divert your eyes from things that repulse you. The back of the cashier's stand cuts into her butt, dividing her in two and causing her fat to pile on the stand like newspapers waiting to be delivered. That can't be comfortable. It must leave lines on her skin the same way my lawn chairs tattoo the back of my thighs.

Leann's stringy, dirt-colored hair usually hangs in her face, but some days, like today, she pulls it back on one side with a tiny pastel-colored plastic barrette, the kind my mother uses on her Shitzu. Her teeth are straight, but yellow, and the only makeup she wears is a garish green eyeliner.

Leann calls for a price check and waits, picking at her nails. I don't have time for this. I'm already late. I'd skip it, except the donuts make everyone else at the office somewhat indebted to me. The fashion magazines catch my attention, and I mentally compare myself to each of the cover models. I look up to see Leann roll her eyes at the nervous woman who says she doesn't need the olives anyway so forget the price check.

When the man in front of me steps up, Leann nods at him. He teases her. It's charitable flirting. I arrange my groceries on the belt and smile blandly at the man as I reach over his groceries for a plastic divider. He looks me over appraisingly and starts to say something, but is cut off by Michael Jackson's "Thriller," a telling ringtone for a balding white man.

I'm not certain of the next chain of events. I remember Leann wrestling with the change drawer. She can't slip the credit card receipt in the slot because something is blocking it, so she begins shaking the machine to shift the contents. The oversized metal Valentine's Day card attached to the lane pole begins to sway as Leann's bulk rattles the cash register. Sometimes events happen in slow motion and your brain freezes and you simply watch the train wreck or the car accident as it happens, never moving to avert disaster. I see something large crash towards me. I wonder briefly why I don't move out of the way. Then everything goes black.

I feel a funny floating sensation, like I'm a balloon lifting off. I see the nasty linoleum grocery store floor receding from view, and it's all eerily surreal until a powerful surge, kind of like the time I touched the static ball in physics class, rushes through me and I'm slammed back to reality.

When the grocery store comes back into focus, something has shifted. I'm standing behind the register, which is crazy because I can see myself clearly lying on the floor as blood pools around my head. The manager kneels next to my body frantically stuffing magazines under my head. I know I'm not dead because I hear my own voice asking, "What happened?" No one answers. A small black guy appears next to my body and says, "Shit!" in a voice that seems more annoyed than horrified, before picking up the Valentine's display that inflicted this trauma.

As I watch myself, all I can think is the blood is ruining my newest Anne Taylor jacket and I'm not doing anything to prevent it. I'm just lying there growing whiter. But then I realize I'm not lying there, I'm standing here. To verify this fact I look down at my hands and notice that they have deep creases at the wrists. I shiver and try to refocus. My head is pounding, and as I bring my hand to my head, I'd almost swear I brush by boobs. I've never been more than a 32A, so the shelf I encounter doesn't make sense. But then again, none of this makes sense because how can I be standing here with a throbbing head if I'm lying on the ground covered in blood?

I try to move, but I'm trapped in the cashier stand. When I turn to get out, I feel my stomach press against the bars from the bag rack.

Another checkout clerk, the older one with the mustache whose hands always shake when she bags groceries, looks right at me and says, "You alright, Leann? That Valentine display clocked her good, huh? Lotta blood. Guess it weren't attached to that pole so tight."

This cannot be happening. Somehow I'm trapped in the body of Leann, and that doesn't make sense. I need things to make sense. I'm a practical person. I don't read science fiction; I don't believe in God; and I'm not the least bit superstitious. I'm in control of my life, my future, and most certainly, my body. This cannot be happening.

When I try to move, I have to wedge my hips out of the checkout booth. People swarm the lane and someone produces a blanket. When I step out into the exit aisle and look at myself lying on the floor next to the rack full of chewing gum, chocolate bars, and travel-size hand sanitizers, my world begins to spin. I stumble back to the bench where old men typically sit waiting for their wives. It's been cleared by the excitement of my accident. I sit down, shocked that my butt doesn't completely fit on the bench, and watch.

Emergency personnel come and lift me on to a stretcher. Someone opens my purse and finds my identification. I listen to the woman mispronounce my name. It's Carin Fletcher. Carin sounds like *Car-in*, just like it's spelled, but no one ever says it right. They always say *Karen*, and so does the woman with the orange hair and black roots as she places my purse next to me on the stretcher. The "me" on the stretcher appears to be unconscious now. The "me" on the bench can't utter a sound.

After the ambulance leaves, the manager comes and sits next to me.

"Leann, I need you to tell me exactly what happened."

I look at him like he's nuts, because he must be. This can't be happening. I read his name badge. It says *Vernon Slick, Assistant Manager*. I don't say a word. I just allow my mind to fumble along with this. I stare at him. He sighs and opens his cell phone.

"I'm going to call corporate and let them know what happened. You look a little spooked. Maybe you should go lie down in the break room."

I don't move. I just watch him like he's a science documentary. I'm fascinated, but completely uninvolved. When a voice comes on the line, he gets up and begins to pace the aisle, explaining what's happened. When he's finished, he yells, "Phyllis, come take Leann back to the break room. Have her lie down for a few minutes. And somebody take down the rest of those damn Valentine promotionals before anybody else gets hurt."

The other cashier, the one with the mustache, puts her hand on my shoulder and looks down at me kindly. When I don't move, she puts her other hand under my elbow and lifts. My elbow rises with her, but the rest of me remains on the bench anchored by the extra two hundred pounds and the shock of what is happening. She lets go of me and says, "C'mon Leann, don't make a fuss. The registers are backin' up." Her expression is equal parts frustration and pity.

I don't know what else to do, so I heft myself off the bench and follow her. My thighs rub together uncomfortably, and more than once I knock into customers as I figure out how much space I require. Right in front of the canned tuna, Phyllis stops and asks, "You alright? You look kinda sick."

I just stare at her, wondering when I'm going to wake up. She shrugs. "I gotta get back to my register." She turns and scurries back up the aisle.

I sigh and wait. I close my eyes and try to relax my body—maybe I'm hallucinating. I take deep breaths. A woman with an overflowing shopping cart stops in front of me. She's watching me expectantly, and I think she's about to explain it all or shout, "Gotcha!" and point to the reality show cameras. I stare back at her and she raises her eyebrows. I don't know what she wants me to say, so finally I blurt out, "What the hell's going on?"

She glares at me and growls, "Can you let me by?"

I'm blocking the aisle. I try to apologize, but really there's no explaining myself, so I back up against the cans of tuna and let her by. I'm not sure how it could be possible, but this is real; I'm not dreaming. I can click my heels together and take all the deep breaths I want, but I will still be this fat woman with hair in my eyes and sweat behind my knees. I wander the rest of the way down the aisle towards the back of the store. I find a hallway I've never noticed before, tucked between the seafood and the butcher shop.

I enter through the door that says, *Employees Only*. Two well-worn couches slump together in front of a small TV set. Lockers cover one wall and I find the one that has Leann's name on it. Inside is her purse. It looks big enough to hold a small child. I search it for car keys. I have to get out of here. The purse contains nothing except a paper clip with ten dollars and a driver's license, a small pack of crayons, her green eyeliner, a baggie full of bus tokens, and a house key. I look at her license. Leann Marie Cane. She's twenty-three, the same age as me. Finding no car keys, I take the ten dollars and put the purse back.

I make it to the front of the store without encountering any employees. I walk too close to a display and my hip takes out a package of toilet paper, sending the entire pyramid of paper tumbling, but no one reacts. Phyllis is busy at her checkout, and Vernon is squinting at the register in Leann's spot, so I duck out through the express lane.

Outside it's cold, and I realize I have forgotten to bring Leann's coat. I hug myself, horrified and at the same time intrigued by the fat rolls that engulf me. We have no taxis in our town, at least none that take people anywhere but the prom, so I look around for a bus stop. I've never noticed it before, but it is right on the corner next to the store. Several people, laden with blue plastic shopping bags, wait under a sign. I stand with them. When the bus arrives I realize I didn't bring the bus tokens. I offer the driver my cash, but he waves me on. He knows Leann and apparently considers her good for it.

I fill an entire bus seat, side to side, front to back. It's uncomfortable and a bit claustrophobic and I wonder briefly what would happen if the bus were in an accident. Would I be wedged in here and left to burn to death? Would the other passengers band together like Christopher Robin and Rabbit and pull me out of the tight spot? The bus makes a stop, and it dawns on me that I have nowhere to go. If I go to my apartment, how will I get in? No one will recognize me, and I don't have a key hidden anywhere.

If I go to Scott's house he won't know who I am. Scott is my on-again, off-again boyfriend. We've been together, at least the way we do *together*, for three years. We will never get married, but he is my fall-back guy. He's the one I turn to as a date for important events, the friend who will go see just about any movie with me on a rainy Saturday. Some nights when we both haven't got dates, we hang out together, drink too much, and more times than I would care to remember, end up in bed. I don't know what else to do, so when the bus stops just a block from his place, I get off.

Scott works noon to eight on Tuesdays, so there's a good chance he'll be home. As I approach his neat little ranch-style house, I try to think of how to explain this. Here I am, this enormous woman wearing a Shop N Save smock and no-brand sneakers proclaiming to be Carin. He'll think I'm nuts.

When Scott opens the door, he hesitates, confused. "Yes?" he says impatiently.

"I need to talk to you."

"Do I know you?"

I nod enthusiastically. "This is going to sound really crazy, I'm sure." He scowls at me, but doesn't say anything. "You know Carin?"

"Uh, huh. Did she set you up with me?" he starts to smile, figuring this is a joke.

"No, no, no. She didn't. Listen, I don't know how else to say this, other than to say it, so . . . here goes. Today, I was at the grocery store and a giant heart fell on my head. I switched places with the cashier. Which is why I look like this, and now I'm her. But I'm not her. I'm me. Carin." I wait for his reaction.

He looks even more confused and maybe a bit irritated, but is quiet, trying to figure out if this is a joke. So I plunge on. "Ask me something only I would know."

He folds his arms in front of him. "Look, I've got the game on." He starts to close the door.

"Wait!" I have to convince him. I touch his chest. I know things no one else would know. "I know you have three kinds of toothpaste on your sink—cinnamon, mint, and baking soda and you choose which one to use based on how your day went. I know you're thinking of getting a dog, but you're afraid it will pee on the rug if you leave it alone all day. You wear boxers, not briefs. You run the same five-mile loop through the park every day, circling the duck pond twice so it will be exactly five miles."

Now he doesn't just look confused, he looks scared. I take my hand off him.

"Sorry, I don't mean to freak you out. I just don't know who else to turn to."

"How do you know all this? Who are you?" He searches my face, squinting. I can smell the garlic from the pizza he's been eating. "Your name badge says Leann."

"But it's me—Carin. I don't know where else to go." I can feel the tears starting. Tears have always been my best weapon. I step back, relaxing, thinking he believes me.

He slams the door and yells, "Lady, you're nuts, and if you don't leave I'm gonna call the police." Of course he thinks I'm crazy. At this point I think I'm crazy.

Now the tears come. I need to find me. I need to find out if I'm even alive.

I return to the bus stop, but nearly an hour passes with no buses, so I have no choice but to walk. It's a slow go because I have to stop and rest pretty much every block or my heart starts beating too fast and my lungs begin to burn. By the time I reach the hospital my feet burn and sweat covers me like condensation on a cold glass in summer. At the reception desk a woman smiles at me and asks, "How can I help you?"

A million answers to that question come to mind, but I say, "Can you tell me if Carin Fletcher is here?"

She looks at her screen. "Yes, she is. She's in room 403. Is she a friend of yours?"

She gives me a visitor's badge and points me in the right direction. In room 403, I find myself sleeping, so I enter quietly. I stand next to the bed and look at the bandages on my head. My face is barely recognizable.

The me in the bed opens her eyes. I know she knows. The fear in her eyes betrays her. She is Leann in my body. Finally she says, "I don't know who you are."

"I don't know what's going on here, but I want my life back."

She continues to stare at me.

"Don't you want your own life back, too?" I ask. Now that I've lived her life for half a day, I can see why this might not be a certainty.

For a moment, I see worry skip across her face, but then she says again, "I don't know who you are."

Just then my mother comes in.

"Carin, do you have a visitor?" I can tell my mother is repulsed at the sight of me. Leann is not the kind of person she would expect me to have as a friend.

She stares at me expectantly, and Leann says, "I don't know who the hell she is. Tell her to leave."

"There's no need to be so rude."

"Mom, she isn't me," I say, turning to her and taking her arm. "I'm Carin."

She looks down at my hand on her arm. Her face is weary, worn. She looks like she's aged a decade since I saw her last week. Finally, she says, "Who are you again? How do you know Carin?"

I look at Leann, imploring her to own up. Leann frowns and looks out the window.

"I'm your daughter." I want so badly for her to recognize me, to wrap her arms around me and tell me this is all some crazy fluke. But she can't see past the hulk of my body. I stumble with the words to explain, "Mom, I'm trapped inside this body and she's not me! I don't know what happened. You have to believe me!" My voice cracks. My lips tremble and my shoulders shake. Tears stream down my face as I silently beg her to recognize me.

Now she visibly recoils from me, horrified. She looks at me, shakes her head, and reaches for the nurse's button. "You seem to be a very confused young lady."

"I can prove it. I've spent a lifetime with you." A million images of my mother fly through my mind, but I can't seem to articulate a single one. Finally my brain settles on the image of my mother studying my school picture in tenth grade. I'm wearing a neon green headband and purple eye shadow, stick-on sequins fixed to my left eyebrow, and a practiced smirk on my lips. She'd sent me to school in a plaid sweater vest with a matching headband. Her disappointment and horror were so huge that she simply walked to the fireplace and dropped my entire picture packet in the flames. I remember my fury and her silence. And she says nothing now, as she turns her back on me and puts her hand on Leann's head as if checking the bandages.

A nurse enters the room. "Oh no, we've got too many people in here. Ms. Fletcher can't have all these visitors. Someone will have to leave."

"That person will leave," my mother says without looking at me.

I don't move. I just stare at her as the tears stream down my face and the knowledge that my own mother has no idea who I am strangles me.

"I was born on August 13. It was a Friday. You always said that made me lucky."

My mother turns to look at me. She is alarmed. I'm frightening her.

"Please leave," she says quietly. She is near tears. I can't do this to her. I let the nurse guide me out of the room. I think if given the choice, my mother will choose an unknown person in a normal body over her own daughter inside this fat suit.

I sit on a bench in front of the hospital; it creaks beneath my weight. I consider the fact that no one in the world recognizes me. How is that possible? I was on the homecoming court in high school. I have lots of admirers and acquaintances, but do I have a single true friend? When the sun begins to set, it is not the temperature that makes me shiver, but the realization that I have nowhere to go.

It's too cold to sleep on this bench, so I slowly walk the eight blocks back to the store. I feel disconnected, like I'm living a nightmare or existing in a parallel universe.

When I walk into the store, the red-faced manager, Vernon, is on me immediately. "Where have you been? You can't just leave; we have to fill out an incident report."

"I'm sorry," is all I can say. I follow Vernon back to the office and sit obediently while he tells me what the incident report will say. Then he asks me to sign it. I reach for the pen and write Carin L. Fletcher in my neat script.

He picks up the report, glancing at it, about to put it in the file folder, but then he stops. He stares at the signature. "That's the name of the woman who was injured."

"I know. That's me." I stare at him, daring him to question me. At this point, what have I got to lose? My real body's been carted off to the hospital, taking with it my money, keys, and last shred of sanity. My best friend doesn't believe I'm me, my own mother doesn't recognize me, and I'm stranded in a body I wouldn't want to look at, let alone inhabit. So, really, what have I got to lose?

Vernon looks at me again and says, "I know this has been a traumatic day. I think you should go home now and get some rest." He watches me and I watch him, then he asks, "What makes you think you're Carin Fletcher?"

It occurs to me that he has nothing to do with this. He's not the wizard behind the curtain. He's just a sad, mid-level, incompetent grocery store employee who probably wants to get home to his outdated frozen dinner and his TV Guide. So I sigh and say, "I'm exhausted; I'm not myself."

"Leann, I don't know what to think. I'd like you to go home for the night. Get some rest and we'll take care of this tomorrow. I think you're on at three, but if you could come in a little earlier, we can take care of this. Fair enough?"

I nod and try to look appreciative. It takes a long moment for me to realize he's dismissed me. I heave myself up, try to shake his hand, which only confuses him, and find my way back to the break room. I open Leann's locker and take out her coat and purse. The coat is thin and smells like cigarettes. The pockets are stuffed with the free mints you get from restaurants. Grabbing the baggie of bus tokens, I head back to the bus stop. The bus is crammed with whiney kids, fussing and screaming. I hate kids. Their noise makes my head hurt. Nothing makes sense. I'm exhausted and confused. I can't sleep on the street, and I have no money for a motel room. There is nowhere else to go. I study the address on Leann's license.

When I arrive at Fairside, one lone building looms in the dark, looking tired and crumbly. Building F. I stare at it, wondering what happened to buildings A–E. I find apartment 12 on the third floor. I'm exhausted, sweating all over, and much to my shock, I stink. Whatever deodorant Leann uses isn't holding up. I stand outside studying the door, unable to make myself open it. At this point, I would pray if I was religious. But I'm not exactly tight with God, still I figure he might have a hand in this. I just want my life back. Or if I can't have it back, I want to know what I should do. I am not Leann. I don't want to be Leann. I open my eyes, but the dinged-up red door to the apartment has not magically transformed. I take a deep breath. What if I just stood here? What if I stood here until my body gave out and I collapsed and an ambulance had to come and take me away? How do you stop being who you are?

I take another deep breath and put the key in the door. The door sticks, and when I finally manage to open it, a small face peers up at me.

"Mama! What are you doin' home?" A little boy with tight black curls and a smile overflowing with dimples launches himself at me and I have no choice but to catch him. No one has ever been so happy to see me, ever. "Mama's home!" he screams.

A teenager approaches us. She is so skinny her collarbone pokes through her sweater. Her eyes are caked with heavy black makeup and her eyebrows are studded with multiple piercings. She scowls and says, "You still got to pay me for the whole night. I need the cash."

She rolls her eyes and brushes past me. She slams the door and I'm alone. Well, not technically alone because the small excited boy is squirming to get down out of my arms. I place him on the floor and he immediately takes off, yelling, "Come see what I done on *Starscraper*! I totally killed 'em. Ain't a single one movin'!"

I stand still, frozen. What am I doing here? It never occurred to me that Leann was a mother. Does this mean she's married? There's no ring on her finger. This cannot be happening. I want to throw myself down on the floor and cry, but I'm not sure I can do that in this body. Besides, I might not be able to get back up. I turn to leave, but a small voice from behind me says, "Mama?"

I turn back to face him.

"Ain't you gonna come see?"

Now, this is the point when my reality shifts. As much as I don't want this to be my reality. To this little boy, right now, I am reality. I am Mama, heaven help us. He needs me to be Leann. Like I said before, I don't like little kids. I get especially freaked out when they cry, and this little guy's face is starting to wilt. So I pull it together, mustering enthusiasm to say, "Of course, I'd love to see what you're doing with skyscrapers."

He looks at me skeptically and says, "Mama, you know it's called *Starscraper*." And then he turns, so I follow him. A worn couch with no legs leans against a wall. In front of it sits a coffee table that appears to be an old door balanced on cinder blocks. The walls are barren except for marks and holes where previous tenants have hung pictures. Leann is clearly not an interior decorator. I watch the little boy. He's small, but seems sturdy. His face is smeared with ketchup and his filthy fingernails look longer than mine. The computer could be one plucked from my high school fifteen years ago. Half the screen is fuzzy. It sits on a welcome mat in the corner. The little boy cradles a keyboard and frantically presses the arrow keys to move a small spaceship around the screen. I think of my brand-new laptop sitting on my polished cherry rolltop desk at home. I completely maxed out my credit card buying that desk, but it was perfect for the little nook in my foyer. The laptop was a Christmas gift from my parents. They're still holding out hope that I will do something with the English degree they financed.

There is a smell in the apartment reminiscent of the Goodwill, the locker room at the Y, and McDonald's. I feel a draft blowing low across the floor, but glance around and see no windows to close.

Exhaustion hits me and I collapse on the couch that looks equally tired. The cushions sink to the floor as it swallows me. It may be difficult to get up from this position without some assistance. I watch the blinking lights on the screen and consider my situation. This child complicates things.

And who is this child? He must have a name and his mother would know his name, so asking him is really out of the question. I look around for hints and spot the tiny kitchen. A child's drawing hangs on the fridge. His name must be on that artwork. I get off the couch with great effort. I'm certain Leann is much better at maneuvering this body than I am.

I turn on the light in the kitchen to reveal a refrigerator, microwave, and milk crates crammed with boxes of Tastykakes, cans of

Spaghettios, and lots of empty plastic take-out containers. Ramen noodle packages are stacked precariously on top of the small fridge, and several have fallen to the floor. On the counter, sample-size packets of every imaginable condiment fill a shoe box.

I look at the crayon pictures on the fridge. Each one contains a house, a sun, a little boy, a father, and a mother. In some pictures, a dog sits next to the little boy. The boy is tiny and the parents have large faces with mouths shaped like big O's. I remove one of the pictures and flip it over. *Trevor Cane* is written in black crayon. Under the name is *Mrs. Olsen, grade 1.*

I go back to the living room and ask, "Trevor, what time is bedtime?"

Without a glance at me, he says, "It's whenever Jillian says 'go to bed.'"

"What time is that?" I ask again. I don't want to mess him up by letting him stay up too late on my first night as his mother. He looks at me, eyes wide open with wonder at this woman who looks like his mother, but doesn't talk or act like his mother.

"I don't know. I can't tell clocks," he says, still watching me even though loud explosions come from the computer.

I look at my watch, which isn't on my wrist, and say, "I think it's time to get ready for bed." I wait to see his reaction. He drops the keyboard and gets up.

"I want a snack first," he says. I watch as he opens a box of store-brand Froot Loops and retrieves a napkin from one of the milk crates. He carefully spreads the napkin and fills it with Froot Loops. Then he pulls up the corners of the napkin like Santa's sack and takes his snack back to the couch. He flips on the TV and starts watching the news. I'm amazed.

I find my way to the bedroom where a double bed sags in its frame, shadowed by a dinged-up headboard and covered by a faded flowered bed spread. Next to it is a Scooby-Doo sleeping bag and an Incredible Hulk pillow. I head to the bathroom. One dangling light illumines a cracked mirror over a sink littered with brown paper towels, the kind you find in public restrooms. Under the sink are more packs of paper towels, most likely pilfered from area restaurants. The toilet is filthy. Ten or fifteen gigantic toilet paper rolls, the kind meant for industrial dispensers, are stacked like tires and for a moment I consider how much fun it would be to roll one down a hill, leaving a long white line behind it. I wonder if Trevor has done this, since one roll sits atop a huge pile of unwound toilet paper.

What stops me in my tracks is the can of shaving cream and the man's razor. Next to them is a bottle of Old Spice and nose hair clippers. Oh My God! Is a man about to walk into this apartment and assume I'm Leann? My heart races as I call to Trevor, "Trevor, is your daddy coming home tonight?"

After a long pause, a little head appears in the doorway. "Why would Daddy be here tonight? It's Tuesday. He ain't ever here 'cept Friday and Saturday." He disappears.

Relief. So I have three days to get out of this before I have to deal with a husband. What is his name? What does he look like? I don't even want to think about him. But apparently I won't have to, until Friday, since the apartment has no phone.

I stare at Leann in the mirror. It is scary. I undress carefully, watching the portion of Leann I can see in the tiny mirror as I go. I'm astounded at the way my flesh pools around my middle and sags over my knees. My breasts droop a bit, and they're much bigger than any breasts I ever had or imagined. My butt actually feels square. Is that possible? I look for something redeeming. The feet are gross—covered in calluses and bunions, no wonder they hurt so much. I consider Leann's elbows, shoulders, and finally settle on her neck. It's not bad. Considering how much extra weight she carries, her neck doesn't have rolls. Besides the extra chin or two hiding her neck, it isn't bad.

All my life I've always been that girl who can eat anything and stay thin. Not that I do eat anything—I'm compulsive about healthy eating now, but I wasn't always. It used to make all my college friends jealous that I could polish off an entire carton of Ben & Jerry's, drink bottles of wine every weekend, snack on Reese's cups and barbeque potato chips and never gain an ounce.

I decide to take a shower. I smell, and I need to do something familiar. I love showers; they are my safe place. It takes five minutes for hot water to appear, and then it lasts less than three minutes. I crash into the wall in my hurry to get out when it turns icy. Rubbing a circle clear in the mirror, I comb my hair. It feels like playing hairstylist with the mannequin head I had as a little girl. I set the comb carefully on the rim of the sink and watch the tears roll down my reflection.

In Leann's bedroom, I look through cardboard boxes stacked in the corner, stepping over the clothes that litter the floor. I find an XXL T-shirt and shorts. I'll have to search for underwear tomorrow.

Back in the living room, Trevor's *Starscraper* battles have not ended.

"Trevor, I thought I told you it was time for bed."

"You did," he says without flinching.

"That means you should get in bed."

"I will," he says, still not moving.

I stand and watch for a few minutes, waiting. He doesn't move. I try to imagine what my own mother would do, but since she wouldn't even be able to stomach the apartment for starters, I decide channeling her won't help. I've had just about enough of this day and I can feel my anger crowding my control. The computer's on/off button is too close to the floor for me to reach, so I yank the power cord out of the wall.

"Hey!" he yells.

"It's time for bed."

"That ain't fair. I ain't done."

"You are now."

Trevor glares at me; gone is the sweet face, the dimples, the adoring eyes. He is all anger now. He stomps past me and crawls into his sleeping bag. I follow him and stand in the doorway.

"Don't you need to brush your teeth?" I ask.

"I already did," he mumbles.

"When?"

"Yesterday," he says without a trace of sarcasm.

"You need to brush your teeth every day, Trevor," I say, trying to sound like a mom.

He climbs out of the sleeping bag, stomps past me, and heads for the bathroom. "Since when?" he tosses back at me with his mouth full of toothpaste.

Later, lying in bed listening to Trevor's soft snores, I can't sleep. On one side, the bed feels like it has a pipe running through it and on the other side there is a huge hole. I balance precariously on the edge of the hole with my back against the pipe and consider the possibility that this is hell.

ᴎ ᴎ

leann

If it weren't for the skinny lady with nasty red lipstick hangin' on the bedrail, I'd think I was in heaven. The bed is soft like fresh marshmallows and everything's all in order just like the hospital on *Fairmont Park*, my favorite soap opera. As soon as she sees me lookin' at her, the skinny woman starts cryin'. I don't know who the hell she is or why she's bawlin'. Hell, I don't even know how I got here.

"Oh, Carin. I thought we'd lost you. Oh baby, how do you feel?"

I try to sit up but my head explodes in about a million pieces, so I lay back down. I'm fading back to la-la land when a nurse comes in.

"Hey, look who's back among the living!" she says in a sing-songy voice just like Nurse Cadigan's on *Fairmont Park*, heck she even looks a little like her. I look around to be sure there ain't no cameras rollin'.

The nurse takes my arm and wraps a band around it to take my blood pressure. I remember them doin' that when Trevor was born. The bizarre thing is my arm looks like all the air's gone out of it. I hold it out and stare at it. She keeps movin' it back to the bed.

"It's okay, dear. Your rings are with your clothes. Everything's fine."

Only everything is not fine 'cause the skinny lady keeps callin' me the wrong name and my arm shrank. I can't understand anything she's sayin', so I close my eyes and pretend to sleep.

Once she leaves, I hold my arm up in the air and check it out. It's still skinny. I lift the other one and it's just as skinny. What happened to me? I feel for my belly, but it ain't there. My boobs are gone too.

I can't reach my legs, but I lift them up a little and they look different too. I don't know what the hell's happened. I always been fat. How can I not be fat? Am I dead? Have I been in a coma for two years, like Wendy on *Fairmont Park*?

The skinny lady comes floatin' in like an angel, only I figure angels don't wear so much makeup. She takes my hand and looks at me like I'm the damn winning lottery ticket. I'm pretty sure she wants me to say somethin'.

"Hi," I say.

"Oh Carin, you gave us quite a scare. I've never been so frightened. Your father even canceled his golf game and sat here all morning."

I watch her, but I don't know what to say. I ain't got no pop, so I don't know who she's talkin' 'bout.

"I ain't got a pop," I say and shrug my shoulders. "Who are you?"

The skinny lady starts cryin' and ringin' the nurses' buzzer over and over. When the nurse comes in, she pulls her away from me and whispers loud, like I can't hear.

"She doesn't seem to remember who she is. She doesn't even know who I am. I need to speak with a doctor right now. Maybe we need a neurosurgeon."

The nurse nods, looks at me all sad like, and takes off. The skinny lady comes back to the bed and starts pettin' my arm. It's gettin' on my nerves 'cause her hands are ice cold, but I let her 'cause it seems to make her happy.

"Look, you're real nice and all, but I think you're confusin' me with somebody else."

She smiles a fake smile and keeps pettin' my arm. "Sweetheart, you've had an accident. Your memory will come back soon. Maybe you should just try to sleep."

"An accident? What kinda accident?" Last thing I remember was workin' an extra shift at the Shop N Save. Usually I work nights, but I needed some extra cash. I was gonna get my hair done. I thought it might make Leroy happy. Lately he ain't been so nice. I hate workin' day shift. All the damn customers. Last thing I remember, some stupid woman didn't wanna wait on the price for her fancy olives, and then that snooty chick who buys the organic crap got in line. It's funny, I don't remember much after that, just that ugly Valentine's display falling off my lane marker. Was the bus in an accident? Did someone shoot up the Shop N Save? They say when people have real traumatic events, they block things out. That happened on *Fairmont Park* once. Somebody shot up the hospital and Nurse Cadigan couldn't remember a damn thing.

"Honey, a display fell on your head while you were shopping. It hurt you pretty badly, but the plastic surgeon says you'll never know. Your hair will cover any scars."

What the hell is this crazy woman talking about?

"Where was I shoppin'?"

"The grocery store—the Shop N Save. You were in line and a large display fell. It hit you before you could react."

Now I know she's confused 'cause I don't *shop* at the Shop N Save, I just save.

"Lady, you have me mixed up with somebody else. How many people did that display nail? Maybe I just look like this Carin chick."

"Oh, honey, you were the only one hurt. I know this is all a big shock. I'm going to see if the nurse can give you something to help you sleep."

Leroy sometimes brought home pills like that. I'd take 'em on crazy nights when he carried on. I know I shouldn't 'cause of

Trevor. Oh shit! What'll happen if I ain't there tonight? He might get scared. And Jillian, that witch, she'll probably call Leroy and he don't like to be called when he's workin'.

I don't have time to think on these things 'cause a doctor comes in and keeps askin' me stupid questions like what day it is, what my name is, and who the president is. I think it's Tuesday, and they all looked freaked out when I say my name is Leann. And who the hell cares who the president is, anyways? I don't know what happens next, cause everything gets kinda fuzzy and I nod off.

When I wake up, it hurts my head too much to move, so I just lie here tryin' to figure this out. Some kind of crazy shit has happened. All my life I wanted to be somebody else. I wished I was pretty. I wished I weren't so damn fat. I wished my daddy was around. If he was, maybe mama wouldn't be so pissed off all the time. Maybe he woulda helped me with my spelling and my math. Maybe I wouldn'ta been so stupid.

The only thing I liked 'bout school was the library. It was real quiet and clean. I used to sneak outta class and go to the library and read the books. My teacher hardly noticed I was missin' since I never made any trouble and I didn't talk to anyone in class. They called me Blubber Butt and Fatty Leann. I didn't want to be friends with them anyhow.

Then one day the principal called my mama and told her I'd been cuttin' class. She whipped my behind so hard it bled. I never went to the library again. In fact, I stayed out of school as much as I could. I told Mama I had a stomachache or a headache. If I said I had a sore throat she would make me gargle salt water, so I stopped sayin' that. I stayed home and watched TV and ate chips. Mama worked at the chip factory, so we had all the chips we could eat. She brought home cases of broken chips.

Some days I'd sit on our stoop and dream my life was different. I'd dream I had two brothers who beat up the meanies at school. And a dad who helped me with my homework and read me stories and tucked me in at night. But instead I got a mama who yells at me. God, she hates me. Always has. All she cares about is that stupid church.

I'm still thinkin' on this when a cute guy dressed like he's goin' to a funeral comes in. He looks all worried. I watch him, but don't say nothin'. He sits down next to my bed.

"Hey, Carin," he says, real quiet. "How're you doing?"

"I'm okay, 'cept everyone keeps callin' me Carin. That's not my name."

"Baby, you had an accident. You just don't remember."

"What don't I remember? Who are you? Who is that lady who keeps comin' in here cryin' all the time?"

He looks surprised, like I hurt his feelings or somethin'. Wow, never has a guy who looked so respectable given a shit what I had to say.

"I'm Scott. And that woman is your mother."

"Oh." This is good to know. I look at him to see if he's messin' with me. He seems like he's tellin' a truth. "Tell me something else about who I am."

He smiles. "You're a beautiful woman and my best friend. Your parents love you very much."

"Where's my pop?"

"Well, he was here, but he had a meeting in Vegas, so he had to catch his flight. He waited until they said you'd be okay before he left."

Great. I finally have a dad and he's an asshole. How could he leave without even talkin' to me? I don't know what's goin' on here, but no one ever called me beautiful. And I ain't never had a best friend. He might look like a dork, but I'll take him. Maybe I'm dreamin' all this, but whatever is happenin' is better than my hellhole of a life. Might be better for Trevor anyways. I'm not a very good mom.

"Do I have any money?"

He looks like he don't wanna answer my question.

"Sure, you do. You make a good salary at the insurance company where you work. They give you benefits, if that's what you're worried about. Your insurance will cover all your hospital bills. And I'm sure you can sue that store for all it's worth."

I ain't never had insurance, Christ, I ain't never even had a bank account. And I could sue, just like Kenny did on *Fairmont Park*. Made him richer than God.

A nurse comes in and takes another reading from my skinny arm. I ask her for a mirror. She looks in a drawer and pulls one out, the kind Cinderella uses. I hold it, but don't look yet.

"She needs to rest now," the nurse tells Scott. He kisses my cheek and leaves.

My cheek kinda tingles where he touched me. I'm not used to all this touching. I scootch up in bed. Seems like half my body is missing. This skinny version feels a little flimsy. I hold the mirror up and look. I slam it back down on the bed.

Oh my God. This ain't me! What the hell happened? I take a breath to calm myself and look again. Holy shit! Somebody switched bodies. That only happens in movies. Maybe I'm on a serious high. God knows what Leroy brings home in them pills. Maybe it's something that makes your mind crazy.

I slowly lift the mirror one more time and look at myself real careful like. I'm that snooty girl who shops my line. My eyes are brown. I always wanted a doll with brown eyes. My doll had blue eyes. Well, one blue eye. The other eye was stuck shut and I never knew what color it was. Mama said she was winkin', but I knew she got that doll from the Goodwill. I guess I'm kinda pretty. My nose is real small and I have some freckles. Always wanted freckles too. Trevor has some, but he got them from Leroy. All I've ever had are moles. I don't know what my hair looks like 'cause all the bandages, but my eyebrows are kind of reddish brown. Maybe I'm a redhead. I used to ask Mama if I could dye my hair red and she never let me. Once I started at the Shop N Save, I used a box of Red-Hot Red, but Leroy hated it, so I dyed it back to brown and after that it felt like straw, so I cut off most of it.

All this thinking makes me tired. I put the mirror down and close my eyes. I want to sleep but I got the spins somethin' awful, which ain't fair since I didn't have nothin' to drink.

I can tell someone is in the room. I have this weird feelin' it's not Scott or my skinny mama. I turn my head and it's me. Only I'm lyin' here in this bed, so someone else is in the me standing next to me.

"I don't know who you are," I manage to say.

She's cryin' and lookin' at me like I did this. Like this is my fault.

"I don't know what's going on, but I want my life back," she says.

I ain't ready to give her this life back. I ain't ever had it this good. I like this life where people are nice to you and you have money and a skinny body and a geeky guy who calls you beautiful. Nope, I'm not tellin' nobody nothin'.

She steps closer and says, "Don't you want your life back too?"

My heart hurts a bit when she says this. Trevor's the best thing in my world, but I know I ain't no good for him. Leroy's always sayin' that. I can't help him with his school work. He don't even have no friends. I was thinkin' I should start takin' him to the park, like he's always askin'. Just most days I'm too tired and I know all those other mothers at the park are lookin' down their noses at me. And what if Trevor gets hurt? Leroy says I'm makin' Trevor a pansy. Most days it's just easier to turn on the TV.

Maybe Trevor's better off with this woman. She'll probably read him books and help him learn to play baseball like he's always askin'. Trevor wouldn't know who I am lookin' like this, all skinny and perky-nosed and tiny. It would freak him out. I got to figure this out and then maybe I can go find Trevor.

I want her to leave so she stops remindin' me of Trevor.

"I don't know who you are," I tell her.

And then my skinny mama comes in. She looks at me and I try to look like she thinks her daughter looks.

"Carin, do you have a visitor?" She's watchin' the fat me. She's grossed out. I feel like I might cry, so I look out the window.

"I don't know who the hell she is. Tell her to get out."

"There's no need to be so rude. I'm sure she means well."

Then the fat me speaks. I slide my eyes over and watch her. "Mom, she isn't me," she says and grabs my skinny mama's arm. "I'm

Carin," she insists. The skinny mama don't like this. She looks like she might throw up. She stares at that fat hand on her arm.

"Who are you again? How do you know Carin?"

The fat me catches me starin', so I look back out the window.

"I'm your daughter! I'm trapped inside this body, and she has my body. I don't know what happened. You have to believe me!" I look to see if skinny mama believes her and see that the fat me is cryin'. I hold my breath, waitin' to see what she'll do. She stares at the fat me, kind of takin' stock. She definitely don't like what she sees 'cause she shakes her head and reaches for the nurse's button.

"You seem to be a very confused young lady. I'd like you to leave."

"You can't do this, I need you. I can prove it. I've spent a lifetime with you." She's cryin' now, but my skinny mama is a tough bitch. She don't break. She turns and looks at me and starts messin' with the bandages on my head. I hate when she touches me.

The nurse arrives. "Oh, no, someone will have to leave. Ms. Fletcher can't have all these visitors."

"That person will leave," says my mama, never lookin' at her real daughter.

The nurse takes her arm and shows her out. "Okay, sweetie, you'll have to come back another time.

"I was born on August 13. It was a Friday. You always said that made me lucky." I can feel my skinny mama freeze up. This is freakin' her out. I hope she won't give in. She turns to look at the fat me.

"Please leave," is all she says. Man, she really is a bitch.

I'm shakin' like crazy and the nurse brings an extra blanket. She shoos my skinny mama out of the room, thank God. I ain't got nothin' to say to her and I'm sure sooner or later she's gonna figure this out.

The bed is so comfortable and my head is throbbin'. My shakin' finally quits. I just want to sleep, but my mind ain't finished. Just before I drift off, I have a thought—maybe this is heaven.

chapter 2

I wake from an awful dream in which I suddenly became fat and married with a kid, roll over and immediately fall in the hole I'd managed to avoid all night. The nightmare is real. Fingering the fat that encases me, I listen for Trevor's snores and hear none. What I do hear is the television. I find Trevor in front of the TV, completely dressed, wearing a backpack, and once again eating Froot Loops out of a napkin sack.

He squints up at me. "Why're you up?"

I'm not sure what to say to this. "What time do I normally get up?"

"I don't know. I ain't here."

"Oh," I say and turn for the kitchen, desperate to find coffee. Of course the only coffee to be found is instant coffee in little sample packets. I heat water in the microwave and hold out little hope as I stir the instant granules into the water. Normally, I buy my coffee at Irma's, a coffee shop next to the gym. The coffee is rich, dark, and potent. This is not that, but it's all I have and I need coffee to face this day.

As I force a few sips down, Trevor appears in the doorway. "Bye, Mama," he says.

I don't know what Leann's normal goodbye would be, but then again, apparently she isn't usually awake to tell him goodbye. I say, "Have a nice day at school."

Trevor smiles. He hesitates, and then says, "Have a nice day at work." His face fills with dimples and he turns and runs out the door. I hope that he's safe. Maybe I should walk him to the bus stop. He's awfully young to be headed out on his own. *Stop this,* I tell myself, *He's not your kid!*

It takes over an hour to find something to wear. It's not that Leann doesn't have many clothes. Mounds of clothes cover the floor, but they are dirty, worn out, and most don't fit. I finally settle on a long sweater that hangs past my hips and some loose stretch pants. If this were a normal day in my life, I'd be at the gym showering and getting dressed for my job at Barnhart's Insurance Agency, where right this minute someone is probably arranging to send me flowers and calling a temp agency to fill my spot.

I find a bottle of CoverGirl foundation. The Noxzema-like smell takes me back to high school when I spent hours in the bathrooms with my girlfriends, caking on the makeup, only to wipe it all off on the bus ride home. I touch my doughy face. Is there any point to makeup in this situation? Zits cover my chin. I pick at them for a minute before I hear my mother's voice screeching, "Stop that! Do you want to have scars for life?"

I'm so hungry it hurts. I look in the kitchen and find the only options are cereal, canned pastas, cheese curls, peanut butter, and Tastykakes. The fridge is full of soda, a few lite beers, more condiment packets, and a jar of pickles. I opt for the pickles and then tear open a Tastykake.

I decide to go for a walk and consider my options for the day. I can't exactly show up at work like this. I don't have a key to my real apartment and there's no way I can convince the super that I'm me. He barely speaks English.

I walk slowly down the sidewalk considering my options. Moving this body in any way makes it sweat. It's exhausted simply walking down the stairs of the apartment building.

If I go back to the hospital and make a scene, I could end up committed. Knowing my mother and her ability to block out reality, I'm not certain I could convince her that I'm really her daughter. Leann doesn't seem likely to corroborate my story. Am I really trapped in this nightmare?

I stop and shake my head, squeezing my eyes shut. I double over and punch at my sides. I hate this body. "This is so freakin' unfair!" I yell. A man walking on the other sidewalk glances at me and hurries on his way. I straighten up and take a deep breath. Maybe this is God, or whatever, teaching me a lesson. Maybe I need to prove that I have learned the lesson before I can have myself back. Aside from completely losing it, this seems to be my only option. I will prove that I can handle life as Leann. I head back to the apartment to look for clues.

As I let myself in, my earlier enthusiasm is lessened by the stale smell that greets me along with my own scent after walking up two flights of stairs. I apply some fresh deodorant and look for clues about my husband.

The men's clothing I find is all different shades of flannel and size 46. So, he's a sizeable guy and has no taste.

I wash out a few pairs of Leann's underwear in the sink and hang them on the shower rod. I'm awestruck by the size of them. They could be sails for the remote control boats that race on the river each Sunday. Scott and I used to pick up bagels and coffee and watch the races, marveling at the kind of grownups who would build and race toy sailboats. I'm only able to unearth four pairs of underwear, which is cause for some concern. I can't handle life, especially this life, without clean underwear.

I pull heavy, smelly curtains away from the only window in the living room. There are dumpsters directly below and several pawn shops across the street. A mail truck parks in front of the building. Remembering the mail key hanging on a hook on the refrigerator, I grab it and hurry down the stairs to the box.

Opening Leann's box, I find two envelopes. One is addressed to *current resident*, but the other is to Leroy Jefferson Cane. Leroy. I once had a dog named Leroy. He was a mix of hound dog and poodle, and he was neurotic. My parents hated him because he peed on everything. I came home from school one day and my mom said he must have run off. She didn't seem upset. She told me she would get me a goldfish.

The envelope for Leroy is an electric bill. I open it and discover that Leroy and Leann haven't paid their electric bill in two months; if they don't pay it this month, the power will be turned off. I hadn't considered finances. I realize Leann and Leroy are obviously not well off, but just how poor are they? I trudge back up to the apartment to look for a checkbook or a bank statement or something. I find nothing. How is that possible? How can Leann be living on the ten dollars in her purse and the meager groceries stacked up in the crates?

All my searching has made the place even messier, so I start cleaning. Cleaning supplies are not in abundance, but I scrounge up a broom, dust pan, and an old T-shirt of Leroy's that looks like it belongs in the trash. I'm exhausted at the outset, but I manage to make things a little more orderly. I feel kind of proud at how organized the place looks, but then I remember I have to be at work! I have to sign the incident report.

It's nearly two and my shift starts at three. My stomach hurts. I don't think I've ever been this hungry. It feels almost other-worldly. But this body is too fat. I can't stand the struggle of just existing like this; I feel like I'm moving underwater. The hunger is a physical pain to the point of distraction. Leann's kitchen contains nothing healthy, but I've got to eat something. I grab one Tastykake and fill an empty soda can with water and head out the door.

I make it to the store with two minutes to spare. Vernon spots me right away.

"Leann, I need you to come to my office once you clock in."

I look at him blankly and follow him to the back of the store.

"Where's your apron?" he asks when we pause at the employees' break room.

The apron! It's lost somewhere in the dirty clothes pile next to the TV.

"It wasn't dry yet," I stammer out. "I had to wash it last night and the dryer must have stopped."

Vernon scowls. "Well, I'll see if we have any extras." He turns to go to his office and I push open the door to the break room.

"What a big scene yesterday!" says a skinny guy with a closely shaven head and one Mickey Mouse earring. "What the hell,

Leann? Was it really an accident or did you crack her head open on purpose?"

I have no idea how to respond to this person. He seems mean, but maybe this is the way they relate to each other. "It was an accident," I mutter and look around for the time clock. I don't see it.

"Man! Maybe I should run someone over with the lift and then I could go home early too! What do you think Leann, you could take out another customer with the St. Patty's Day decorations and I'll run one over and then we can go get it on at my place?" He laughs.

I'm horrified. Is he flirting? Is he being cruel? I have no idea how to interpret this exchange. So I say nothing. I put my purse and coat in Leann's locker and walk around the periphery of the room looking for the time clock.

"Did ya lose somethin'?" asks the Mickey Mouse earring man.

"Uh, where's the time clock?" I stammer.

"Did ya crack your own head too? Duh, it's in the hallway where it's always at." He flicks the remote through several stations and laughs to himself.

I race out of the room as fast as Leann's body will let me, knocking into the edge of the couch on my way.

Figuring out the time clock doesn't take as much time as it should because Phyllis arrives to punch her card at the same time. I watch her carefully and then do the same with Leann's card. I've never seen a time card anywhere but the movies.

Vernon Slick is on the phone when I knock on his door. He waves me in and roots around on his desk until he finds the papers he's looking for. He's arguing about a shipment of potatoes that arrived already sprouting as he holds out a piece of paper. I take the paper and look at him blankly. He holds up one finger and then starts rummaging through his desk drawer for a pen, listening intently and nodding to the caller on the phone. I spot a pen hiding under some Ding Dong wrappers on the edge of his desk and pick it up. He smiles and motions for me to sit in a chair.

I read over the report. The blame is placed firmly on my inhuman strength. But the report also excuses my behavior by stating that I couldn't have known the outcome of my actions. I want to argue for Leann. I'd like to defend her, but right now I'm more than a little annoyed with her, so I sign Leann's name, place the paper and pen on Vernon Slick's desk, and back out of the office.

Now what? I have no idea how to work in a grocery store. I have no idea what Leann normally does at this point. I'm immobilized by indecisiveness, a foreign predicament for me. Should I go back and wait for Vernon to finish his call and then ask what I need to do? Should I go to the front of the store and look around for an obvious task? I don't know how to operate a cash register, although I'm looking forward to having the opportunity to use the scanner gun and control the conveyor belt—two things I've fantasized about doing since I was a kid. Before I can decide, Vernon appears again.

"Thanks for not making a fuss. I just want you to know, I'm not holding you responsible. I know it wasn't intentional."

I would certainly hope Leann didn't plan to split my head open. Vernon Slick's tone and his relief make it clear he was entertaining the idea. Is Leann a hostile person? If people talked to me the way they talk to her, I think I might be. No time to sort that out now. I nod at Vernon Slick.

"Mr. Slick, I think the shock from the incident has affected me. I can't remember what I'm supposed to do here. I can't even remember how to operate the register."

Vernon Slick looks confused. He hesitates, not sure if I'm kidding.

"Maybe you should spend the afternoon stocking shelves, Leann. It's pretty slow right now. Why don't you check with Jimmy and see what needs to be done."

"Jimmy?"

"He's in the back unloading the bread delivery. Tell him I told you to stock shelves and set up endcaps today."

Even though I have no idea what an endcap is, I nod knowingly at Vernon Slick and head to the double doors leading to the back of the store. I'm hoping Jimmy isn't the rude man with the Mickey Mouse earring.

It's quiet in the storage area. The cold air smells of diesel fumes. I hear noise near the big garage doors in the back corner. I head off in that direction. I'm happy to see Jimmy is not the same weaselly man I encountered earlier. In fact, Jimmy is a tall, strong-shouldered man with a baseball cap who, from the back at least, is somewhat appealing. He's wearing blue coveralls and high-top sneakers. I forget that I'm a whale of a woman and approach him, "Excuse me, Jimmy, I need a little direction." I smile my best helpless woman smile and twirl the ends of the hair that has fallen in my eyes.

He drops the rack of bread he is holding and turns to look at me.

"Hey, Leann. You scared me."

"I'm sorry. Vernon wants me to restock shelves and set up endcaps today."

"Okay, start with the soups. That sale over the weekend nearly cleaned us out and everything's all mixed up on the shelves. I'll bring you out a pallet in a bit."

I nod and smile sweetly. He looks confused and gives me a weak smile before bending over to pick up the rack he dropped. I pause to admire his efforts and then sigh, remembering that I must weigh over three hundred pounds.

I spend the rest of the hour rearranging soup cans and creating a soup pyramid on the endcap, which I learn is the product display at the end of the aisle. I actually enjoy placing the clear plastic shelves between the cans and lining up the cans, labels out, in a balanced row. It reminds me of playing Jenga as a kid. I loved that game, though it always made me anxious.

My feet are killing me. Leann needs to buy some better shoes. The only shoes in the apartment are the worn tennis shoes I'm wearing and some ridiculous red fuck-me pumps. The pumps are brand new—stiff and shiny and full of potential, except I can't imagine this body teetering on those shoes. Maybe Leann doesn't walk in them. Frightening thought. The idea of Leann having sex reminds me that Leroy will return on Friday. I wish I had a clue about their relationship. Does Leann love him? Does he love Leann? Seems odd that they don't even talk during the week. Will I be expected to have sex with him?

"You, okay?" asks Phyllis, the cashier I met yesterday. I shake my head to rid it of the images of a flannel-clad trucker with a beer gut pulling back the sheets.

"I'm fine."

"You looked really freaked out there for a minute. How come you ain't workin' the checkout?"

"Vernon told me to restock shelves today."

"Poor you. Is he mad at you about yesterday?"

"I don't think so." I consider asking Phyllis how to operate the register. Maybe she could teach me.

"I'm on break, you want a cigarette?" she asks as she heads off down the aisle.

I don't know if it's okay for me to take a break, but I don't know that it isn't, and I need more information about who I am.

"Sure, that'd be great." I follow Phyllis out back and join her on the milk crates stacked up against the building. She pulls out two cigarettes and hands one to me. After lighting her own, she hands me the lighter. I put the cigarette between my lips and flick the lighter. I try not to inhale, expecting to erupt in a coughing fit just like I have the other times I've tried cigarettes, but I inhale smoothly and feel my body begin to relax. Hmmm. I'm a smoker. What other habits does Leann have that I don't know about?

"So, you heard if that girl from yesterday is gonna make it?" Phyllis asks.

"I don't know. Maybe," I speculate.

"Wow. I bet she's gonna sue the Shop N Save. I would. Poor girl. She comes in here all the time. Kind of snobby, always buyin' all that overpriced organic shit."

"Yeah, I've seen her before. I didn't think she was that bad." I feel the need to defend myself.

"Hmmpf," Phyllis replies.

How can I ask Phyllis about Leann, without sounding like a nutcase? I wonder if she'd believe me if I told her I had amnesia. I wonder if she knows what amnesia is. I've got to do something; I can't keep rearranging soup all week. If I don't figure out how to operate the register, I'm going to get Leann fired, which would be alright with me, except I don't know what else Leann can do.

"Phyllis, can I tell you something?"

"Uh, huh," she replies without looking at me.

I can't figure out what to say. Phyllis turns to look at me.

"Is something wrong, Leann? You in some kind of trouble?"

I take a deep breath and spin my story.

"Well, actually I'm not okay at all. Yesterday, after that woman fell, my mind went kind of blank. I can't remember anything."

"Ya mean you don't remember seeing all that blood?"

"Not the blood. I mean I can't remember how to do things—like operate the register. I can't remember what my life is like. I can't even remember what Leroy looks like."

Phyllis levels her eyes at me skeptically. "Honey, I hate to tell ya, but Leroy ain't worth rememberin'. Whatcha mean you can't remember? You weren't the one got dragged off to the hospital."

"I know it's weird. But I'm telling you the truth, Phyllis. And I'm scared to death Vernon will fire me if I can't work the register."

"This is weird, Leann. You should see a doctor."

"I can't afford a doctor. Besides, I feel fine; I just can't remember anything before the accident."

"Oh, shit, I've got to get back on my register." Phyllis glances at her watch and gets up to leave.

In desperation, I grab Phyllis' sleeve. "I really need your help."

Phyllis sighs and looks down at me sitting on my milk crate. I barely fit on it and I think it might be permanently attached to my back side. I let go of her sleeve and try not to grimace as I grasp the walls and heave myself up.

"Tell you what. Come up front with me and bag, and I'll try to explain some of it to ya. Maybe it'll all come back if you just get to doing it again."

"Thanks. I mean it." She shakes her head and I follow her inside.

Phyllis and I work together through the pre-dinner rush. It doesn't seem that hard. The coupon stuff is a little confusing to me, seems like a lot of effort for only a few cents. I'm a great bagger, but I knew I would be. I'm also good at identifying vegetables and fruit. When Phyllis can't figure out what kind of pepper the customer has, I save the day. And later, when I'm able to identify the herb in question as cilantro, she is really impressed. "When did ya get so good at produce?"

"I'm interested in vegetables," I say, and Phyllis looks at me like I'm nuts.

We have a short dinner break at 8:00. I cruise the salad bar and fill a plastic container to overflowing. I put back the apple I had selected after my salad comes to $4.97, since I'm guessing Leann's ten dollars has to last all week. I'll pack my dinner tomorrow.

Phyllis and I eat in the break room with Jimmy. Jimmy has his nose in a book and eats a ham sandwich he brought from home. He's still wearing his baseball cap, but he's turned it around backwards. A small tuft of light brown hair sticks out through the band like a horn. Freckles dot his nose. A fresh milk mustache glistens on his upper lip and there's a small patch of stubble on his jaw where he missed shaving this morning. He never looks up at us through the entire break, which lasts only fifteen minutes.

Luckily, it's slow and I help Phyllis instead of opening another register. By the time we leave at eleven, I feel fairly confident I can handle a register tomorrow. I'm also exhausted, and my feet hurt so badly I have to walk on the outer edges of my shoes. This has the added benefit of keeping my thighs from rubbing together. I don't know how Leann has survived so long in this body.

The bus is late. As I make my way to an open seat, I hear muffled pig noises. At first, I wonder if someone has brought a pig on the bus with us, but then I realize that the noises were for my benefit. I look around and scan the faces, but no one will meet my eyes. I slump down in my seat, hoping the farmyard imitator won't see my tears.

When I enter the apartment, I'm expecting to find the tattooed, raccoon-eyed teenager from last night, but it's eerily quiet. I spy a note on the table.

Had to go. Trevor's asleep. —Jillian.

I look in on Trevor; he's asleep, burrowed deep in his Scooby-Doo sleeping bag. Dirty dishes crowd the table and sink. I look for the Tastykake box and pull out a chocolate cupcake, eating the filling with my fingers and licking off the frosting before throwing out the cake. I eat the filling out of three more cakes. Then wash the dishes and leave them to dry in the sink.

I need to gather more information about Leroy. I find a junk drawer in the kitchen that I missed this morning. It's crammed with matchbooks from girly bars and truck stops. I search through the lost buttons, paper clips, corroding batteries, playing cards, dice, and finally—jack pot—an expired driver's license!

Oh my god—he's so old! Leroy Jefferson Cane is twenty years older than me and Leann! The picture on the license is nearly ten years old. He has a mustache and dark eyes. He looks dangerous, but maybe that's just the facial hair. Guys with facial hair always seem like they're hiding something. His hair is a rumpled mess and covers his ears. He is six three and weighs 210 pounds. I'm surprised to see "organ donor" printed in green on the bottom of his license. I wouldn't think someone like him would be so selfless. But then again, what do I know about him? Not much. He's shacked up with a twenty-three-year-old woman he impregnated at age sixteen. He has no books, no pictures, no evidence of a life lived. He travels for his work and collects match books from less than pristine places. And Phyllis doesn't think much of him. Right now, Phyllis is about the only friend I have in the world, so I trust her judgment.

chapter 3

I wake to the television blasting in the living room. Trevor is watching the news. Why would a six-year-old watch the news? I stumble out of bed and am shocked once again when I look in the mirror. Leann looks even worse when she wakes up. She looks much too old to be just twenty-three. I use the corner of a washcloth to dab rubbing alcohol on my face, hoping it will work like a toner and help with the doughy effect created by too little sleep and a horrible diet. The lumpy pillow doesn't help matters. The alcohol does wake me up, but it makes every one of my zits sting and blare bright red.

Travis perches on the makeshift coffee table, just inches from the television. He's dressed, wearing his backpack, ready for school. He's cutting out pictures from magazines and placing them carefully in a plastic bag that appears to be stuffed with them. He looks surprised to see me. "Hi, Mama. Why are you up?"

I start to sit down next to him on the coffee table, think better of it, and collapse on the couch instead. "I just wanted to spend a little time with you," I say, watching him carefully for reaction. He raises his eyebrows, but lowers the volume on the TV.

"Are we moving?" he asks, without taking his eyes off the screen.

"No, why would you think that?"

"I don't know. Every time I like a place, we have to go."

"You like it here?"

"It's okay," he says, finally turning to look at me.

"What do you like about it?" I'm really curious. I certainly haven't found one redeeming quality to this apartment.

"I don't know. The kids are nice. The TV comes in better than at the last place." He pauses, shifting his gaze away from me. "Jillian lets me do stuff."

"What kind of stuff does Jillian let you do?"

"You know, stuff."

Actually, I have no idea what "stuff" a six-year-old would do. So I press further.

"What stuff, specifically?"

Trevor looks at me cautiously, sizing me up for motives. He puts the empty box on the table, looks back at the TV, and says, "She lets me sit on the fire escape with her, and sometimes we drop ketchup packets on people."

I'm relieved. I don't know what I thought he was going to say. She lets me smoke pot? She lets me watch porn?

"Does that make people angry?"

"Sometimes, but Jillian just cusses at them."

"Hmmm. Maybe you shouldn't do that."

"Why not?" I'm at a loss here. I remember building dirt bombs in the road for cars to run over when I was his age. I get the ketchup packet thrill.

"Never mind. I'm glad you like it here. Can I ask you something else?"

He nods, sneaking a peek at the television, his attention divided between it and me.

"Do you like it when your daddy comes home?"

Now Trevor wrinkles his forehead and looks away. He doesn't say anything. I'm afraid I've stepped over some kind of line here. I wait.

Quietly he asks, "Ain't Daddy coming home?" He looks scared.

"Sure, he's coming home. I just wondered if you miss him when he's gone, if you wish he was here more."

He thinks about this, picking up his spoon and flipping it around in his hands.

"I don't really miss him, but it's okay when he's here. He brings me candy and magazines."

I don't know what to say to this. I'm not gaining any more real information about Leroy, but candy and magazines are thoughtful.

"What do you do with the magazines?"

He nods at his pile. "I cut out the stuff I like."

The microwave alarm goes off and Trevor jumps up.

"Bye, Mama." He's gone. This kid is so independent. When I was six years old, my mom dressed me, walked me to the bus stop, and waved as the bus pulled away. In fact, I'm fairly sure she laid out my clothes, fixed my breakfast, and packed my lunch until I was in high school. Either Trevor is pretty exceptional or I was pretty spoiled.

I spend the better part of the morning putting together something decent to wear. I wish Leann had some real makeup. I find a stash of Trevor's old school papers and read them over my breakfast of chocolate cupcakes and Coke. He's a good student. His handwriting is neater than mine. And his highly developed imagination is obvious. How can a kid left alone with a morbid teenager in a smelly, dank apartment for hours on end be this bright? Maybe that's his escape. Or maybe he doesn't know any different. When I was a kid, we had a kitten that would let us do anything to it. A neighbor kid and I dressed it up in doll clothes and put it in a stroller. We carried it around in a pillowcase. We cut all its whiskers off and painted its white paws with permanent black marker. It never scratched us. It never complained. When guests would remark on what a tolerant cat we had, my mother would say, "It doesn't know any different."

I pick up the plastic bag of pictures and pull a few out. There's one of a family on a beach, another of a little boy hugging his grandpa, and lots of pictures of dogs. He's creating a bag full of dreams. I spread the pictures out on the floor, studying the happy people, the perfect food, the beautiful places. Isn't this what we all want? Trevor deserves these things more than most of us.

Around 11:00 a.m., I start feeling restless. Why doesn't Leann work a day shift? What does she do all day? It's crazy to work from three to eleven and leave Trevor with that freak show Jillian. I've been through the whole apartment, and I haven't found any hobbies, not even a book. I decide Leann's body needs some exercise. I can't bear the thought of putting any extra miles on these feet, so I lower myself to the floor to attempt some sit-ups. I'm barely able to lift my head. I feel something contracting beneath my voluminous middle, so I lift my head and think about abdominal muscles. After ten excruciating attempts, I manage to flip myself over and rise up on my hands and knees. Pushups are out of the question, but I'm able to lower my upper body down and push it back up again while on my knees. Normally, I can do fifty pushups, no problem, but in Leann's body, I feel triumphant when I squeeze out ten modified pushups. This meager effort wipes me out, so I climb up on to the couch and stretch out.

Once again, I ponder this crazy situation. Why haven't I gotten a sign? Surely, this is some kind of test, some kind of trick. How can Leann and I be the only ones in on this situation? Leann must be loving my body. God, I miss it. I wonder if she's out of the hospital yet. Maybe I can call and check on her when I'm at work. Doesn't she miss Trevor?

For lunch I eat pickles, frozen corn, and some stale crackers. I fantasize about the lunch I would be having any other Thursday at Leon's. Hawaiian panini and a blue cheese and pear salad, with mango iced tea. I wonder what Marta thinks of the new me.

Marta Malone and I have met for lunch the first Thursday of the month for six years. She is my only friend who is married with children. She had a storybook wedding two years ago and then got pregnant on her honeymoon, but we have always met for lunch, except when the baby was just born. We were college roommates, and when Marta announced her engagement before we'd even graduated, we promised that we would not be like so many other friends and let our lives pull us apart. Our monthly lunches have kept us together, although I have to admit our lives have definitely spun in different directions.

I love listening to her stories about the baby, but some days it just seems so God awful boring. Of course, I've spent many lunches unloading about my latest break up, only to see Marta staring out the window, not really following my dissection of each word the man of the month uttered. To be honest, we have both been canceling Thursday lunches as often as we make them. Still, I like to think we have a real friendship. Surely, Marta will notice something amiss.

I shove some Tastykakes and a packet of ramen noodles in my purse for dinner and decide to leave early for work. As I'm headed down the stairs, an elderly man pokes his head out of a door and calls, "Hey, Leann, tell that man of yours he owes me twenty bucks."

I turn and shrug and then lumber down the rest of the stairs.

"You tell him to pay me. I need my money!"

Oh Leroy, I hope you are much better in person. I know walking to work today is a bad idea. My feet have not recovered from yesterday's walk, but I need to unload some of this weight. I stop every few blocks to sit on a bench and rest my feet. When I get to the Shop N Save, it's only 2:30, so I lay down on the couch in the break room for a quick nap. This doesn't work out because the obnoxious guy with the Mickey Mouse earring, whose name I learn is Franklin, comes in for his break.

The name Franklin doesn't seem appropriate. I think someone named Franklin should be neat, nerdy, and incredibly normal. This man is none of those things. He smells of stale smoke, his Shop N Save smock is covered in some kind of black grease, and he's whistling the tune to *Jeopardy*. He spots me on the couch and leers.

"You know I like my women larger than life, Leann. I bet you're just waitin' for a taste of Franklin."

He stands over me and I stare at him. I try to convey all the disgust I feel, but he just laughs and mutters, "You are such a crazy bitch. I know you want me."

Franklin turns on the TV to a soap opera and sits on the end of the couch, pushing my feet out of his way and picking his nose at the same time. I close my eyes and try to imagine what Leann must be thinking. If I were her, I'd never come back. This thought scares me to death, so I pull myself up off the couch and go in search of Vernon Slick. Maybe he knows whether my body is still in the hospital.

I knock quietly on the manager's door and it swings open with a loud squeak. Vernon Slick is on the phone complaining about the last order of bags, which have been splitting, forcing us to double bag everything. He waves me in. The solitaire screen is still up on his computer. Phyllis told me that's what he does when he thinks no one is watching, but other than that the computer collects dust. He's afraid of it and he can barely work the computerized registers. I step inside, but stay near the door. Finally, he finishes his phone call and turns to me.

"Leann, how are you today? Do you think you'll be able to get back on a register? The folks at corporate have looked over the reports and I think I convinced them not to tarnish your record with a reprimand. I assured them you were very sorry."

I'm incredulous he could be holding Leann responsible for any of this. So many responses come to mind, but all I say is, "Is that woman out of the hospital?"

"She is, but they've moved her to a rehab facility because apparently she can't remember anything. They think her memory will return as she heals."

Perfect. Leann is much smarter than she looks. Now she can learn all she needs to take over my life.

"Oh," I say and feel the life going out of me. Vernon Slick rushes around his desk and puts his arm around me.

"You shouldn't take this so badly. She's going to be fine, and I know you'll be extra careful in the future."

I shrug Vernon's arm off and turn to look at him. I want to smack his smug, condescending face. He really thinks I'm stupid.

"It was not my fault, Mr. Slick," is all I manage to say, but I don't know that, do I? I scowl at him and leave without saying all the things I'd really like to say.

I work register the whole shift, right next to Phyllis. I'm proud to say that I do pretty well. I only goof up a couple of times and Phyllis bails me out each time. I find a rhythm to the work and grow annoyed at the people who can't load my belt fast enough. I help the elderly customers put their bags in their carts and ring for Franklin to help them load their cars. He always arrives scowling, but pushes the carts outside. When he returns, he says each time, without fail, "Stop callin' me up here to help these lazy old people, bitch."

I act like I can't hear him and Phyllis giggles and says, "You're makin' Franklin so mad, Leann! Be careful though, girl, he's not someone you want as an enemy."

I can't figure how Franklin could be dangerous. He's awfully stupid, and I've got at least 150 pounds on him.

It is almost 9:00 p.m. when Scott steps into my line. I hadn't seen him enter the store. He has frozen pizzas, Cokes, Pecan Sandies (my favorite), a *TV Guide*, and condoms. Hmmm . . . wonder what he's up to. I finish the customer in front of Scott. As his groceries float up the conveyor belt, I stare at the condom package. We have an awkward moment when I look up and realize he is watching me watch his condoms. I smile and a nervous giggle slips out. He smiles back and then gets out his wallet to find his credit card.

I bag everything up, being careful to bury the condoms underneath the pizzas and crush the Pecan Sandies with the Coke cans. I watch as he slides his credit card through the reader and say, "Will this be debit or credit?" When I say this, a light seems to go on in his head. I want to believe he's realized I'm Carin, but that's not it.

"Hey, you're that girl who showed up at my house."

I smile again. "I think maybe I got you mixed up with someone else," I say without meeting his eyes.

His confidence grows, "No, you told me you were Carin."

"Who's Carin?" I ask hoping to confuse him.

He's not confused.

"You didn't tell me you worked here. Were you here when she had the accident?" The accident. It doesn't seem so much like an accident anymore. Seems more like a major nightmare or a really bad reality show.

I nod.

Sadness flickers across his face.

"She was my friend."

"What do you mean was? Did she die?"

"No, she didn't die, but she's different. I think something happened to her brain. Her mom says that she'll regain her memory. She doesn't remember me."

"That's too bad."

He frowns and gathers up his groceries.

"Have a nice day," I call as he leaves. I feel bad about the Sandies, but Leann doesn't deserve them anyway. And why does he need condoms? Isn't Leann taking my birth control pills? Or are they for someone else?

At my last break, I decide I need to get some air. Seeing Scott is a reality check and I'm feeling freaked. I wish for the millionth time that I was back in my own body. I suppose I took Scott for granted. We had some great times, but I never took it seriously. We were both waiting for real love to turn up in our lives. I push the door to the alley open. I walk past the milk crates, lean against the wall, and look up at the sky. It's a clear night and, despite the lights coming off the loading dock, I can make out several constellations.

"Can you see the little dipper?" asks a voice above me. I turn and see Jimmy crouched down in one of the garage doors.

I scan the sky. "I think that's it, right there." I point up and Jimmy cranes his neck to see.

"Hmm. Maybe. Which one has the north star in it, the big dipper or the little dipper?"

Now, I'm over my head. "I don't know. Actually, I can barely pick them out."

"Me, too. Some nights I put together my own constellations and give them names."

I giggle.

"Stupid, right?" he asks.

"No, I don't think so. I think if you don't know, sometimes it's just better to make it up."

We watch the stars for several minutes in silence. I turn to say something, but he's gone.

Riding the bus later that night, I realize how completely alone I am. No one knows this is me and I don't know anyone Leann knows, besides Trevor. Of course, there's Jillian, although I don't think she thinks much of Leann. I don't know if Leann has a mother or father. Does she have sisters or brothers? Does she have a best friend? If a giant Valentine heart fell on my head right now, who would come to the hospital with Pecan Sandies for me?

I look up and meet eyes with a cute guy about my age. He's dressed for a date. He looks away quickly. If I was in my own body, I would have smiled at him, maybe even started a conversation. But no one maintains eye contact with Leann. No one encourages her to connect with them. I feel truly alone. If it weren't for Trevor, I could leave. I could start a new life somewhere. Trevor does have a father, so technically I could leave. My momentary enthusiasm fades as I realize Leann has no money. If she has a bank account, I can find no evidence of it anywhere. Tomorrow is payday at Shop N Save. Franklin has talked of nothing else except how he's headed out to play the ponies this weekend. Says he'll come back a rich man on Monday. I wonder why he'd come back if he was a rich man.

It takes longer tonight to haul myself up the stairs. It's exhausting being Leann. I can hear a TV blaring a *Seinfeld* rerun as I enter the apartment. Jillian gets up and rushes past me before I take off my coat.

"Later," she mumbles as the door shuts.

I wonder what her story is. Where did Leann find her? She looks young enough to be in high school. I turn off the TV and sit on the couch. I take off my shoes and rub my sore feet. What I need to buy first with my paycheck are some decent sneakers. My stomach rumbles. The rumbling has become almost constant. I pull myself up and head to the kitchen to find a snack, but then stop myself. If I'm going to be stuck in this body, I've at least got to get rid of all this weight. I pour a big glass of water and drink it as I head into the bathroom. I study Leann's face in the mirror. Will I ever think of this face as my face? Will it always be my face? I put the glass down and pull my skin tight across my jaw bone. What shape is it under all that fat? I hold back the extra chins with one hand and look. Not bad. Leann might not be too bad under all this.

ल ल

leann

They moved me to some fancy rehab place. Back at the hospital they kept askin' questions, and I didn't know the answers. So now they all think I have amnesia. Scott and Brenda (that's Carin's mama) have been here a lot.

Scott's a pain in the ass. He's cute and all, but God, what a wuss. He keeps cryin' and sayin' how he loves me and don't want to lose me. At first, I thought it was kinda sweet. The tears and all. But Christ, he's a man. Quit your bawlin'. He don't act like a man. Maybe he's a transgender like the one on my soap. This guy Jerry used to be Jill. Completely disgusting, but after a while you forgot he was ever a girl. Scott reminds me of him.

Life here would be pretty sweet, what with the all-you-can-eat menu, the free cable, and the comfy bed, 'cept the nurses keep comin' in here and drilling me on stuff. Stuff I never learned in school, like the presidents, the planets, and then they ask me about Carin's life and sometimes I just make up shit to mess with 'em and sometimes I look at 'em sad like I'm all broke up that I can't remember. It pisses me off when they come in right when I'm tryin' to watch *Fairmont Park*. It's kinda at a crucial time right now. Jake just found out that Pamela lied to him about their kid and he might not be the father. They're waitin' on paternity tests to find out. And Jake already changed his will. See, Jake is dying of cancer too. Today's episode is almost over and right when the doctor comes in with the results, they go to commercial and then that perky nurse shows up and snaps off the TV.

She's still grillin' me when Brenda shows up. Will this woman ever quit? She's brought more photo albums of Carin in elementary school and high school. She was a homecoming queen. I look at the pictures and wonder what it would be like to look like that. I didn't make it too far in high school 'cause of Leroy.

I met Leroy at the arcade. I used to do my face all pretty with Mama's makeup and wear the jean jacket I stole from my cousin. It was too small, but I thought it made me look older. I'd swipe the laundry quarters and spend afternoons at the arcade. It was better than school. I hated school. The classes were boring, and I didn't really have any friends. I was sorta friends with Wanda, this girl who had all kinds of tics. She was nice. One time when we were sittin' together at the loser lunch table, I invited her to cut out with me and go to the arcade.

"Why do you want . . ." she paused and shrugged her shoulders three times, "to do that?" She grimaced and squished her mouth from side to side; she really was a freak. But pretty much the only friend I had.

"C'mon, Wanda. The place is crawling with cute guys," I lied, 'cause I knew the only guys in the arcade were the weird ones who talked to themselves and stank like BO, 'cept on Fridays when the Catholic boys school let out early. "Don'tcha want to get out of this hellhole?"

"I couldn't do that," she said, and her shoulders started workin' overtime. That meant she was thinking 'bout it. "Maybe I could meet you on Saturday."

"Whatever," I said and rolled my eyes before getting up and takin' my tray to the window. The group of guys that liked to harass me got up from their table. They surrounded me as I sorted out my utensils and dishes at the window.

"Hey, Leann baby, want to meet us under the bleachers after sixth period?"

I tried to ignore them. The one time I did meet them under the bleachers, they had touched me all over and knocked me to the ground. One of them had got my pants and undies down around my ankles, but they'd been scared off when the maintenance guy started up the blower to clear off the bleachers for the game that afternoon. Ever since then, they didn't leave me alone.

"Yeah, sweetheart, plenty of you to go around." They thought they were funny. I turned and stepped on the toes of two of them as I shoved my way past. They laughed and called out to me, but I kept walkin'. I'd figured out that if you walked like you were headed somewhere, you could walk right out of the school and no one would stop you. We lived one block over from the school, so I headed home to catch my soaps before I went to the arcade.

They were just boys. What I wanted was a man. I went home and discovered Mama had been to the grocery store, so I grabbed a box of Twinkies and watched *Fairmont Park*. I loved Edgar. Now, that was a real man. He was tall and strong and always showed up just when Victoria needed him. She was a real whiner. I'd have been much better for Edgar.

When the final credits rolled, I dug in the laundry jar and found half a roll of quarters.

The arcade was deserted. It was a Tuesday, so no Catholic boys. A woman with two bratty kids was tryin' to drive the speedster, but other than that no one was there 'cept the guy that sometimes came in and ate at the snack bar. He nodded to me, and I smiled at him. He was older, but he looked mysterious. Most days he talked up the lady behind the snack bar. She was old and wrinkly and smoked all the time. One time I bought some nachos and she gave me extra cheese. That was nice. When no one else was in the arcade but me, she'd open the back window and smoke cigarettes. It was like we were in on a secret together, 'cause she knew I'd never tell. I looked at her knowingly and she winked. I think that was why she gave me extra cheese.

I plunked my first quarter in and warmed up on the Ms. Pac-Man game. I was barely through the third level when I could tell someone was standing behind me watchin'. I glanced back and it was the guy from the snack bar. He sidled up next to the machine.

"You're pretty good at that."

I nodded and concentrated. I got nervous when I had an audience, even if it was just a bunch of little kids. I lost one of my Pac-Men and the down-the-drain melody trilled.

"Tough luck," he said. "How come you ain't in school?"

I glanced at him, wondering if he was one of those school cops, but he didn't look like a cop one bit.

"I don't like it," I said and got back to the game.

He laughed. "I never liked school much either."

It was hard to concentrate now, because he leaned closer and I could smell him. He smelled like cigarettes and cheeseburgers and a little like the old guy Mama made me sit next to at church.

"You wanna get out of this place?" he asked.

I stopped playing and my last Pac-Man got swallowed up. I looked at him. I couldn't tell what he wanted. I didn't think he was like the guys under the bleachers.

"Where do you wanna go?" I asked.

He smiled and offered his hand. I felt my heart flutter. No guy had ever held my hand. And what could be bad about holdin' hands?

I followed Leroy out to his truck that day. He showed me the cab and let me talk on the CB radio. We laughed. And then he drove me home in his big rig.

After that I started skipping school whenever he was in town. At first we just drove around or sat in the truck and talked. He liked to hold my hand. But one day, he showed up with a new truck. It had a bigger cab than the old one.

"Isn't she sweet?" he asked. "Gotta real bed back here, and a TV. C'mon, Leann, what do you wanna watch?"

I climbed back with him. I didn't weigh so much back then. I had to buy my clothes in the plus sizes, but I wasn't as big as I am now. Leroy turned on my soap and lay down on the bed. He patted the spot next to him. He took my hand like he always did and it was just perfect. My soaps and a real guy who liked me.

I thought my heart would burst. I felt all the things that Selma talked about when she was explainin' to Judy about how much she loved Edgar even though Edgar was always chasin' Victoria. The flutterin' feeling only got stronger when Leroy let go of my hand and put his hand on my thigh. I thought my undies was catchin' fire. We stayed like that 'til the first big commercial break. And then Leroy rolled onto his side and looked at me.

"I know I'm a lot older than you, and all, but I'd sure like to kiss you."

No one had ever wanted to kiss me. I looked at him and I felt like I was gonna cry.

"Go on, then," I told him. And he did. He kissed me. I didn't even notice my soap start back up. We kept kissin' and kissin' until it was dark outside and my lips were swollen fat. And while he was kissin' me, Leroy was just ticklin' my boobies, right through my shirt, and that was too much. I thought I was gonna explode.

From then on, we met a couple afternoons a week. My mama suspected something, and she'd check the laundry money expectin' I took it. I'd just smile like the canary and think about Leroy. When my periods stopped comin', I didn't even notice. I'd probably missed three or four when Mama finally said something.

"Leann, you need to cut down on all them sweets. You're gettin' fatter than a hog at the state fair."

I thought about this. I was eatin' a lot. But I was hungry a lot. My boobs had gotten bigger, but I thought that was just from all the attention. The next day at school, I went to the library and pulled out a book on babies. I read the symptoms of pregnancy and I tried to figure out when my last period was. I couldn't remember. It said your boobs get all swollen and tender and just yesterday I had swatted Leroy's hand away because I thought he was being too rough with 'em.

When I told Leroy, he freaked.

"You mean you ain't on the pill?"

I looked at him blankly and burst into tears. "Leroy, there's a baby growin' in my belly. Our baby."

"How do you know it's mine?" he asked. And it was just like that scene with Jake and Pamela on *Fairmont Park*. Only I knew this baby was Leroy's just like Pamela knew hers was Jake's.

When I told my Mama, she tracked down Leroy and told him he had to do the Christian thing. My mama is tiny and Leroy's bustin' over six feet, but when she pinched the back of his arm and threatened him with words I never heard, even from her, he got down on a knee like she said and asked me to marry him.

We got married the next weekend in the pastor's office. Mama and the secretary were the witnesses. Mama scowled through the whole thing. I was wearin' a dress my Aunt Betty found for me at the Goodwill. She couldn't come for the ceremony 'cause she was workin' down at the Quikmart that day. I think that was the happiest day of my life. It weren't no wedding like Edgar and Victoria had, but it was still a wedding.

Me and Leroy got an apartment behind the Laundromat the next week. I loved bein' pregnant and married. I didn't have to go back to school no more neither. Mama told me I was a married woman now and I needed to take care of my husband and my baby. I loved the sound of that—my husband. I worked hard at growin' a real nice baby too. I ate everything I could get my hands on. I knew I was eatin' for two, so I didn't want my baby to be hungry. By the time Trevor came, I was as big as a house, but I knew once I weren't pregnant no more I'd go back to my regular size, just like Pamela did. And that baby made Jake love her even more. I was hopin' that would be the case with Leroy, since he hadn't come home as much and he hardly ever wanted to hold my hand.

But I stayed fat. Trevor cried all the time, and Leroy still didn't come home much. We changed apartments a lot. We'd stay in one until the notices changed from white to yellow to pink and then we'd move, usually in the middle of the night to some other part of town. Once or twice we stayed in the cab of his truck. I liked that a lot, especially when we got to ride with him on one of his runs. Leroy'd get all pissed though if Trevor cried, and he did that a lot.

Once Trevor got old enough for school, Leroy found the apartment we're in now. It's paid for up front 'cause of some business associate of Leroy's. He never tells me their names, says I don't need to know. Sometimes they come to our apartment, but Leroy makes me stay in the bedroom or go somewhere with Trevor. A lot of times it's Sunday morning when me and Trevor are at church. I don't know what kind of business associate you meet with on a Sunday morning. I don't ask, though, 'cause Leroy don't like a lot of questions. And he don't seem to like me much anymore either, says I keep getting stupider and fatter. But I don't think I'm much different.

When Leroy's happy, we still have good times. He brings home beer and sometimes other stuff. It's stuff I don't really want to do, but if I don't go along, Leroy gets real mad. I do like how the pills make me feel. Everything seems better. I don't like the weed so much, it stinks and Trevor gets upset. Those times are just about the only time Leroy and I get into any loving anymore. I miss the loving. I miss holdin' hands and kissin'.

chapter 4

In the morning I wake to quiet. No TV this morning. I glance at the clock on the floor next to Trevor's sleeping bag, thinking I must have slept late, but it's only 7:45 a.m. Trevor should still be here. Why is it so quiet? I find him sitting at the table drawing. He is drawing a picture of a truck.

"Wow," I say, admiring his work. "That's a nice truck."

"It's Daddy's truck," he says. So Leroy drives a truck. That explains a few things, except why we seem to be so broke. I walk to the kitchen and look for something to eat.

"Are you excited to see him tonight?" I try to sound cheerful.

"I guess." Trevor is non-committal.

I watch him for a minute as he signs his name.

He catches me watching and asks, "Are you okay, Mama?"

"What do you mean?"

"You ain't grumpy and you ain't sleepin' so much."

"Am I usually grumpy and sleepy?"

"Yeah."

"Oh." He's no longer looking at me. He's studying his picture carefully. I walk over and put my hand on his shoulder. He looks up at me, almost frightened. Does Leann ever touch this child?

"I'm going to try not to be so grumpy, and maybe if I don't sleep so much I'll get to see you more."

Trevor smiles, but looks worried. The microwave alarm goes off. He places his drawing in his bag of cut-out pictures and heads for the door.

"That's pretty neat how you set the microwave alarm every day."

"I don't. Jillian does that for me. Bye."

He's gone. Jillian sets the alarm for him? Maybe she isn't a teenage zombie after all. Maybe her mother never got her off to school in the mornings either.

Learning to live Leann's life is kind of like learning a foreign language. I've never mastered any foreign language, despite trying most of them—Spanish, French, German, Latin, even Chinese. I was horrible. Absolutely no ability, a lot of desire, but that didn't translate at all. I feel like I'm beginning to master Leann's language. I'm already starting to have moments when I think like her. It's spooky. When I look at Trevor, I feel something. I think it's responsibility, but maybe it's the outer edges of love. How could she walk away from him? He's part of her. Maybe after I meet Leroy, I'll understand. Maybe I'll understand whether she's ever coming back.

The mound of clothes I stacked up next to the TV on Wednesday is still parked there. It is time to deal with that, mostly because I'm hoping all of Leann's best clothes are in the stack. I've done all I can with the clothes I've found on the floor. Checking the roll of quarters, I find about seven dollars. I resist the urge to head to Starbucks, load all the dirty clothes into pillow cases, and carry them to the stairs.

The old guy who yelled at me yesterday is sitting outside his door in a lawn chair. He's eating a Pop-Tart.

"Where is he?" he asks as I start down the stairs.

"I don't know, but I'll give him your message when I see him." I smile sweetly, struggling with the bags of laundry. Halfway down the next flight of stairs, I stop and turn.

"Hey! Where is the closest Laundromat?" I call up to the old man.

"Hell if I know." My heart sinks, and I turn to continue down the stairs. But then he adds, "You can use my washer, if you'll do my clothes too."

An hour later, I'm hanging out Mr. Giovanni's clothes on the line that runs out the window between our building and a pole in the empty lot next door. I finish hanging Mr. Giovanni's things and sit down with him at his table while my clothes finish. I don't know how I'll dry them, but at least I've saved seven dollars.

"How long have you lived here?" I ask.

"Let's see. I came here when Shirley was still alive, so that's at least nine years ago. It's probably been twelve years, I think. Twelve years in this hellhole, I've seen a lot."

"When did Leroy and I move in?" I ask.

"You can't remember?"

"Things with Leroy get kind of fuzzy."

He hesitates and then says, "I think you came here about a year ago. Yeah, that's right. You got that place when Gerome got thrown in the slammer. I guess you're kind of subletting, in a way."

"Why did Gerome go to jail?"

Mr. Giovanni rubs his forehead. "Now, you must know about that. Gerome got in trouble for selling dope to the school kids. It was a big deal. The police came in here with guns and dogs. Scared the bejesus out of the rest of us. They took Gerome off in handcuffs. Next thing I know, Leroy is explaining to the landlady that he's Gerome's cousin, never mind that Gerome is black, and you move in here with that little boy of yours."

"Lucky break, I guess." I think about this. So Leroy has a friend that deals pot. Does that mean Leroy smokes pot? Does Leann?

"I think the washer quit."

I gather up my laundry, thank Mr. Giovanni, assuring him Leroy will return his twenty dollars when he gets home. I hang our clothes on every piece of furniture I can and use string I find to rig up a clothesline. Nothing's going to look too great without an iron, but at least they'll be clean. It's past noon, so I eat lunch—cheese curls, pickles, and dry macaroni. I really hope Leann's paycheck is big enough to buy some groceries. I can't eat like this much longer. Gathering up a packet of ramen noodles and a can of Coke, I decide to leave for work early. I've got the laundry money and a desperate need for real coffee.

Twenty minutes later, I'm sitting at a table in Irma's Coffee Bar on Sixth Street, sweating and studying the coffee menu. Several waitresses are working the section where I sit, but no one approaches me. Maybe it's the Shop N Save apron. I remove it and fold it neatly in my purse. After nearly fifteen minutes, I realize that no one is going to offer me service, so I flag down a waitress.

"Excuse me!" I call. A young blond girl, wearing a tight skirt and a black Irma's Coffee Bar T-shirt stretched across her ample chest, glances in my direction but continues to talk with three young businessmen at a corner table. I wait. When she leaves their table, I try again, "Excuse me!" She cuts across the room obviously avoiding me and ducks under the bar. I get up and follow her. If I wasn't so huge, I would duck under the bar too. She has her back to me and is intently measuring beans into a canister.

"Excuse me!" I say one more time. She doesn't flinch. I can't help myself. I pick up the nearest object—a sugar dispenser. I fling sugar at the waitress and begin screaming, "What the hell is the matter with you? Can't I get any service here?"

She turns and throws her hands up trying to shield herself from the shower of sugar I'm unleashing. Suddenly a man grabs my arm from behind and takes the sugar dispenser.

"Ma'am, I'm the manager. I'll have to ask you to leave."

He is a pudgy little guy. His tangled hair is dusted with dandruff. He's at least two inches shorter than me and has a large pimple on his forehead that's as big as a third eye. I fix my gaze on his monster blemish and say, "All I wanted was a cup of coffee, and this waitress wouldn't serve me."

"Phil, I didn't see her," says the waitress, who is wiping sugar off of her shoulders indignantly.

I glare at her. "You saw me, but you were too busy flirting with the corner booth."

"Ma'am, you'll have to leave now. You're creating a disturbance." His voice squeaks a little on the word disturbance. He's terrified that I might not leave. He glances around to see who is watching. The entire coffee bar is watching, of course.

He releases my arm and puffs up his chest, trying to be a more substantial presence. I look down at him. There is so much I'd like to say. Like, you are a peon. You think that you're in charge here, but you aren't. No one is. At any moment, you could be knocked on the head by a giant Valentine and your whole world could change. On second thought, looking at him carefully, that might be a good thing.

Phil and the waitress are both watching me, waiting to see what the fat woman will do. I know in a better world, I would have returned to my table and insisted they serve me, but I'm already blinking repeatedly to hold back my tears, and the last thing I want to do is cry in front of the entire coffee shop, which is now collectively holding its breath to see what I will do.

As I'm walking down the street, the tears come. I want my life back. This is too hard. I sit down on a bench and fish around in my coat pocket for a tissue. I find a Roy Rogers napkin and dab at my face. Then I lean back on the bench and close my eyes. I just want this to be over.

"Hey girl—are you alive?" asks a raspy voice.

I open my eyes. An old woman glares down at me. Her face is covered in wrinkles that gather around her jaw and mouth. She reminds me of the Grinch.

"Move over, you're taking up the whole bench. This is my bench. I don't know why you had to park your fat ass right here."

I take a breath, preparing to heave myself up and move on, but I don't. I turn to her.

"That wasn't very kind," I say.

"Huh? What did you say?" she croaks back at me.

"I said that wasn't very kind, what you said."

"What'd I say?"

"You said I had a fat ass."

"You do."

She's right, but I feel I need to speak up for Leann.

"And you have a wrinkly face."

She narrows her eyes at me. Then she throws her head back and laughs a huge belly laugh. I look around to see if people are staring. No one even glances in our direction as they hurry past. I watch her laugh and laugh. Finally, she wipes her eyes, takes a deep breath, and looks at me.

"You're alright," she says. I feel a little lighter as I haul myself off of the bench. The old woman is grinning as she takes over the seat. She opens her bag and pulls out her knitting and gets to work.

I don't say anything else, but I smile to myself. It's time for me to get to the Shop N Save. I walk to the store feeling a tiny bit better. I wish I had some coffee, but at least I have a little dignity now.

The coffee in the break room is no better today. I spit it out after one sip. Then I dump the whole pot, and make a new one. As I wait for it to brew, Jimmy comes in. He looks at the coffee pot and raises his eyebrows.

"I just put a new pot on," I answer his unspoken question.

He nods and sits down on the couch. He pulls a book from his back pocket and starts reading. I stare at the coffee maker. The silence is obvious.

"What are you reading?" I venture.

He jumps and looks around at me. I guess Leann doesn't normally talk to him.

"Just something," he mumbles and goes back to his book.

The coffee finishes and I pour a cup, walk over to the couch and hold it out for him. He looks up at me, startled, and accepts the coffee.

"Thanks." He tucks the book in his pocket and then heads back out.

I sip my coffee slowly, watching the clock. I have three minutes until I have to punch in. I'm determined to have a better attitude. I will stand up for Leann. For me.

But it is difficult to be pleasant after standing for six hours without a break. Gone is the triumphant feeling I had only yesterday, when I was able to bag groceries single handedly and zip through coupons on the first swipe. I can feel sweat seeping through the underarms of my shirt and my feet are throbbing. It is difficult not to be angry when Vernon sends Phyllis off to take her break while my line is six deep. And when I have to lean back and allow the back wall of the cashier stand to support my fat rolls in order to stay on my feet, I feel like a freak. No, a freak trapped in hell.

Finally, at 9:45, Vernon motions me to take my break. Why is it that people leave their shopping until Friday evenings? Don't they have better places to go? I sure wouldn't be here if I weren't trapped in this oversized body and this unfortunate life. I fill a bowl with fruit from the salad bar, which is swarming with fruit flies. I don't even bother to take it up to the register. If Vernon wants to charge me for this barely edible fruit that is going to be thrown away at eleven, then he can come track me down.

The cold air feels heavenly as I push the side door open and sit on a milk crate. The fruit is inedible, and I toss each piece into the woods behind the store. Some of my throws go much farther than I've ever thrown. Leann has a decent arm.

"Nice shot," calls a voice from the loading dock. Jimmy is sitting on the edge, dangling his legs over and lighting a cigarette.

"Thanks," I say as I tear open the ramen noodles and begin crunching on them dry. My loud crunching echoes off the dark woods, so I try to just suck on the noodles to soften them up. This causes me to nearly choke on the dry pasta and I erupt in a coughing fit. Jimmy doesn't move. When I finally manage to get a good breath again, he says, "You okay?"

Speaking is impossible, so I nod, embarrassed, but he can't see my nod in the dark. He jumps down from the dock and approaches me.

"I'mpf, okay," I manage to squeak, which causes me to begin coughing again. Jimmy pats my back pretty hard and noodles spray out of my mouth. I'm mortified. Finally, my coughing stops and I put my head in my hands. This day can't get much worse.

Jimmy doesn't say anything, but he pulls up another crate and sits down directly in front of me. I look up and am startled by how close he is sitting. In my few days as Leann, no one has been this close to me.

"Are you crying?" he asks.

I shake my head, but his kindness starts my tears flowing in torrents. I wipe at my face with my sleeve. Jimmy pulls out a handkerchief and hands it to me. It's an honest-to-God hankie, like my grandpa always carried. I stare at it, embarrassed, and finally take it. I wipe my eyes and blow my nose. When I'm finished I don't want to hand it back to him all snotty, but it seems wrong to keep it. So I just hold it in my hand. I look up at Jimmy. He is looking off in the direction of the loading dock. I'm sure this is not how he would like to be spending his break.

"I'm sorry. I'm a mess," I say quietly.

He looks back at me and says, "Everybody's a mess, really."

That makes sense. But I'm a mess on a completely new level, and I realize I can't explain that to this guy who seems really sweet.

"Hey, I have to get back to work. Are you gonna be alright?" He starts to stand up.

I nod and hold his handkerchief up.

"Nah, I got plenty of those. My grandpappy sends me a twelve pack every Christmas."

Jimmy jumps back up on the loading dock and disappears into the mouth of the store. I hear a machine start up. I better get back to the checkout. Pressing my hands against the wall for support, I raise myself up. So much for dinner.

I finish out my shift and linger in the break room, hanging up my smock. I clear off the table and find a paper towel and wipe it off. Then I open the refrigerator and toss out anything that looks moldy, organizing the remains in neat rows. Phyllis comes in, sees me and says, "Hey, I'm surprised you're still here. Usually you're the first one out on Fridays. Got to get home to your man." My heart starts racing. I have managed to block the thought of Leroy all day long.

I wait until I'm on the bus to open my paycheck. When I finally do, I'm shocked. How can Leann make so little? I sigh and push the check down deeper in my pocket. I try not to think about Leroy.

Putting off the inevitable, I get off the bus several stops before mine and begin walking slowly. As I approach the building, I say silent prayers that everyone will be asleep in the apartment. I wish I could go somewhere else, but I can't think of anywhere. It's too cold to sleep outside. The Shop N Save is closed now. Maybe I should have asked Phyllis if I could go home with her.

Outside the door, I hesitate. Men have never scared me. In fact, I have always been amazed at how easy they are to manipulate. They all truly want one thing. It's not just sex either. They want to be admired and desired. The same things women want, really. All my life it's been so easy to tease them along. Flatter them, give them a taste of what they want, and they'll do anything you ask. But I don't know how to do this as Leann. None of the men I've encountered have reacted to me in the way I'm accustomed to. They rarely even meet my eye. On the other side of this door a man expects something from me. Hopefully not sex, but he does expect me to act in a certain way. If anyone is going to know I'm not Leann, it'll be him. He's her husband.

I put my key in and open the door. The whole place smells different. I can't explain what it is, but it's not the innocent smell of Trevor, or the incense-infused smell of Jillian, or even the rancid smell of the dirty clothes pile. It smells dangerous.

Leroy is sitting on the couch with his feet on the coffee table. He's drinking a beer and watching TV. He doesn't look up when I enter. Should I say something? I set down my bag and coat near the door and watch him. He takes a swig of his beer, but his eyes don't leave the TV. I move towards the bedroom. The clothesline I hung earlier is gone.

"Hey, bitch!" he calls. "Ain't you gonna say hello?"

I could say the same thing to him, but I turn back around and say very quietly, "Hello."

"Where's your paycheck?"

I reach for my coat and fish out the measly check. Leroy is holding out his hand, still not looking at me. I place the paycheck in his hand and in a flash he grabs my arm and pulls me down to him. I stumble over the makeshift coffee table, knocking the door off the cinderblocks, and land sprawled across his lap.

He laughs, "Now that's what I'm talkin' 'bout."

I push myself up to my knees and look at him. He chuckles and stuffs the paycheck in his jean pocket. Then he pats the couch next to him. "Don't you want some quality time with your ole man? I know you missed me."

I sit down carefully and lean as far away from him as I can, which is difficult given the structure of the couch. He doesn't say anything, and I don't either, but he puts his hand on my knee. It's the hand holding his beer.

"Hey, make yourself useful." He knocks the empty beer can against my leg. In all my life, I have never waited on a man. Never. Not even on Scott when he was recovering from tonsillitis or my dad on Father's Day. But I keep my mouth closed, climb up off the couch, and go to the kitchen. The sink is full of dishes and the counter is littered with takeout boxes.

"Me and Jillian had a little supper tonight before she left." I freeze. Jillian is probably about the same age Leann was when she had Trevor. Maybe this guy is a pedophile.

I look in the fridge and find several six packs of beer. Considering the condition of Leann's finances, that beer could have bought my lunch all week. I take out a beer for him and one for me. Maybe this will all seem easier if I'm not completely sober.

When I sit back down on the couch, Leroy looks at me. He squints at me, so I squint back. He hesitates. "You look different. You didn't get your hair cut did you? Jesus, Leann, we ain't got money for stuff like that."

"I just styled it differently, that's all." He continues to stare at me. I stare back. He really is old. His face looks weathered and his nose is redder and more bulbous than his driver's license photo. He's tall and muscled—like a man who does physical work for a living, but a beer gut spills over the top of his jeans. Girls might have been attracted to him when he was young, but I can't imagine giving him a second glance now.

"Why the hell was the laundry lyin' all over the place when I got here?"

This morning seems like a lifetime ago.

"Mr. Giovanni let me use his washer, but I didn't have anywhere to dry everything."

"What the hell you doin' in Mr. G's place? Jesus Christ, Leann, he's a crazy old man. Why'd he let you use his washer anyway?"

"I did his clothes too."

"Great, next you'll be cleaning his place and God knows what else. Jesus, what's so fuckin' hard about doing the laundry?"

"I didn't have any money to do the laundry and it's way too far to carry everything. Next time, you do the laundry!" I'm sick of this guy. What an asshole! I try to jump up, but have to grab the back of the couch for support. After I regain my balance I grab my beer and storm out of the apartment. So much for effect. Outside the door, I take deep breaths and try to calm down. I don't have my key, but I'm not about to go back for it. I sit down on the top step and sip my beer. Is this really happening? Am I crazy?

Behind me the door opens. "You done?" asks Leroy, looking purposefully calm. "'Cause if you are, get your fat ass back in here and clean up the kitchen. I got buddies coming over tomorrow morning. We're gonna discuss a business proposition." He over-enunciates the word proposition, making it sound sleazy. I can't imagine what kind of business proposition Leroy would be mixed up in, but I also don't want to sleep outside, so I get up and go back in the apartment. As I pass Leroy I tell him, "You owe Mr. Giovanni twenty bucks."

"Ha! He's a nut case. He's been saying I owe him twenty bucks ever since we moved in here."

I just want to get the kitchen cleaned up and go to sleep. I don't know where I will go tomorrow, but I need to get far away from this disgusting man. Behind me, Leroy turns the TV up louder and opens another beer.

chapter 5

〜〜

When I wake in the morning, I'm still alone in the bed. I breathe a sigh of relief. Trevor is not in his Scooby-Doo sleeping bag, so I creep out to the living room to find him. He is playing on his computer with the sound off and Leroy is lying across the couch with his jeans undone. His mouth is open and a small stream of drool is puddling on his shoulder. I shudder and head back to the bathroom.

While I'm showering and considering what I should do next, the bathroom door opens. I tense up and wait. I hear the toilet seat bang against the toilet. A minute later, the toilet flushes and I jump back as hot water scalds me.

"Gotcha!" calls Leroy as he exits, leaving the door open so cold air rushes in.

I do the best I can with Leann's hair and find some humongous stretch pants and a long black T-shirt that says *Don't Mess With Texas.* Most of the clothes that I washed yesterday are now balled up and still damp in the corner of the bedroom. I pull out a few pieces and hang them over crates to dry.

Leroy yells from the kitchen, "Where the hell's my eggs?"

I poke my head out of the bedroom and ask, "What eggs?"

"You know I like my eggs on Saturday. What the hell am I supposed to eat?"

"Maybe you can eat Froot Loops like Trevor and me," I suggest, stepping back into the bedroom. A moment later, Leroy appears in the bedroom.

"What the hell's gotten into you Leann? This ain't right. I work all week on the road. When I come home on the weekends, I expect food in the fridge and the damn laundry done. What the hell you been doin' all week?"

I take a breath. I take another breath. But I can't do it. I can't be the quiet, passive wife here. Leann shouldn't take this and I'm not going to either.

"I work all week too, for your information. And I can't make eggs materialize from nothing. I don't have any money, how am I supposed to buy eggs?"

"Duh, you work at a grocery store."

"But I have no money!"

"You never needed any money before. You're the one started all this. You waste the money I give you for food on shit we don't need. If you didn't do that you wouldn't have to lift anything from work. Why's this week any different?"

I want to scream, "Because I'm not Leann! How the hell was I supposed to know you eat eggs on Saturday?" but instead I turn my back to him and make the bed. I won't let him see my tears.

"How come there ain't no Twizzlers in the cupboard either, you too high and mighty to pick those up?" he says, stepping in to the room.

I'm still reeling. My mind can't catch up with this. Leann steals food? That's why we have nothing to eat? How is this possible? Doesn't someone at the store know? Now that I think of it, who would? Leann works at night. No one else is working but Phyllis and Jimmy by the end of the night. Vernon almost always leaves early. It would be easy for Leann to take what she needed at break and put it in her locker. Who would know? Is this why she works at night?

"I can't steal." I say this without turning around, terrified.

Leroy laughs a hard, brittle laugh. "Don't tell me you went and found God while I was gone this week."

"I'm not going to steal."

"Well, that ain't my problem, but you better cut back on the damn Tastykakes. You're fat as a house anyway, don't know why you eat that shit."

He turns and goes back to the kitchen, banging dishes on the counter for emphasis. I stay in the bedroom until I hear his friends arrive.

I grab my purse. "C'mon, Trevor, we're going out," I say. I have no idea where we'll go. I just know I need to get far away from this man.

Leroy and his friends don't even acknowledge me. They're sitting around the table and someone has brought a box of day-old donuts. Trevor helps himself to one and Leroy smacks his hand away. "Dang, boy, those aren't for you."

I approach Leroy and say firmly, "I need some cash."

He looks at me and raises his eyebrows. "Don't we all." He laughs and his friends laugh, too.

I don't move. I just stare at him.

"Leroy, you better give the lady her money or you ain't gonna get some tonight," says a heavyset guy wearing lots of flannel and chewing on an unlit cigar. He chuckles to himself and eyes me with a wink. Leroy pulls out his wallet and hands me five dollars.

"That's not enough," I tell him. I pick up Trevor's hand in mine. It is soft and he grips my hand right back.

Leroy pulls out ten dollars and says, "That's enough. And get some groceries 'cause there ain't nothin' to eat in this damn place." He turns away, dismissing me.

It's cold and my hands are practically numb before I figure out where to go. I buy Trevor a pancake breakfast at McDonald's.

"I love pancakes, especially this kind," says Trevor, spreading butter on his pancakes. "McDonald's is my favorite food place."

I sip my stale black coffee and nod.

He takes a bite and says, "Yum! These are the best pancakes I've ever had."

I think of the French toast pancakes served with real cream and raspberries at Irma's on Saturdays.

"How come you ain't eatin'?" he asks.

"I'm not hungry," I tell him, even though my stomach would argue otherwise. Even in this condition, I can't eat at McDonald's.

"This is the best Saturday, ever!" he says as he slurps up the syrup left in the little plastic cup. He smiles at me with syrup on his nose and then runs off to the Playland.

I sip my coffee and consider my options. I still can't believe Leann steals their groceries. That explains the big empty purse and the night shift. But if she's going to steal food, can't she come up with something better than Tastykakes, cheese curls, and peanut butter?

I couldn't steal the food if I wanted to, so I'll have to find another way. When I was a kid, I once stole a lip liner from my mom's friend. I was so afraid of being caught, I don't think I ever used it. I came across it buried in the bottom of my underwear drawer when I was cleaning out my dresser to leave for college. I can't imagine stealing anything. Aside from the lip liner, I've never even wanted to. If I needed something, I just asked my parents. They bought me almost anything I wanted and if they didn't, well, then I just asked my grandma. I wish Leann had a rich grandma. I wonder if she even has a grandma.

The only solution is for me to get another job. I don't know much about anything except insurance and even if I tried to get a job, what would my résumé say? High school dropout with experience as a cashier at Shop N Save? I look out the window and watch the sky. It's going to rain. I wonder what Leann is doing in my body. If I was in my body, I'd be at the gym right now playing racquetball with Scott. Then we'd head out for lunch somewhere and end up shopping or going to the movies. Unless, of course, one of us had a real date. I wonder what Scott is doing today.

By 11:00 Trevor has finally had enough of Playland, and the manager has walked by my table six times. She's stopped asking if I need anything, and now she just scowls at me. It is time to move on. The rain is coming down in a lazy drizzle. Trevor and I stand in the tiny entryway of the McDonald's between the doors, as I try to figure out where we can go. My gym is only a block or so from here. I can't resist finding out if Scott has convinced Leann to play racquetball. I hold Trevor's hand as we walk the few blocks. We stop in front of the gym.

"What's this place?" he asks.

"This is a gym, where people come to exercise."

"What's exercise?"

"Moving your body. You know, like running or climbing." I swing my arms back and forth to mime a running motion and the fat on my arms slaps against my sides. Horrible feeling.

"Why would they come here to do that? Why don't they just play at the park?"

"Good question." I smile and lead him inside.

The front desk receptionist frowns when she sees us. "Can I help you?" she asks.

"We just want to look around," I say and start to walk past her desk. She scoots out from behind it in a flash and blocks our way.

"Are you interested in a membership? I can have one of our associates get your information and take you on a tour."

"I just want to look around," I persist.

She grimaces. "Sorry, we can't allow that."

Who is we? I don't see anyone else here. "OK, I guess I could talk with someone."

"Let's just take this cutie-pie down to the Kiddie Korner, our childcare room, and I'll call someone to help you." Trevor looks at me, eyes wide. I mouth the words "cutie-pie" to him as we follow the woman down the hall. He giggles.

We settle Trevor in the Kiddie Korner, where he is overjoyed to see the toys and nonstop Nickelodeon. I follow the receptionist back to the desk and wait while she calls someone. Bruce appears. He's the personal trainer who originally helped me develop my free-weight workout. The workout I could do in my sleep if only this body wasn't so cumbersome. Bruce is incredibly buff and very gay, but all the women here think he's just picky. I know about the gay part because he once asked Scott out. He looks me up and down and then puts out his hand.

"Hi, I'm Bruce. Let's get you started on your journey to fitness."

I swallow a giggle. Journey to fitness. He can't be serious. I follow him back to his office to fill out paperwork. I don't know Leann's social security number, so I write in mine and take out her license to get her birth date, gambling that they don't really check these things. Her birthday was only a month ago. I wonder if anyone baked her a cake. Next it asks for my fitness goals. Hmm. Learn how to operate this size-24 body? I write *lose weight and feel better* on the line and hand the form back to Bruce, who reads it over.

"Membership begins with a four-hundred-dollar initiation fee. How would you like to handle that—cash, check, or charge?"

I gulp. "I'm not sure yet if I want to join. Could we look around first?"

"I'm jumping ahead of myself. Of course we can. Right this way."

Bruce shows me the Nautilus room, the weight room, and the pool, and then waits outside while I check out the women's locker room and sauna. Several women are changing when I enter. They stop talking and turn to look at me, then look away quickly and resume their conversation as if I'm not there. I pretend to look in some lockers and open the sauna, only to startle a few naked old women. Leann is not here with my body.

I stop in front of the mirror and look at myself. This is the first full-length mirror I've encountered since I became Leann. I'm used to looking at part of me, one bit at a time. Seeing my entire body is startling. I am huge. I look like a Weeble. Those were one of my favorite toys as a child. I hum the "Weebles wobble, but they don't fall down" tune from the commercial. And then the tears come.

I step away from the mirror and hide inside a toilet stall. I sob and sob. I don't even care that the women outside can hear me. I cry so hard I begin to shake and my nose is running. I miss me. I miss my crooked nose and my long hair and my confident body. I miss running in the morning and sleeping on my stomach at night. I miss lattes and goat cheese. I miss people treating me like Carin. I don't want to be Leann. I miss my apartment, my boyfriend, my life.

I hear a soft knock on the stall. "Excuse me, are you alright?" asks a familiar voice. I know that voice. I wipe my face with toilet tissue and then open the door slowly. Gina, the aerobics instructor, in all her spandex glory, is standing in front of me. My friends and I have always made fun of her behind her back. She's perky and sweet and always dressed head to toe in pink. She does teach a tough class, though. I don't know anyone who can do more leg lifts.

"Can I call someone?" she asks gently.

"I'm sorry; I was just having a moment. I'm okay."

"Bruce was worried when you didn't come out."

"Tell him I'll be right out, I'm sorry."

"You sure?" She looks genuinely concerned.

I nod and move to the sinks to splash some water on my cheeks.

A few minutes later, I emerge from the ladies' locker room with a swollen face and a runny nose.

"I thought I'd lost you," Bruce jokes, looking worried. We continue the tour, passing by the empty racquetball courts, the aerobics room, and the Pilates class, and end up back in the personal training center. Bruce asks me to step up on the scale so he can get my vitals. I want to protest for Leann's sake, but at this point, I really don't care. The scale reads 376. Even I'm shocked. I was guessing more like three hundred. Bruce takes more really embarrassing statistics involving a device that looks like salad tongs, then measures my height and takes my blood pressure. He looks at my shoes and says, "Maybe we can have you come back to do the treadmill test when you have your workout shoes."

We head back to his office to finish the paperwork. As he settles at his desk, I blurt out, "I can't afford it, but I really need to be here. I could do anything. I could work the desk. I could wash towels. I'd even clean the locker room." I don't know what makes me say this. Maybe it's a need to be in a familiar place. Somewhere I am still me.

Bruce doesn't say anything for a moment. He seems crest-fallen. "I see," he finally says and opens his desk drawer. He hands me an employment application. "I think they might need some-one in the Kiddie Korner. Let's see what we can do."

I expected him to turn me out on my tail, especially after my stunt in the ladies' locker room. They must be desperate for help. Or maybe he just feels sorry for me. Either way, I don't care.

An hour later, I retrieve Trevor from the Kiddie Korner, where I'm the newest employee. I'm jubilant. We stop in at the Shop N Save with the few dollars I have left to buy groceries. Trevor ate so many snacks in the Kiddie Korner, he's burping animal crackers and tells me repeatedly he's stuffed. I, on the other hand, haven't had anything but black coffee, and my whole body reverberates with hunger. We say hello to the manager at the front desk when she waves us over.

"Hi, Leann, come to do some shopping?" Her name tag reads "Sheila" and she seems desperately sweet.

"Hi Sheila. How's it going?"

"It's really slow, but I heard you were jammed last night."

"It was crazy. Hey, is there an employee discount?" I'm hop-ing we get a discount, of course Leann would know this, or maybe not since she normally takes a one hundred percent discount.

Sheila looks at me quizzically and says, "It ain't changed. It's still ten percent. But we got some great buys in the daily discount rack. Harv just loaded it up."

"Thanks," I say smiling brightly, and head off in what I hope is the direction of the daily discount rack. I've never actually shopped from the daily discount rack. I think it's somewhere in the back near the bakery. Today I need every discount I can get.

We buy lettuce, outdated salad dressing, noodles, pasta sauce in a dented can, some day-old French bread, and a dozen eggs and get out with thirty-two cents to spare. I'm relieved; I was ter-rified I'd be one of those people who have to put items back while everyone watches.

When we arrive back at the apartment, it's empty. I breathe a sigh of relief and get to work making a spaghetti dinner. After doctoring the sauce with spices that are several years outdated, I cut up some bread and bake croutons. Trevor sits on a milk crate watching me, crunching on dry pasta.

"I didn't know you could cook," he says.

"Of course I know how to cook."

"I ain't never seen you cook before. I wish you cooked every day."

I wish we had food to cook every day. This is one meal, but what about the rest of the week? Somehow I have to get more money out of Leroy. I start tomorrow at the gym, so hopefully Trevor can fill up on snacks again.

Trevor and I are just sitting down to eat spaghetti, garlic bread, and salad when Leroy walks in the door.

"That smells good!" he says as he sits down. He looks at me expectantly. I guess I'm supposed to go get his dinner. I don't want to start a fight, so I dish him up pasta and salad. I set it down in front of him and wait, expecting at least a thank you.

"I don't eat leaves. Why the hell did you buy that stuff? You never eat it either. God, I swear something is screwy with you."

Have to give the guy credit. At least someone has noticed I'm not acting like Leann. I smile and say, "It's good for you. You should try it."

Leroy looks at me skeptically, but doesn't say anything. He just shakes his head. He does eat a few bites of salad, I notice. After dinner, Leroy disappears. Trevor and I watch an interesting show about snakes on PBS. At nine, I tell him it's time for bed.

"It's way too early."

"We're going to bed early tonight. I have to work tomorrow at the gym."

"Do I get to go to the gym too?" he asks, hopefully.

"Yup, so we both need to get to sleep."

After we are in bed, Trevor asks, "Can you read me a book?"

"Do you have a book?" I haven't seen a single book in the entire apartment.

He jumps up and runs out to the living room, then walks back in with his backpack. He pulls out a library book and hands it to me triumphantly. He smiles and snuggles in bed next to me. The book is called *How I Became a Pirate.*

"Do you like pirates?" I ask.

"Duh, Mama, I'm going to *be* a pirate."

"I forgot," I say and open to the first page.

We read the book three times. By the third time, Trevor points out all the words he knows and shouts out every pirate phrase. Yawning, I nudge him off the bed. "Shiver me timbers, it's time for bed, matey." He giggles and crawls into his sleeping bag.

I'm almost completely asleep when I hear a voice. "Mama?"

"Yes?"

"I had fun today."

"Me too," I say, although fun isn't what I would call it. I do feel good about today. I lie awake wondering how Leann can just leave this child.

ᔓ ᔕ

leann

Didn't take 'em long to figure out there was nothing wrong with me at the rehab place. At least nothing they could fix. So I'm all set up in Carin's place now.

When Scott and Brenda finally leave, I get a good look at the apartment. It's twice as big as mine and Leroy's. It's so neat you'd think Mr. Clean lived here. Maybe Carin's got a housekeeper like on *Fairmont Park.* Victoria has a housekeeper, but she don't want Edgar to know so she sneaks her in after he leaves in the morning to go home to his wife. This place is clean like that.

I pretended my head hurt so they'd leave. They wanted to stay and take care of me. That creeped me out. I like the idea of someone takin' care of me so long as that someone ain't either one of them weirdos. Scott is a real girlie-guy and he keeps saying goofy things that he thinks are funny. He looks all sad when I stare at him like he's the dumbass he is. And Brenda, she just gets on my nerves. She lurks around me like a shadow and can't shut up about how I need to put on makeup and wash my hair. It's my hair, not hers. Well, maybe it's not really my hair, but for now anyways.

I get up off the couch and check out the bedroom. The bed has so many pillows you can barely sit your ass down. But the closet! The girl has some clothes! I yank off the sweat suit Brenda brought to the rehab center for me and pull out a slinky black number with a slit up to the belly. I find a full-length mirror in the bathroom. It's unbelievable. I have to keep making motions to be sure it's really me in the mirror. I don't have any boobs. I look like a doll. I pull the dress off and stare at Carin's body. It is so pretty and so perfect. No rolls, and no stretch marks crisscrossing the tummy. I turn around real slow like. What a great ass. I look down at my legs and like how there ain't no dimples, no cottage cheesy stuff on the thighs.

The whole drive over here, Scott and Brenda tried to say all kinds of cheery things, like how my boss was hoping I'd be back and how some friend I have lunch with all the time wants to come by and bring her kid. That got me thinking 'bout Trevor and how I got to get back to him. But he'd never know me like this. No one would. I'd like to get all dolled up and go to the arcade. I bet boys would notice me now. And Trevor, he knows how to take care of hisself. He'll be alright. I ain't been such a great mama anyway. I love him, but I don't do the right things.

Leroy says if I don't watch out, Trevor'll grow up stupid just like me. I don't know if I'm as stupid as he says. It's just 'cause he's got a diploma and I had to drop out on account of Trevor.

Trevor needs somebody who'll do stuff with him. He always wants to go to the library and I never take him there. It brings back too many memories. And I never let him have any friends come over. Leroy says no strangers in our house. He's real para-noid like that. Maybe he's afraid someone will steal Trevor in the night. That happened on *Fairmont Park*. Some crazy lady stole little Emma in the middle of the night! And Netty and Bill went 'bout crazy tryin' to get her back.

Sometimes Leroy yells at Trevor for stupid stuff and I don't say nothin'. Lately Leroy's had a short fuse and he's a little free with his fist. He really clocked me last week. I was harping on him about taking me with him in his truck like he used to, and he smacked me good. I should've asked nicer. Mama says kids are resilient—meaning they bounce good—so I'm hoping Trevor can bounce back from Leroy's meanness. At least he has a father. My daddy weren't never around.

Brenda said Carin's daddy will be home from Brazil next week and he's gonna take me out for lunch in The Towers, wherever the hell that is. I ain't never had a dad.

chapter 6

My first day in the Kiddie Korner doesn't go so great. I've never been very good with kids. And now I have a new handicap—my size. I never truly appreciated how difficult it is for someone of this weight to get down on the ground without hurting herself. Had I known, I probably would never have attempted to sit in the circle with the children to play duck-duck-goose, which apparently isn't an appropriate game to play in a small space with a slippery linoleum floor.

Trevor helps me out by going first, but he doesn't help me out one bit by tapping my head ever so gently and whispering "goose." I'm a competitive person, so my first instinct is to leap up and run him down. Following this instinct without considering the great effort it takes to get up from the floor is not only a mistake, it is dangerous.

I'm sitting the only way that is physically possible once I lowered myself to the floor—leaning back slightly with both legs thrust out in front of me. After Trevor picks me, I turn to the side and struggle to raise myself on my hands and knees. I try to bring a leg up underneath me, but my mind and my body are at odds.

Meanwhile, in his haste to get around the circle as fast as possible, Trevor slips on the linoleum floor and crashes headlong into a crib, whose occupant begins screaming hysterically. Trevor starts crying too and looks to me, but I'm marooned in this position. The rest of the kids take my inaction to mean I'm inviting them for a pony ride and they pile on. In my frustration, the first thing that pops out of my mouth is, "Get the hell off me!" At which point, Denise, the Kiddie Korner supervisor, who is trying to comfort the crying toddler, comes running over and pulls the children off of me. I crawl over to a chair and use it for support to get myself vertical again. I'm huffing and puffing and Denise is glaring at me as she gathers the children around the table for a coloring activity.

When the children, including Trevor (the traitor), are happily coloring, Denise approaches me. She smiles tightly. Before she can begin her lecture, I cut her off.

"I'm sorry. I'm not used to having so many kids climb on me. But I really do love kids and I promise I'll try much harder from here on out. And I know I shouldn't say *hell*."

Denise cringes and looks to see if the children are listening. I grimace and try to look remorseful. Not for the first time, I consider that this *is* hell. To be surrounded by small children and forced to kowtow to a grumpy, frumpy woman whose only power exists in this Kiddie Korner is a certain hell. She probably doesn't even have a college education. Of course, at this point, I don't either, so I should probably drop my superiority issues.

Somehow I survive the day, but it is more physically challenging than I ever imagined. I remember babysitting kids when I was a teen. I just ate snacks and watched TV. This is much harder. I hold a sleeping baby for over two hours while her mother is in the Boot Camp class I used to take. It's so strange to be on this side of life at this gym. I know this baby's mom. She's one of those rare mothers who still has the glamorous job and the gorgeous body. I spend two hours rocking her baby. Every time I try to lay her down in the crib, her eyes fly open in panic and she begins to cry, so I continue to hold her even though my arms ache.

Rocking that baby, watching Trevor build block castles with his new friends, I realize that this motherhood thing is real work. I don't know why anyone signs up for it. It does more to you than give you flabby ab muscles and droopy boobs. Your mind is divided between what you want and what they need. You're no longer the priority. But why did this baby's mom have a baby if she's just going to toss her in child care seven days a week?

I'm probably being judgmental. According to Scott, this is one of my weaknesses. We always used to argue about that. He's right, which I guess I always knew. But that's the thing about being judgmental: in order for that gig to work for you, you also have to always be right. So admitting he's right would mean that I'm wrong, and I've never been comfortable with being wrong.

Ever since I became Leann, I'm aware of how much I'm being judged by others. They look at me and they see weakness. They see someone who is lazy. At least that's what I imagine when they stare at me and then look away as soon as I meet their gaze. Children also stare at me, but they don't look away. One little boy asked me today why I was so fat. He wasn't judging me necessarily, he was just curious. I didn't know how to respond. First I said, "That's not a very nice question." He wrinkled his brow, but was still waiting for an answer, so I said, "I don't know. I just am." He nodded and went back to playing cars with the other boys.

But it made me wonder, why is Leann fat? She doesn't have any money for food, so you'd think she'd be skinny. I'm sure she qualifies for food stamps. I wonder how that works.

Trevor and I have just finished eating leftover spaghetti and salad for dinner when Leroy comes in. I watch him as he eats the leftovers I put in front of him. He tries to smile at me, but it's kind of gross because his mouth is full of food.

"Leroy, I was wondering how come we don't get food stamps?"

"What?" he yells, spraying food all over the table. "You don't think we have enough to eat? You sure look like you're eatin' enough. Why the hell do we need a handout?"

"I think we'd qualify for them, and I'm not going to steal our food anymore."

"Talk to Mr. G. He got the damn food stamps last year. He said all he got was a loaf of wonder bread and a jar of peanut butter. They tell you what you can buy with them stamps. It's not a free-for-all. Besides, the damn welfare office is clear on the other side of town. How you gonna get there?"

"I'm sure I can take a bus. I could go tomorrow."

"Hell no! No child of mine is going to be raised on welfare."

"That's just stupid," I say and turn to leave.

"No, you're just stupid if you don't see they don't pay you enough at that damn store. We deserve to get the food for free. And don't forget my eggs this weekend. And the Twizzlers."

I lie on the bed. My feet ache and I'm crying again. I hate this life. How does Leann stand it? Doesn't she get to do anything fun? She must have been doing something during the day. Maybe she has a boyfriend or a hobby I haven't discovered yet. Maybe she has a friend she visits. Her life can't be this bleak, can it?

I've almost fallen asleep when I feel Leroy sit down on the bed. I freeze.

"Is something going on? You ain't actin' like you."

I don't know what to say. I want to say, "Yeah, I'm not me. I'm Carin. I have a life. I have money and clothes and things and people and so much more than this. So it's taking me a while to adjust."

Instead I mumble, "I just don't feel good."

"You're not preggo are you?"

"No!"

"Good, because I'd have to assume you was cheatin' since we ain't done it in forever."

Good to know. Quite a relief.

"I'm not pregnant, I just don't feel good."

"So? When has that ever mattered before?"

I sigh. C'mon Leann, you sure haven't given me much to work with here. I stick to my point.

"I started another job today."

"You what?" Leroy's voice rises and he jumps back up off the bed like it's on fire.

"I started a job. In a day care at the Lotus Gym on Sixth Street."

"Why'd the hell did you do that? All them people who got nothin' better to do than run like rats on a machine? How're you gonna do that job and watch Trevor?"

"It's not like I watch Trevor much anyway. Jillian does. Besides, if I have to work when he's home I can take him with me. He likes it there."

"Yeah, they have free snacks," says Trevor as he plops down on his sleeping bag.

"Hey, boy, we're talking here. Go watch TV," Leroy orders.

"I'm tired and it's my bedtime," Trevor insists.

"Out!" says Leroy in a mean voice. I want to tell him to talk nicely, but I'm afraid to make him any angrier.

"Leann, I don't know what the fuck you're up to, but you better not be thinkin' a leavin' me. You wouldn't survive two minutes without me. You're too stupid. You're lucky I married you in the first place." He sits back down and puts his hand on my shoulder. It makes my skin crawl and it's all I can do not to fling it off.

"Speaking of that, ain't it about time? I need a little something."

"Leroy, I don't feel good. I can't."

He jumps up quickly.

"Jesus Christ, Leann. What the hell you good for? You used to be fun. Heck, you're just a kid, but you act like an old woman." He stomps out of the bedroom and I hear the apartment door slam. Why would Leann have married this man? More to the point, why would Leann ever have slept with this man?

chapter 7

Ⅰ discover the answer to both of those questions the next morn-ing. I'm busy trying to make myself look presentable before heading to the Kiddie Korner. It's just a few minutes after seven. Trevor is watching TV, backpack on, eating the last of the spaghetti, when we hear a knock at the door. He jumps up and runs to it.

"Grandma," he says, quietly, backing away from the small, pointy woman who barges in waving a cigarette.

"Hey you little shit—why ain't you in school?" Her voice is worn raw from complaining and cigarettes. "Where's your useless mama?" She looks up and I wave from the bedroom doorway.

"Where the hell were you this weekend? Why weren't you in church? You too busy sittin' on your fat ass and screwin' that old man?"

I'm taken back. Leann goes to church? How was I to know? I've seen no evidence in her life to indicate that she's a churchgoer. And what kind of grandmother talks like this?

"I started a new job on Sundays, so I probably won't be able to go anymore."

Leann's mother flies across the room so fast that I have no time to react. She slaps me across the face a lot harder than you would think possible for a woman only four foot ten and at least sixty by the look of her. Her wrinkled, stained face is staring at me as I hold my cheek, her hand still raised. I back away into the bedroom.

"You don't need to hit me."

"Someone needs to knock some sense into you. You're a damn embarrassment, Leann. The least you can do is show up for church. Your life is spilling over with sin and you can't come to the Lord's house on his day and beg for forgiveness? I'm disgusted with you."

"Sorry to disappoint," I say, still keeping my distance.

"You are more than a damn disappointment. Lord knows I did everything for you and look how you turned out—fat, ugly, stuck with a kid and an old man for a husband and you're only twenty-three. No, 'disappointment' don't cover it."

I watch as she flicks ashes everywhere, waving her arms to dismiss me. She walks to the sink and tosses her cigarette. Then opens the fridge and takes out Leroy's last beer. She pops the top and starts chugging it.

I don't know what to do with this. This woman is possibly the cruelest creature I've ever encountered. How can she talk to Leann like this? Has she done this all her life? I guess if your choices are a bitter, mean old woman and a stupid, bossy old man, I'd go with the guy too. But there had to have been another choice.

The microwave alarm goes off and Trevor runs out the door without saying a word. I have less than an hour before I need to be at work. I'm not sure what this woman is expecting. I fix myself a cup of instant coffee. She doesn't say a word, just sits at the table, lights another cigarette, and finishes off the beer with a burp.

"So what's this job that's more important than the Lord on Sundays?"

"I'm working in a child care center at a gym."

"So you'll be congregating with a bunch of heathens that don't even bother with church? I remember when everything was closed on Sundays. I don't know why they ever changed that. Probably because them liberal God-haters are in charge. It's the Lord's Day and the only place people need to be is church. And that includes you, Leann. You better show up next Sunday or Pastor Mitch will be coming to call, you hear?"

I nod and drink my coffee, scalding my tongue. I grab the last of the Twinkies and put on my coat.

"I'll try to be there if I can. I've got to get to work."

She follows me out of the apartment. I watch as she gets in a beat-up, mustard-colored Cadillac and speeds off still puffing on her cigarette with all the windows closed. She seems like a comic book character to me. I visualize her driving through space in her Cadillac filled with smoke. Actually, she channels the Wicked Witch of the West pretty well too. What a nasty woman. Poor Leann.

Today's shift in the Kiddie Korner goes much better than yesterday. I manage to refrain from yelling any obscenities at the children and actually enjoy holding the babies. My belly is so large, some of the babies fit stretched out full length across it and I hold them against me with one arm. They smell really good, too.

Trying to save money and get some exercise, I walk to the Shop N Save. My feet hurt before I even step up to my register. I survive the day but resolve to buy better shoes with my very first paycheck from the gym. When I get home, Jillian is furious that I didn't leave anything decent to eat. I ask her what would be "decent" and she says I could at least buy some chips. I can't afford anything, not even chips. I promise to leave something tomorrow and ask what Trevor ate. "I don't know. Something." Great.

ᔕ ᔕ

leann

A big fat check's been sitting on the kitchen table watching me. It's enough to buy me pizzas and vodka for years. Only problem is I don't know what to do with it. I ain't never cashed a check before. Leroy always takes my check to cash. He gives me money for groceries and when I run out, I just grab some freebies from the store. Trevor likes his cheese curls and I'd die if I don't have my Tastykakes, but that shit costs more than the money Leroy give us. Course, he'd never do without his Twizzlers. Some weeks I don't need to steal anything, but lately I been doing it a lot more.

I'd never have to do that again, if I knew what to do with this check.

I don't know how banks work. Brenda says the Shop N Save just wanted everything settled quietly. So Carin's dad made 'em pay up. Brenda says he's gonna sit me down and tell me how to invest it wisely. I don't want to invest it wisely, I want to cash it. I've figured how to get cash out of credit cards. I just ask 'em to put more on the credit card and give me the money. They can do that. So far I got three hundred bucks in a sock in my drawer. I wish I knew what to do with that check.

Today I'm supposed to meet Lawrence, Carin's dad. I talked to him once on the phone, but that was back when my head was first bashed in and I don't really remember much except him clearin' his throat a bunch of times.

I tried on all the pretty hats that Brenda bought for me. It's drivin' her near crazy that my hair is all chopped off. Carin's got lots of pictures of herself all over the apartment, like she can't remember what she looks like. Her hair was pretty—kinda brown and red and gold all mixed up together. She musta dyed it 'cause that can't be natural. The hats look silly, but I find a baseball cap in the closet and put that on to cover the bald spot and stitches.

I take a bus to my old neighborhood. I just want a glimpse of Trevor. I sit on a bench across the street from where he catches the bus. I'm so nervous I'm shaking. And now here he comes walkin' up the street. All swagger and cuteness. Oh, I just want to go scoop him up, but that might freak him out. I taught him not to mess with strangers and that's what I am, a stranger.

I watch him drop his backpack on the ground and pick up a straw under the bench. He starts poking the straw in the holes on the sidewalk. Then he looks through the straw up at the sky. I take a picture of that with my heart and wish I could use that big fat check to buy a camera. Trevor's looking at them big puffy clouds. I look up at them too and when I look back, I can't see Trevor anymore 'cause the bus is blocking my view.

Lawrence told me to meet him at the offices on Montrose Avenue. I catch the next bus and work my way uptown. When he sees me, Carin's dad grabs me in a stiff hug. He is all angles and points, this man. It's like hugging a damn board. But it's something.

He smiles. "Well, young lady. You are a lucky woman, it seems."

This makes no sense. "I ain't sure it's so lucky to get cracked on the head by a valentine."

He frowns and leads the way into a maze of offices. My mind wanders around as he and another man in a suit talk about "investments" and "portfolios" and other crap I don't under-stand. In the end, they want me to give them the check and sign a bunch of papers, but before I do, I want to know I'll be getting plenty of cash. Just in case I figure out how to get Trevor back. Kids is expensive. Maybe I can send Trevor to a fancy boarding school like Ashley sent Jim-James to on my soap.

"Before I sign anything, I want to know how much cash I get each month."

"You have a monthly stipend that should be enough with your salary to live comfortably, but you can always take out money if necessary, though there would be a penalty." He pushes a paper with the number figure on it across the table to me.

"I need twice that." I'm shooting for the moon here, but I don't plan on setting foot in that office of Carin's and I need money so I can figure out how to get me and Trevor out of this town.

Lawrence chimes in. "That seems excessive Carin. Your mother and I have been over this. You can live easily on this, plus some yearly dividends that will allow you to travel."

"It's my money, ain't it?"

"Well, of course . . ."

"Then change it or I'll just take the check and cash it somewheres."

The men get all worked up over that, but they talk some more and then new papers pop out of the computer. I look over the papers carefully. The words make no sense, but I'm looking for the number. I find it and sign everything.

As we're walking out, Lawrence says, "Carin, I think you were a little disrespectful and rude in there. I don't know what's gotten into you, but I suppose this has been a difficult time. Still, you're going to profit nicely from it. You should appreciate that and all that people are doing for you, particularly your mother. She's having a tough time of it."

I don't want to listen to this puffed up man lecture me.

"Tell her I'm fine, Pop. I don't really need her help. I'll see ya." I turn and hurry off before he can give me another one of his boney hugs or offer to buy the lunch he owes me.

Later, Scott drives me to the bank and helps me figure out how to get money out of Carin's bank account. I can't believe these people will just give me money for nothing. It's like a-whole-no-ther world.

When I climb into bed, I can't shake the feeling this is all a huge scam. Someone's gonna figure it out. And then I'll have to pay it all back, and how could I do that?

chapter 8

In the morning I ask Trevor what he had for dinner and he says, "I had those curly noodles in the orange pack." He means the ramen noodles. That was the last pack. I don't know what he'll eat tonight. I've got to find something. I remember helping my mother pack emergency boxes at her church. The boxes were given to desperate people when they came to the church for money. My mother said the boxes were better than giving money because they couldn't use it to buy alcohol or drugs. I get dressed and leave even before Trevor.

I find the church with only two bus transfers. I won't have enough bus tokens to get through the week now. The church is locked. I ring the bell, but no one answers. I lean against the door and look up at the sky. Why does everything have to be so hard? As if to answer, it starts to rain. A cold, drenching rain. I push myself up against the doorway trying to get out of it, but I'm much too big to be shielded by the meager overhang. Finally, a man comes up the steps with a key.

"Can I help you?" he says brightly.

"I need food for my little boy," I say. I know I sound cliché, and he probably thinks I want money for drugs, if my mother is to be believed, but he smiles and invites me inside. I follow him down a long hallway, past the sanctuary that smells like my grandmother's perfume.

He unlocks a closet and asks, "How many children do you have?"

"Just one—he's six."

He pulls out one of the emergency boxes and carries it to an office. He sets it on the desk and fishes around in a drawer for something. He hands me an envelope.

"I hope this will help. It has information about resources that the county offers. Oh, and here," he reaches into another drawer and pulls out a roll of bus tokens.

I thank him again, and he walks me to the door. He asks my name and without thinking I tell him Carin.

"Carin, I'll pray for you."

I hurry to the bus stop with my box of food. The rain has slowed to a persistent trickle. I make it home and leave the box of food on the table. None of it is perishable (or very healthy). No chips, but the store brand cheese curls might appease Jillian.

I'm late for work in the Kiddie Korner and Denise gives me a short lecture on reliability. She pronounces it "REE-liability" which irritates me. I'm the most reliable person in the world. I apologize and promise I won't be late again.

My shift at the gym is 9:00 a.m. to 1:00 p.m. on weekdays. That leaves me with two hours before I have to be at the Shop N Save. I'm sitting on the bench just outside the Kiddie Korner, rubbing my feet and considering my options, when Bruce sits down beside me.

"Leann, right?" he asks brightly.

I smile at him. He really is a nice guy. It's too bad he's gay. I wish straight guys could be more like gay men. Gay men are much more attentive. They remember names, and they notice when you get your hair cut.

"Bruce, right?" I counter.

"Right you are. How's the job working out?" He gestures behind us.

"I'm figuring it out. I like the babies."

He smiles.

"So, are you ready to start your journey to fitness now?"

I hadn't even thought about my journey. I've been too focused on my survival. But now that he mentions it, exercise might be just what I need.

"I'd like that, very much. But I don't have any workout shoes. These are my only shoes, and they really hurt my feet. I can't afford anything else right now. Maybe when I get my first pay-check I can get some."

Bruce considers this. "What size are you? We have a huge box of sneakers our members donate to be recycled. Some of them look barely worn. Maybe we can find a pair for you." He gets up and motions for me to follow.

I've donated all my old shoes to this gym for years. I never even cleaned them up before I dropped them off. They were smelly and dirty, but he's right, they were barely worn out. I bought new sneakers every four months, like clockwork. I have a thing about working out in the right footwear. In the closet at my apartment I have no less than six pairs of workout shoes: running, aerobics, racquetball, weight lifting, walking, and hiking. I've probably spent more on workout shoes than Leann makes in four months. Seems like overkill at this juncture of my life. I follow Bruce to the big cardboard bin near the entrance.

Bruce lifts the box and carries it to his office. I don't know what size shoe Leann wears, so when I sit down and take off mine, I check the bottom. It's been worn completely off, ditto for the inside tag. I tell Bruce I don't really know what size I am. He pulls out a few pairs of shoes and starts untying the laces. We find two pairs that fit me. It feels great to have decent shoes on my feet—even if they are used.

"Okay, Leann, let's get started!"

Bruce spends the next hour with me. He has me do a tread-mill test. I'm sadly unable to walk for long without my heart rate getting too high.

Next, Bruce steers me towards the recumbent bikes. I used to log nearly an hour on one of those bikes every day. It was the first machine I hit each morning. I loved them for the view. I liked to watch the muscles in my legs work and sitting on the bikes offers a clear view of the free weight area filled with men to admire. It's a great way to start the day.

"Now, swimming would be another excellent choice. We do have a lap pool, so you might want to consider that," he advises.

I nod and sit gingerly on the bike machine. Putting this body in a swimsuit is something I really never want to experience. When I wedge my feet on to the pedals, my knees are forced to bend at an uncomfortable angle and my waistband digs into my middle so hard I can barely breathe. Without missing a beat, Bruce reaches between my legs and adjusts the seat. He has to wedge his hand between my massive thighs to reach the lever. I cringe, but he seems unfazed. The seat slides back and my legs straighten out. Bruce notes the seat adjustment on my chart.

Next, Bruce shows me several Nautilus machines. I really want to do the free weights, but he is insistent that this is the place to start. After he finishes setting me up on six machines, we go back to his office and he writes out my schedule.

"So you'll start tomorrow with twenty minutes of cardio and twenty minutes of weights. And then you'll add five minutes of cardio every week until you're up to one hour. After a month, we'll look at your weight workout again."

I smile happily. It feels good. Bruce smiles at me and continues, "Now, I don't want you to get discouraged. Let me know if you can't keep up with this. It might prove a little overwhelming at first."

"I can handle it. I can absolutely handle it." I'm excited. I can't wait to get back here tomorrow, but when I get up to leave I feel how sore my body is already. And I still have an eight-hour shift that starts in less than thirty minutes. I thank Bruce and make my way gingerly to the bus stop. I carry the extra shoes in my purse. I donated Leann's shoes at the gym.

I'm getting used to my job at the Shop N Save. I feel like a real cashier. I try to be friendly and helpful, but most customers don't even look at me. They keep their eyes focused on their food and their money. I'm pretty much an obstacle to them. Every now and then, someone nice gets in my line. Many people seem surprised if I speak to them. I forget that Leann, the Leann I used to know, never spoke to anyone.

A few elderly customers come in every day. One woman, Geraldine, loves to talk. She gives me a running itinerary of her day while I bag her groceries. I love when she talks about her grandchildren. She is so proud. One of them is a six-year-old boy, so I pump her for information.

"What kinds of books does he like to read? Does your daughter let him play video games? Does he make his own breakfast?" She answers all my questions and seems delighted to do it. I think Trevor is probably smarter than her grandson, but I'm sure I'm biased. Her daughter only lets her grandson play video games for thirty minutes a day. I'm not sure how I could enforce that with Jillian in charge of almost all of Trevor's time in the apartment. Geraldine tells me that her grandson could make his own breakfast, but his mother doesn't like him to do it because he makes such a mess. I smile and think proudly of how well Trevor handles the task of feeding himself. Of course, his basic dish is Froot Loops out of a napkin. Still, he doesn't spill many.

At break time I head outside. I think about the food in the box I left in my kitchen and hope Jillian hasn't eaten all of it before I get home. Tonight for my dinner I'm eating little packets of stale saltines I found in the back of the cupboard and cream cheese packets from the salad bar. I'm so hungry it actually tastes delicious.

"Quite a meal you got there," says Jimmy as he jumps down from the loading dock and walks over. He pulls his baseball cap down tighter and sits on a milk crate.

"It's all I had at home," I say, embarrassed to think he was watching me squirt cream cheese packets into my mouth. I unwrap a mint for dessert and offer him one. He takes it and puts it in his pocket.

"How long have you worked here?" I ask. He cocks his head at me, seeming surprised, but doesn't answer. We sit in silence for what feels like a long time. Being Leann has taught me to say less. Since I don't know what she would say, I tend to be quiet. It's amazing how much people will say if you're quiet. No one likes silence, although Jimmy seems quite at home with it. I'm just about to get up and go back in when he says, "I've been here since I quit high school. That'd be five years, I suppose."

"That's how long I've been here," I say with enthusiasm. Now here is a fact about Leann that I do know, thanks to Leroy.

"Huh," says Jimmy. He's not impressed. The fact that Jimmy started working here about the same time as Leann makes me wonder if they were friends. Maybe he's noticed that I'm not acting like Leann. Five years is a long time to work with someone. If Jimmy thinks anything, he doesn't say. He gets up and jumps back on the loading dock. "Hey," he says as he disappears into the darkness. I don't know if the "Hey" is his way of saying goodbye or if he is saying hello to someone in the loading bay.

I recognize a small flutter of physical attraction building in me. Is this my interest or Leann's? I wonder how that works. It's my mind, but it's her body, so who controls the physical reactions? Jimmy is cute and mysterious, but he's definitely weird and he never graduated from high school. Not my type and besides, I'm married, right?

I'm curious what Trevor and Jillian had for dinner. When I get home, I stand in front of the door, blocking Jillian's escape.

"How was your evening?"

"Peachy. Gotta run." Jillian tries to move around me, but I shift my weight sideways and she can't get around me.

"Did you have a nice dinner?"

She rolls her eyes and sighs heavily. "We ate."

"What did you eat?"

"Since when do you care? We left plenty for you," Jillian shoves past me, squeezing between me and the door frame, and I let her go. Not that I wouldn't rather throttle her.

I inspect the food box. It contains three boxes of macaroni and cheese, which would be great if I had the butter and milk required to make them. Five cans of SpaghettiOs-type meals and five little cans of potted meat line the bottom of the box. How do you eat potted meat? On crackers? That must be why they put in the huge box of saltines. I'm guessing that Jillian and Trevor had peanut butter sandwiches and cheese curls for dinner, since the bread and peanut butter have been hit pretty hard and the cheese curl bag is empty. Canned vegetables, a bag of dried beans, some generic cereal, mashed potato flakes, and a big can of applesauce complete our week's supplies.

My body is craving something to eat, but everything requires more effort than I can make after the day I've had, so I fix a peanut butter sandwich and open the applesauce. I'm still hungry, so I open the green beans and eat them straight out of the can.

Lying in bed, I think about money. Why does Leann have to give Leroy her paycheck? Why doesn't he give Leann more money? What is he doing with all his money? If he's driving a truck, why do I have to steal food for us to eat? I thought truckers made good money. No way is he a real trucker. Maybe he's a drug trafficker. Of course, if he was, we wouldn't be living in this dump.

I drift off to sleep imagining Leroy has another life during the week with another wife squirreled away in another dumpy apartment. But that doesn't make sense either.

ᑭᑫ

leann

Carin's fridge is full of healthy crap. Brenda said she filled it before I got here. I eye the cookies Scott left behind. He came over last night and wanted to make pizza for me. It was just pizza in a box. I told him my stomach hurt. He was all "poor you" and shit, but at least he left. After he was gone, I cooked up the pizza and tried to eat the whole thing. My stomach started hurting about half way through. Normally, I can put away one all by myself. Sometimes at work, Franklin gives me the damaged stuff Vernon tells him to toss. One time it was a whole case of pizzas that was kinda smashed. I ate those things for a week. One every day for lunch. I guess Carin's stomach ain't as big and it won't fit. So I threw the rest out.

I tear open the cookies, but they got nuts all through 'em so I toss those too. Usually, I just pick off the nuts, but these ones are cooked right in. Everything else is rabbit food. I shut the fridge and that's when I see the stack of takeout menus under a magnet. I call the Italian place and order a big plate of lasagna, cheese rolls, and a two-liter bottle of Coke. Then I rattle off the credit card number. As the lady takes down the card, I notice they have desserts and order a cheesecake too.

An hour after my food gets here, I end up in the bathroom puking up the cheesecake. As I'm kneeling by the toilet, I hear the front door open and Brenda's voice calling, "Carin, sweetie, everything okay?"

I don't answer. I freeze. Maybe she'll think I'm out and go away. But she finds me.

"Honey, what happened? Should I call the doctor?"

"I'm fine," I say into the toilet.

"You most certainly aren't fine."

"Yeah, I am."

She takes my arm and yanks on me. "Let's get you in the shower and clean you up. Scott will be here in a little while and we can't have him seeing you like this."

This woman is nuts. When she gets me upright, she starts to pull my shirt over my head like I'm some little kid. I clamped my arms down and shout at her, "Don't touch me. I can take off my own damn clothes!" But right then my stomach heaves, and I lunge for the toilet again.

"I realize you're sick, but that is no reason to talk to me like that, young lady. I'm your mother!"

I wipe my mouth with my sleeve and look down at the toilet. It is all I can do not to go psycho on this lady.

"Just leave me alone. I don't want your help. I'm sick of you bitching at me to wash my hair, change my clothes, put on makeup. I'm not a baby. And I'll take a fucking shower when I want to!"

"Well, I was just trying to help. And this is the thanks I get!" She turns and marches right out of the apartment. Shit, if I'd known it would be that easy to get rid of her I would've yelled at her back at the rehab center.

chapter 9

Wednesday
I'm so sore I can't even imagine working out. I'm disgusted with this body for betraying me after only one workout. My legs ache, and even with new shoes my feet are throbbing. My sides hurt, and I can barely lift my arms to shoulder height. Still, when I finish my time in the Kiddie Korner, Bruce is waiting for me.

"I thought you might try to sneak out today. I bet you're sore," he says, all smiles as he pats me on the back. I hate it when guys pat you on the back. Men really shouldn't do that. I'm a woman, not your buddy.

"Hi, Bruce. I don't think I can do it today. Everything hurts."

"Tell you what, just do some time on the bike and then maybe a couple machines. It's important that you do something. Get the routine started."

I sigh. I look down the hall to the exit. I look back at Bruce and he takes my arm and steers me towards the machines.

"C'mon, you'll feel better once you get moving."

I seriously doubt that, but I don't seem to have a choice. I sit down on one of the bikes, but have to climb back off because I forgot to adjust the seat. Once settled, I slowly pedal. Every muscle in my legs hurts and I don't have any tension on the pedals at this point. God, this is depressing. But I keep going. I think about Trevor and how much more I'll be able to do with him once I lose some weight. I think about Leann and how she must be enjoying my body. I hope she isn't smoking in it.

I think about Scott and how sad I feel for him. He does care about me, after all. I think he was just as scared as I was to reveal how he really feels. That's always been my hang-up. I will never be the first one to say "I love you." Never. If the other person doesn't feel that way, you look stupid. I have never been a vulnerable person. Leann is completely vulnerable all the time. Look at the way people treat her. Just going out in public makes her vulnerable. She can't hide her size, so she suffers unfair abuse. I guess I get that. No one ever buys the "you can't judge a book by its cover" lesson they give you in grade school. Most of us totally judge the book by its cover. It sucks to be fat.

Before I know it, I have pedaled for fifteen minutes and resolved to take a stand for Leann. I'm not going to let people treat her like crap anymore. Just because I'm stuck inside this body, it doesn't mean it's all I am. I feel more confident and move the tension to one on the bike. I will pedal for five more minutes. The sweat is pouring down my face, but today I have time for a shower. I can't wait to have unending hot water.

I'm startled out of my shower fantasy by Scott. He walks into the cardio center and hops on a treadmill just to my left. He quickly accelerates until he is sprinting on the machine. I can only see the side of his face, but he looks upset. He pumps his arms and then pushes a few buttons until the machine is moving so fast it's vibrating. I watch his legs. He has really nice legs—completely defined, every muscle and tendon shimmering under the skin. I would love to touch those legs again. I'd like to trace the path of his muscles. Wow, I'm getting myself all excited, so maybe I am in control of Leann's body. I'm definitely turned on watching Scott run. So what's with all the funny feelings around Jimmy?

By the time I reach the Shop N Save, I feel inspired. I worked out two days in a row. Two days. I'm on my journey to fitness. I will make Bruce proud. When I'm putting my things in the locker, Franklin comes up behind me and puts his hands on my hips and says, "Hey baby, we got a couple minutes before my break ends."

I smack his leering face. He laughs and grabs his cheek. "So that's how it's gonna be? I like it!"

I glare at him and he backs out of the break room, still laughing. Jerk. What is his problem? Did Leann actually welcome his advances? She has absolutely no taste when it comes to men.

The afternoon goes by slowly. I talk with customers, even writing out my pasta salad recipe for an older man who is cooking for a first date. He thanks me and leaves with his groceries and a big bunch of flowers. Lucky man. Lucky woman.

At break time, I unpack my dinner—saltines and potted meat. It looks like dog food, but doesn't smell too bad. I remember I had a friend who used to love to eat this stuff mixed with ketchup. I'm eating in the break room today, so that I can use a plate and knife. The glaring lights and blaring television are not relaxing. When I finish I step outside for a few minutes of air. I suck on a mint and look at the stars. It's a clear night and not as cold. I can smell spring coming.

I bump into Jimmy as I'm headed back up front to my register.

"Hey," he says.

"Hi," I say and we both just look at each other for a moment.

"I just had break," I say.

"I'm going out now. You see any stars?"

"Lots. I think you can even see the Milky Way."

"Huh. I'll check it out." He nods, shoves his hands in his pockets, and walks past me.

My heart is beating quickly, which is silly. I have no interest in a man who wears coveralls to work and can't carry on a conversation longer than three sentences. This silly fluttering must be Leann. She truly can't pick 'em. He is cute, though, I'll give her that.

The rest of the week goes much the same. Rush to the gym, hold babies, clean up toys, work out (sadly I can't do much more than I could on Wednesday), shower, rush to Shop N Save, rush home, duck out of Jillian's way, and collapse into bed. I'm left with no time to consider what Leroy is up to and no time to confront Leann.

Now it's Friday night and I still don't have a plan. I'm sitting on the milk crates out back, hoping Jimmy will show up (why?) and considering my options. The best one I've come up with so far is to get Leroy drunk and make him talk. My other thought is to break into my apartment and threaten Leann with the baseball bat in my coat closet. But I can't kill her because then I won't have a body to go home to. Besides, neither plan is possible with Trevor in tow.

"You look like you're a million miles away," says Jimmy. We seem to have developed an unspoken agreement to meet for dinner on the milk crates each night.

"I'm not really that far," I say, smiling stupidly at him. Tonight I'm eating the macaroni and cheese I cooked this morning. Instead of milk and butter, I used water and vegetable oil. It tastes pretty horrible, but it's better than another night of potted meat. I left a note for Jillian to heat it up and open the last can of vegetables for Trevor. They've been existing on peanut butter and saltines since the bread ran out.

We eat in silence. Jimmy burps, loudly, and it echoes off the trees. He says, "Oops," and I start to giggle. The giggle turns to hysterical laughter. Jimmy looks at me like I'm nuts, but soon he is laughing too and then just to prove his point, he burps again, but much louder. I wish I could burp, but I've never been able to make a sound. My mother taught me when I was young—ladies don't burp. I've trained my body to swallow burps before any real sound comes out. It kind of hurts, but I don't know any other way.

When we've recovered, I say, "I wish I could burp."

Jimmy looks at me like I have three heads. "Impossible! Everyone can burp," he assures me.

"I can't," I tell him.

"Yes, you can. I don't believe you've never burped."

"Not out loud. My mother would never let me."

"But what about when your mom's not around?"

"Nope."

"Never?"

"Well, maybe once when I was really drunk."

"Here, take a drink of my Coke and then burp."

I'm doubtful, but take a big gulp. It tastes so cold and sweet I want to drink the entire thing. The caffeine hits me too and I feel a physical rush. Then the biggest burp I've ever heard comes barreling out of me. I look at Jimmy shocked and we both start laughing. I forgot that I'm not Carin. Leann can burp with the best of them.

Jimmy points to the can again and I swig the rest of it and let out another huge burp. We are still laughing as we make our way back into the store. I'm wearing a leftover smile as I step behind my register and flick on my light. I look up, and standing in my line is my mother.

She doesn't look at me. I stare at her as I pass her groceries over my scanner. She finishes loading the belt, and then waits by the credit card machine. She doesn't ever help bag her own groceries. I've never understood this. In fact, we argued about it. I told her how much better it is to bag your own. That way you know where everything is and it's easier to unload them. She looked at me like I was crazy and insisted, "It's not my place to do that, dear. It's the cashier's job. How would it look if I bagged my groceries?"

My mother loves to be waited on. She pays someone to clean her house, not because she doesn't have time to do it herself, but because she thinks it's beneath her to clean it. She has her parties catered for the same reason. I had to figure out how to clean my house once I was on my own. My mom was astounded to find I could cook and clean—as if these were foreign skills. She would walk into my apartment and make a fuss over a meal or new paint on my walls—like I'd brought my kindergarten project home to show her. And here she is, waiting for me to bag her groceries.

"There you go, Mrs. Fletcher," I say as I load up her last bag. She looks up at me, startled. I'm not sure if she remembers me from the hospital. I'm hoping she'll speak to me. I need to hear her voice and so far all she's done is nod at every comment I've made. She looks at me carefully, trying to figure out whether to acknowledge me. I'm not the kind of person Mrs. Brenda Fletcher would associate with.

She nods again and says, "Thank you," before turning quickly and pushing her cart out of the store. I watch her go. Do I miss her? I suppose. Even though I can see clearly now that she is critical and snobby, she is my mother. I guess I'm like Trevor that way. No matter how rotten your mother treats you, no matter how much she ignores you, she's still your mother. You still want to love her.

It's not that my mother doesn't love me. She just has this need to make me into her. And believe me, I tried to be her. She is beautiful and elegant and incredibly classy. All my life I've tried to be those things too. I do think they are admirable qualities and worth striving for, but sometimes they miss the point. Sometimes it's more important to be loved than to be beautiful. This is becoming quite clear to me as I live this odd, lonely life of Leann's. The problem with the way my mother lives is that she misses out on so much. She spends her time making sure everything is "just so" and consequently she's not really living. It's more like rehearsing.

I think maybe I was doing that too. I thought if I made my life look absolutely perfect, then I would be happy. It was part of the plan. My mother does love me, in her own way. She just doesn't know me. And I'm beginning to think I don't know me either.

It seems awful that my own mother doesn't recognize me for who I am. Or that she and Scott haven't figured out yet that Leann is not me. Neither of them can hear anything I'm saying when I'm in velour pants and a Shop N Save apron. How is it that I've lived twenty-three years and not a soul in the world can recognize me for me without all the trimmings?

On my way home from work, I stop at a check cashing store. They take a portion for their troubles, but I want to keep some of the money I earned before I hand it over to Leroy. I stop at 7-Eleven and buy Twizzlers and eggs and even some donuts. In the morning, I'll go back to Shop N Save and buy more groceries with this money. I hide some of it in my sock and put half of it in my pocket to hand to Leroy.

It's well past midnight when I turn my key in the lock. The lights are off in the apartment and I can hear the TV running. I call quietly, "Hello?" I creep to the kitchen and put the eggs in the refrigerator. I open the Twizzlers and eat one while I decide whether I should sleep on the couch or chance waking Leroy up. I know sooner or later I'm going to have to sleep in the same bed with him, but I'd prefer it to be later. Before I know it, I've eaten half the bag of Twizzlers. Somehow the sugar and the chewing feel comforting. I put the rest of the Twizzlers in the cabinet and leave the donuts on the table. I opt for the couch.

~ ~

leann

I click off the TV and put the rest of the bagel on the coffee table. I've discovered the limit to how much I can eat before this body gets pissed off and starts puking. I been in this apartment a couple days now and I'm bored shitless. Once the soaps are over, which is when I used to go to work, there's nothing to do.

Mostly I order takeout food and read Carin's journals. That girl is messed up. She writes about how fat she is or how some guy used her or how her friend Marta, the one with the kid, is so boring. Sometimes she writes about Scott. Maybe I should show him. She said she ain't gonna marry him ever. She likes him, but she don't love him. That's what she says. She's always blubbering about Brenda too. First she's mad, and then she's all "poor mother" this and "poor mother" that and talking about how she's from another *generation*. Like *Star Trek*? I don't understand half of what she writes, but I like reading it. It's the real insides of someone besides me.

Carin's got lots of books. Sometimes I look at them, but I'm kinda afraid to read them. I haven't read a book in a long time. Mostly, I try on her clothes. I look pretty good. It's still hard to believe that's me in the mirror. Only I know it isn't. I'm working up the nerve to go out like this, but it feels weird. I feel real small, like I might blow away.

I find some vodka in the freezer and mix up a drink with my leftover Dr. Pepper. Don't taste so great, but it gives me nerve. I put on the shortest skirt in the closet and a lace-up shirt, laced real tight, which kinda makes me look like I have boobs. Carin has got some kick-ass shoes, but I'm nervous about the real tall ones. My special red ones at home hurt my feet. Leroy had them made special, but he didn't know my size. They're our secret. Jillian put them on once and I caught her. She laughed, but Leroy smacked her around good. Teach her to mess with my stuff.

It's almost nine o'clock when I decide I'm going out. I drink another glass of vodka and head out. I ask the maintenance guy downstairs and he tells me which way to the mall. I have a car, but I ain't never driven before. Leroy let me drive his big truck once in a parking lot. That was a long time ago. I didn't do so great. I couldn't figure out the gears. I look around the parking lot, but I don't know which car is Carin's, anyway. That's kinda funny and I laugh. It echoes across the empty parking lot.

I find a bus stop and buy some tokens out of the machine. I keep dropping them and instead of picking them up, I watch them roll off the curb into the street. When I get on the bus, I go to the back, like always. Hardly no one is on the bus. I get off at the mall and make a beeline for the arcade. It closes at ten, which I forgot. I ain't been here in a long time. Leroy didn't like me going there. He said guys would try to pick me up and they just want one thing, but most guys avoid me, so I don't know what he was worried for.

The place is loud and gangs of kids are roaming around in packs. Most of them are younger than me. I look for a game I know, but everything is loud and flashy. Kids are dancing at one machine and I watch them. A funny-looking guy with a tattooed neck comes over and stands next to me. He wants to know if I want to play the game I'm leaning on. I think the vodka is hitting me 'cause everything seems to be moving real slow.

We start playing and then it's my turn and the tattoo guy rubs up next to me and I think he's got a hand near my ass. Can't be sure 'cause, like I said, everything's starting to get fuzzy. It's been a long time and I'm all weirded out by the tattoo guy, so I lose pretty quick. He laughs and starts his turn. I look around and feel like everyone is staring at me. A big guy near the change machine is looking at me all hungry like. And the nice lady in the snack bar must not be working, 'cause a black kid is behind the counter flirting with a bunch of skinny white girls.

I think maybe I should leave. But before I can make a move, tattoo guy nudges me. It's my turn again. This time when I'm playing, I definitely feel his hand on my ass. It don't necessarily feel bad, but I don't know what I should do. I ain't never had a guy, except Leroy, try to touch me since those jerks at school. He'd be so mad if he saw me now. Course, he wouldn't know it was me.

I ask tattoo guy what his name is and he says, "Austin." I tell him I ain't never known anyone named Austin, seems like a girl's name. Austin asks me if I want to check out his ride. This seems funny and doesn't make sense to me, but I follow him. I'm starting to feel sick anyways, and I think I should go home.

An hour later, Austin drops me off at my apartment and wants me to give him my number. I don't think just 'cause you have sex with a person you need to give him your number. Besides, I don't know my number. Something else to figure out. I tell Austin I'll see him at the arcade and climb out of his low-rider truck. I thought you jacked up trucks, but Austin's near about drags on the ground. Go figure.

chapter 10

〜 〜

When I wake on the couch, Trevor is sitting on the floor about five inches from the television screen. He has the sound down low.

"Hey Trevor," I say, smiling at him.

He looks worried. "I ate a donut," he says, cringing.

"Good, I bought them for you."

"You did? I thought maybe they were for Daddy's friends."

"Nah, they can get their own donuts," I tell him, sitting up. "Is Daddy still sleeping?"

Trevor looks at me quizzically and shakes his head. "I don't think Daddy slept here last night."

"He didn't?"

"He went out right after he told me to go to bed."

I get up and inspect the bedroom. The bed is still made just the way I left it. No Leroy. I'm relieved, but my relief turns to panic when I hear the front door slam open while I'm in the shower.

"Hey, Bitch! Where are you?" he yells. Then he's standing in the bathroom and he pulls the shower curtain back. "What the hell happened to you last night? You were off work at eleven and still not here at midnight!" He's looking at me, waiting for my answer, but I'm frozen. I am horrified to be standing naked in front of him. I know he's seen this body, but not this body with me in it. I pull the curtain closed again.

"I had to make a couple stops."

He rips the curtain off the rod and glares at me. "What kind of stops? And where's your paycheck?"

I shut off the water, pull a towel from the rack, and try to cover myself as best I can. Leroy hasn't moved, he's still glaring at me, waiting for my answer. I can see water splattered on his T-shirt, his face is red and his eyes are blood shot. My heart skips a beat. Is he high? I measure my words, but I don't back down in my tone.

"I cashed my paycheck. I needed to buy some groceries and Trevor needs a decent coat. I put the rest of it in the jar on the counter. I wanted to make sure you got your eggs and Twizzlers, so I stopped at the store after I cashed my check."

"Since when do you handle the money? You can't handle money. You're too stupid, we've been over this. I give you the money you need."

"Why can't I handle my own money?" I'm really curious; it's not a rhetorical question.

"You don't need to ask me why. You'll just use it to buy McDonald's and booze. Or crap from the dollar store. You're the only person I know who can spend fifty bucks at the dollar store."

Interesting. What could Leann possibly want at the dollar store? I've been living in this body long enough to know she craves salt and sugar, so the fast food make sense, but the dollar store?

"Maybe I've changed," I say defiantly, meeting his stare and holding it.

"You sure as hell have changed. I don't know what's gotten into you, but I don't like it." I don't say anything. I just continue to match his stare. Finally he turns and walks out, muttering, "Crazy bitch."

I kind of like that he thinks I'm a crazy bitch. Maybe I am. I should be. I try to replace the shower curtain, but most of the holes are torn through. I finish my shower. When I leave the bathroom, Leroy is gone, but so is Trevor. I panic. I don't want him to have Trevor. He's high or drunk, or something. I dress as quickly as I can, but then don't know what to do. I don't even know where he parks his truck. Trevor. So I pace and then I get the Twizzlers back out and finish them, along with several donuts. Finally, I can't take it anymore, so I put on my coat and find my sock of money and shove it in my pocket.

Mr. Giovanni is sitting on his landing when I come out. "Need to do some laundry?" he asks, hopefully.

"Actually, I do, but right now I need to find Trevor and Leroy."

"They left a bit ago. Heard Leroy's bike start up."

He has a bike? Does that mean Trevor is on his motorcycle with no helmet and a crappy winter coat? That son of a bitch. I can do nothing about it, so I go to the Shop N Save and carefully buy groceries for our week. I buy plenty of bread and milk and cereal. I shop the day-old cart and the sales and manage to get enough for our meals. I didn't think about how I was going to get it all home without a car. As I wheel the cart into the parking lot, I consider my options. I could take the cart and walk home, or I could leave some of the stuff in my locker and bring it home in stages. Or I could make several trips. I'm still undecided when a car pulls up in front of me.

"Hey!" the driver calls.

It's Jimmy. He's wearing his baseball cap, but he's dressed nicely in a clean shirt and dress pants. I've only ever seen him in coveralls. He looks handsome.

"Hi," I say. He drives a beat-up old Pacer, the kind of car that looks like a tick. It has to be twenty years old, at least.

"You waiting for someone to pick you up?" he asks.

"Actually, I was trying to figure out how to get my groceries home. I don't have a car."

He doesn't even ask me why I would buy so much if I didn't have a way to get it home, he just hops out of the car and loads my groceries into his hatchback, then pushes the cart back to the cart corral and walks towards me. "Get in," he says.

I climb in. The seats are cracked and the carpet is completely bare. It doesn't look like anything works on the dashboard. Jimmy revs the engine a few times and then pulls out kind of quickly. "It stalls if I try to use first gear," he explains. "Where do you live?" he asks. I give him directions. Jimmy nods, but doesn't say anything.

We drive in silence. When we stop at the light I say, "I really appreciate this."

"I was picking up my paycheck. I didn't have a chance to get it last night, I had to be somewhere."

I wonder if he had a date, but don't ask. When we get to my place, he offers to bring the groceries up, but I'm terrified Leroy will see him, so I just have him unload them into the building entrance. He looks at me and nods.

"Thanks again. I don't know what I would have done without you."

"You'd have figured it out, I bet. I'll see ya." He gives me a quick smile and pulls away from the curb, the Pacer jerking as it struggles to get going.

It takes me three trips to get everything up to the apartment. I'm covered in sweat, head to toe. Leroy is still not back. I put away the groceries and then take some clothes to Mr. Giovanni's place. He offers to let me share his clothesline, since he doesn't have many things to wash. I start the washer and join him on the couch watching baseball.

"It's kind of early for baseball, isn't it?"

"I get the baseball channel. These are spring training highlights."

"You like baseball?"

"I love baseball. I played minor league when I was a young man. Loved the life, but then I settled down and got married. Always wished I'd gone back."

"Do you have any children?"

"Nah, my Shirley couldn't have any. We spoiled her nieces though. They're all grown now, and ever since Shirley passed they don't come around much."

"I'm sorry to hear that."

"How old's your little boy?"

"He's six," I tell him, worry rushing back at the thought of Trevor.

"He looks like his dad, I think. Too bad," he smiles at me apologetically. "He's sweet though and he seems very responsible.

I see him come down with his backpack in the morning. He don't talk to me much; bet his daddy tells him not to. That Leroy is bad news, no offense now."

"None taken. I agree. He's not the best."

Mr. G watches me, measuring his words. "Why are you stuck with him? Don't you think you can do better?"

Such a good question. And I've only got the vaguest idea of why Leann stays with him. I'm beginning to see she has a somewhat addictive personality, so maybe she's addicted to him. Or addicted to being treated badly. Or maybe she just doesn't have any self-respect. I wish I knew. I don't know how much longer I can stay with him. I guess it comes down to choices. Leann doesn't have many. She's kind of stuck here, and for the moment, I am too.

"I don't know why I stay here. Maybe someday I'll leave."

"Well, you better leave before he gets you into his trouble, is all I can say."

"What kind of trouble is he in?"

"I don't know, but I can smell trouble and he stinks."

I couldn't agree more, but I don't say so. I get up to move the laundry.

By five o'clock, Leroy and Trevor are not back. I've baked cookies, made four casseroles for Trevor and Jillian to heat up during the week, and fixed the shower curtain using duct tape. I heat soup for dinner. Even without my workout, I feel as though I ran a marathon. But I had to do something with all my worry about Trevor. Finally, the door opens and Leroy and Trevor walk in.

"Good, you made dinner. I'm starved," says Leroy.

"Where have you been?" I ask, trying not to sound angry.

"Out," says Leroy, and he disappears into the bathroom. Trevor looks at me and shrugs. "We went to some guy's house and I watched TV and Daddy did something in the basement. He bought me McDonald's for lunch," he says cheerfully.

"Did you wear a helmet on the motorcycle?" I ask.

"Why?"

"I think it's a law that you have to."

"Daddy says helmets are for sissies," says Trevor, turning on the TV.

I dish up three bowls of soup and set out sliced apples and cheese. I fish out the crackers packets from Leann's stash of restaurant freebies.

"Trevor, turn off the TV and come eat with me."

Leroy is still not out of the bathroom, so we start without him. When he joins us, he snorts in disgust. "This is dinner? I'm going out," he says and leaves. I divide his soup between Trevor and me.

Trevor spends the entire evening watching TV, cutting out pictures from the latest bunch of magazines, and playing with a small toy slingshot he got with his Happy Meal from McDonald's. If I was really his mom, wouldn't I be making him do something more redeeming? He's watched TV his entire day. I remind myself that I'm not his mom and go back to planning my encounter with Leann tomorrow.

After I finish work in the Kiddie Korner at 2:00 p.m., I plan to ask Denise to let Trevor stay at the center until five. That way I can talk to Leann without Trevor around. I have to keep him out of her sight so I can play the worry card on her. Maybe if she thinks I'm not taking care of him, she'll relent and own up to who she really is. After spending the past two weeks in her apartment, I shudder to think what my apartment looks like by now.

I surprise Trevor with microwave popcorn and convince him to turn off the TV. "Don't you have a new book from school we can read?" I ask.

He grins and shouts, "I've got three new books!" he rummages in his backpack and produces three books that are torn and bent and held together with packing tape. We have to get to a library soon.

"Where did these come from?"

"Ms. Olson gave 'em to me. She said I could keep 'em."

The books are beat up, but they're classics. The first one is *Are You My Mother?* by P. D. Eastman. I remember this book from when I was little. We snuggle on the couch, and each time I read "Are you my mother?" my heart aches. Does he know? Could he know? If anyone should recognize Leann for who she is, it would be him. If he does know, he doesn't let on, just burrows into my side and asks me to read the others.

Later, after we turn off the lights, I lie awake listening to Trevor's soft breaths as they slow to sleep and wonder if I could be his mother. If this situation never resolves itself and I'm stuck here as Leann forever, could I be his mother? I don't know what I'm doing. I could seriously mess this kid up. And he's so good. Better than I would be if I was in his situation.

I know now I had it good as a kid. I resented the way my mother dressed me up and showed me off and expected perfect grades and seamless manners, but at least she was paying attention to me. At least she was investing in who I would become. She had a plan for me. I don't think anyone has a plan for Trevor. He's an excuse for Leann's life and a nuisance for Leroy's, but no one is looking past today. They aren't considering what a life in this dingy apartment, ignored by adults and the TV ringing in his ears, will do to him.

Leroy returns at some point during the night. I've gotten so used to him sleeping on the couch or not coming home, I had forgotten to worry about him getting in the bed. When the bed shifts and I feel myself rolling towards the middle, I'm instantly wide awake. His leg presses against mine and he throws his arm around my middle. I remember sleeping snuggled like spoons with Scott and holding his hand in mine and pressing his fingers to my cheek. I loved the way our bodies curved together. Sleeping over at Scott's was much better than sleeping with Scott, if that makes any sense. Leroy's hand dangles in the air since his elbow can't clear my girth. He presses himself against my butt and I'm shocked and appalled to feel his excitement poking me. I can smell alcohol on his breath and cigarettes on his clothes (which he hasn't bothered to change before getting into bed, so now the bed will stink like him all week if I can't find somewhere to do laundry tomorrow). I stay frozen and try to breathe slowly so he'll think I'm asleep.

Leroy's arousal is short-lived and soon he is sleeping. I lie awake for hours before I quietly inch myself down to the bottom of the bed and crawl out. I tiptoe around Trevor, who hasn't moved, and stumble to the couch. I want to sleep, but my heart is racing. My mind is wild with fear. What if next time he isn't so drunk? Will I have to have sex with him? What if I say no? Did Leann ever tell him no? I've only seen glimpses of his temper, but I've seen enough.

chapter 11

Trevor appears next to the couch, startling me awake.

I have the urge to hug him, but he is already reaching for the TV remote.

"Maybe we could do without the TV today," I suggest.

"Nah," he says, and settles on the floor in front of the set.

I sigh and get up to get dressed. Lucky for me, Leann's clothes are still hanging in the bathroom to dry. I pull on sweats and pin my hair back. Hard to believe that only two weeks ago I spent at least an hour getting dressed every day and now I can do it in two minutes. Maybe I need to buy some makeup with my next paycheck. And hair products. But I guess food is more important.

I snap off the TV. "Get dressed sweetie, we're going out for breakfast." I don't really want to blow any of the few dollars I have left, but I also don't want to encounter Leroy this morning. With luck, he'll be gone by the time we get back tonight. I need to figure out what his routine is. So much is assumed around here and I don't want any more surprises.

I'm starving, but refrain from ordering anything at McDonald's as Trevor digs into a pancake breakfast. The smells are making me physically ache. I've got to eat something. When we get to the gym, I swoop on the complimentary bagels and cream cheese donated by a fitness equipment company. Trevor goes skipping back to the Kiddie Korner as I help myself to a bagel loaded down with half a bar of cream cheese. I can't seem to eat it fast enough. It's only when I've managed to shove the entire thing in my mouth that I look up and see Scott walking in. He glances at me and grimaces, bypassing the bagel table. I grab two more bagels and stuff them in my jacket and head back to the Kiddie Korner. I can't believe how quickly I ate that bagel and I really can't believe how much I wanted to eat several more. I have got to force some discipline on this body. The physical desire for food is spooky. I've never dreamed about food so much. I've been hungry before, but not like this. This is crazy desperate and the relief is pure.

The day seems to drag on and I never have an opportunity to ask Denise about keeping Trevor. I sneak out twice to watch Scott working on the weights. He catches me staring at him and looks away embarrassed. I can't help looking at him. He's the only link to my real life anymore. I wonder if I ever really loved him. I do miss him, but I think I just miss being with someone who knows me.

I finally ask Denise about leaving Trevor in the Kiddie Korner. She tells me it's against policy and a parent must be in the building. I tell her I need to visit someone in the hospital and they don't allow kids, but she is unyielding. I think she likes being able to tell me no.

When we get outside, I'm surprised to find it sunny and warm. Being in the gym is like being in a cave. I take Trevor's hand and head to the bus stop.

"Where're we going?" he asks.

"I need to see a friend." He doesn't ask what friend. I guess anywhere is better to him than that apartment.

As we approach the stop for my apartment, Trevor points out a playground I'd never noticed before. I was more focused on the jogging track that circles it.

When the bus lurches off, I still don't know what I'm going to do. We walk over to the playground. It doesn't take long for Trevor to make friends with two kids playing in the sandbox. Their mother is on a bench reading. I sit down on the other end. The bench lurches my way and nearly lifts her end off the ground. She glances at me and smiles a reserved smile. I grin back and shrug.

I ask, "What are you reading?"

She takes a deep breath, I've definitely annoyed her. She looks at me and I can see she is patronizing me with her kindness.

"*Little Women*," she says, and turns back to her book.

"I read that in high school, I think."

She nods, keeping her eyes on her book.

"How old are your kids?"

Now she sighs and sets down her book. "Do I know you?"

Rude. Rude. Rude. That's what she is, but suddenly I have an idea.

"Actually, I just moved in. My husband died. Trevor and I are making a go of it alone." When did I become such an accomplished liar?

She catches her breath and sets her book down, watching Trevor with watery eyes.

"That's so sad. How old is your son?"

"He's six."

"My boys are seven. They're twins actually, although they don't look like it. Joey is so much bigger than John."

"Wow, twins. I can't imagine dealing with that."

"I can't imagine living with your tragedy. I wish I could help you."

I pause as if I'm thinking and then say, "Actually, you could. Can I leave Trevor with you for about fifteen minutes? I need to run up and talk with someone in the apartments about a babysitting job."

She looks flustered and I can tell she doesn't really want to say yes, but I've trapped her. Clever me.

"Well . . . we can't stay much longer, but if it's only fifteen minutes, I guess I could keep an eye on him."

"Thanks so much!" I get up too quickly and her end of the bench thuds down again. I wave to Trevor, but he doesn't see me as I head for my apartment building.

Luckily, the entrance door is wedged open by a rock. All the tenants use this trick when they're carrying in groceries. Once inside the building, I head for the stairs. It was my habit to walk up the five flights to my apartment, but that might be difficult now, I realize. I doubt I could make it past the second floor. I head to the lobby and take the elevator. Mike, the super, is cleaning the floor. Mike is from some Middle Eastern country and I'm fairly certain his name isn't Mike, but that's what his shirt has always said. He must be in his forties, although his bushy black hair and tawny skin make him look much younger. I can't remember him ever being in a bad mood. "Can I help you?" he asks, straightening up and setting his mop down.

"I'm here to visit someone."

"Who?"

"Carin Fletcher."

"Yeah? How you know her?"

I don't know what to say. "Uh, we're friends."

"Huh?" he says, knowing I'm not my type.

The elevator opens and I get in. He is still watching me.

"She maybe not know you. Something not right with her head. She had accident. I hear she get rich suing big company."

As always, Mike offers too much information. I smile at him and wave as the doors close.

I reach my floor and walk down the hall to my door. I take a deep breath and press the bell. No one answers, so I press it again. What if she isn't here? This is my only chance to talk to her. I press the bell over and over and over. I can feel tears ready to spring. I can't do this much longer. Someone approaches and the peephole cover slides open. I duck out of view.

"Who's there?" It is downright eerie to hear my own voice on the other side of the door.

I ring the bell again.

"Who's out there? What the hell do you want?"

"It's me," I say.

After a long pause, I hear footsteps retreating. I push the buzzer again. And again and again. She won't answer, so I pound on the door. I pound until sweat pours down my face. I start kicking the door and yelling, "Leann, open the door, please!" Several other doors open and my old neighbors look at me. Soon, the elevator opens and Mike approaches me.

"Hey lady, she not want talk to you. You bothering other tenants. I think you go." He reaches for my arm. I jerk it away and glare at him. This is my apartment! This can't be happening. Maybe I should knock on my neighbors' door across the hall in 5F. Let them know about the UPS guy who stops by every day when the husband is at work. I know it doesn't take thirty minutes to deliver a package, and who gets that many deliveries anyway? Or maybe I should report the activities of 5C, where the smell of marijuana is so strong you can get high just waiting for the elevator. None of these people have the right to complain about a fat girl knocking on her own apartment door. But what can I do? I follow Mike to the elevator.

"What's happened to Carin?" I ask innocently.

"She got hit on head by some crazy lady at Shop N Save and now she going to be rich."

This doesn't make sense, but before I can ask another question, Mike continues.

"She never come out, but pizza guy deliver every day. Her mother real angry and sad. She always cry when she leave. Her boyfriend, Mr. Scott, always nice guy, but she not remember him. He comes by, she slams door. Poor man. He sad."

When we get to the door, I turn and apologize to Mike.

"It okay, everybody go a little crazy sometime. You smoke?" He gestures to the cigarettes in his pocket.

I shake my head and start to leave, then turn and say, "Actually, I'd love a cigarette."

Mike and I sit on the brick retaining wall in back of the building. I wait for the nicotine to relax my body, and when it does I start to cry.

"You sad?" Mike asks.

I nod and keep crying. We sit like that for a while. I want to pump Mike for more information, but the air has gone out of me. It can't get much worse. Then I remember Trevor. I jump up and stomp out my cigarette. I thank Mike and hurry off.

"You come again, maybe she remember you," he calls as I round the corner of the building. I can see the playground, but my feet will only take me so fast. It looks deserted. What have I done? Where is Trevor? I feel fear shoot through my entire body.

This is much worse than when Leroy took him yesterday. This is my fault. I'm responsible for that sweet little person and I forgot about him. How can you forget about a child? I stumble through the sandbox calling his name and looking frantically in every direction.

I turn and start for the pond, panic seizing my soul as I look at the sun glinting off the water. The pond is usually so relaxing, but now it looks menacing. A car horn blares, but I cannot turn to look because I think I see something moving in the water. I'm almost to the water's edge when I hear Trevor's voice call, "Mama! Over here!"

Relief. Sweet relief. Now the tears that were seeping out earlier come in torrents. I hug Trevor and pull him to a bench so I can sit down and breathe. My breaths are coming quickly now and I hug Trevor tightly.

"Where have you been?" asks a sharp and angry voice.

I turn to see the mother of the twins approaching us, arms swinging in agitation. Her boys stand at the edge of the park, watching. She reaches me and stops, hands on hips, waiting for an answer.

I can't speak. I just keep crying. She does not matter to me. I've lost my life, my friends, my family, and I thought I'd lost Trevor. I cling to him and stare at her.

"Well, I'm glad you turned up. I was getting ready to call social services." She turns to leave and then says, "Trevor, it was nice meeting you. Say hello to your daddy for me." She looks pointedly at me and then stomps off.

"Mama, why did she think Daddy was dead?"

"I don't know, sweetie, I think she's a little nuts." I hug him tighter.

I'm much relieved to arrive home to no Leroy. Of course, no evidence betrays that he lives here when he's gone, the same could be true of when he is here. Still, the whole place seems to be breathing easier. I had planned to bake a chicken for our dinner and then use it to make meals for the week for Trevor and Jillian, but now it is nearly 6:00 p.m. I put the chicken in to bake and open up a can of Raviolios left from the church box. I manage to convince Trevor to eat some salad by letting him dip his leaves in ranch dressing, just like the carrots. Getting a few vegetables in him feels like victory.

I try to get Trevor to move his sleeping bag up to the bed, but he refuses, telling me, "Daddy would be mad." Even when I assure him Daddy won't know and I won't tell him, he still refuses. He does climb up with me to read. We read his three books and then he convinces me to tell him a story. I've never told a story. Never. I feel put on the spot.

When he's settled in his Scooby-Doo bag, I ramble through a much butchered version of Goldilocks but Trevor doesn't correct me, not once. In my version they eat tortellini with clam sauce and sleep on a pillow top mattress. Turns out it's fun to tell a story when you have such an undiscerning audience. When I'm finished, Trevor says, "Mama, I like the way you tell it. What's a turtleini?"

I smile in the dark and peer over the side of the bed at his sweet face. "Someday soon I'll cook some for you, promise. You'll like it."

"Does it really have turtles in it?"

I laugh. "No, sweetie, no turtles."

"Promise?"

"Absolutely."

I know I'm not his mom. I do. But, God, right now I kind of wish I were.

⌇⌇

leann

I have a wicked hangover. I don't even remember what I drank. I been working my way through Carin's liquor cabinet. She had a lot of fruity crap and since that's all that's left, that's probably what I drank last night. I've learned that this new life makes much more sense if I'm drunk. I know I should be happy that I finally ain't so fat and I have a nice place to live, but I don't know what to do. I can't go to the insurance agency where Carin works because I don't know shit about computers and that's what Scott says I do all day. If I stay here, Brenda shows up and about drives me bonkers.

Lately, I've been bumming cigarettes off Mike, the building super. He's pretty nice. I like his wife. She don't speak no English, but she likes me. Some days when I go down to get a cigarette, she sits with me on their patio. They have the basement apartment and Esperanza has set up a nice garden. She can grow anything, I think. Anyways, I smoke and, since she don't understand nothing I'm saying, I tell her everything.

Last night, Mike was off fixing a toilet somewhere and Esperanza invited me in. I was carrying my latest drink I made with melon vodka and peach schnapps. I offered her some, but she shook her head no and went and got Mike's cigarettes. I really should go buy some, but I ain't been out since my time at the arcade, and I'm afraid I'll see Austin. We sat outside and she drank her tea and I smoked Mike's cigarettes.

"I know you think I'm Carin, but I ain't. I ain't told nobody. My name is Leann and I'm married to Leroy and I don't look like this. I'm taller." She looks confused, but nods at me to keep talking.

"Anyways, I work down at the Shop N Save, you know, the grocery store." When I say this, she nods real fast like she knows the store. "I weigh, like, a lot more than this, and I got a kid, Trevor. Trevor's real great. I wish I could see him." I take a swig of my drink and then the tears start flowing. Esperanza, she just watches me and pushes a napkin across the table. I pick it up and smile. No one's ever been so nice to me. If my mama found out about all this, she'd beat me senseless.

And then I'm talking. I tell Esperanza about Trevor and what he was like when he was a baby—how he smelled like love and looked at me like I was the best thing he'd ever seen. How my mama smiled at me after he was born and squeezed my arm, like she was proud or something. When I finish my cigarette, Esperanza hands the pack to me and pats my hand. She wants me to keep them. I thank her and go back up to my apartment.

A note from Scott on the door says he'd come by to see if I wanted to go to the movies. Jesus, can't this guy take a hint? I let myself in and refill my drink. Then I sit down to read more of Carin's journals and light a cigarette. I'm working my way backward through the journals. She was in high school now and the shit she was worried about is crazy. She was always scared people wouldn't like her. I coulda told her that people like you when you're pretty. People sure like me more now. She was hot after one boy and then another. She cheated on some test and almost got suspended. And she had sex for the first time with some guy named Rick. And then she blathers on and on about cheerleading try outs. It gets real boring, so I order pizza. I been ordering so much, the guy at Aldo's recognizes my number and just says, "The usual?" Sometimes I trip him up and change my order, but I almost always order extra cheese, extra sausage. I just get a small now, so I have to pay extra for delivery, but that's okay since the credit card keeps working. I ain't never been filled up with just a small pizza, but this body is real different than mine.

This morning I couldn't get up, 'cause every time I moved I felt like I would puke. I ain't never been one to puke, but this body can puke over anything. I took some Tylenol and went back to bed, but now it's afternoon and someone is pounding on the damn door. And they won't quit. I crawl out of bed and pull the sheet with me. I'm naked. I been sleeping naked 'cause I like the feel of this body and I don't know how long I'll have it. I like touching all the flatness.

When I get to the door, I look through the peephole. Ain't no one out there, so I yell, "Who's there?" I don't hear nothing and now I'm pissed 'cause my head is throbbing and the damn knocking got me out of bed. "Who's out there? What the hell do you want?" And then I hear her. Or I hear me.

"It's me," is all she says. And that's all I need to hear. I don't want to see her. I don't want to talk to her. She can keep that fat, ugly body. I don't want it anymore. In fact, I don't want any body any more. I march back to the bathroom and upend the Tylenol bottle. I don't know how many it'll take, so I scoop them all up and swallow them. Then I go to the bedroom and finish my drink from last night. I light a cigarette and wait.

chapter 12

~ ~

I spend the morning at the gym holding babies. Only today it's not nearly as much fun. The first little girl I rock to sleep easily, and I'm able to slip her into one of the cribs with no problem. The next little boy will not stop crying. He cries so much and so hard that he throws up all over me. We page his mother and then I go to the ladies' room to try to get the smell out of my hair.

I rinse my hair and duck my head under the hand dryer. I eye the scale in the corner. I can't really say whether I've lost any weight. I did exercise quite a bit, if twenty minutes of slow walking on the treadmill and ten minutes of even slower biking counts. Plus hiking all over the park yesterday looking for Trevor was some serious exercise. But I find myself eating at every available moment. As if finally having a little food in the apartment was the green light to gorge. Sometimes I'm literally surprised to discover I'm eating. Almost like the food has some kind of magnetic control over me. I'll be sorting through the dirty clothes trying to find something that will fit and suddenly I'm tearing the wrapper off a Tastykake. Very weird. I eye the scale. No one's around, so I step gingerly on to the black matted surface. I adjust the weights, horrified to slide the 350-pound marker into place. I adjust the other measure and gasp.

Three seventy. I step off and step back on and check again. I lost six pounds! Six pounds! Never in my life have I lost that much weight in a week! This totally makes my day. I resolve to stop eating so much junk. Denise pokes her head in the locker room. She looks at me, raises her eyebrows, and leaves. I don't even care that she caught me standing on the scale with both arms raised in triumph. I am triumphing.

Later, I meet with Bruce about my journey to fitness and tell him I've lost six pounds.

"That's great, Leann. You're on the road now!"

Please stop with the journey metaphors. He gives my shoulder a gentle squeeze and marks it down on my chart. I'm extremely grateful when he doesn't take body fat measurements. He increases my times on the cardio machines and takes me through the Nautilus machines again, fine tuning the weights. Between monitoring my journey with Bruce and actually working out, I barely have thirty minutes to shower and get to work. I arrive on time, but with wet hair and a red face. My reflection in the bathroom mirror is frightening, but I borrow some of Phyllis's lipstick and head for my register.

The afternoon creeps by and even with the momentary joy of my weight loss, it is hard to maintain a good attitude. Everyone seems grumpy today. A teenage boy in my line plops down a girlie magazine and a pack of gum and says, "Mondays suck." I've grown accustomed to being ignored by teenage boys, so I don't know if I'm more surprised by his words or his purchase. His face is still innocent, not even a hint of facial hair, and he looks everywhere but at me while attempting to smile. He's not old enough to buy this magazine, of that I'm certain. But I'm less certain of an actual law forbidding the sale. I look to see if Phyllis is busy and see her arguing over coupons with a mother of twins. I sigh and look at him again. I try to size up whether this is a regular purchase he makes or if this is the one time he's screwed up his nerve to buy the magazine. He doesn't seem tall enough to reach the high shelf where the magazines are kept. He keeps smiling at me with his unfocused gaze as I try to figure out what to do.

I pick up the magazine and flip through it. Just nakedness. Nothing too raunchy. I guess he's going to see all this sometime. Well, not exactly this. It could warp his expectations. No one looks like this. I sure tried. I look up at him again and he is staring at me. He looks terrified. He even picks up another pack of gum and tosses it on the belt as if that will sway me. Maybe he thinks I work on commission. Either way, who am I to mess with his day and his fantasies?

He pays and when he grabs his bag, I hold on to it and look at him. I wait until he meets my eye and then say, "Women don't look like this in real life. Just in case you wanted to know. These pictures are altered. If this is what you're looking for then just keep buying magazines."

He yanks the bag out of my hand and mutters, "Crazy bitch."

Next time I'm carding him. If there isn't a law, I'll make one up.

At break, Franklin follows me outside and pulls up a crate a bit too close for comfort. He lights a cigarette and looks over at me as I pull out my chicken salad sandwich.

"Could you move away if you're going to smoke?" I ask.

He laughs and blows the smoke directly at my sandwich.

"I mean it."

When he just scowls and looks away, I put my sandwich back in the bag, haul myself up, and move closer to the loading dock. Franklin watches me, waits until I take out my sandwich again, and then gets up and moves closer to me.

"Hey, Leann, when you and me gonna do the nasty?"

I'm horrified. I fix him with my angry eyes and say, "There is not a chance in hell that I will ever sleep with you."

He laughs. "C'mon, you know you want it."

"Franklin, I don't want anything from you. Nothing. Nada. Not a thing." If I could think of another way of saying it I would, but I've exhausted my vocabulary, so I just glare at him to be certain he gets it.

"Yeah, you do. You know you do."

I have nothing to say to this. Why does this impossibly horrible person think I have any interest in him?

"Oh girl, you just playin' hard to get. I get it. But you know I like a fat girl."

I close my eyes and try to will him away. He starts making all kinds of noises that I imagine are supposed to be sexy, but mostly they sound like he's in pain. I've completely lost my appetite and am packing up my dinner when two feet appear at my eye level on the loading dock. White high-top sneakers and black socks.

"Hey, you still haven't unloaded the bread order. It's not your break time." Even with the black socks, Jimmy looks like a knight in shining armor to me.

"Shit, man, you ruin all the fun. I was just about to score here. Why you gotta be such a party pooper?"

Jimmy just looks at him and waits. Franklin kicks a box off the loading dock as he shuffles into the building. Jimmy sits down on the edge of the dock. He doesn't say anything for a minute. Finally, he takes a deep breath, and asks, "Are you and Franklin friends?"

I don't know if he's Leann's friend, he doesn't act like it, but he certainly isn't my friend. I decide he shouldn't be her friend either.

"No." I say and look away. I hate what Jimmy is thinking. I wonder how much he heard or how much he knows. Maybe Leann has always flirted with Franklin. Maybe they have something going on. I can't tell if Franklin is just a big talker or if he's actually interested in wooing me in his own way.

"Don't let him bother you," Jimmy says with finality in his tone. Then he gets up and goes back in.

I sit for a minute and wonder if that means Jimmy is going to say something to him or if he just wants me to stick up for myself so he doesn't have to.

chapter 13

‹∿ ∾›

The next morning, Trevor has a notice for me to sign. It says we have a teacher conference scheduled for this Thursday at 2:00 p.m.

"Trevor, how can your teacher have a conference with me when she's supposed to be teaching you?"

"She won't be teaching me, Mama. We don't have school."

"What?" I shriek.

"It's conference day. No school," he says simply. I quickly scrawl a signature that is mostly illegible and hand it back to him. He puts it in his backpack and produces another paper. It's a permission slip for a field trip to a museum.

"Wow, Trevor, this looks like fun," I say as I scrawl Leann's signature again.

"I need fifteen dollars, too," he says hesitantly, pointing to the information at the top of the paper.

"You need it today?"

"Maybe you can bring it to the conference," he suggests, hopefully.

"I'll do that. I can do that," I assure him. I only have twelve dollars left. I'll have two paychecks by Friday. Hopefully, the teacher will be able to wait. I give him a hug and then the microwave alarm goes off and he runs for the door.

At the gym, I'm sweating on the bike and trying not to be bothered by the way my sweat pants are digging into my waist when Scott arrives fresh from work. I see him talking to Bruce.

Sometimes Scott works out during the day. It's usually because he's chasing a new girl.

I can't cycle another moment. I feel like my pants are cutting me in two, so I climb off the machine and get a drink from the water fountain. I decide to skip the machines today. I turn from the fountain and crash into Scott. He holds his hands up to his chest to soften the blow and then holds my arms for a moment to steady me.

"Sorry! I didn't mean to sneak up on you," he says. "Hey, it's you!"

I think he recognizes me, but then he says, "We keep running into each other. Literally."

I try to laugh, but only a small grunt comes out. Nice. I nod and shake my head, not sure what I'm trying to convey, and then head for the showers. I'm almost to the locker room when Bruce calls, "Leann, wait! I've got your training sheet. You need to write your times down." He hands me the sheet. Scott is programming the elliptical machine for his workout.

"How did those weight adjustments work out for you on the machines?" Bruce asks.

All I want to do right now is get far, far away from here, but somehow I can't lie to Bruce's earnest, kind face.

"I haven't done them yet."

"Oh, well then let's get to them. I've got a couple minutes while Scott warms up."

I let Bruce take me through the machines. I try to keep my eyes focused on what I'm doing, but they keep wandering back to Scott. I wonder if I mentioned a few things about our lovemaking if he would be convinced it was me. Maybe he's already given up on Leann and moved on. After all, we were never serious. That wasn't our thing. If the situation was reversed and Scott was stranded inside some enormous fat guy, I guess I wouldn't want to believe him either. But that seems horrible. Was I only ever attracted to his outside? That is a painful question. I think most people wouldn't even consider the inside unless they are turned on by the outside. Does that mean my life as Leann will be filled with men like Franklin?

Scott finishes on the elliptical and waves to Bruce.

"Gotta run, Leann, you're doing great."

I smile and look past him to Scott. Scott meets my eyes and seems confused. Bruce reaches him and gives him a hearty pat on the back and they head for the free weights.

That night I eat my dinner inside, not just because it's raining, but I figure I have less chance of encountering Franklin's taunting if I'm in the break room with the deli ladies. They meet in here each evening and compare notes on all their physical ailments. It's painfully boring and incredibly depressing. They compare their spider veins, their hemorrhoids, their bunions, their cholesterol levels, and the biggie—their arthritis. Then when they finish they begin comparing their husbands' ailments. It's almost a sport. Who can have it the worst? Whose legs look the most like a map of New York City? Who has more toes bent at horrible angles? Who has to take the most pills just to survive their day? Oh my God, it might be better outside with Franklin.

I do my best to ignore them and study the posters on the wall. They are meant to be inspirational, but the only one that hits home is the desperate kitten hanging on a bar with the caption *Hang in There*. The edges are curled and split. I bet it's been taped to that wall for twenty years. On the side of the vending machine is a calendar. The pictures are of mountain ranges. As if anyone who works here is ever going to scale any of those mountains. Leann's life is turning me into a cynic.

chapter 14

On Wednesday morning, I oversleep and wake to the sound of someone beating on my door. I stagger to the kitchen and look at the microwave. It's already 8:30. Trevor is long gone. And the beating continues.

"Dammit, Leann! Open this door! Get your fat ass out of bed and open this door! I mean it! I could freeze to death out here. I'm an old woman!"

The last thing in the world I want to do is open the door for Leann's mother. The last thing. But what choice do I have? She won't give up. I have thirty minutes to be dressed and at work. I decide to press my luck. I quickly find clothes to wear and stuff my workout clothes from yesterday into a grocery bag. I stink pretty bad. I'll have to use the hair spray in the women's locker room to mask the smell. It's amazing the things a person will do when they are desperate and don't have a washing machine. The hairspray makes the clothes a little stiff, but it sure knocks out the smell.

The entire time I'm getting dressed and gathering my stuff and putting on my shoes, Leann's mother is screaming. When I finally open the door, she glares at me and blows smoke in my face. I walk past her and start down the stairs. I find it takes a certain amount of time to get my large body moving each day. It always seems to be a few steps behind my mind. I have to adjust to its pace and then, once we're in sync, I can speed up. Because I move slowly and this grumpy old woman is so skinny and energetic, she easily moves past me and stops at the bottom of the stairs, blocking my way.

"Where are you going? You think you can just ignore me? Like you're ignoring God? Dammit, Leann—look at me when I'm talking to you. All I've ever asked of you is that you go to church. I don't care what you do with your pathetic life, but I'll be damned if I'm going to let your soul burn in hell. You hear me? You better get yourself to church this week. Your life depends on it!" With that, she turns on her heel and speeds off in her Cadillac. Is she serious? Did she just threaten me? I truly have bigger issues to deal with than an angry mother and church attendance. I push it out of my mind and move as quickly as I can to the bus stop.

The bus is late and I arrive at work ten minutes late. Denise is on me the moment I walk in.

"Leann, we expect employees to arrive on time. This is the second time you've been tardy. How are we going to handle this?"

"I'm sorry. My mother came by and I couldn't seem to get away from her."

"Look, I feel we have truly bent over backwards to make you welcome here. If you are going to continue to disregard the chance we've given you, this isn't going to work."

She can't possibly be threatening to fire me because I'm ten minutes late. I look at her bony, sallow face. She needs this power. She needs me to grovel. I can do that. Once upon a time I wouldn't have, but right now, in this place, groveling seems to be my best option.

"I'm sorry, Denise. I do realize the gym has given me a great chance here. I promise I won't be late again." Denise smiles her I'm-so-superior-and-aren't-I-so-nice smile and pats my shoulder.

"I know you are doing the best you can. I'm sure it won't happen again." She walks away and I stick my tongue out at her retreating back. A two-year-old standing at the Play-Doh table sees me and sticks his tongue out at me. I laugh and retreat to the infant room. All the babies are sleeping except one. She's watching a mobile and talking to herself. I wonder what she's thinking. Her life is so simple right now. Everything revolves around what she wants. If she's hungry, uncomfortable, sleepy, bored, whatever, someone will jump to help her. I would love to be taken care of like that. Maybe we spend our entire lives trying to get back to that point where all our needs are met without so much effort on our part. I suppose few ever achieve it, unless you count the old people in the rest homes. And they don't seem so happy.

That night, I head to the break room for dinner again. I just can't decide how to deal with Franklin. He's been leering at me all day and making little sucking noises whenever he passes me. I can't tell if this is his attempt at flirting or if he's mocking me. Either way, I'm just not up to it. I'm about to push the door open and join the deli ladies when Jimmy steps out of the back storage area.

"Hey, are you on break?" he calls.

I nod.

"Are you gonna come out back?"

"I don't think so."

"Are you mad at me?"

I'm confused. "No! What makes you think that?"

"You didn't come out back for break last night."

"I didn't know you were expecting me."

I swear Jimmy blushes. There is no way that at 370 pounds I can make a man blush like that. But it sure looks like it. He doesn't say anything and turns to go.

"Wait! I'll come!" I hurry after him.

"You don't have to," he says to me when I follow him into the storage area. "It's just you usually do. I didn't know if it was because of what I said about Franklin."

I catch my breath. What a good man. I can't believe he actually cares how I feel. He's actually thought about it. For some crazy reason, I have to blink back a tear before saying, "Thanks for making Franklin go away the other day. I don't know how to handle him."

We sit on crates on the loading dock. Jimmy looks at me quizzically. I guess he's trying to see if I'm serious.

"I thought you and Franklin were friends," he says as he takes a bite of his sandwich.

"Maybe we were once. But not anymore. Actually, he scares me a little."

"Franklin?" Jimmy smiles at this.

I smile too, but I'm serious, so I say, "He's really creepy."

"He's too stupid to be dangerous. Really, I would know. I know his older brother. Known him since grade school. Franklin's all talk."

"That's good to know." Jimmy looks at me again with a question on his face. But he doesn't ask it.

We eat in silence for a while.

Finally, I have to ask. "Do I seem different to you?"

He turns and looks at me carefully. "No, not really. Are you different?"

"I am. I'm very different. Remember when that woman was hit by a Valentine's display heart a few weeks ago?"

"Sure I do. I had to clean up all that blood."

"Ever since then, it's like I'm someone else completely. Does that make sense?"

"I don't know. I guess that happens."

He doesn't say any more, and even though I'm dying to talk about this with someone, I don't want to scare him off, so I drop it for now. But I smile to myself, happy to know someone knows my secret, even if he really doesn't.

~~ ~~

chapter 15

Thursday morning dawns crisp and clear. The air, even in the apartment, smells like spring. It makes me think of my daffodils. Last fall I planted one hundred bulbs outside the entrance to the apartment building. I did it on the weekend, early on a Sunday morning so no one would know and no one could protest. I don't know why anyone would be bothered by daffodils, but you never know. Communal living brings out the worst in people.

Trevor is parked in front of the TV. He's still in his pajamas.

"Hey bud, get dressed," I tell him, startling him.

"Mama, I don't have school, remember?" He smiles his adorable dimple-filled grin and I just want to squeeze him.

"You don't have school, but I have to go to work. You'll come with me."

"To the store?" He wrinkles his nose.

"I haven't figured that out yet, but you'll come with me to the gym first."

When I asked Jillian to come pick up Trevor at the store when she gets out of school, she said, "That ain't part of the deal. Guess I'll see ya Friday."

I wasn't successful in my attempts to switch schedules with someone, but Vernon told me if the evening is slow, he'll let me go at seven. Vernon is a throwback from the old days. He doesn't understand why we don't all eat, sleep, and breathe the Shop N Save. I imagine he'll live out his days at the Shop N Save and someday he'll retire and they'll give him a nice watch. Not sure yet what I'm going to do with Trevor for four hours at the Shop N Save. I'm hoping it will come to me.

Trevor is happy to be in the Kiddie Korner. It's swamped with kids, lots of kids his age. I guess Trevor is not the only kid who doesn't have school.

I skip my workout today since I have to be Trevor's mom and attend the teacher conference. I don't know what happens at these conferences. I remember when I was a child, my own parents always came home with knowing looks on their faces. I would ask what the teacher had told them and they would say it was none of my business, which isn't entirely fair considering they were talking about me at the conference. I was an excellent student. That was expected at my house. My parents would have accepted nothing less from me. I had friends whose parents paid them ten dollars for every A they got. I approached my own parents about the same deal and they looked at me like I had three heads. Of course I would get As. That's what a Fletcher would do.

Walking into the brick building and down the salmon-colored concrete block hallways brings back so many memories. It smells like cheese and mayo sandwiches, fresh packs of crayons, and floor polish. I was good at school. Everyone liked me, especially the teachers. I was very good at appearances. I've always wished life was more like elementary school. It was easy when you knew what was expected of you.

I follow Trevor to his classroom. The construction paper owls dangling from the ceiling in the kindergarten hallway watch me with their big eyes. Even they seemed to know I'm faking this. Their expressions, lopsided yarn pieces, question my presence. As we turn down his hallway, Trevor points out his handiwork. His happy face peers out upside down from a bat body on one wall and I instantly recognize his "garden of learning" project. His careful tulips and smiling daisies dot the outside edges and a big truck fills the center of the paper.

We walk into his room and his teacher waves us over to her conference table. On the way, Trevor shows me his desk. All his supplies are lined up neatly inside—crayons worn down to nubs, a pencil stub, and part of a Santa Claus eraser. We sit down at the table, and his teacher asks if he'd like to work at the art center while she and I talk. He jumps up, excited to paint. She reminds him to put on his smock and then turns to me. I instinctively cower. I can sense she is about to reprimand me, but it's hard to focus on what she's saying because I'm precariously balanced on a chair designed for a six-year-old. I hold the table for support. The chair is invisible beneath my huge bottom. It's cutting into me and already beginning to hurt. I nod as Mrs. Olsen goes through the test results from Trevor's latest math evaluation. Apparently he's pretty good at math. That's a good thing, since I'm not. She hesitates as she begins to talk about his reading. I try to listen, but I'm incredibly distracted by the effort of sitting on the tiny chair. I think she's telling me that his reading is not so hot.

"If you could read with him more at home that would really help. Maybe take him to the public library? I know at our fall conference you said you aren't such a big fan of reading, but they have story time programs at the library."

She's waiting for my answer. I love to read. I do. My book shelves in my apartment are crammed with books. How can anyone not be a fan of reading? I'm momentarily furious with Leann for handicapping Trevor this way and for giving this teacher the impression that I'm not a fan of reading. I take a deep breath and try to explain.

"I don't know why you would think that. I love to read."

Mrs. Olsen is visibly startled. She had been leaning in towards me and now she leans back in her chair, cocking her head to the side, appraising me.

"Really? In the fall, I distinctly remember you telling me it's my job to teach Trevor to read. I believe you told me books were boring."

I gulp.

"I would never say that! I love to read."

"But Trevor tells me you don't have books at home."

"Well . . . money is kind of tight right now. But I do love to read. We've been reading the books you've sent home. Trevor really enjoys them."

At this, she finally smiles and leans forward again. She reaches below the table and pulls out a plastic bag bursting with books.

"I'm so glad to hear that. I found a few more books for Trevor to have. You can keep these." She hands them towards me and when I let go of the table to take them I'm suddenly unstable and lurch to the side, nearly coming off the chair. I manage to take the books and set them next to me. Mrs. Olsen smiles and makes a note on Trevor's chart.

"Mrs. Cane, this is wonderful. It could really help Trevor. His reading scores are slipping below grade-level, but I'm sure with a little effort he will be up to grade-level by the end of the year."

"What happens if he isn't at grade-level by the end of the year?"

"Well, you have several options. It would depend on his other scores. He still has several standardized tests to take before June. But if his other scores are below grade-level also, we would need to talk about retaining him. Another option is sending him to summer school. Lots of parents do that—even if their children aren't struggling. It gives them a leg up."

"Can you send home information about summer school?" I see Trevor's head snap up when he hears this.

Mrs. Olsen is obviously pleased with my question and makes more notes.

"Now, the other thing we need to address is Trevor's school supplies. He's very careful and doesn't waste a thing, but he is down to just a few crayons and one pencil. The social service committee has school supplies for children who might need them. I know in the fall you told me that wouldn't be necessary, but I was hoping you might reconsider and apply for the supplies."

She doesn't meet my eye as she says this. Totally ridiculous that Leann won't take any help. If anyone in this world needs help, it's her.

"How do I apply?"

Mrs. Olsen's head pops up from where she's been scribbling notes and a big smile comes over her face. She pulls out a form from Trevor's file and hands it to me.

"I've already taken the time to fill out the entire form. All it needs is your signature and I bet we can have new supplies here tomorrow!" Clearly, this conference is going much better than she expected.

"Do you have similar programs for field trip costs?"

By the time we finish at the school and catch a bus to the Shop N Save, I have only five minutes to spare before my shift starts. I take Trevor to the break room and show him how to work the TV. He doesn't need my help—he's ahead of his grade-level when it comes to remote controls. I give him a dollar in change to buy snacks from the vending machine and tell him we'll get dinner when I'm through. I instruct him not to talk to anyone and if someone asks him what he's doing here, he's to say he's waiting for his babysitter to pick him up. Then I punch in and head up front.

All goes well for an hour. I even manage to sneak back and check on Trevor several times, and Phyllis clearly adores him. But then Franklin discovers him. When he passes my station on his way to collect carts, he whispers, "Vernon know your kid's back there?"

I glare at him and he laughs as he heads outside. I try to focus on my work, but I keep screwing up orders and when Franklin passes me again, he says, "What'll you give me to keep your secret?" raising his eyebrows and making a suggestive movement with his hands. A few minutes later, Vernon is striding towards me purposefully.

"What's this I hear about your son being here with you today, Leann? You know we can't be responsible for the care of a young child. That's your responsibility."

"His babysitter is late. She should be here any moment," I stammer.

"She needs to be here now," Vernon says firmly. "Leann, please take care of this right now." Franklin passes behind him smiling at me and making rude gestures towards Vernon. I can't do anything about it until my line dies down. When I finally get a lull, I hurry back to the break room. To my horror, Vernon is just coming out.

"I'm glad your babysitter arrived, Leann. I'll do my best to get you out of here by seven, if possible," he says as he passes me.

My babysitter? What the hell is he talking about? I open the door to the break room and Trevor is nowhere to be seen. I'm about to panic when I hear a voice calling my name.

"Leann, back here."

Jimmy waves me back to the storage room.

"Your kid's back here with me." I follow him. We walk to a tiny booth near the huge truck doors at the far end of the storage room. Inside, it's toasty warm and Trevor is perched on a stool playing a small handheld game.

"Hi, Mama. Jimmy's letting me use his Game Boy. But he says I have to use it in here or it won't work."

I look at Jimmy, puzzled. He closes the door to the booth and turns to me.

"I heard Vernon was going to kick him out and figured he'd be happy back here. He's a nice kid."

"Jimmy, I don't know how to thank you. You totally saved me." I shake my head, amazed.

Jimmy ducks his head down and says, "No biggie. He's not a problem. I've got to get back to work." His walkie-talkie beeps loudly at this point and he walks off to answer the page from the front office.

I poke my head back in the booth.

"Trevor, you okay?"

Trevor nods, intently focused on his game. I slide the booth shut and hurry back up front. Vernon lets me go at about seven fifteen. I punch out and go to find Trevor. He and Jimmy are sitting on one of the forklifts eating peanut butter crackers.

"Mama—watch!" Trevor yells when he spots me. Then to Jimmy he says, "Can I show her?"

Jimmy smiles and scoots back on the seat. Trevor climbs up in front of him and the machine roars to life. They guide it to the nearest stack of pallets and lift a pallet of cat litter from the stack and set it down in the aisle. Jimmy turns to Trevor and gives him a high five. Then Trevor jumps down from the machine and comes running over to me. I take his hand.

"Thank you!" I shout over the machine to Jimmy.

On the way home, Trevor wants to stop at McDonald's. I figure I'll be rich tomorrow, relatively speaking, so we splurge. I'm worn out from the effort and worry of the day, and for once this doesn't make me hungry. I watch Trevor scoot through the human version of a hamster habitat and sip my coffee. I know having coffee at this hour will keep me up, but my mind hurts and I'm hoping caffeine will help.

Today at that conference, I really felt like Trevor's mom. I wanted to be Trevor's mom. But I'm not. Or am I? Maybe my entire other life is a fantasy. Maybe I've always been Leann and I'm only now waking up.

I spy the payphone in the back hallway, glance at Trevor one more time, and head for it. I drop in all the change I have. I have no idea how a payphone even works, but I remember seeing people dropping in coin after coin in the movies. I hear a dial tone and most of my money comes banging down to the coin return. Bonus. I dial my old number. The phone rings and rings and finally a voice answers. It's my voice except it sounds kind of lifeless.

"Hi," I say.

I listen to the silence on the other end, but she doesn't hang up.

"I went to school today for Trevor's teacher conference." She doesn't say anything.

"I thought you'd want to know how he's doing. He's struggling with reading. I'm trying to help him with that." She doesn't say anything.

"What the hell's wrong with you? Don't you care about him? You're his mother. How can you just walk away?" My voice is becoming shrill.

I think she's going to continue to be silent, but then I hear my shaky, sad voice come through the receiver.

"He's better off with you."

Wow. What do I do with that?

"But I'm not me, I'm you and you're me and this just totally sucks. How did this happen?"

"I wished it," she says very definitely.

"You can't wish things."

"My life sucked. Trevor's life sucked. And now it doesn't."

"Yes, it does," I insist. "This is no way to live. I hate it. I want my life back."

She's back to silence. I frantically think of something to say to get her talking. "Did my friend Marta call?"

"Some nervous woman called and left a message. Said her kid was sick. Said she figured you were busy anyway."

So much for Marta. I try another topic.

"What is Leroy's problem? Is he always so mean?"

"He's messed up," she says.

"Messed up how? On drugs? In the head? With the police? How is he messed up?"

"He's not like he used to be."

I find it hard to believe he ever had any very redeeming qualities.

"What did he used to be like?"

She sighs. "He used to be nice to me." This thought apparently wakes her up because she blurts out, "I'm done talking. Don't call me anymore."

"Wait! I have more questions!" She's still on the line, so I press on. "What does he do during the week? Where does he go?"

"He drives a rig for Floral Foam and Heavenly Herbs. He has runs all over the country."

"What's Floral Foam and Heavenly Herbs?"

"They make that green shit that goes under flower arrangements, plus herbs, you know."

The way she says "herbs" implies something different.

"Herbs, like lavender or oregano?"

She laughs. "Yeah, that shit." And then the phone goes dead.

I drop more coins in the phone and dial again. The phone rings and rings. She must have turned off my answering machine. That's all I'm going to get. I wish I'd thought to ask her more important questions like: Do you have sex with Leroy? Does he just yell or is he dangerous? What's with the pickles and Tastyka-kes? Whenever I'm put on the spot like that, my mind goes blank.

I gather up Trevor and we head home. He's tired from his big day. He's not used to being so physically active. He takes a bath and climbs in his sleeping bag without much fuss. I go to find the books Mrs. Olsen gave us, and when I come back he is already asleep. I watch him for a minute. I feel so connected to him. He is the only bright spot in this entire nightmare.

The coffee won't let me sleep. I pace the apartment, willing it to tell me what it knows. I feel unhinged. I don't want to say *crazy* because I'm kind of afraid of that word. I knew a girl who went crazy once. She used to lock herself in the bathroom stall at school and talk to someone. Only she was the only one there. She swore someone was in there with her, but we couldn't see him because he only appeared when the door was closed. You could hear her inside laughing and telling bizarre stories of things I really hope she never did. Eventually, Ms. Templeton, the vice principal, would arrive with the guidance counselor and they'd make us all leave the bathroom. Then Monica would disappear for a few weeks. She'd be back eventually, all glassy-eyed and quiet. But sooner or later she'd end up back in that bathroom stall again and the whole process would repeat itself.

Now I think maybe she wasn't crazy. Maybe something happened to her like what has happened to me. Maybe this is going on all over the place and we just don't know it until it happens to us. I've known people who underwent complete personality changes. You think it's because they found Jesus or they gave up caffeine or they had some other kind of life-altering experience, but maybe they aren't really themselves anymore. Maybe they are someone else trapped in another person's body. God, I do sound crazy.

Am I crazy? I feel pretty certain if I approached someone like my mom or Marta, I'd sound nuts. I think I'm stuck in this body for now. Until some other cosmic shift occurs. The only chance I have at getting my life back would involve Leann being willing to give it back. And after living her life for three weeks now, I'm positive that isn't going to happen. I wouldn't give it back. But what about Trevor? He's the only thing that makes this life bearable. He needs me. I don't know how Leann can walk away. Maybe it's because she's strung out on drugs or beaten down by her mom and Leroy and the rest of the world, I don't know. But that's no excuse. Trevor deserves better.

If I'm sticking around (like I have any choice), I need to know what's really happening here. Leroy is not a normal truck driver hauling floral foam and herbs. Or if he is, he isn't hauling the kind of herbs that are legal. Of that much, I'm certain. If he is, he certainly isn't spending his profits on this dump. But what's he spending it on?

〽 〜

leann

I feel less and less real. I sleep until I can't anymore. My mind won't stop twistin' into odd shapes and strange stories, so I get up and start another day. Takin' the whole bottle of Tylenol sure didn't kill the pain, or me for that matter.

Carin's mother has stopped callin' every morning. Since I never answered the phone, she finally figured out I didn't want to talk to her. Smart lady. Now she just drops by and slips notes under the door or sends packages through Mike.

"Carin, hope you're feeling better today. Call me for a little retail therapy! Love, Mom"

What the hell is "retail therapy"? The woman is nuts.

Most days I play solitaire until it's time for my soaps. And drink coffee. Carin has a great machine. Scott showed me how to use it. She has a whole case of little cups of cappuccino and other shit and I just plop one in and out pops a cup of good stuff. I drink a bunch of those in the morning instead of eating. Nobody has good breakfast takeout.

Before my soaps start, I order some food from the deli. Mostly I get fruit salad or soup 'cause it makes me feel better. Esperanza is teaching me about that. Some of Carin's clothes were getting tight and I figured I better do something. Sometimes I have lunch with Esperanza. I feel bad eatin' her food, so I leave money under the placemat. She won't keep it if I hand it to her.

I'd probably never leave the house if it weren't for Trevor. Some mornings, I get up and fix one of them little cups and then catch the bus to his stop. I just watch him. But it's hard. I really want to touch him. Once, I actually sat on the bench beside him. I wanted to hear his voice. I couldn't bring myself to talk to him, but when he got on the bus I heard him say "good morning" to the driver. It made me happy. I must've sat on that bench for an hour, 'til some lady sat down and started talking to me. I can't get used to people talking to me. I don't know what to say, so I mostly leave.

Today, I'm puttin' on blue jeans 'cause Esmeralda invited me to help her in her garden. She's planting new seeds. I think she likes having somebody to talk to, even if I just talk and she just listens. I have a lot to talk about today; last night the phone rang, and I don't know why but I answered it. I meant to ignore it, but before I knew it my hand picked up the phone.

She started rattling on as soon as I put the phone to my ear. I figured I'd be quiet and she'd go away just like her mama, but then she started talkin' about Trevor. Said he's real good at math but he's bad at reading. Knew that, she's no genius.

Then she asked me why this happened. Her being stuck in me and me being stuck in her. I been thinkin' on that a lot. Mostly in the morning before I open my eyes. I figure God made it happen. God, or somebody like God. I ain't never been that sure of God. I figure if he's tight with a nasty old woman like my mama, he ain't quite right in the head. So I don't really pray, I just wish. I wish to God, or whoever. I always wished my life would change. That I'd stop bein' so fat. That Leroy would be more like Edgar on my soaps. But I wished mostly that Trevor would be a good boy and be happy. I figured God, or whoever, knew that weren't ever gonna happen if I was in charge, so he swapped me out for somebody smarter. He gave me two of my wishes. I ain't fat as a house no more, and Trevor got a shot at growin' up good.

But Carin didn't believe me. Then she started in about Leroy. He must've smacked her around or something 'cause she wanted to know what's wrong with him. Damn, everything's wrong with him, but it didn't used to be. He used to be sweet. That was before he started likin' all them drugs and Jillian. I tried to tell her that, so she'd see a good side of him, but I could tell she didn't believe me, so I just hung up. She called back, but I just let it ring.

Down at Esperanza's place, I tell her about that call. Mike weren't around, so I could say what I liked. I tell her that Carin is helping Trevor read better. And I tell her 'bout seein' Trevor at the bus stop. He looked happy. And then I start crying 'cause he don't need me no more. He's all took care of. Trevor don't need me. So I cry like a baby.

And Esperanza, she gets her Kleenex box. And she puts her hand on my arm and we just sit like that. So much for planting seeds. Mike comes in then and sees me all sad and pulls out his cigarettes. He waves me outside and lights us each one. I don't want to leave Esperanza. I like the feel of her hand on my arm. I like how much she likes me.

Mike looks at me and shrugs. Then he says, "So, your head all better, yes?"

I nod.

"But your heart, it's not?"

I nod again. And then we smoke in silence.

chapter 16

~ ~

The next morning I oversleep. I wake up when Trevor slams the door on his way out. Shit! I can't be late again. I jump up and pick clothes off the floor. I used to agonize about what to wear but now I've resigned myself to the fact that I look bad in everything, so I just don't look in the mirror. I pull back my hair in barrettes, splash water on my face, squirt a blob of toothpaste in my mouth, and run out the door.

I make it to the gym on time. Thank God. Denise gives me the hairy eyeball—I must look worse than I imagined. It's only when I'm rocking Dylan, my favorite baby, that I realize I'm wearing red stretch pants, a maroon tunic with the Tasmanian Devil on it, and green socks.

The morning goes by uneventfully, except I fall asleep while I'm rocking Dylan and wake up with a start when someone clears their throat just behind me. It's only Teresa, who's newer than I am. I mumble "thanks" and then spend the next half hour alternately blinking and holding my eyes open as wide as I can to keep from falling asleep.

When my shift is over, I bolt for the employee locker room. I'm just changing out of my Tasmanian Devil shirt when Denise appears by my side. I jump and try to hold the shirt in front of me. I'm mortified that Denise can see all my rolls. She hands me two neatly folded navy blue shirts.

"These just came in. They're employee shirts for you to wear to work. We had to special order your size." She smirks at me and turns to go. I don't say a word. "Bitch" is what I would say if I could. I put the new shirts in my locker. I plan to wear one to the Shop N Save. It will go better with my red pants than the Tasmanian Devil shirt. If only they had employee socks. Socks are what I need.

I remember once, a few years ago, I was eating at Cracker Barrel with my friend Wendy. Wendy is the thinnest person I know, mostly because she's a chain smoker and allergic to pretty much everything that tastes good, like chocolate, peanut butter, nuts, milk, wheat. Anyway, we were at Cracker Barrel because our friend Lorie worked there and gave us free cornbread and sweet tea. Next to us, a table overflowed with loud, colorful, obese women. They carried on as if they owned the place, constantly asking Lorie for soda refills and extra butter. Every dish they ordered was drowning in gravy and grease. After cleaning their plates, they ordered dessert. Wendy and I watched them in disgust. I remember Wendy saying, "If I was that fat, I wouldn't leave my house. I'd be too embarrassed!" We were so smug. I told Wendy, "If I ever get that fat, promise you'll lock me up and make me diet." We made a pact to never allow each other to become obese. "I'd rather die," Wendy said.

Looking back on that conversation now, from the vantage point of Leann's body, I feel horrible. I'm uncomfortable in Leann's body, but at the same time, I feel a sense of pride. I am a person. I see how people cringe when I sit near them on the bus. I'm not accustomed to men ignoring me. I'm alternately a circus freak show or invisible. People don't want to see me, but some can't help staring. I feel like yelling, "What makes you think you're so much better than me?" But I know that they do feel better than me. I felt that way. These people who walk so widely around me, who won't meet my eyes, they think I'm worth less than them. My presence, my appearance, makes them feel good about their own appearance. At least they don't look like me.

As I'm walking slowly on the treadmill, I see Scott enter the gym. He disappears into the men's locker room. I finish with the treadmill and move over to the Nautilus equipment. I'm lying on my belly, balancing on a narrow bench while attempting to curl my leg back and straining under the new weights Bruce has assigned, when I hear Scott's voice.

"Hey, is that you?" he says.

He can't possibly be talking to me. I'm mortified that my gigantic ass is on full display. I close my eyes so I can't see him in the mirrors.

"Aren't you the girl from the Shop N Save?" he asks. He is now standing right over me. I'm not sure what to do. If I try to turn over, I'll definitely wobble right off this bench. Normally, I put my hands on the ground and pivot my body to get my knees on the ground and then stand up, but Scott is standing right where my knees would land and the other side of me is a mirrored wall. I open my eyes and look for him in the mirror. His eyes meet mine and I can see he's waiting for an answer.

"Uh-huh," is all I can manage.

"I thought so," he says. He's still looking at me. Now what? What am I supposed to say to that?

He looks like he wants to say more. Finally, he kind of shakes his head and turns to go start his workout. "Well, have a good workout." I watch him retreat in the mirror. When he's busy adjusting a bike, I slide over and get my knees on the floor. I rest for a minute with my hands on the bench, like a Catholic in church.

"Man, it must be really bad if you have to say your prayers," says Bruce merrily. He reaches out and grabs my elbow and helps me up. "Are the new weights too high for you?"

"They're fine," I assure him. "I just needed a minute."

"Everything else okay?" he asks. He really does seem concerned. Why are all the good men gay?

"I can handle it. But I better get moving if I'm going to get to work on time."

"I thought you already finished work."

"I have another job that starts at three."

"Oh," he says, looking at me sadly. "You're a hard worker, Leann. It'll pay off someday. I know it."

"I hope so," I say as I turn and make my way to the showers.

When I arrive at the Shop N Save, Phyllis grabs me and pulls me aside. "The police are here," she says breathlessly.

"Why?" I say, fear gripping me. I don't know why, but every time I see the police my heart races. I've never done anything glaringly illegal except when I was a kid and had a fake ID. I guess the reaction is left over from those days.

"Vernon thinks someone's been shoplifting." When I don't react, she says pointedly, "Someone who works here."

"Oh," I say and my heart sinks. I haven't taken anything since I've been in charge of Leann's body, but maybe Vernon has finally figured out that Leann has been stealing groceries on a regular basis. I wonder if anyone else knows. I look back at Phyllis. If she knows, she's not letting on. She's scanning the lounge and evaluating the possibilities. The deli ladies are passing around a tube of Icy Hot. Franklin is parked on the couch with the remote in his hand, surfing through the channels and increasing the volume every time one of the deli ladies glares at him.

"Everyone is being interviewed. They've got Jimmy right now," Phyllis whispers. This is clearly the biggest event to have occurred in her lifetime. I've never seen her so animated. Sweat is beading on her forehead.

Franklin looks back and notices me. He whistles low and turns the volume down. Eyeing me, he smirks. "Guess the shit is gonna hit the fan now huh, Leann?"

I bolt from the room. Franklin knows. He knows Leann was stealing groceries. What will I say? If they make me put my hand on a Bible, do I have to tell the whole truth? But whose truth? Mine as Leann or mine as me in Leann's body? I only know what I know and I know I haven't taken anything. I don't steal. I march up to my register with a new determination. Nothing can happen because they can't prove anything. Unless they have surveillance tapes. What if they do?

I try to focus on my register, but I'm nervous and keep screwing up. I have to call the manager-on-duty, Charlene, over three times to use her key to fix my mistakes. When a bag I have just filled rips open and spills a carton of eggs all over the floor,

Charlene rushes over and shoos me away. She calls for Franklin to clean up the mess and tells me to take a break.

For once, I'm not hungry. Which is a good thing since I didn't have time to pack any dinner. I need some air. The police detective is still in Vernon's office. He's working his way through the deli ladies. It's only a matter of time. What if Franklin told them about me? What if I go to jail? I wonder if Leann has ever been to jail. She doesn't seem to have too many morals, so it's possible.

I pace back and forth behind the loading docks, wishing I had a cigarette. I eye the half-smoked butts on the ground around me. I'm not that desperate. Finally, Jimmy appears.

"Hey," he says as he jumps down from the loading dock and approaches me. "Need a smoke?" He offers his pack.

"You are my savior," I say quickly as I snatch the pack out of his hand. He has his lighter ready before the cigarette is even in my mouth. I raise my eyebrows and say, "And a gentleman." Jimmy makes me feel like myself, not the me trying to be Leann. Being around him is the only time I feel like I'm not nuts. Like I'm who I am and not some fat, desperate thief who neglects her child and is married to a bully. I lean back on the wall and let the nicotine relax my body. Jimmy watches me.

"What's the matter?" he asks, cocking his head to the side, still staring at me.

"Now there's a loaded question," I smirk as I take another puff.

"How so?" he asks innocently.

I laugh to myself and stare up at the stars. "I wouldn't know where to begin and even if I did you'd never believe me. Not in a million years. I'm not sure I'd believe me."

Jimmy doesn't say anything. He seems comfortable with that answer. We watch the stars and he smokes his own cigarette. Finally, I figure I have to get back inside and face whatever is coming. Just before I reach the door, I hear him say, "I'd believe you."

As I'm signing onto my register, Franklin leans over my credit card machine and says, "You're toast." He laughs as he heads outside to round up the carts. I take a deep breath and try to remember I'm not the Leann who stole groceries. I'm the Leann who would never steal groceries. I'm the Leann who is working two jobs and trying to figure a way out of her sorry life.

Later, after too many minutes of dread, I hear Vernon's voice on the intercom calling me back to his office. When I reach his office, the door is open. He's sitting behind his desk and a rotund police officer is perched on the corner. The officer's shirt is littered with crumbs and a few still stick to his chin.

Vernon stands up and walks around his desk, nervously holding out a chair for me. I nod and sit down.

"Detective, this is Leann Cane. She's been a cashier here for over five years. I think you might remember her from the incident with the fallen display a few weeks back."

The detective looks at me. I read his badge. It says Lt. Friedel.

"Hello, Leann. I just have a few questions for you." I don't like him sitting on the desk. It forces me to look at his crotch. Why can't he sit in a chair like a normal person? I look up and try to focus on his face, but his moustache is stained with red sauce from his dinner, and the knowing smile he gives me makes my stomach heave. I look down at my lap. I think this makes me look guilty, so I try again to look at him. I focus on his eyebrows. They are bushy and multi-colored.

"Leann, you may have heard that Mr. Slick called me here to do an investigation. According to the sales records and inventory, we believe someone is stealing food from the store on a regular basis. We think this person may be an employee."

I try to look surprised, but don't say anything.

The detective seems disappointed when I don't respond.

"Do you know anything about this?" he asks. He and Vernon look to me expectantly.

"No." I'm not lying because really I don't know anything about the specifics of when and what Leann stole.

"Are you sure?" asks the detective.

"Yes," I say and continue to stare at his eyebrows. He consults his paperwork. He writes something on his notepad. Then he adjusts himself on the desk corner.

"Well, another employee here seems to think you might know something about the thefts." He looks at me again expectantly and Vernon leans forward in his chair.

"I don't," I say as firmly as I can.

"You don't know anything at all?"

"No."

"So you won't mind if we check your locker?"

I know nothing is in my locker but my gym bag and lots of condiment packets. I don't think you can get in trouble for having too many condiment packets. After all, they give them out free.

"Sure, you can check my locker," I say confidently. But after I say it I wonder if they will bring an entire CSI team in here and dust for evidence. Could they tell if Leann had Tastykakes and peanut butter in the locker a month ago?

Both men have nothing to say to that. Finally Vernon speaks, "Well then, we'll just have to see what comes of this. You can go back to your register."

"And young lady, please think about the fact that Mr. Slick is willing to allow the person who is taking things to make restitution. He's willing to settle this without my help if someone comes forward on her own and confesses."

I hate it when anyone calls me young lady and this guy is such a creep, I want to say all kinds of things to his ugly, crumb covered face, but I just say, "Is that so?" and leave.

Back at my register I'm relieved. They don't have any evidence on Leann. They just have the fact that things have been disappearing and Franklin's accusations, whatever they might be. Still, I feel like everyone is watching me. They must all know. Of course they do. How could Leann be doing this for so long and they not know?

When it's time to close, I grab my paycheck and fold it carefully into my pocket. I need to get home so I don't piss off Leroy again. I buy some eggs, Twizzlers, and a bag of apples and head home.

When I enter the apartment, Trevor is still awake. He's playing on his computer. Leroy is parked on the couch watching some kind of reality show. He looks up when I come in and studies me. I wave and take the groceries to the kitchen.

"You get my eggs this time?" he asks.

"I did."

"Twizzlers?"

"Yep."

"Well then give them to me, Bitch."

Why does he have to do that? I hand him the Twizzlers and glance at Trevor. I say quietly, "I wish you wouldn't use that word in front of Trevor."

He laughs, biting off a piece of Twizzler and looking at me with it hanging half out of his mouth. "What? Bitch? Why can't I call you Bitch?" He raises his voice intentionally. His face is full of contempt, yet the Twizzler dangling out of the side of his mouth just makes him look stupid. Trevor glances up at us. It's useless. I walk over to Trevor and touch his head.

"It's time for you to be in bed."

"In a minute. Just let me finish this battle."

"Hey boy! Your mother said get to bed, so get your ass in bed!" Leroy yells. Trevor jumps up and races for the bedroom.

"You don't need to yell at him," I say, glaring at Leroy.

He watches me and viciously bites off more Twizzler. I clear the dishes off the table and take them to the kitchen. I turn around to get the rest and Leroy is blocking my way.

"What makes you think you can talk to me like that?" he asks. I try to get around him and he grabs my arms and pushes me up against the sink.

"I'm talking to you, Bitch. You can't just ignore me. What the fuck is wrong with you? You're acting weird, Leann. Like you're some high and mighty person. Like you're better than me. Is that it? You think you're better than me now? You got another job. You don't steal anything anymore. You suddenly care about Trevor's bedtime and my language? What the fuck is going on?" He's shaking me as he yells.

I'm terrified. Never in my life has anyone ever treated me like this. But this man is big. He could hurt me. Words stick in my throat. I want to run away, but I know I can't. I have to calm him down. I start crying. Tears have always worked for me with men. Leroy looks even more shocked at my tears than my words. He shoves me aside roughly and I crash into the microwave. It beeps.

"Get out of my way, Bitch, and quit your crying. You must be on the rag. I don't know why else you're actin' so crazy." He opens the fridge and takes out another beer. He looks at me in disgust and shakes his head, but he goes back to the couch. I hurry to the bedroom and crawl into bed. I pull the covers over my head and try to curl into a ball. My stomach doesn't allow me to do this. I hate all this fat. I am not fat. I am not this person. I try to cry softly so that Trevor won't hear me.

chapter 17

When I wake up in the morning, Leroy is gone. Trevor tells me that he left early. I take a long shower and mentally make my shopping list. Today I'm going to buy some things to make my life here a little less miserable.

Trevor and I start at the Kmart, where I buy him a coat and pick up a coffee maker and some makeup for me. I usually buy my makeup from the counter at Macy's, so it's hard to choose a foundation and lipstick from the millions of choices at Kmart. I go for the cheapest.

Our next stop is my hair salon. I can't afford the perm Leann's hair needs, but a decent haircut will do wonders. I ask Sharon, who has cut my hair for years, if she can cut it without the shampoo and blow dry. I don't tell her I can't afford it; I just say we're in a hurry. She purses her lips, but since she doesn't have anyone else waiting, she agrees. I tip her the best I can and we head to the library. Trevor is carrying a stack of old magazines the receptionist let him have. I'm sure there will be plenty of pictures of beautiful people in those.

It turns out Leann doesn't have a library card and Trevor has never been to the public library before. I fill out the form to get a library card. Luckily they don't want much information other than name and address and telephone. I make up a phone number.

Trevor picks out three books. I don't want to go home, but we are too loaded down to go anywhere else. It's a beautiful day.

"Trevor, let's take this stuff home and then go have a picnic. We can take the books to the park with us." He loves the idea.

I can hear the music coming from our apartment before we are even halfway up the stairs. Loud blaring bass that makes the whole building shake. Mr. Giovanni is not sitting in his customary spot outside his apartment and his folding chair is gone. As we reach our landing, the music is even louder because the door is standing wide open. It's country music, which shouldn't surprise me. I'm stunned by what I see inside the apartment. Leroy is dancing around with a cigar hanging from his mouth and a drink lifted high in the air. He sees us and starts to yell greetings. The cigar falls out of his mouth. He ignores it and comes running to greet us. He grabs the bags out of my hand, flings them on the couch (my coffee maker!), and puts his arms around me. Now he is dancing me around the apartment. Trevor is standing in the doorway with a grin on his face. Leroy stinks from the cigar, which is slowly burning a hole in the ugly yellow carpet, and of booze. He has another funny smell on him too. Almost like a barn. He's yelling, "We're rich 'cause I'm so damn smart!"

I pull away from him and go to retrieve my bags off the couch. He turns the music down, and as I try to walk by him, he grabs the packages and says, "C'mon, Leann, don't you wanna know how much I made today on the ponies?" I'm dumbstruck by this because I've been under the impression that he doesn't trust me with financial information. I can't imagine he plans to share his earnings. I look at him blankly, but Trevor rushes over.

"Daddy, how much did you win?"

Leroy grins, still looking at me. "My boy, we are going out to eat."

Which means exactly what? Heaven help us. I have to go out in public with this sorry excuse for a man.

"Now?" I ask. Leroy seems to wake up.

"Yes, now. What's your problem, Bitch? Can't you be happy? Ever? I got me some serious cash and we're goin' to celebrate. What's in these bags anyway?" He pulls out the skin cream, makeup, and shampoo one by one. He looks at each one and then tosses it back over his shoulder on the couch. Some of the bottles hit the coffee table with a horrible noise. I'm afraid to move. "What's all this? Why do you need this shit? You spent my good money on this crap? Who you getting all dolled up for?" He grabs my arm, digging his fingers in painfully. I pull the other bag out of his hands. I'm not going to let him break my coffee maker. I yank my arm away.

"I'm not seeing anybody. What's so wrong with wanting to look decent? Maybe I'm tired of looking like crap. I'm glad you got money, however you got it. But it's not like you share any of it with me. You dole it out like I'm a complete imbecile." I'm on a roll here, and Leroy stares at me like I'm an alien. At this point I have nothing to lose, so I go on. "I'm sick of you bossing me around. I'm sick of living like this. I bought these things with my money. My money!" I stare at him, daring him to deny me my coffee maker. I hold on to it for dear life. He glares at me and then he turns on his heel and starts grabbing up all my cosmetics. He walks over to the door and flings them down the stairwell. I hear the bottles clattering all the way down. I'm shaking with rage, but I know he is much stronger and I have pushed him to the limit.

"Where's your damn Shop N Save check?"

I find my jacket and pull out the check. I hand it over to him.

"I need money for groceries, Leroy."

"I thought you had your own money now."

"I need to feed Trevor."

Leroy looks at Trevor, who is standing back against the wall near his computer. He looks terrified.

"I'll feed Trevor. C'mon boy. Let's you and me go out and celebrate. At least someone in this family appreciates me."

"Trevor and I have plans," I say, looking at Trevor, pleading with him to agree.

"Change them. He's coming with me."

"He can't."

"He's my son and I want to take him out for lunch. What's your goddamn problem?"

"Then I'm coming too."

Leroy shakes his head. "No, you ain't. You're too good for us. Besides, I wouldn't waste my good money on you." He reaches in his pocket and pulls out forty dollars. He flings it at me. "You can go do your damn grocery shopping."

I watch them leave. I'm powerless. I feel like I might hyperventilate. From the window, I see they are only walking down the street to the deli. Guess he didn't make that much money if he can only afford a cheesesteak.

I clean up the cigar and send it down the garbage disposal. It has burned an oblong black spot on the carpet. He was really happy. I suppose the old Leann would have been happy too, right? Wish I knew. Suddenly I feel like I can't breathe. I have to get out of here. I grab my coat and head out. I see some of my makeup in the corners of the stairwell, but I don't stop to pick it up because I've got to get out of this building or I'm going to explode.

The fresh air hits me and I take my first deep breath. I start walking. I need to talk to someone. But I have no one. I think through the list of people I know. Phyllis seems a bit shallow for this and she would never understand it. I think Jimmy would listen, but he might think I'm completely nuts and I'd lose the only friend I have. Bruce is much too focused on my journey to fitness. Without realizing it, I find myself walking much farther than I have before. I'd like to just keep walking. Like in *Forrest Gump*. The only reason I don't is Trevor. I can't leave him alone with that man. I finally stop to catch my breath and look around. I'm near the church where I got the free food. How could I have walked that far? I cross the street and walk up the steps. The door is unlocked. I creep inside. It's dark. The only light spills out from a door to the side of the pulpit, making the candlesticks on the communion table glow. I walk halfway up the aisle and sink down in the red plush cushions of a pew. The air is still warm from the people who filled this space last. Were they here for a wedding? Maybe a funeral. Someone's been here.

I close my eyes and breathe in the calmness of the place. I feel some of the pressure that has been choking me begin to dissipate. I wish I could leave it here. I open my eyes and study the stained glass. The place is covered in it. The windows and doors are a shower of color. As clouds pass over, the sanctuary gets bright and then dark again. I'm captivated by the pattern of light and darkness.

"Hello?" Someone calls from behind me. I turn around quickly. It's the priest who gave me the food. "Can I help you?" he asks.

I stand up and walk towards him. "I'm sorry," I stutter. "I was walking by and I just . . . it's nice in here. I guess I was just taking a breather."

He smiles. "This is a good place for that. I was closing up. Almost locked you in."

"I'm sorry. I'll get going." I start to walk past him and he says, "I've seen you before, haven't I?"

"I was here to get some food for my son."

"That's right. It was raining something awful that day."

I smile but don't know what to say.

"Do you need more?"

Forty dollars won't get me many groceries, and I don't have much left from my paycheck after my shopping spree this morning. I need fifteen of that for Trevor's field trip. At this point, I'll take all the help I can get.

"I could use some."

"But that's not why you're here, is it?"

Suddenly I want to tell this man everything. I don't care if he thinks I'm crazy or not. I just need to tell someone.

"Can I talk to you?" I ask.

"Of course. Let's sit down." He leads me to the front of the sanctuary and we sit in two big chairs that look like they're made for royalty. It seems strange to be sitting in the front of a church. I look out at the pews. It must feel powerful to look out over those pews when they're filled with people. I wonder if he likes preaching. All those people watching you, waiting to hear what you have to say. Waiting to be condemned or forgiven.

Before I can change my mind I spill my entire story. I tell him about Leann stealing and about Leroy and his funny money and how I doubt he could be a real trucker. I tell him how amazing Trevor is and about his bag of dreams. I tell him how much I hate that he's left alone with Jillian, who must have her own demons. I tell him about Vernon Slick and how he blamed me for the accident and now he thinks I've been stealing, which I have, only it wasn't me. I tell him about Leann's awful mother and about Scott not believing me and about trying to see Leann in my apartment. I can't tell if he believes anything I'm saying, but he's paying attention, occasionally asking a question to be sure he understood me correctly. Finally, I tell him how Leroy flung my makeup down the stairs and how I ended up here. When I'm finished, I feel tired. Like I could sleep for days. I take a deep breath and close my eyes. Father Frank, as he's told me to call him, takes my hands. He asks if he can pray for me. I'm startled. No one has ever prayed for me before. So I shrug. He bows his head, so I bow mine. I expect him to start talking, but for a long time he is silent. When he does speak, his voice is soft and gentle, almost a whisper.

"Father, we know you hold us in the palm of your hand. Guide your child, Carin, and comfort her. Surround her with people who will help her and who will love her. Be with Trevor. Protect him and grant him your grace. Help Carin know that you love her spirit. That you know her spirit and you celebrate it. As do I."

When he is finished, all I can think is, "Is that it?" He's not going to help me. It feels better knowing that someone knows, but it doesn't change anything. That truth sinks my soul. I'm in this alone. Doesn't seem like God can do anything but be my cheerleader and maybe give me a couple lucky breaks.

We walk back to Father Frank's office and he gets me a box of food. I thank him. He tells me he will continue to pray for me and to come see him again. He gives me a card with the information for a women and children's shelter and the abuse hotline number. He asks again if he can do anything else for me. I realize he can't do anything. Nobody can, except me.

I walk the entire way home in a daze. It's late afternoon now. I'm too tired to go to the grocery store, but I can't walk in with this box of food. Leroy will be furious that I took a handout. When I reach the building, I walk slowly up the stairs. My makeup is no longer all over the stairwell. I knock on Mr. Giovanni's door. He opens it a crack, and when he sees me he smiles and opens the door wide. "Leann! Good to see you!"

"You, too. Hey, can I leave this box of food with you until tomorrow night?"

He looks curious, but agrees to keep it for me. I'm about to leave and he stops me and hands me a plastic bag. When I look inside, I see all my makeup and skin care stuff.

"You didn't need to pick it all up."

"Nonsense. He's an idiot. He has no right to throw out your things."

I leave the bag with the food box. I don't want to set Leroy off again today. I thank Mr. Giovanni and head to my apartment.

Inside the apartment, I find Trevor and Leroy. Leroy is subdued. He's talking on a cell phone. He's huddled over the coffee table, looking at some notes he's scribbling. He slams one hand against the sofa and shakes his head. He says, "I thought they said they were good for it? You gotta help me make this right!" Again he slams his hand on the sofa and curses. He hangs up the phone, glares at me, and says he's going out.

When he's gone, I scrounge around in the cupboard for some dinner. I cook up the tiny bit of pasta that's left and divide it between two bowls. Trevor doesn't eat much. He says he had a cheesesteak and fries earlier.

"Did you have a good time?" I ask.

"It was okay," he says reluctantly.

"I'm glad you did," I say firmly. I don't want him to feel guilty for having a good time with Leroy. "What else did you do today?"

"We went to see a guy with a bunch of dogs."

"Wow? Did you get to play with them?"

"Nah, he said they were really mean."

"That's too bad."

"It was okay. Daddy bought me ice cream because I was so good when he was talking."

"Did you go anywhere else?"

"We stopped at someone's house and Daddy showed them the plants he hauled this week. He said he needed to make sure it was the right kind."

"Really? Did you see the plant?"

"Uh, huh, but I think it was just leaves from the plant. Daddy told me it was none of my business."

"What did he do with it?"

"He gave it to Jillian."

Now I'm confused. Why would Leroy give anything to Jillian?

"Did she like it?"

"I guess so. She kissed Daddy."

I knew it. I should report him and get him locked up for statutory rape. But I guess to do that I'd have to prove he was having sex with her. I'm still pondering this development when Leroy comes back. He grunts at us and goes into the bedroom. Later, when I'm tucking Trevor in, I see that Leroy is passed out across the bed, still wearing his clothes. He stinks. I sleep on the couch.

～ ～

leann

There ain't nothing to do on Saturdays. Sundays either. At least, I don't have to go to that crappy church with Mama. So that's good. But my soaps ain't on. During the week, I hang out with Esperanza, but on the weekends she and Mike go to visit their kids. Esperanza is teaching me lots of stuff. She tells me in Spanish, but she shows me with her hands. I'm learning stuff like cooking and gardening. She even showed me how to make a bracelet using teeny tiny beads. And she showed me how to make soap and lotions. I never knew a person could do that. I thought you had to buy that stuff at the store. I think Esperanza can make anything. When I'm with her I don't feel so weird in this body. I feel more like me.

I wander around the place, snooping. I've looked at most everything. Today I look at all the books. There are hundreds of them. Ain't no way Carin's read them all. Probably just trying to impress that powder-head boyfriend. I pull a book off the shelf. It's a story, I think. The title don't make no sense, so I open it up.

I start reading the story. It's slow going at first. I ain't read since school, which was boring as shit. This is different. It's a story. Just like my soaps. I take the book to the couch and keep on reading. Before I know it, lunch time has come and gone. I need to stop to order my lunch, but decide to just eat some cereal instead so I don't miss anything.

It takes me all day, but right around midnight, I finish that book. And I feel so smart! Memories of the library at my grade school come back. I loved the library smell. It was like the inside of my lunch box, just-Xeroxed papers, and a little like my basement. It was a nice smell. I remember that the books was free. I watched kids come in and take a book off the shelf and just walk out without paying and I liked that. I liked being able to take what I wanted.

The librarian in the plaid skirts believed I'd bring them books back. She believed everybody would. I doubt they did, so you'd think she'd change that policy. Sometimes I'd take out a whole stack. Just 'cause I could. I don't know why I stopped reading. I guess 'cause Mama started working at the snack factory and let me watch television when she weren't there. She figured I'd get in less trouble. She'd set out a couple bags of the free chips and tell me to turn on the TV and then she'd be gone. I'd watch until I couldn't keep my eyes open no more and then I'd sleep on the couch. She'd wake me up and holler at me around midnight and I'd clean up the chips and get in bed. I could never sleep and a couple times I tried to read, but we shared a bedroom and Mama would yell at me to turn off the damn light. Guess my life got too busy for books after that.

But not anymore. My life has no busy in it. My life has room for lots of books.

In the morning, I pull all the books off the shelves and start sorting them into piles: books that look good, books that look okay, and books that look boring as shit. I fix some cereal and just start reading. I got a lot to do today.

chapter 18

~ ~

In the morning, Trevor and I creep out of the apartment early.
I know on Sunday mornings they offer bagels at the gym,
so I pick up orange juice and coffee at the 7-Eleven and we head
to work. We settle on the bench across from the reception desk.
Trevor eats two cinnamon and raisin bagels, picking out the rai-
sins and carefully setting them on the edge of his Styrofoam plate.
I nibble on a plain banana nut bagel and sip my coffee. Each time
the receptionist scowls at me, I smile sweetly and raise my bagel
in salute. Trevor is focused on balancing his bagel plate on his lap
and doesn't notice.

Work in the Kiddie Korner goes by quickly. Now that the
weather is starting to warm up, fewer kids come to child care each
weekend. I hope Denise doesn't decide they need fewer staff too.
But they can't predict rainy days, so I think I'm safe.

Later, I settle on one of the stationary bikes with a magazine.
Just like the Kiddie Korner, the fitness center is also deserted.
Scott comes in midway through my workout. I'm feeling really
good and have biked longer than I've ever biked. I wore longer
shorts today and that is saving my thighs from the incessant rubbing. Or maybe they aren't rubbing together quite as tightly as
they usually do. I'm getting used to this body. The rolls around
my middle don't freak me out nearly as much as they used to.
Except at night. I can't get used to them lying there beside me like
a puppy.

Scott smiles shyly at me and climbs on a bike a few seats
down from me. I try to focus on my magazine. Sweat is pouring

off of me. After a few minutes, Scott calls out, "How are you doing today?"

I keep looking at my magazine and ignore him, but he is undeterred. He asks again, louder. I sigh and put down my magazine. What could he possibly want with me? The Scott I know would never voluntarily speak to someone who looks like me.

"I'm good," I say quietly and turn back to my magazine.

"I like Sundays," Scott begins. I glance over to be certain he's still speaking to me and he smiles. "There's hardly anyone here."

I nod, smile tightly, and turn back to my magazine. I've got to get off this machine. My legs are starting to feel like sand.

"I used to come in here with a friend, but she doesn't come anymore."

My curiosity is piqued. I venture, "Why doesn't she come in here anymore?"

"I don't know. She doesn't really talk to me anymore. It's like she's changed, ya' know?"

I nod.

"She doesn't seem to care if I'm there or not."

It breaks my heart. He is so sad. Never in a million years would I have thought Scott could be so torn up over me that he would be talking to an obese woman sweating on an exercise bike.

"That's sad," I say, and finally stop my bike. My legs feel like they might seize up, and it is extremely difficult to get off the bike. I manage it awkwardly. Scott is watching me. My heel catches as I swing my leg off the bike and now I'm hopping on one leg. I'm sure I'm going to hit the ground, but I manage to hold onto the handle bars and right myself. I smile at Scott and he gives me a thumbs up.

I work through all of the machines today. Scott works on the free weights. We keep catching eyes in the mirrors. It's embarrassing. I know he's worried that the fat girl thinks he likes her. I can just hear him now. It was horrible how we talked about people at the gym. We were so judgmental. I never really thought anyone was paying attention, but now I realize they were. Everyone thinks everyone else is looking at them. I thought that was only unique to the beautiful people. As I walk through the weight machines, squeezing between the ones stationed too close together, I'm conscious of all the other people. I think they are cringing at my size and feeling sorry for me. In reality, they are probably worrying what everyone else is thinking about them. They can't imagine a fat girl is looking in the mirrors and worrying what they think. I know this because even when I was thin, I worried what everyone thought. Fat or thin, we're all starring in our own show.

I stand in the shower, wishing I could stay here forever. Hidden behind the shower curtain, letting the hot water cover my body, I'm happy. Just for a few moments. I feel healthy and hopeful. I know the moment I walk out and struggle to cover myself with the pathetic little towels the gym gives out, I'll feel awful again. I open the shower stall. Only a few women are left in the locker area. I feel their eyes and their pity on me. I hold the towel up in front of me, and after I pass them I switch it around to cover the back of me. I dress quickly in front of my locker, not really drying off because that takes too long and exposes too much.

Trevor and I stop by the Shop N Save on the way home. We stuff our cart with items from the sale rack. He wants more snack food and whines when I won't buy it. I try to explain to him about eating healthy. Forty dollars doesn't go far and I still need to pay the fee for Trevor's field trip. Trevor wants Doritos. He says a girl in his class brings a new bag on the bus every day. She doesn't share with him. He wants to bring his own bag to share with everyone but her. I tell him that won't change anything. He says, "I know, but I want to do it anyway." I know the feeling.

Leroy is gone when we get back and never comes home at any point in the night. Is he with Jillian?

chapter 19

Our weekday lives have begun to slip into a routine, occasionally interrupted by unpleasant visits from Leann's mother. I try to get out of the apartment as fast as possible in the morning, since that seems to be the most likely time for her to show up. One day I came home to a nasty note taped to the door. Luckily, her pen ran out of ink, so she didn't finish her thought, just poked holes with the pen in the bottom of the paper.

At the Shop N Save, I've been managing to avoid Franklin for the most part. He still scowls at me when he comes up front, but I've stopped calling him to assist customers and do it myself if I'm not busy. Several customers have made me their favorite cashier. They line up in my lane even when Phyllis' line is shorter. I like these people. They see me as competent, helpful, and interesting, even if other people don't. My mother is one who regularly chooses my line. I'm always extra careful with her things. She never says much, but she has started smiling at me. I like this relationship with her.

On Tuesday night, Jimmy joins me for dinner. He and I have fallen into the routine of eating together. He's the quiet type, but somehow that doesn't feel awkward. Mostly, he lets me talk. It occurs to me that I don't know much about him.

"Jimmy, do you think you'll always work here?"

He looks up from his sandwich and pauses mid-chew. He looks back at the building as if he's deciding right this minute. Finally, he swallows and says, "Nah. It's alright here, but I want to do other things."

"Like what?" I ask. I'm curious. He seems much too smart, and even kind of wise, to be working as a stock manager at the Shop N Save all his life.

"I think I might like to work at the Home Depot." He smiles at this thought and goes back to his sandwich.

I'm disappointed by this. I was figuring college or, at the least, his own business. How could he aspire to wear an orange apron and spend his days in a warehouse? I press him. "Really? You don't want to do anything else?"

"Well, I'll probably end up working in my Uncle Hal's business, but I don't much want to."

"What does he do?"

"He has the funeral home up on Eighth. I work for him some now on the weekends if he gets busy. I drive the cars. It's okay, but everyone's so sad and fragile. It makes me nervous. I don't think I'd want to be around that all the time."

"Isn't there anything else you'd like to do?" I ask hopefully.

Jimmy thinks for a minute. "I like jukeboxes," he says quietly, not meeting my eyes.

"Jukeboxes?" I ask. I'm confused. What does that have to do with a career?

"Yeah. I like fixing them up. Music sounds different on a jukebox—stronger, more real. Maybe I could open up a shop someday." He watches me carefully. He looks vulnerable at this moment. He's waiting for me to respond, but I'm not sure what to say. I can't imagine there's a big market for jukebox repair. In fact, I don't remember seeing a jukebox anywhere other than the old diner near the home where my grandma lives. That one never worked. We used to stop at the diner after visiting grandma, and my parents would argue like always, and I'd go to the jukebox and flip through the selections. I liked the way you pressed a button and another layer flopped down with more music to choose. But that jukebox rarely worked. And the times it stole my quarter, my mother would never let me complain about it. She'd say, "It's just a quarter. Don't make a fuss Carin." I haven't seen a jukebox since my grandma passed away ten years ago.

"I don't know, Jimmy. I guess someone's got to fix the jukeboxes."

He smiles at me. "Nah, it's stupid," he says and takes another bite of his sandwich.

"If it makes you happy, it's not stupid."

He looks at me surprised. He doesn't expect such optimism from me. I smile and climb down from the loading dock. I'm sure Phyllis is getting annoyed by now. She always lets me eat first, but then she gets all out of sorts because she had to wait. I wish people would say what they really want.

～ ～

leann

Today I read so much my eyes start to ache. I even miss my soaps because I'm all distracted by the story I'm reading. It's a love story and it's just so damn sad, but happy too. Sometimes I start talking out loud to the girl in the book. She does some dumb stuff. I'd do different, but she don't listen to me.

This morning I talked to Trevor. I was real careful. I knew he weren't gonna talk to any stranger, so I said I knew his mama and Leroy. He wondered if I was going to see his mama.

"I am," I said and he smiled.

"Good, 'cause she needs a friend. I think she's lonely."

"How you doing, Trevor? Your mama take good care of you?"

He nodded and squinted at me. I could tell he wanted to figure out who I was.

"How's the bus ride? The other kids nice to you?"

"Mostly they're fine, except this one girl, Cecelia. She eats her Doritos on the bus and won't share."

"You like them Doritos, don't cha?"

"How do you know that?"

"I just remember is all. Would you like it if I brought you some?"

He thought on this. Then nodded his head and smiled. The bus pulled up, and he was gone.

I sat down on the bench and I just cried 'cause I miss my baby so much. And I realized this morning that he don't miss me at all. He don't even know I'm gone. I'm gonna bring him them Doritos tomorrow.

chapter 20

On Thursday, I push myself on the treadmill. I raise the incline and have to grip the side bars to keep from falling off the back of the machine. The problem begins as I struggle to keep up. Before I realize it, I've migrated to the back edge of the machine. I desperately try to reach the buttons on the control panel to slow the machine down. I try to run, but I stub my toe on the belt, lose my balance, and get flung off the back of the machine. I bang my head on the machine behind me and try to ignore the stifled giggle I hear from a woman on a machine a few feet away. Scott appears in front of me and offers his hand. I'm mortified. If I give him my hand and he tries to lift me from the ground, he'll probably just end up on top of me.

"Let me help you," he says.

"I'm okay. I just need a minute," I tell him and act like I'm comfortable sprawled here between two machines with a power cord grinding into my back.

"Do you want me to get Bruce? Are you hurt?" He seems sincerely concerned.

"I'm fine, really. Go back to your workout." Go away, go away, go away. Can't you see how embarrassing this is? Can't you just leave the fat girl on the ground and pretend you didn't see, like everyone else?

Scott looks around helplessly and finally he squats down next to me.

"I've been watching you," he says.

I'm not sure how to take this. Why on earth would Scott be watching me? I look at him skeptically, trying to figure out his motive. His face looks innocent enough.

"Really?"

"Yeah. You're doing really well. You're so committed, here every day. And you've lost some weight too, haven't you?"

God, now that's an embarrassing question. Scott should know better than to ask a girl if she's lost weight. Except, I guess, if said girl weighs more than he does. I'm not sure how to respond. Finally, I opt for honesty.

"I'm trying really hard. I have lost a little weight."

"I think you've lost more than a little." He smiles at me. Then he stands and again offers his hand. Awkwardly, he heaves me upward.

"Thanks."

"No problem. Anytime," he says, then grins at me and heads back to the weight area.

Weird encounter. It's almost like he knows something.

After my shower, I walk tentatively towards the scale. Amazing how that machine holds such power. The power to destroy a day, a mood, a life. When I was growing up, I obsessed over every ounce. I weighed myself several times a day. I let it control me and dictate my every move. Funny, now that I weigh as much as a horse I don't even think about it. It's all relative, I suppose. Gingerly, I step on the scale and look down. It's hard to see past my stomach. I should use the other scale, the one like they have at a doctor's office, but it's been moved to the hallway and I'm not up for another fat girl sideshow. I lean forward and try to look over my belly. The arrow wiggles and then settles on 335. No way. I know it's probably been weeks since I weighed myself, but that's a lot. This is encouraging. I can do this.

When I get to the store, Vernon has called a meeting. Everyone is crammed into the break room. I manage to squeeze in next to the soda machine. I can't really see past the deli ladies in front of me. Vernon starts the meeting. "Hello, everyone. I'll be brief, because I know you're all anxious to get to work." I, for one, am not the least bit anxious to get to work. I'm anxious about what he's going to say. I'm guessing it's about the big investigation.

"As most of you know, there was a detective here last week. He was here at my request. It has come to my attention that food has been disappearing from the store on a regular basis. I'm not sure how long this has been going on. Our new inventory system was only put in place six months ago, so we're working with limited data. However, the interviews did reveal a few things. First of all, we believe some employees are taking food and neglecting to properly pay for it. Sometimes it may be a misunderstanding, I understand that. However, from this point on, any employee who takes food without properly paying for it will be prosecuted to the full extent of the law."

Two of the ladies in front of me whisper to each other and then one turns to look at me. I raise my eyebrows in wonder and surprise. She turns quickly back around. Vernon is not finished.

"Also, any employee who reports a theft will be rewarded financially. I'm sure that we won't have any occasion to use this reward system, but I want you to know it is in place. Thank you for your time. Now, let's get back to work."

Go team. Vernon really knows how to rally the troops. Everyone is whispering to each other as they exit. Franklin stands next to the door trying to catch my eye between people exiting. I'm studiously ignoring him. I'm examining the calendar taped on the side of the soda machine. When I'm the only one left, Franklin walks over and says, "Now I can make some money off you, Leann. I know you been stealing food ever since you started here. Back when you treated me nice, I didn't mind looking the other way. But not anymore. You don't want to be my bitch? That's fine. But you just wait, 'cause Franklin's gonna hang you up. You're gonna be begging me someday soon, wishing you could have a piece of me. Wishing."

"All I'm going to wish, Franklin, is that you disappear. Poof! Like that!" I wave my hand in the air to illustrate and walk past his angry face.

That night, I'm climbing carefully into bed, trying to make as little noise as possible, when I hear a small voice say, "Mama?"

I freeze. Is he talking in his sleep? "Mama?" he says again. Nope.

I roll over to his side of the bed and peer down at him in the darkness. I can see his face lit up by the bathroom light slipping under the door.

"You're supposed to be asleep."

"I know, but I'm not."

"Are you feeling okay?" Please don't let him be sick.

"Uh-huh. Mama, can I ask you something?"

"Of course," I say, watching him. He looks up at me very seriously.

"Mama, did something happen to you?" My heart stops. Of course, he knows. If anyone on this earth would know Leann, it's him. I don't know what to say. I cannot tell him that his mother abandoned him. That she's currently housed in a different body and is choosing not to return to him.

"What makes you think that?" I ask.

"I don't know. You're just different. You don't act like you."

"Is that a good thing or a bad thing?"

He doesn't answer for a while. A few minutes pass, but his eyes are wide open, searching the ceiling and occasionally flitting over to see if I'm still watching.

"I guess it's good, but it's weird. Do you love me?"

"Yes, yes, yes!" This I do know. No matter what has happened here, I know I love this child with all my heart. He smiles.

"Now you need to go to sleep because you have school tomorrow." I brush the side of his head with my hand and he closes his eyes. I roll over and try to find the comfortable spot on the bed.

I'm finally drifting off, when I hear him say in a quiet, small voice, "Is she coming back?"

My heart is stuck in my throat. I don't know what to say. I have to say something, so I say, "I don't know, but I'm here. I will be here for you." I guess this answer is okay, because soon I hear his sweet snores. I'm glad I worked out so hard today, because my body is too tired to allow my mind to sort this one out right now. Sleep comes.

~ ~

leann

I'm at the bus stop early today. I don't want to miss him. I've got a bag of Doritos and a Coke ready for him. I want to give him more, but I ain't figured out how to do that yet. If I hand him a pile of money, that wouldn't be right and people would get suspicious.

I think maybe Trevor's gonna miss the bus, but then I see him turn the corner, hustling his little self so he makes it. He sees me and looks around like someone's watching. I hope he didn't say nothin' to Carin.

"Hey," I say and smile real big.

He smiles back and looks around again, worried.

"I brought you something."

"Ya did?"

I hand him the bag with the Doritos and Coke. He opens it and smiles, but closes it fast and looks around again.

"Told you I were gonna bring it."

"Thank you," he says, all polite. I told him about being polite.

"Now, that's just for you. Don't you go telling nobody I brought it, okay?"

He nods and smiles. Makes my day. I watch as the bus pulls up and he climbs aboard. He sits in a seat near the front and then turns to wave at me. My sweet boy.

I stay on that bench for a while, my heart aching. I can't figure how I can fix this. I don't want my body back. I don't want ole Leroy and that sorry-ass apartment back. I just want Trevor, but I figure Carin ain't gonna go for that. I decide to get a move on, else I might run into Carin herself. Not ready for that. I gotta think on this.

I hurry back to the apartment; I got a lot of books to read.

chapter 21

〜〜

It's Friday morning. I study my face in the mirror. There's only a few minutes left before I have to get to work. My skin looks better. I'm getting used to the size of me. I feel a little better too, not so nutso. I've been avoiding sugar. It seems to be a trigger for Leann's body. One bite and I go on automatic pilot. I have to have more or I get really angry. It's nuts. Maybe it's what an alcoholic feels like. Leann is a sugarholic. I wonder if there are support groups for that.

The lipstick I bought is too bright for this skin. I wish I could get to my own makeup. I've got over twenty-five shades neatly arranged in a drawer. I examine my yellow teeth. It's all that smoking. I wonder when Leann last went to a dentist. I run my tongue over my teeth now and they feel filmy. I brush my teeth thoroughly and pull my hair back in a hair band. I check myself in the mirror one more time. Not bad.

The morning flies by because we are swamped with kids. Apparently it's spring break for some of the preschools. I organize a coloring contest and this keeps the kids busy until they realize I don't have a prize for the winner. So we play follow the leader and, much to Denise's shock, I lead them out of the Kiddie Korner and down the hall. She runs along next to me saying, "We really shouldn't take them out of here. What if a parent needs to pick them up?"

"I'm not taking them cross-country, Denise, just down the hall and back." I smile and continue marching, periodically waving one hand or pausing to turn in a circle, which causes all the children to pile up like cars on the freeway. We make it back to the Kiddie Korner unscathed. Denise is fuming. The kids want to play again, so I let them take turns leading, but since they can't leave the room, they soon lose interest. We switch to Simon Says and play round after round until I think my brain is going to fog over. I wish life worked like Simon Says. "Simon Says, give me my life back."

I'm ready for Scott today. He arrives right on time and climbs on the bike next to mine. He's so close I could reach out and touch his arm. I want to touch him so much, it's almost unbearable. I have to take deep breaths and force myself to look away. What is this? Since when have I ever been so hot for Scott? I usually need a few beers in me before he starts looking so appetizing. I try to focus on my magazine and wait for him to say something. I know he will. For some reason, he can't resist me. Maybe it's the freak factor. I don't know what he's up to, but I'm hoping he'll tell me what Leann is doing in my body.

We ride along for five minutes, but besides the initial smile and raise of eyebrows, he hasn't said a word. I can't take it any longer.

"So, how is your friend? The one that had the accident?"

He looks startled. He puts down his magazine and looks at me. "Uh, she's not so great," he says.

"That's too bad. Hasn't she recovered?"

"Well, physically, I think she's alright, but mentally she can't remember anything. She can't remember who she is or her family or any of her friends. And the worst of it is, she won't let us help her. She refuses to talk to any of us. She just stays locked up in her apartment. I don't think she ever goes out. Even her own mother can't get her to see a psychiatrist. Her mom called me yesterday and said Carin wouldn't open her door, but she knew she was in the apartment because she could smell Chinese takeout. Which is odd because Carin never liked Chinese food."

Yes, I did. I just never liked the place where he liked to go. It was filthy and every dish tasted the same. I'd like to set him straight, but I put on the most sympathetic face I have and say, "That's just awful. If she doesn't go to work, how does she pay her bills?" I hope she isn't getting all my furniture repossessed.

"Money's no issue. She was given a settlement. She won't ever have to worry about anything. She never returns my calls and hardly ever wants to see me. We used to be best friends. More than friends." He looks so sad. I never imagined he would react like this to me cutting him off. We always promised if either of us found someone special, we would back off. Our relationship was comfortable, but it was never serious.

"I'm sorry," I say, and I mean it. I'm so sorry I led him on like this. I wish he'd been honest with me sooner. I wish I had known. I just never considered him seriously.

He searches my face. Maybe there's a hint of recognition. I'm about to die from being on the bike so long, but I don't want to look away to adjust the tension.

"I miss her," he says quietly.

"Maybe you have to let her go." I climb off the bike carefully, trying not to kick Scott as I swing my leg over.

"Maybe," he says. Then he sighs and smiles a little. "Sorry to unload on you like that. You don't even know me."

"I know you better than you think," I say, and turn before he can see my smile. I put a big effort into my weight routine, knowing Scott is watching me. If I don't look at myself in the six thousand mirrors coating the walls, I can imagine I don't look the way I do. I focus on the muscles that I'm working and the weight I'm losing. I have an awesome workout and feel pretty good as I head back to the locker room.

Denise stops me to give me my paycheck. "Leann, it's against our rules for anyone other than parents to take the children out of the Kiddie Korner. So in the future, please remember that." Even Denise isn't going to dampen my spirits. I tell her I will remember that and apologize for violating such an important rule. She scrutinizes me carefully, trying to see if I'm being sarcastic, decides I'm not, and smiles back at me. "See you on Monday," she says cheerfully.

I'm always jumpy at work on Friday nights. I'm terrified of what I will find when I get home. Leroy is completely volatile and unpredictable. I've never been married, but I assume married people have sex on a regular basis. So that means Leann and Leroy haven't had sex in over a month. I don't think I've ever gone that long. This means sooner or later, Leroy will expect it. And if I keep refusing him, I don't know what will happen. He scares me. That's the bottom line.

I wish like hell I could get out of this place. But I have no options. I can't go to my mom; she'd have me committed. I can't go to my apartment, Leann won't open the door. I can't go to Scott's; he has a completely different idea of who I am. It is unbearably sad that no one recognizes me. Why is it the only person who knows I'm not Leann is Trevor? He's the real reason I can't just run.

I'd planned on getting a manicure and a perm, but Leroy's been giving me less money for groceries because he says I have my own money now. I have to focus on getting out of this situation. I'm saving most of the money I get at the gym. I keep it in my locker, rather than bringing it home where Leroy might find it. I wish I could make Leroy leave. I don't understand what makes him come home every weekend.

As if in answer to my prayers, Leroy is not home. Jillian is furious.

"Where the hell is he?"

I shrug and step back to get out of her way. For once, she's not in a hurry to leave. She picks up her purse, but then flings it back down on the table.

"I don't want any more of his weed this time, I want some cash." She glares at me.

"I'm sorry Jillian. I don't have any money. Leroy handles that."

"How can you be such a stupid cow? Don't you know he's running around on you? I don't know why you take his shit. He don't even like you. He thinks you're a fat, useless bitch. If you'd never got pregnant, he wouldn't be here."

I swallow this, even though a fury rises in me. How dare she talk to me like this? And how the hell does she know what Leroy thinks?

"My relationship with Leroy is none of your business, but your relationship with him is. What's going on between you two? Are you sleeping with him?"

She laughs and picks up her purse. She's dismissing me.

"What do you think? Why would he want you, when he can have me? Just tell him, I want the cash he owes me, not some second-rate weed he can't sell. Got it?" She's almost out the door when she says this, but turns around and waits for my answer.

"What kind of second-rate weed?" I'm confused. She laughs again and starts to leave. I follow her to the stairwell. "Is Leroy dealing drugs?" Her cackle echoes off the walls and all through my brain. I sit down on the steps and listen as her heels click their way down to the bottom. A hopelessness starts to settle in. I think I might sit on these stairs all night long, but I hear a door open and then Mr. Giovanni pulls up his lawn chair.

"She's something, that one. Trouble, I say."

"Do you know her?"

"Do I know her? I hear her. I hear her yelling at Leroy all the time. She wants more all the time."

"More what? More drugs? More sex? More money?"

Mr. Giovanni chuckles softly. "All those things. I tell you, that one is trouble."

"How old is she?"

He thinks for a minute. "I know her Uncle Stan. I remember when she was born. She must be about fifteen."

"Fifteen?" I'm incredulous.

"Well, she thinks she's older, I'm sure."

"What's the deal with her parents? How come they don't supervise her?"

"Supervise her? They can't control their own lives. Stan says the mother is a drinker and his brother just tries to stay out of her way."

We sit quietly thinking on this.

"Mr. G, is Leroy dealing drugs?"

He looks up, "I can't really say. I know he doesn't drive a real truck anymore."

"Then what is he doing all week?"

"Oh, he might drive a truck, but he's not moving paper towels or liverwurst."

"You mean he's using his truck to deal drugs?"

"I can't say. I just hear things. I'm old, you know? I don't get out much. I just hear things."

I have got to get out of this situation. But not tonight. Tonight I'm tired and I don't want Leroy to catch me out here talking with Mr. Giovanni.

"Thanks, Mr. G." I haul myself up. All those extra weights today are getting to me. Every part of me is stiff.

I can't sleep just yet. So much is spinning around my brain. What the hell is Leroy doing? What does Jillian have to do with it? And why does he need my paycheck if he's dealing drugs? We should be rolling in dough. I wish I could find some of it. I will keep saving my gym paycheck. One way or another, we will get the money to escape. No more waiting around for Leann to come back. I've got to get the hell out of this situation.

∿ ∿

leann

He's bangin' on the door again. Pain in the ass. I'm at the best part in my book. Vanessa is about to confess to Todd how she does love him, she didn't mean all that stuff she said before. She's not running off to marry some prince, she wants to be with ole Todd after all. I knew that's what she wanted a couple chapters back. It just took her some time to figure it out. These damn books are no different than my soaps. I guess Carin and me do have something in common. We like the love stories. Her books are full of them. One after another. Every now and again a mystery sneaks in, kinda like my shows. They got mysteries sometimes too. Keeps 'em interesting.

Now this damn fool is knockin' on my door. Shoutin' stupid stuff. He's worse than Rick on yesterday's episode. All sad and pining for Lisa. Guess I gotta open the door. I bend down the corner of the page and close my book.

When Scott gets inside, he looks all around like he's missing something.

"Whatcha lookin' for?" I ask him.

"Oh, nothing. Your book shelves are pretty empty. Are you cleaning out?"

"Nope. Just readin' a few things."

He stands there waiting for something, but I don't know what. So, I just wait. I know he'll get nervous and start talkin' soon, and sure enough he does.

"I've been worried about you. It's not like you to just hole up in this place and never go out."

"Oh, I go out," I tell him.

"You do?"

"Yeah, I go out in the mornings."

I can tell he wants to know what I do when I go out, but I ain't gonna tell him.

"Look, I came here to tell you something. Can I sit down?"

I nod and we sit down on the couch. He takes my hand. He's all clammy.

"All these years that we've been friends, I haven't been honest with you or with myself. I said we were only friends, but after all you've been through this past month, I've realized that wasn't true. You mean more to me than just a friend. I love you Carin. I think I always have. I want us to be together. I know you don't remember everything about us, but you will. I know you will." He's gettin' all choked up. If he starts bawlin' I swear I'm gonna scream. I don't need this. "So I just wanted to tell you that I can wait. I'll wait until you are ready to love me too."

What do I say to that? I don't want him to wait. He's nice and all, but he's not my type. I wish I was strong like Victoria, I'd just tell him what I really think. But I'm not strong. Nope. So, I just nod.

"You don't have to say anything. I just needed to tell you that. And if you want me to go, I will. But if you don't, I'd really like to stay."

I want him to leave, but he's so damn sorry and sad, I can't kick him out. I tell him maybe we can watch some TV together. It's getting late, so we watch the end of a movie and then the news. I can tell he wants to sleep in my bed, but I say I ain't ready for all that, so he sleeps on the couch. He's like a damn stray. And I'm the damn fool who let him in.

chapter 22

ᔕ ᔕ

I sleep soundly. I never hear Leroy come home. When I wake, he's asleep on the bed next to me. He's wearing underwear and nothing else. My stomach turns. The tighty whities have strings hanging from the elastic and they cut into his side. My stomach lurches. I need air. I crawl out of bed and find some stretch pants and a sweat shirt. I grab my sneakers and head out for a walk. I don't want to piss off Leroy, so I leave a note on the table.

It's a beautiful day. One of those early spring days that teases you. I'm sure tomorrow will be cold and miserable. I wonder about the bulbs I planted outside my old apartment. It's more than a mile or so from here, but with all the exercise I've been getting, I think I can make it. It's early and only a few cars are on the road. I look up and wave at the drivers, but only an elderly man waves back. The rest look right through me. They don't want to acknowledge the fat woman trying to exercise. I wave more frenetically at them. Smiling like a lunatic. This produces a confused look and a half-hearted hand lift from the next driver. Now it's a game. A minivan crammed with kids rolls to a stop as I pass by an intersection. I wave at the kids. They look at me and laugh, so I stick my tongue out at them. The mother yells something at them, and they all sit back down in their seats. A small girl in the back sticks out her tongue and then waves as they pull away. It's not much to ask. People just want to be seen. I need to know I'm here.

I'm still a good ways off from my building when I see the daffodils. They are glorious, waving in the wind. I planted them in groups of five so they would look like mini-bouquets. When I reach the building, my emotions well up. I miss my life, but I can't imagine it without Trevor. I've never been needed so much.

I've always been more or less a decorative ornament to the men I've dated and certainly for my own mother. Most of the girl-friends I've had would drop me if they saw me now. Scott was kind of my best friend, but that was never going to be forever. When I was a little girl, I had a couple best friends. I don't know where they are anymore. Most of them moved on and got married. They have kids. Our lives just don't mesh anymore. I lived in a different world. The world of work and men and looking good and doing what you want when you want regardless of how it affects anyone else.

That's probably why they all dropped me. If you're a mother, or even just a wife, you have to consider so many other things before you consider what you want. Your needs and wants are readily sacrificed. And you don't mind. Trevor's not even my kid, but I would give up just about anything if it meant keeping him happy and safe.

I look around and see no one, so I snap off a bouquet of daf-fodils. And then another and another. Now my arms are full of daffodils. I'm about to start walking back when I see Scott's car in the parking lot. Guess Leann's warming up to him. I'm surprised at how hurt I feel.

It's harder going back. My legs are tired and I worry about what I will find when I get back to the apartment. And I can't stop thinking about Scott sleeping with Leann. But the daffodils are beautiful. When I bought my bulbs, the man at the garden center told me that deer hate daffodils. He said that's why you see them blooming in the woods. You never see tulips, deer think they taste great. No one wants the daffodils.

I make it to the apartment building, but the stairs seem like a mountain so I lean against the building and catch my breath. The mustard-colored Cadillac pulls up with a screech. Oh God. I can't believe Leann has never told this woman to shove off. I guess when so few people are invested in your life, you can't be too picky. I sigh as I watch her leap out of her Cadillac. For a woman of her age, she sure moves fast. She doesn't look happy as she approaches me waving her cigarette.

I smile. I will charm this woman if it kills me. "I'm glad you stopped by. I have some daffodils for you." I separate out a bunch and hold them out to her.

"Where'd you steal those?"

"I didn't steal them. They're mine."

"Like hell," she says, but takes the flowers anyway and seems to soften a little.

"Since you ain't goin' to church, I thought I'd take my grandson to services tomorrow."

Scary thought. I doubt Trevor wants to spend any time with this woman. I can't think fast enough, so I buy some time.

"Why don't we go up and ask him," I suggest, waving her to the stairs. I'm curious to see Leroy's reaction to her.

"Is that louse up there?" She can only be talking about Leroy.

"I think he is."

"Then I'm not going anywhere near the damn place. You're Trevor's mama, you decide. I would think saving his soul would be a priority." She stares at me intently.

"I think we should ask him. I don't know if he wants to go to church."

"I don't give a shit if he wants to go to church. He needs to go to church and I'm his grandmother. I wasn't really asking anyway, I was telling." She takes a final puff on her cigarette and tosses it on the sidewalk. She turns to leave, calling back, "I'll be here at 8:45."

As the car starts to pull away, she stops and rolls down the passenger window. She leans across the seat and says, "Make sure he's clean." And then she screeches off.

At 8:45 I will be on my way to the gym. I wish I'd just told her no. She has a way of rolling right over you.

Leroy is at the stove cooking his eggs when I enter the apartment. Trevor is parked in front of the TV, munching on cereal. He jumps up when he sees my flowers.

"Cool! Flowers!" He reaches out and I give him one daffodil. Leroy snorts and says, "Where'd you steal those?"

"I just found them," I tell him as I search in the crates for a glass to put them in.

"What's the occasion?" Leroy asks as he dumps his eggs on a plate.

"No occasion. It's just a gorgeous day and I felt like flowers," I say as I arrange them in a coffee cup. The stems are too long. Leroy stands at the counter eating his eggs. He pulls an army knife from his pocket and holds it out to me, "Here," he mutters between mouthfuls.

After I shorten the stems, the daffodils look beautiful in the cup. I set them in the center of the table and start to gather up the papers that Leroy left. There are notes scrawled in his illegible handwriting, racing forms and schedules of some kind.

"Hey, don't mess with that shit," he says, waving at me. I stack them in a pile, but leave them for now. He doesn't generally leave anything of his around, so I'm curious. Maybe I can look at them later.

I never get the chance. While I'm in the shower, Leroy leaves and takes all his papers with him. When I ask Trevor about it, he shrugs. I'm relieved I don't have to spend the day with Leroy. He never asked for my paycheck either, so I'm hopeful today we can get some real groceries. After I eat, I tell Trevor to get his shoes. We're not staying cooped up in this place all day.

I cash my Shop N Save paycheck and head to Goodwill. It's not very far away. I'd never noticed it in all my years of living here, but I drove past it nearly every day. I guess you don't see what you're not looking for. Inside we find all kinds of treasures. I buy jeans and sneakers for Trevor and a warm up in size XXL, perfect for me to wear to the gym in the mornings. Trevor picks out some books and a set of Legos that are missing the directions. We spend nineteen dollars and have two big bags to carry. Amazing what you can find for less than twenty bucks. I can't believe I never knew about this place. Then again, the old me wouldn't have dreamed of shopping here. The closet in my apartment is stuffed with designer clothes and over fifty pairs of shoes.

We haul everything back to the apartment. I tell Trevor I'll be right back, grab a handful of daffodils, and head to Mr. Giovanni's. He is happy to see me and carries on over the daffodils. "No woman has ever brought me flowers! They're beautiful!" He smiles and squeezes my arm.

"Mr. G, I'm going to take Trevor to the park down the street for a picnic. Would you like to join us?"

I can tell he's delighted, but he plays hard to get. "I've got so much to do. Won't your husband mind if an old man tags along?"

"I don't know where Leroy is. Anyway, he's not invited. Come with us!"

"I'm not sure these old bones can walk that far. It's such a long way."

"It's only two blocks. You can make it. We're going to stop at the deli and get sandwiches. You can get one too, my treat." I saved so much at Goodwill, I'm feeling generous. "It's the least I can do for using your washer so much."

"Nah! I can get my own sandwich. You need money for your little boy. Let me find my sweater."

"I'll get Trevor."

After we order sandwiches and a bag of Doritos for Trevor, we walk to the park. I'm still tired from my trek this morning, and Mr. Giovanni moves slowly, shuffling his feet, so it takes us a while. Trevor is patient, walking with us and holding my hand. I know he can't wait to get to the park, but he never rushes us. I get the feeling he hasn't done this much. Maybe he's waiting to see if it's for real.

While Trevor races around the playground playing tag with two kids from his class, Mr. Giovanni and I settle ourselves on a bench in the sunshine. Mr. Giovanni leans his head back and closes his eyes. He lets the sunlight shower his face. "Ah. Now this is nice," he says. He opens his eyes and winks at me. "How is it that we've never done this before?"

My mouth is full, so I shrug my shoulders.

"You've lived next door for a while, yet until recently you never said much to me." He pauses and looks over at me. "Were you scared of me?"

I consider this and chew my sandwich. Hard to believe Leann never found refuge in this gentle man.

"I guess I've changed. I'm a new person." I smile at him. It feels good to divulge my secret. "I'm sorry we weren't friends until now."

"I always worried about you in that apartment alone all day with the TV blaring. Not healthy for a young woman. And him yelling so much." Mr. Giovanni shakes his head.

So Leann did stay holed up in that apartment. What a sad life. She must be completely freaked out. It dawns on me, Leann may not be as happy in my life as I think she is. She probably doesn't know what to do. But at least she's got satellite TV. Her apartment has crappy cable that Leroy stole from the people downstairs by splicing wires.

"I'm thinking of leaving him," I say quietly without looking at Mr. Giovanni, as if we might be overheard.

"You should," he says just as quietly. We both know how difficult that will be. We eat in silence. Then Mr. Giovanni gets up and produces a baseball from his coat jacket. He and Trevor play catch. Trevor is not very good, but Mr. G. is patient and shows him how to follow the ball as he catches it and to not brace for it.

We still have to go to the grocery store, so at three o'clock we gather our stuff and walk back to the apartment.

"Lovely afternoon," Mr. Giovanni says over the blaring stereo coming from our apartment.

"Thanks for the company," I say.

"And thanks for the ball," Trevor grins, holding the ball up.

"You take care of that now," says Mr. Giovanni as he opens his apartment.

I can tell Trevor doesn't want to open our door any more than I do. So I take his hand and in we go. A strange, hairy man is sprawled at the kitchen table rolling a joint. The room smells of marijuana and Leroy lounges on the couch with Jillian asleep in his lap. Still holding Trevor's hand, I turn around and head back out the door. Leroy calls in a sleepy voice, "Hey babe, the party's just getting started."

I have never smoked marijuana. Never once. I've never even wanted to. I believed all those prevention programs in high school that tried to scare you with stories about how you can end up dead or worse—completely alive but inside a body that can't move, like my Uncle Mike who has Parkinson's disease.

Trevor doesn't say anything as I drag him along the street. We walk to the bus stop. I don't know when the next bus is, so we sit down on the bench to wait.

"Sorry about that," I say.

"It's okay. He does that sometimes."

"Does he do that a lot?"

Trevor shrugs his shoulders. "I don't like the smell."

"Trevor, what Leroy, I mean, what Daddy is doing is illegal. He's not supposed to be doing that."

"Then why does he do it?" Trevor looks up at me. Leroy may be his father, but I'm not going to condone his behavior. Trevor deserves better.

"I don't know. I wish he wouldn't."

We sit for another fifteen minutes. The bus still hasn't come. I begin to worry that there isn't service on Saturdays. But then it rounds the corner and I realize I don't have the foggiest idea where we are going, except away from here. The bus is almost completely empty. When the stop for the Shop N Save comes up, I pull the cord.

As we walk across the parking lot, I'm still undecided. If we buy groceries, where would we put them? I don't know when we can go back to the apartment. So instead of making a decision, we just wander the store. Trevor picks out some Doritos. I'm not up to arguing, so I put them in our cart. At the bakery we pick out day-old cookies and a coffee cake. I want something healthy, so I drag Trevor to the produce section and we both hit the salad bar, only Trevor's plate has nothing but fruit and pudding and a whole scoopful of sunflower seeds. "That looks healthy," says a familiar voice behind Trevor.

"Jimmy! What are you doing here on a Saturday?"

"I could ask you the same question." He smiles, and I believe he is genuinely happy to see us. He's wearing cargo pants with green paint all over them, and his baseball cap is turned around backwards. His face is speckled with paint and he looks like he might have the first sunburn of the season.

"We're just grabbing a few things for dinner."

"Me too. I haven't eaten all day. My cousin's a slave driver. Been painting her shed."

"Green?" I ask.

He looks down at his splattered pants, and grins. "How'd you guess?"

"We're running away," says Trevor. My heart stops. And I look at him confused. "Right, Mama? We can't go home."

"That's not exactly right, Trevor . . ."

"You said at the bus stop that we can't go home until Daddy's friends go away."

Jimmy doesn't miss a beat. "Then you'll have to join me. I'm waiting for my pizza back at the deli, and then I was going to kick back on my porch and watch the water."

"You live at the beach?" Trevor asks.

"Nah, but I have a stream in my backyard."

Thirty minutes later, we unpack our food on Jimmy's tiny balcony overlooking the train tracks, and, indeed, a small stream. Jimmy drags out a kitchen chair for me, which is good because I'm not sure his rickety lawn chair with the rusted arms will hold me. Trevor eats two pieces of pizza, slurps down his pudding, and then asks if he can go down and check out the stream. Jimmy walks him down and waves at me from the yard below.

He is such a sweet man. The amazing thing is, when I was my old self I would have never given him the time of day. Now that I'm Leann, I'm guessing he's not going to give me the time of day. But he is very decent. That I know.

Trevor spends the next hour building a dam. Jimmy helps him for a while, hauling the bigger rocks, but now he plops down next to me and gets back to his pizza, which is cold and hard.

"So what's up with Leroy?" he asks quietly.

"He and a bunch of his friends were smoking pot at the apartment. He's having some kind of party. I just couldn't stay there with Trevor."

"Does he do that on a regular basis?"

"I don't know," I answer honestly.

Jimmy raises his eyebrows but doesn't comment. We watch Trevor slip and land in the stream. He grins up at me and yells, "I'm not real wet, Mama, just my leg!" Jimmy gives him a thumbs up and he gets back to searching for stones for his dam.

I take a deep breath and look over at Jimmy. I watch his jaw working his pizza. He is so simple. In a good way.

"You don't worry about much, do you?" I ask.

"What's to worry about?"

"Everything."

"You can only worry so much, ya know? It doesn't do much good. Doesn't change anything. I worry about some things."

"Like what?"

"I worry about my folks. They're getting old. I don't know if they have money put away. My dad won't talk about it."

"What would you do?"

"About what?"

"If they didn't have any money?"

"I guess they'd have to move in here."

I look around. "I don't think they'd fit."

"You know what I mean. I'd find a place where we all could live."

"You don't worry about yourself?"

"I go to work. I eat. I read. I sleep. I help out my uncle sometimes. Not much to worry about. I was thinking of getting a dog. I'd really like a dog. A big one, ya know? One that can catch a Frisbee."

I nod. "I just wish it were easier."

"It could be."

I turn to look at Jimmy, but I can't read him. He takes a bite of his pizza and meets my eye. He raises his eyebrows in question. But what does he want? I shake my head. "I don't think so. This can't get any easier."

Jimmy chews for a while, then says, "Why don't you just leave Leroy?"

"It's not that simple. Where would I go? I don't have any money. He takes everything. And I have Trevor to worry about too."

"They have places. Shelters."

"I can't go live in a shelter. I can't do that to Trevor."

"What? And living in a house with a bunch of dopers is better?"

He does have a point.

"I'm going to leave. I'm working on it. I just have to pull together some more money."

"If you need money, I can lend you some," he offers. I look up at his clear blue eyes and I can see that he means it.

"No, I'll get it. I have a plan."

"That's good. You shouldn't keep living like this."

When it gets dark, Trevor comes in. He is filthy from head to toe. I use a wash cloth and wipe him down as best I can. Jimmy lends him a T-shirt that comes down to his knees. I take his clothes to the laundry in the basement and wash them with quarters Jimmy loans me. While the clothes are in the machine, we watch a movie. Trevor stretches out on the carpet and falls asleep before the movie has hardly begun.

At eleven, I figure we better get back. So Jimmy picks up Trevor and carries him to the car. We drive in silence. When we get to the building, Jimmy offers to carry Trevor up, but I won't let him. God knows what Leroy would do if I showed up with Jimmy.

Turns out I was worried for nothing. When we get to the apartment, Leroy is out cold on the couch and Jillian is gone. The hairy man is sleeping, slumped over the table. I put Trevor in the bed and crawl in next to him. It's hard to sleep. My mind is busy thinking of what I'm going to do next.

chapter 23

I sleep fitfully, worrying that Leroy or the strange man at the table will wake up and discover us. When the sun finally begins to rise, I sneak out of bed quietly and pull on clean clothes. I gently wake Trevor. I tell him it's important we not wake the sleeping men in the living room, and we creep towards the door. As we pass the table, the stranger opens his eyes momentarily, but closes them as if the effort of lifting his lids is too much for him. I look over at Leroy on the couch. His bottom half has sunk into the gulf between the cushions and he is hugging the couch cushion under his head like a life preserver. He doesn't move. I can't even tell if he's breathing. So with a final glance at the man at the kitchen table, we slip out.

Our first stop is Dunkin' Donuts. Trevor picks out two glazed donuts with multi-colored sprinkles. I order a coffee for myself. We park ourselves at a booth next to the counter where a group of old men are having a heated discussion. Trevor giggles when one of them lets out a huge burp. I'm deep into the local Lions Club gossip when Trevor interrupts my eavesdropping.

"How come you don't volunteer in my class? Everybody else's mom does."

I wrinkle my brow and turn my attention back to Trevor.

"I wish I could, honey." I sip my coffee and hope he'll leave it at that.

"Why can't you?" Trevor's tired whine grates my nerves. I remember my own mother volunteering in my classroom. She always did the big parties. She loved that stuff. She could make a cake in the shape of just about anything. Each party got bigger and bigger. All the other mothers were afraid to volunteer—she was too much to compete with. I had mixed feelings about her presence. On the one hand I was happy to have her attention, but on the other hand I was embarrassed by her over-the-top efforts, especially as I got older. When I reached fifth grade, I asked her not to volunteer anymore. She was angry, so I suggested she just come in to help the teacher and not do the parties. But she said if I didn't want her doing the parties, I must not want her there at all.

"I work during the day. If I didn't, I'd come in. I would. I'm sorry."

He looks at me and frowns, then turns his attention back to his second donut. I decide to pump him for information on Leroy.

"Trevor, where does your daddy take you on Saturdays?"

He creases his brow for a moment, and then says, "Sometimes he takes me to the track."

"The race track with the horses?"

"Uh-huh. They have Butterfingers and Twizzlers in the machine there, so Daddy makes me buy him a Twizzlers and sometimes he lets me get a Butterfinger too."

"Nice. What does Daddy do at the race track?"

"He watches the TV and yells a lot. Sometimes he talks on the phone. Sometimes the lady in the window pays him."

So he gambles. Could explain why we're broke. Betting on racehorses is a losing proposition. I've never understood the attraction. I worked on a racetrack one summer when I was in college. I thought it would be glamorous and couldn't wait to be near the horses. I did the books for the track vet. He was a drunk and couldn't keep his hands off me.

When I ventured down to the clubhouse, it was a depressing sight. It could be the middle of the afternoon on a Tuesday and you would see such desperate people. I liked driving past the barns in the morning before dawn, though. They were bustling, their lights glowing in the darkness. Horses whinnied and pawed in their stalls. Grooms made lap after lap, leading horses shrouded in steam and dripping with sweat. They seemed otherworldly.

But truth be told, when the sun came up the people who worked on the backside of the track were desperate and dirty. The people who came to bet were also desperate, but their dirt was more on the inside.

It's time to get to work. I take Trevor in the ladies' room under protest and try to wipe most of the icing off of him. He is a sight. His hair still has leaves and pine needles tangled in it. He looks like an orphan just off the set of *Annie*. I rub at a few spots, but it's hopeless. The dirt between his fingers and under his nails seems to be permanent. When I sigh, yet again, Trevor looks up at me and smiles. "Can we go to Jimmy's river today?"

"Not today, sweetie. I have to work and then we better get home so you can see your dad."

"I don't have to see him," Trevor says and looks away.

"He'll want to see you," I assure him, not at all sure that he will.

Trevor doesn't say anything else. We walk in silence all the way to the gym. Leroy is awful—mean, arrogant, thoughtless, and lots of other horrible things, but he's his father. I know Trevor wants to believe he's good. I wish that he was.

After I finish at the Kiddie Korner, I decide to squeeze in a workout. Trevor is busy building a Lego warship. When I ask him if he minds if I go exercise, he shrugs his shoulders and turns back to his project.

Scott is on one of the bikes, pedaling furiously. He has on headphones and sweat pours off him. I don't think he notices me as I climb on a bike two seats over, but the moment I start pedaling, he removes his headphones and calls over to me. "Hi, Leann!" I wave and begin thumbing through the magazine I borrowed from the rack. Scott seems determined to talk with me.

"So do you like working here?"

"It's a job," I say, trying to sound as boring as possible so he won't continue talking to me. I can't get over seeing his car at my apartment building yesterday. It seems to get more painful each time I see him. He is a reminder that my life is nuts. Some days I can be completely Leann. I believe I'm her and I don't even think about my old self, but Scott instantly takes me back to my real life. At least what I think was my real life. I'm having my doubts. Maybe I'm really crazy. Maybe I've always been Leann.

"So what is it you do here?"

"I work in the Kiddie Korner, supervising the rug rats."

"And you have a rug rat of your own?" So he's noticed.

"I have a son named Trevor. He's great."

"I always hoped I'd have kids," he says wistfully.

"I know," I say.

He laughs. "How could you know that?"

I laugh nervously. "I guess I just assumed a man like you would want children."

He stops pedaling. "A man like me? How can you know what I'm like?"

Shit. This isn't going well. "I don't know. You just seem like you'd make a great dad."

He starts pedaling again, but stares at me carefully.

"I don't know. I wasn't really sure I wanted kids, but now that I'm getting more serious about my girlfriend, I feel differently."

What? Now I'm his girlfriend?

"I didn't know you had a girlfriend."

"Well . . . not exactly. But I'm hoping that changes. It's complicated."

He looks up, scrutinizing me again. It makes me uncomfortable and I go back to my magazine.

"Do you have a boyfriend?"

"No," I say. Oops. I guess I do. "Well, actually I'm sort of married."

Scott leans back and smiles. "What's 'sort of married' mean?"

"Hard to explain, but it's not serious."

"Is he your son's father?"

"Yeah, that's it."

"So do you live with him?"

"Kind of."

He laughs. "How can you be sort of married to someone and kind of live with him?"

"It wasn't my idea," I blurt out. "I didn't have a choice."

"I think we all have choices and no one does anything they don't want to."

"You believe that?"

"I don't know. I'm just in a weird place is all. Sorry I'm telling you all this. You don't even know me."

"That's okay. I don't mind. People seem to tell me things." Which is true. Phyllis is always telling me things I really don't want to hear. People who come through my checkout tell me stuff they seriously shouldn't be telling a complete stranger, like which foods are an aphrodisiac or how they need to eat more fiber because they can't poop. I don't need to know these things. I wonder if it's because I'm so large, or maybe it's just that I'm only a checkout clerk. I'm safe. I'm not anyone who will judge them. In fact, maybe they think they're being kind by trusting me with their most unsavory secrets. I don't know. I just know that when I was Carin no one told me anything, including Scott, apparently.

I move to the Nautilus machines and crank through my workout. My mind is busy sorting through the past twenty-four hours, and I'm barely conscious of what I'm doing. Leann is wreaking havoc on my life and all I've done is improve hers. You'd think she could work a little harder. On my way to the showers, I stop to use the phone at the desk. I dial my number, not expecting anything. I've called it at least five times this week and she doesn't answer, so I'm shocked when I hear my voice answer, "What?"

"Why would you answer my phone like that?"

"It ain't your phone," says an eerily calm voice.

"It is my phone and you know it. While we're on the topic of my things—why can't you be nice to my mother and Scott? I've been nothing but nice to all your people, except Franklin because he's a jerk."

"What's the matter with Franklin? He was always nice to me."

"Nice? He treats you like crap."

"Better than your damn mama treats you," she counters. Now I know my mom can be awful, but in light of the circumstances, I'm sure she's on her best behavior.

"My mom loves me. Why would you say she doesn't treat me well?"

"She's a bossy bitch. Always telling me what to do. Always complaining about my hair, my clothes, what I eat."

"That's just how she shows she cares."

"No, that's how she shows she's a bitch."

"You really can't complain about my mother. Your mother is like the Wicked Witch of the West."

"Look, your life's pretty shitty, so don't be making comparisons."

"MY LIFE??" How dare she? How can she even begin to compare them? "Your life sucks. Leroy is a horrible person and everyone else treats you like crap. I'm stuck in this enormous body that craves sugar and cigarettes all the time. If you think it's so great, how come you don't want it back?"

She is silent.

"And leave Scott alone."

"I am."

"I don't call sleeping with him leaving him alone."

"That ain't none of your business."

I don't know what to say.

"How is Trevor?" That's the hitch. If I give her life back, I have to give Trevor back.

"If you want to know, why don't you come see for yourself?"

"I know you're taking care of him."

"How could you know that? You're holed up in my apartment ruining my life."

"I just know."

"Look, this is not going to last forever. At some point this crazy situation will have to right itself. Life doesn't work like this."

She doesn't say anything.

"Leann! What do you want?"

I think she has hung up, but then she whispers, "I just want what everyone else wants," and she hangs up. I stare at the phone. I'm about to call her back, but Trevor comes running up the hall.

"Mama! They're closed. I didn't think you were going to come back!"

I look up and see Denise walking away from us back to the Kiddie Korner. She probably won't be so generous in the future.

"Sorry!" I call to her retreating back. She doesn't acknowledge me.

I didn't realize how late it was. I'll have to shower at home now. Trevor and I head to the Shop N Save to do our grocery shopping. It's another battle of the junk food. He wants it; I don't want to buy it. But it's cheap and it makes him happy, so we agree he can pick out two things. This keeps him busy calculating his best options. He's definitely going for the biggest two things he can find. I leave him pondering the chip offerings in the snack aisle and head to produce. I'd love some strawberries and asparagus, but I can't afford them, so I get lettuce, carrots, and apples.

When we arrive home with our groceries, the apartment looks pretty much the same way it looked when we left. Empty beer cans are piled in one corner with lots of splatters and dings on the wall above them where they've ricocheted off the wall. Cigarettes and ashes are spilling out of two paper cups on the table and a third has fallen over on to the carpet. Pizza cartons are stacked next to the couch where Leroy is calmly watching ice hockey on TV. His hair is wet and he's wearing only jeans. He's a lean, muscled man, except for the beer gut he's developing. It's lapping over the top of his jeans. His large shoulders seem disproportionate to the rest of him. He swings one powerful arm up over the back of the couch. Tattoos label the inside of his arm. I can't read them from where I am, but a snake winds its way around his swollen bicep. He looks up at us, but doesn't say anything.

Trevor approaches him. "Hi Daddy," he says hopefully.

Leroy surveys him and then says, "What the hell you been into boy? You look like you slept on the street." Trevor is visibly crushed. I see his shoulders slump and he looks back to me.

"Go get in the shower, Trevor. You are pretty filthy."

I begin putting the groceries away, trying to make as little noise as possible. After everything is stowed, I begin cleaning up the mess from the party. I hear the TV click off and brace myself.

"Where'd you go?" he asks. "Your crazy mother showed up this morning. Bitch honked her horn until I finally had to go down there and tell her I would kick in her windshield if she didn't shut the fuck up."

Crap. I forgot about her. But maybe Leroy scared her away for good.

"I was at work," I say innocently.

"No, I mean last night. Since when are you too good to party with us?"

"We got some dinner."

"That took all night?" He's standing now and approaching me. I take a deep breath and decide I can be truthful. I didn't do anything wrong.

"I didn't want to be here because of the drugs."

Leroy laughs. "Since when have drugs been an issue for you? You used to beg me for them. You'd do just about anything." He's leering at me and I'm too terrified to speak.

"C'mon Leann, don't you miss our party nights? Don't you want to get naked and put on them red shoes?"

Oh. My. God. My stomach is lurching and my head is spinning. What am I doing here? This only happens in books. Actually, this doesn't even happen in books. I close my eyes and will my life back. Now he is standing next to me.

"Where'd you go last night, Bitch? You find a new sugar daddy? Is that why you're so high and mighty these days? Too good for the likes of me? Don't you forget that I own you." I feel something burst inside me. He owns me? What kind of shit is that? I drop the bag I have been filling with cans and back away from him.

"You don't own me. No one owns me. I own me." I stare at him, daring him to move. He doesn't. We just stay like this for what seems like a long time. Finally, Leroy laughs. It's a huge, sick laugh. In one quick motion he picks up one of the cups filled with cigarette butts off the table and flings it in my face. I'm horrified, but more horrified by his words, "I own you, Bitch. You weren't shit 'til I came along. Don't you ever forget that."

I'm blinded by the nastiness of his words and the ashes on my face. I fumble towards the kitchen looking for a paper towel. I wipe my face and wash my eyes in the sink, willing him to leave me alone. But when I look up, he's blocking my way out of the kitchen.

"You never answered my question. Where'd you sleep last night?"

"I slept here."

"I was here. You weren't."

"Yes, I was. You were asleep on the couch when we came in. Ask Trevor. And I had to go to work this morning before you got up."

Leroy snorts. "Yeah, right. You better not be lying to me, Leann. I don't like the way you're acting lately. You need to remember who you are." He turns and heads back for the couch. I should let this go. I know I should, but I can't.

"You don't know me!" I scream. I know Trevor and maybe the whole building is hearing this, but this asshole has pissed me off. "You don't know the first thing about me!"

Leroy stops and turns to look at me. His face registers shock, and I'm afraid of what is coming, but then he starts laughing.

"I don't know you? Oh, I know you, Leann. You're a fat, ugly girl who wanted a boyfriend. Only you were too dumb to use birth control. So you ended up pregnant and saddled with a kid. What? You dreaming that some other guy is going to want you? You're watching too many of them stupid soaps." He continues towards the couch, dismissing me.

"What makes you think no one else would want me?" I ask, following him into the living room. He laughs again.

"Trust me, Babe. I'm your only shot, and most days I don't know what the fuck I'm doing with you."

"Then maybe you should just leave me." It pops out before I can think it through. He's back up and has a hold on my arm in moments.

"That what you want?" He shakes me. "How the hell would you survive? You're too stupid. Besides, I ain't leavin' my son."

I'm done. I am. It is crystal clear to me now. Trevor and I have to leave. Soon. Leroy is still holding my arm. I can feel the

bruise beginning to rise under his hand. He's waiting for something. When I don't say anything, he drops my arm and pushes
past me to go to the fridge. "I don't know what the fuck's wrong
with you," he mutters. He pulls out another beer and makes his
way back to the couch.

"What's for dinner?" he calls.

I towel off Trevor and help him into his pajamas. I wonder
how much he has heard. But then again, I'm sure he's heard worse.

"Honey, I need you to do something for me," I say.

"What?" he asks innocently enough. I can't believe I'm going
to ask a child to lie for me, but then again I can't believe a lot of
things I've been doing lately. I get down on my knees, which is
quite an effort, and look him in the eye.

"It's really important that you don't tell Daddy about going
to Jimmy's."

"Why? I want to tell him about my dam."

"You can't tell him because he will be really angry we went
there without him."

"Oh," Trevor says quietly and nods his head, understanding.
"It would make him sad if he knew we got to go there and play
and he didn't."

"It would," I say very seriously. "So we need to keep it our
secret, okay?"

"Can we take him to Jimmy's tomorrow?"

"Daddy's busy. I don't think we can take him there anytime soon."

"But I want to show him my dam."

"Just promise me you won't say anything about it unless I tell
you to, okay?"

Trevor sighs and moves away from me. "Okay," he says.

Leroy ignores us at dinner, concentrating on the hockey game
on TV. Trevor is quiet too, but keeps looking at me to see if I'm
ready to tell Leroy about Jimmy's. So we eat in silence. When we
are finished, Leroy goes in the bedroom and packs a bag.

"I'm heading out early this week," he says to Trevor, pointedly ignoring me.

"Where are you going?"

"All kinds of places."

"Can I go with you someday?" Trevor looks up hopefully. I can see how much he loves his dad, even if it's only the idea of a dad. Amazing how loyal children are. You can treat them as badly as you want, and still they come looking for your love. If I take Trevor out of here, will he hate me?

"Nah, you wouldn't like it," Leroy says and turns to go. He pauses and looks back at me. He wants to say something, but he just stares at me. I can't tell if the hesitation is for my sake or for Trevor's. Leroy seems to be evaluating me, deciding if I'm worth whatever it is he has to say. Finally, he shakes his head and mutters, "Crazy bitch," before turning to go.

"What did he say, Mama?" asks Trevor, looking at me.

"He said, 'have a great week,'" I assure Trevor. He looks back at Leroy and yells, "Have a great week too, Daddy!"

Leroy doesn't respond.

I stay up for hours after Trevor goes to sleep, preparing and packing dinners for Trevor and Jillian. I mark everything carefully with masking tape and a permanent marker. After I finish, I began putting the apartment back in order. It's late when I finally collapse into bed. It's hard to close my eyes, because every time I do I see Leroy's angry face. I could leave. He would figure out some way of taking care of Trevor. I have no ties here. But where would I go, the women's shelter? The thought makes me shudder. Once again, staying seems to be my only option. Besides, I could never leave Trevor. He needs me. And I need him.

～ ～

leann

I don't know what made me answer the phone. She calls just about every day. She calls from all kinds of places, but I still know it's her. When I answer, she goes on about my mama. I know my mama's a horse's ass, but I have to stick up for her. She's my mama, ain't she? I tell her that her mama's no picnic either. Is this why she called, just to tell me to be nice to her mama and that pansy Scott? I was nice to him. I let him sleep here, didn't I?

That's what's got her so worked up. She thinks I'm screwing Scott. Maybe I should, that'll fix her. But then it'd be like feeding a damn stray.

She tries to get me worked up by asking about Trevor, but I let it lie. I know Trevor is fine. I seen him. He even seems happy. I figure she's good for him. I'm just sad as hell he don't miss me. She won't shut her trap, so I hang up on her.

I do wonder what will happen. She said this mess has to sort itself out, but I wonder. It don't seem in a hurry to. I'm here in her life and she's stuck in mine and neither of us can figure out how to get back. I guess I may as well start makin' my own plan, seeing as I've read just about every book in this place.

When Scott was here on Saturday, he showed me how to make the computer go to the Internet. Never seen that before. Heard 'bout it plenty, but it ain't never made no sense. I fire it up now and stare at the screen. I don't know what to do. It turns on to a screen that says *Google*. Scott told me Google can tell me anything. I type "Leroy Jefferson Cane" and hit enter.

The first thing that comes up is a newspaper article from last year. That was the time Leroy got busted for transporting illegal substances. He told me they dropped that charge, but right here it says he was released on $100,000 bail. Who paid his bail? And don't that mean he has to go to court eventually? I read further and see that date is almost here. Two months from now. When was he planning to tell me we're movin' again? Damn him. What if I'm still here in this apartment and he and Carin leave and take Trevor? She can't do that. She wouldn't. She ain't gonna run off without her mama and Scott.

chapter 24

ᔥ ᔨ

The next few weeks go by without any real change, except my weight, which continues to go down. I'm still losing weight and most of my clothes are baggy. Still, I don't buy anything new because I'm saving every penny for our escape. Each week, I cash my gym paycheck and hide it in a Ziploc baggie in my locker. I have nearly five hundred dollars. I'd like to have a thousand dollars, so I figure that's only a month or so away.

Leroy is subdued on the weekends. He tries to sleep with me once, but I tell him I'm having my period and he drops it. Most nights he sleeps on the couch or doesn't come home. I don't ask where he's been. Scott continues to talk to me at the gym. I come close to telling him who I am a few times. I'm beginning to think I could convince him if I tried, but more and more I realize it's pointless. He's a good guy, but he's in love with the idea of Carin much more than he was ever in love with me in real life.

It's Jimmy who holds my thoughts. He listens to me and some days I think he knows I'm not Leann. Last night as we were talking, he said, "You're different, Leann. You're not who I thought you were."

"I am different. A lot of days, I don't think I'm Leann," I say, watching his face for a response. He doesn't look up, just nods.

I watch Jimmy during the day. I make excuses to go to the back so I can peer in the window of the loading dock door and catch a glimpse of him. I wonder if he thinks of me as much as I think of him. He always seems cheerful and content. Maybe that's what is so attractive about him. When he looks up and sees me watching him, he doesn't look away, he just winks. This makes me blush.

Mr. Giovanni has been my rock. He's the sanest person in Leann's life. We've spent the last two Saturdays with him, doing our laundry and playing at the park. He has taught Trevor every card game known to mankind. This weekend, I tell him I'm leaving.

"You should," he says without looking at me. He is watching Trevor throw a baseball high above his head and attempt to catch it as it falls back down to him. Most times he ends up covering his head and ducking from the rushing ball.

"He's no good," he says firmly, and I know he's not talking about Trevor and his baseball skills.

"I haven't figured out where to go yet, and I haven't told Trevor. I just know we're going to leave. I'll miss you."

Now he looks at me and I can see his eyes are misty. "I'll miss you. Your boy makes my heart happy." Then he sighs and says, "But you won't be safe with Leroy. I wish I could help. If I wasn't such an old man, I would take care of him for you. Back in my day, men had to answer for their actions. Leroy should get his due. Who knows? Maybe he will." Mr. Giovanni gets up from the bench and goes to join Trevor. I watch them play catch. The smile on Trevor's face is pure. I don't want to break his heart.

On Monday, I approach Vernon about the coming week. Trevor will be out of school for spring break. Mr. Giovanni wants to watch him, but I worry about him babysitting every day. I'm hoping I can get a few days off. Jillian has already told us she isn't going to babysit on spring break. She said it's her time to party. Leroy was there when she said that and he just laughed. He told me to call in sick that week.

"Hi, Mr. Slick," I say as I poke my head in the door.

"Oh, Leann, I forgot you wanted to talk to me. Come in, I've got a couple minutes before I need to make an important call." He's always doing "important" things, but I can't imagine how anything related to this place could really be that important. Importance is relative, I suppose. I walk in and move some papers off the chair near his desk to sit down. He's writing something and doesn't look up.

"What can I do for you?"

"Um, I need a few days off," I begin.

"Out of the question. I'm short on cashiers as it is, with spring break."

"That's just it. My son will be on spring break and I don't have anyone to watch him."

"I'm sure you can make arrangements, Leann." Now he stops writing and looks at me. It's embarrassing, but I feel like I might cry. I open my eyes extra wide to keep this from happening. I'm just tired of everything being so hard. One tear slips out. This makes Mr. Slick uncomfortable and he has to look away.

"I'll see what I can do, but I can't give you the entire week off," he says impatiently.

"Thank you, Mr. Slick," I say and smile at him.

I stand up to leave, knocking a pile of papers off the credenza behind me. I still forget how much room my body requires. I try to clean them up, but he waves me out the door as his phone starts ringing.

I have to admit that the thrill of commanding the conveyor belt and bagging groceries is beginning to wear off. I'm distracted by devising a plan to escape this life. I'm able to ring up most orders on autopilot. I hardly remember the afternoon. It goes by in a blur of register dings and small talk.

My mother comes in near dinner time and stands in my line. She can't help staring at me. I guess I freak her out. I freak me out too. Sometimes when I was a kid, I'd catch her watching me. She'd always look away, but not before I saw the look in her eyes. She seemed stunned. Like she couldn't believe I was real. I always wondered if my parents planned me. They were kind of older when I came along.

Whenever I asked my mother if I could have a sister or brother, she would laugh uncomfortably and tell me she was too old for babies. She was thirty-eight when she had me. She'd been married to my dad for almost twenty years. That's a long time to get settled into a life without kids.

I guess I never realized until Trevor how much more complicated kids make your life. I never appreciated what she must have gone through in adjusting to me. To be honest, I didn't think about my mom much at all. She was always doing her own thing. The only time she intruded into my life was to assert her opinion of what a horrible job I was doing with it. She didn't like my hairstyles, my clothes, my boyfriends, my books, or pretty much anything I liked. I kept her at arm's length and reeled her in when I needed something.

I've only been with Trevor for six weeks and already I feel like I couldn't live without him. Even if this craziness were to get resolved, I couldn't let go of him. I'd need to know he was alright. Maybe that's what my mom needed. Maybe she just needed to know I was alright. The thing is, whenever she was around I always got the feeling I wasn't. I wish I could talk to her now. I wish Leann would be nicer to her.

At break I ask Jimmy, "Are you close to your parents?"

He takes another bite of his apple and thinks a minute. That's one thing I like about Jimmy. He really thinks before he speaks. That's a skill I've never mastered.

"I guess compared to other people, I'm close to my parents. I mean, we don't like, hang out, but I like them. They're good people."

"Huh," I say, and consider this. It makes sense. Jimmy is such a nice person. I bet he was a good kid. Probably did whatever his parents said and didn't cause any trouble. As if he can read my mind, Jimmy says, "Course I was a pain in the ass. I was always skipping school or losing something important."

"You skipped school?"

"Why is that so hard to believe?" he asks, his voice rising.

"I don't know. I just figured you were a goody two-shoes. I can't imagine you breaking a rule."

"I broke plenty of rules, but I didn't break rules just to break them. I only broke them if they were stupid."

"And going to school is a stupid rule?"

"It's stupid if you're staying home to read a really good book or if you're skipping out to go fishing on a nice day."

"That's what you did when you skipped school?" I'm amazed.

"What else would I do?" he asks innocently enough.

"I don't know. Maybe smoke dope or sleep with your girlfriend."

"Did you do those things?"

I consider this. I think Leann probably did cut school to smoke dope. I'm doubtful on the boyfriend or girlfriend front.

"Maybe." Seems like a truthful answer.

"Maybe? Either you did or you didn't." Jimmy is watching me now. He seems very interested in my answer. I can't believe he cut school to read a book.

"It's been a long time. I guess I did a few things I shouldn't have done."

For a moment it seems like he isn't going to let that go, but then he sighs and goes back to his apple. Conversation over. We eat quietly for a while. That's how our dinners go. We don't talk much, which is good because I'm forever trying to sort out what Leann would say. Lately, I've been less concerned with that. If I'm going to be her, then I'm just going to have to be me. I can't keep making up a past I don't remember.

"Jimmy," I begin. When I don't say anything else, he looks up from his peanut butter crackers and swallows.

"What if I told you I don't remember what I did when I was younger because I wasn't me when I was younger?"

He starts chewing again and doesn't say anything. He's doing his thinking thing. He's probably trying to figure out if I'm nuts or if I just don't want to tell him what I really did.

"Who were you?" he asks. Good question. But what do I say? I was Carin Fletcher, a rich blond girl who spent too much time in front of a mirror and dropped her friends the minute a cute boyfriend was available. I was Carin Fletcher, a shallow girl who wasn't really paying attention to anyone but herself. A girl who took too much for granted and never really made much of an effort at anything. Who assumed everything would always be easy. Carin Fletcher, a girl who had a lot of growing up to do. I used to think I would marry a wealthy, handsome man and travel the world, maybe design my own line of clothing or open a trendy boutique. I'd live an exciting, glamourous life. That seems like a charade now. Now, I don't know what I want, but that isn't it.

"I don't know, but I wasn't me. I'm someone different now. I know a lot more. I want a lot more. I don't want to be a grocery clerk forever."

"Everybody is different when they grow up. We all do stupid things when we're kids. That's what kids are supposed to do. Stupid things."

We share the silence for a few more minutes. I want so badly to tell him who I am, but I know I can't. It doesn't make any sense. Shouldn't make any sense. If it did, it would mean our world doesn't make sense. I need to talk to Leann. She's the only one who would understand. I get up abruptly. I have twelve minutes left of my break.

"I gotta make a phone call," I say.

Jimmy doesn't say anything. Just watches me go.

The phone rings five times before she answers it. I don't even bother with introductions. I know she knows it's me. Who else would be calling her from the pay phone at the Shop N Save.

"Don't hang up. I have to talk to you." I take a deep breath and listen for the click. It doesn't come. "Do you sometimes feel like you're going nuts? Nobody else knows what we're going through. Me being you and you being me is crazy. Has it ever happened before? Are we the only ones?" I'm worried she hung up, but then she speaks.

"It feels weird, but I'm getting used to it," she says.

"You can't get used to it. You're not me. Someday this is going to fix itself. It has too. The world isn't like this. You can't stay me forever."

"But what if I do?" she asks, her voice edged with anger.

"Because you're not me. It doesn't make sense."

"Look, you don't want this, maybe I don't either, but this is it. So maybe we have to figure this out. You ain't Trevor's mom. You know that, right? You can't just keep him."

I don't know what to say. I do want this to resolve itself, but now my heart is all tangled up with Trevor's and I can't just leave him. I love him.

"I love Trevor," I tell her.

"Well, that don't matter. He ain't yours."

She's right, but I don't want her to be.

"If Leroy says you gotta pack a bag, you'll tell me, right?"

"Why would he say that?" Leroy barely speaks to me, and he certainly doesn't want to take me away on vacation. "I can't imagine Leroy wants to take me on vacation."

"It wouldn't be no vacation. That's what he says when ya gotta move quick. It means he's in trouble and it's time to move. I gotta feelin' he might be planning something like that."

"I'm not moving anywhere with Leroy!" I can't. I have a job. I have a plan. I'm getting the heck out of here.

"Well, if he does, you gotta call me."

"Leann! What do you know? How do you know this?"

"Never mind."

"I can't never mind! This is my life you're messing with!"

"I think I'm gonna leave," she says.

"Leave what?" I ask. Is she going to leave town? Leave me? God, she wouldn't kill herself would she? What would that mean? Would I get me back or would I be gone forever?

"I don't know. Your apartment sucks. I'm sick of your mama and Scott. They won't leave me alone."

"That's because they love me."

"Well, I don't love them. God, your mama won't quit with her damn nagging. And Scott is just such a sorry ass." I cringe at her attitude. No wonder my mother and Scott are so upset. I could be difficult, but I was never like this. How dare she be so mean to the people who love me.

"I would think you might like people being nice to you for a change," I say calmly and diplomatically. But then my anger gets the best of me. "Your mother is just scary and Leroy is . . . he's just . . . shit. Did Leroy ever hit you?"

She laughs. "Oh, he gets pissed off sometimes. He don't mean nothin' by it. He just gets jealous and he likes to be the boss. Just put on them red shoes and nothing else and you'll make him crazy." My stomach lurches. Enough about the red shoes. There is no way on God's green earth I'm putting those shoes on. The last thing I need is to drive him crazy in a sexual way.

"Leann, Leroy is abusive. He controls you emotionally and he's physically intimidating too. Has he ever hit Trevor?"

"I don't know half of what you're saying. He can be a mean son of a bitch, ya just have to know how to handle him. Sometimes he has to get firm with Trevor, that's how he keeps him in line. My mama's always quotin' the Bible, 'Don't spare the stick or your child will be a dumb ass.'"

"I don't think that's in the Bible. Besides, your mother is not someone I would take advice from."

"Well she ain't your mama."

"No, she's not. And I don't want her to be my mother. I want my mother back."

"Shit, you can have her."

Jimmy walks passed me on his way to punch back in. I smile at him and try to make myself smaller so he can squeeze by in the tiny hallway. He smells good, like fresh air and bread and peanut butter. I wish I was thinner. I wish I wasn't Leann. I wish a lot of things, but right now I have to keep Leann talking.

"Where would you go, if you left?"

"I don't know, but they gave me a whole bunch of money so I could go anywhere."

"That's not really your money."

"Yeah, it is. It's mine. I'm the one got hit on the head."

"Technically, I was the one who got hit on the head."

"Shit. You just want the money, is that it? Well you can't have it. It's mine. And I ain't givin' you a dime."

"I don't want the money. I want my life."

"Don'tcha gotta get back to work or something?"

"Wait! Don't hang up. Where will you go?"

"I ain't figured that out yet. I'm tired of talkin' to you. I got things to do."

"But what about Trevor?" I ask. Silence. She has already hung up. It amazes me that she cares about Leroy. Maybe someone's life just gets so screwed up that they care about the wrong people. They love the very people who are hurting them. Why would anyone care about Leroy? He's horrible. But Jillian likes him too, and so does Trevor. Leroy is horrible. I'm right about that.

I make it back to my register late and Vernon scowls at me from the manger's booth where he has been counting money for the night deposit. I feel disoriented. Calling Leann didn't help. It only made me feel panicky. Maybe I'll never get my life back. Maybe I need to stop trying.

When I get home that night, Mr. Giovanni is sitting in the hallway listening to his radio.

"Pretty late for you, isn't it?" I ask him as I trudge towards my door.

He smiles at me and points to his radio. "They had a rain delay and now they're in extra innings." He's talking about the Cubs. He loves the Cubs. I've never asked him why. He didn't grow up in Chicago.

After Jillian leaves with a roll of her eyes and a smirk, I clean up the dishes from dinner. At least she did feed Trevor one of the meals I made. I'm exhausted, but I go back out in the hall to see Mr. Giovanni anyway. He waves me over and gets up so I can sit in his seat. He pulls out his other chair. The game is finally called, still tied 2-2.

"Not bad," he says. "This just might be their year."

I smile at him. I don't know a thing about baseball, but even I know the Cubs never win.

"How are you tonight, kid?" he asks with a smile.

"I'm tired."

"Then you should be going to bed, not hanging out in the hallway with an old man."

"I know, but I needed to hear a friendly voice tonight."

"That bad, huh? Anything I can do?"

"I don't think so. I think I'm stuck with this."

"No one's ever stuck with anything they don't want to be stuck with."

I consider this. Scott said the same thing. If I don't want to be Leann, I can leave. It's not really that simple, but then again it is. If I don't want to be fat, I can change that. And I am. It's just going to take some time. If I don't want to be with Leroy, I can leave. I can take Trevor and go somewhere. But where?

"I wish it were that easy," I say.

"It is, kiddo. It is. Life is too short. Remember that. I wish someone had told me that a long time ago. Course, I wouldn't have paid them no mind. I was too busy just getting by. Life is too short to just get by. I mean it."

I wrestle myself out of the chair. I've got to get some sleep. "Thanks, Mr. G."

I fold up my chair and lean it against the wall. Mr. Giovanni doesn't move.

"Aren't you going in?" I ask.

"Nah, I want to hear the sports report. See what all those dumbass commentators think of my cubbies." He smiles wistfully and leans back in his chair as he turns up his radio. I don't ask why he listens in the hallway. I guess he's lonely too.

〜 〜

leann

Jesus, she just won't stop calling. I gotta stop answering is what. Why did I pick up that damn phone? She's going on about how I gotta be nicer to her mama and Scott. I ain't bein' mean to them, I just ain't talkin' to 'em is all. Why should I? They don't say nothin' that makes no sense.

Then she's complaining about Leroy. He can get nasty sometimes, and he got a mean hand when he's drunk. But he's not so hard to make happy. She's so smart, she can figure that out. I told her to find them red shoes, the ones Leroy bought special. They hurt my feet like hell, but they sure make Leroy happy. He loved seein' me in them, always made him laugh and get all horny.

I don't know what her problem is. She's the one who gets Trevor. So she's got everything.

I should get out of here. Try out a new town. Leave with Trevor before Leroy gets it in his head to go. I haven't figured out how to make that happen. Leroy will go ape shit if Trevor goes missing. I ain't never been nowhere. But I won't go without Trevor. I may not be the best mama for him, but I ain't gonna let him go neither. I'm learning how to be a better mama. I'm gonna do it right this time. Feed him what he should eat, like the stuff Esperanza's been showing me. I'm gonna read with him, too. Maybe I'll even learn baseball. I have to make him trust me lookin' like this. He's too smart to just go off with a stranger.

I saw him just this morning. Handsome as ever. We talked a little and I gave him his Doritos and Coke. He likes that. I gave him a new magazine, too. It's one of Esperanza's gardening magazines. The words ain't in English, but the pictures are real nice. Said he ain't said nothin' to his mama. Said he's doin' better in school. Said he has a new friend named Jimmy and they played in a stream and built a dam.

I told him I knew his grandma. Told him I knew her well, and that she had a birthday comin' up. He said he always makes a card for her, like I know he does. But he don't know when he'll see her, so I gave him her address; I wrote it down for him on some paper. He put it in his pocket and promised he'd send her a card. Such a good boy.

I decided maybe I should just go on and sleep with Scott. Don't know why he'll keep hanging around if I don't. I still don't really like him, but as long as I have him, Carin ain't gonna run off with Trevor. Maybe we can make a trade. I ain't slept with no one 'cept Leroy and that guy Austin. Leroy said I was the worst fuck he ever had. Maybe Scott won't think so. I'll have to get good and drunk to work up my nerve. I wish I could find someone like Dr. Halliday on my show. Now he's a real gentleman. He'd make a great dad for Trevor.

chapter 25

In the morning, I wake to find Trevor standing next to my bed with something behind his back. "I need to mail my birthday card for Grandma."

"You do?" I try not to look as shocked as I feel waking up to this information. I yawn and study his face. He seems nervous. He's still holding whatever it is behind his back. He nods.

"Did you make it at school?" I ask. He shrugs and looks away, purposely not answering me. "When's her birthday?" He shrugs again. "If you don't know when it is, how do you know you need to mail it to her?" Now I'm sure Trevor looks scared. His lip is trembling and he pulls out the card he's hiding behind his back. It's homemade. A lopsided birthday cake festooned with long crooked candles covers the front. Inside it says, *Happy Birtday Grama!* Colorful balloons float up from each of the letters. I look at Trevor and he is holding his breath, his eyes fixed on me, waiting for my response. Why does he look so scared?

"This is nice, Trevor. I think Grandma will really like it."

"Can we mail it?" he asks. I suppose Leann would know her mother's address, but I don't.

"I don't have her address. Maybe we can wait until she stops by and we'll give it to her then," I say cheerfully, placing the card carefully on the crate next to the bed.

"This is where she lives," Trevor says quickly, digging in his pocket and pulling out a small scrap of paper. He offers it to me. I unfold it and see an address written on a piece of stationery I recognize because I have the same kind in my cherry rolltop desk in my apartment. My heart begins to race. I know where he got this address and how he knows it's her birthday.

"Where'd you get this address?" I ask. Trevor shrugs.

"Who gave it to you?" I ask a little too forcefully. He starts to cry. I hug him and ask again, "Trevor, who gave you this address and told you it was Grandma's birthday?"

"The pretty lady," he mumbles into his chest.

"What pretty lady?" I ask carefully, trying to keep my voice from rising. He doesn't answer me. "Where did you see this pretty lady?" He looks up and there is fear in his eyes. I force myself to smile and try to look as non-threatening as possible.

Finally he says, "At the bus stop."

I want to grill him, but he seems like a deer caught in the headlights. So I choose my words carefully.

"Trevor, I know you know not to talk to strangers. Why did you talk to this lady?"

"She was nice."

"Sometimes dangerous people are nice."

"She knew my name and she gave me Doritos and a Coke."

"What did she say to you?"

He looks around the room, his gaze resting on the card he made. He doesn't take his eyes off it as he says, "She always wants to know if you take good care of me and she wants to know what Daddy is doing."

My heart is pounding and I have to take a few deep breaths before I can say anymore. What is Leann doing? Is she planning on taking Trevor? This life is a living hell and only Trevor makes it bearable. Besides, she's the one who won't come back. How dare she spy on us?

"How many times have you talked to her?" I ask calmly.

"I don't know." Trevor won't meet my eye.

"Well, is it every day?"

"No."

"Every week?"

He looks up at me. "I don't know. She's nice to me."

"Why didn't you tell me about her?"

He shrugs and mumbles, "She said you wouldn't like it if you knew."

I take a few more breaths. "Trevor, you shouldn't keep secrets from your mama."

He looks at me and seems to see right through me. He doesn't say anything. He doesn't even nod. He looks over at his card on the table and asks, "Can we send the card to Grandma?"

I get up. I don't have any place telling him not to talk to Leann. He seems as confused as I am about who his mother is. "Yeah, we can mail it. I'll buy a stamp today."

I walk Trevor to the bus stop, but there's no sign of Leann. Later at the gym, I'm distracted. I need a plan. More than ever I know I have to get out of the apartment. But finding somewhere else to live takes time. And cash. Two things that are in short supply in my life these days. Not long ago my days were wide open. I had nothing to do. Sundays seemed to drag on the worst. I'd come up with a huge to-do list, but then it would seem like too much, so I'd just lay around feeling guilty that I wasn't getting anything done. Scott helped a great deal. He was a wonderful distraction. I'm sorry I never thought of him as more. I guess maybe I did in the beginning.

I don't know what changed. At some point, he wasn't enough. We got along great, sex was pretty good, but deeper down, where it matters, we were too different. He didn't read or enjoy cooking or want to travel. We never agreed on politics. I was interested but ignorant, he was informed but cynical. We held completely different views on religion. He thought it was defining, although he never attended church. I thought it was manipulating but followed my mother to Mass on occasion.

When it came to families, we couldn't have been further apart. He loved spending time with his and wanted one of his own. I avoided mine and never planned on further overpopulating this planet. Actually, I was more afraid of getting pregnant and gaining fifty pounds and losing my perky boobs. So when I think about it, we didn't talk much, at least not about anything that mattered. We talked about other people—the people at the gym, the people in bars, the people on TV. We could talk for hours about other people, but we avoided talking about ourselves because that never got us anywhere. Still, I did love him. He was my dearest friend. But I don't think he can handle this. Or maybe I don't want him to.

I can't think of anyplace Trevor and I can go. I have over six hundred dollars now. That won't get me an apartment or even two plane tickets. I've never been on a train. I wonder if a train is cheaper. I figure if we leave on a Monday that will give us a five-day head start on Leroy. I'm counting on his drug problem to buy us even more time. If he's high or drunk, he'll assume we are out somewhere and he missed us. We need to get out, but I need to be ready. I'm completely unprepared. I've never done anything daring or big. I wish I was clever. I wish I had more nerve.

I'm still deep in thought when something small and hard hits me above the eye. I'm so startled I almost fall out of my chair. I hear giggling and see two small boys hiding behind the chairs on the other side of the drawing table taking aim.

"Hey!" I shout and struggle to get up. Another Lego hits me in the neck and tumbles down inside my shirt. Lovely feeling, a Lego trapped between rolls of fat. That's it. I look around. No Denise. I grab a handful of Legos from the table and fling them back at the little round faces that are now rolling on the floor laughing. Great, four-year-olds think I'm a joke. Just at that moment, Denise appears from behind the sign-in counter. She storms towards me. She grabs a boy with each arm and plops them both on their feet.

"We do not lie on the floor in this room. We also do not make a mess of our toys or create such a ruckus!" Who uses the word *ruckus?* She glares at them, waiting for their explanation.

One boy, lip trembling, points at me and says, "She threw them at us!"

Denise turns to me. I furrow my eyebrows and shake my head firmly.

"We do not throw Legos in this room either," she continues. "Now the two of you will clean up all of these toys, and I mean all of them." She watches them begin their task and then returns to the desk. The boy who spoke up looks at me and I stick out my tongue. This causes the other boy to giggle, which prompts Denise to wheel around. Both boys quickly begin gathering Legos. I head to the bathroom to retrieve the lost Lego.

That afternoon, Bruce helps me with a new workout regime. He takes me through a series of intervals, making notations on my charts. Out of the corner of my eye, I'm watching for Scott. He's late today. After my conversation with Leann, I'm feeling kind of sorry for him. Any opportunity to console him doesn't present itself and I spend thirty minutes sitting in the locker room waiting for my body to cool down and my face to come back to its normal color so I can apply my makeup. I barely get to the Shop N Save in time for my shift. Jimmy is waiting at the time clock when I come in.

"Take your dinner at seven thirty tonight," he tells me.

"Why?"

"Just do. I've got a surprise." he winks and disappears down the hallway. I swear, if I didn't know better, I'd think that Jimmy is flirting with me.

On my bathroom break, I apply my cotton candy pink lipstick and smile at myself in the mirror. I think I look pretty damn good, for a fat girl. I'm still feeling good when I step out of the bathroom and crash right into Franklin. I haven't seen him in nearly a week. He's been out sick. I had hoped he quit, but Phyllis said he had the flu.

"Whoa big girl! I know you missed me, but you don't have to throw yourself at me."

I turn to go.

"What? You don't even ask how I am? I been out sick, coulda been dyin' and you can't even say boo?"

I stop, turn back to him, and say, "Boo!" Then I pivot back the way I was going and try not to listen to his next words.

"You ain't got to treat me like that, bitch. You better start showing some respect. I know things."

What Franklin could know, I have no idea. God knows what Leann did besides steal groceries. It's not fair. I really wasn't such a bad person. Sure, I did some shallow things, a little bending of the law on occasion, but nothing serious. It is entirely unfair that I'm saddled with all the crap Leann did. It's bad enough I have to take on this lumpy, uncoordinated body, but to have to deal with a history I never committed is just unfair.

At seven thirty, I flip my light off and nod to Phyllis. I grab my dinner from my locker and look outside for Jimmy. He's nowhere to be seen. I call softly, "Jimmy?"

"Up here!" His voice comes from the depths of the loading dock. It's still light out, but only barely, and I can just make out his face inside the doorway. He comes over to the steps and says, "Come up here. I've got something to show you."

I struggle up the steep steps, carrying my lunch box. With no railing, the steps are tricky when you are as gravitationally challenged as I am. When I get to the top, I grab the wall for balance and peer into the darkness. A small table covered with a plastic tablecloth holds a box with bright neon lights flashing.

"Listen!" says Jimmy as he gleefully leans down to the box and presses a button. With a click and a pop, music pours out of the box. It's a jukebox. The sound is great. Patsy Cline warbles and echoes all through the storage room. It's beautiful. I close my eyes and lean back against the cool cement. The music swirls all around me. It bounces from the walls and tumbles out into the night. When the song is over, I open my eyes and Jimmy is standing in front of me watching me.

"I knew you'd like it," he says quietly. I smile. I don't know what to say. For a few minutes, I'm not Leann. I'm not Carin either. I'm just me.

"Where did it come from?" I ask finally.

Jimmy visibly swells up. He's so proud I have to smile. "I built it. It's a tabletop juke. Took me the last six months. It can only hold about thirty records. But the sound is great."

"I love it," I say as Jimmy pulls two crates over to the table and we sit down to eat. We eat our dinner serenaded by Nat King Cole, Jimmy Buffet, and Green Day. Jimmy's taste is quite eclectic.

That night, when Jillian leaves she reminds me that she won't be here on Friday because it's the start of her spring break.

"I'm sure you've got all kinds of fun planned," I tell her as I hold the door open.

She sneers at me as she leaves, pausing to say, "Oh, I've got that covered and you can tell Leroy that." I swallow the laugh that is welling inside me. Jesus, is she really thinking Leroy would care? Would he care? This is all too sick for me. I hate that Trevor is too young to understand what a scumbag his dad is. Sad thing is, he may never see it.

Brushing my teeth, I stare at my reflection. Is there any of me in this face? I'm starting to get used to it, even thinking of it as mine. The acne is much better, and my hair is finally long enough to pull back in a ponytail holder, even though it stills requires two or three plastic barrettes to hold all the stray hairs in place. I plucked my eyebrows last weekend, which has dramatically improved my appearance. "It's the little things that make the woman." My mother used to say that. She was big about maintaining your eyebrows and nails. Manners were her other stickler. I remember the fights we had when I was little. Plenty of nights, I spent the evening sitting at the dinner table because I refused to ask to be excused. Every time I got up, she'd come find me and carry me back to the table and plop me on the chair. I don't know when I got too big for her to physically manipulate me, but I guess by then she had the emotional manipulation down. I look at my nails. Between changing diapers and bagging groceries, there isn't much point. Acrylic nails might be a work hazard.

chapter 26

The next morning over breakfast, Trevor reads me his latest library book. His voice punctuates the story with grand pauses as he sorts out a word in his mind. I know not to tell him the word. He wants to figure it out on his own. He's so smart. I wait patiently, but soon I'm off in my own daydream of us living at the beach and spending our days reading books in the sun. Trevor's voice reels me back in. "Do you think there is, Mama?"

"Do I think what?"

"You weren't listening!" he accuses.

"I just got distracted for a moment. Ask me again!"

He looks at me sternly and pulls the book away.

"You weren't listening. My teacher says that if you aren't listening then you just have to miss out."

"That's not fair!" I cry. "Please ask me again!"

He's standing indignantly now with the book clutched to his chest. I reach out and pull him down to me. He stays stiff as a board until I start tickling him and then he collapses in giggles and yells, "Stop!"

"So ask me!" I say, pausing with my hand poised over his belly.

"Okay," he looks at me seriously. "Do you think there really is an Easter Bunny?" What do I say? Will telling the truth about the bunny ruin his life? Should I lie? He didn't ask me if there *was* an Easter Bunny, just did *I think* there was. Big difference. Lately, I think a lot of things that obviously aren't real.

"I think there could be an Easter Bunny," I say hesitantly. "What do you think?" Always good to turn it around on them. I've learned this the hard way at the gym. A little girl asked me where babies come from, and I launched into a mumbling, stumbling explanation of sex. She looked at me with a puzzled expression and said, "I thought they came from God." Much simpler. It's better to keep it simple and be sure you know what's being asked. Most people just want their own opinions confirmed anyway.

Trevor says, "I think there's an Easter Bunny, but he only goes to houses, not apartments."

"Why wouldn't the Easter Bunny visit an apartment?" I ask.

"I don't know. Maybe he can't hop up the stairs."

"Didn't he leave any eggs for you last year?"

Trevor shakes his head. Wow. Leann sucks. How could she deny him the Easter Bunny?

"Well, maybe he got lost. This year we'll leave him some notes in the hallway."

Trevor brightens at this thought. The timer sounds. I set him back on his feet and he gives me a shy kiss before racing out of the apartment. I lean back on the couch and feel good. I feel like a good mom. I can do some things right.

On my way to the gym, I stop by the drug store. I pick out candy, small toys, plastic eggs, and a basket decorated in a baseball theme. I spend twenty-five dollars. That's a lot of groceries, but this is important. I smile to myself as I carry my bag out.

I spend my whole morning rocking the babies. They smell so great. Breathing them in comforts me, makes my life seem not so crazy. I gaze out the front window and see Scott come down the hallway. He glances in at the children, but quickly ducks away. Could he have been looking for me? No, I know Scott. He's only being nice to the fat girl because he thinks I have some kind of connection to the real me.

I remember when I met him. We were at a cookout at one of his co-worker's houses. My friends Matt and Sarah dragged me along. I haven't seen Matt or Sarah since then, come to think of it. That was about three years ago. Matt and Sarah had recently been married. Married friends tend to dissolve out of your life when you're single. The friendship doesn't end abruptly; it just sort of fades away. They don't invite you to things, because you aren't married, and you don't invite them to things, because they are. It's kind of inevitable. After all, who wants a married chick with a big bright ring cramping your style when you're out cruising the bar scene. Not me. Besides, Sarah and I were never really that close.

Anyway, I was bored and ended up hiding out on the front porch to get away from the music and chaos in the backyard. I didn't know anyone except Matt and Sarah. I was perched on the railing and considering leaving when Scott stumbled around the side of the house. The porch railing was about ten feet off the ground and he stopped in front of me and yelled, "Behold, a goddess!"

I didn't know how to respond to him. I remember thinking he was kind of cute, but not really my type and obviously drunk. He was wearing a Def Leppard T-shirt, which was enough to make a girl wonder, but he was also wearing penny loafers and pressed jeans. It was clear he'd never had an older sister or a bossy girlfriend to clarify fashion rules for him. I rolled my eyes at him.

He was undeterred. "Juliet, Juliet, wherefore art thou, Juliet?"

I could tell he wasn't going to go away until I responded. So I forced a smile and said, "Nice try, I'm guessing you didn't major in literature," and went to sit in the swing on the side porch. Next thing I knew, Scott sat down next to me.

"Sorry," he said. "I've had a lot to drink. Let me try again. I'm Scott."

He looked at me with such sorry puppy dog eyes, I took pity. We ended up talking on the porch the rest of the afternoon. He was sweet and funny and I did enjoy talking to him. I remember thinking what a perfect guy he would be if a perfect guy was what I wanted. I never seemed to go for the perfect guy. I wanted the god-like guy. I was waiting for the man who made my stomach do flips and my heart race. Scott just made me laugh, not because he was funny, but because he was so earnest and adorable, which to me is friend material, not boyfriend material. I wish Leann would be nicer to him.

I'm adjusting weights on one of the machines when I hear Scott talking to Bruce. He worked out early today, so he's leaving and I'm just getting started. I watch him through the machine. He's animated and waving his enormous hands around as he speaks. Bruce is laughing, but I can't make out what they're saying. I wonder if Bruce still has the hots for him. Scott finally slaps Bruce on the shoulder and turns to go. He glances my way and I manage a wave. He smiles and heads out of the gym.

When Bruce stops by to check on me, I can't help myself; I have to ask. "Scott was here early today. Did he have a hot lunch date?"

Bruce smiles and says, "Something like that, I think."

That's not enough information, so I press on. "I didn't know he was dating anyone."

Bruce takes the bait. "He's been taking care of a friend who was in an accident, and it sounds like he's about to get his thank you."

My heart sinks. Leann has no right to sleep with Scott. She doesn't care about him. I can't let it happen. I wait for Bruce to move on to the next machine and then grab my towel and run. I don't even take the time to change my shoes; I just hurry out the door. Looking around the parking lot, I don't see Scott's car, so I run for the bus station. Maybe he won't go directly to the apartment. Maybe he'll stop and buy flowers. That would be just like Scott.

When I arrive at my apartment building, I don't see Scott's car. Not wanting to take any chances, I head for the entrance and push my buzzer.

"Hello?" I hear my voice ask.

"Leann, what are you doing?"

"I told you not to bother me. I ain't doing nothing." Pause. Burp. "What do you think I'm doing?"

"Look, I know Scott is on his way over here. What are you up to?"

"I'm just takin' him on a test drive." She laughs. She sounds drunk.

"Are you drunk?"

"Not exactly."

"What does that mean?"

"It means it's none of your goddamn business. Now go away, I don't want to talk to you anymore."

"Leann, Scott doesn't know what's going on."

"Aw, shit. I ain't gonna hurt him. I'm just gonna screw him."

"I don't think that's a good idea."

"Well, it don't matter what you think, does it?" She's slurring her words and sounds on the edge of hysteria.

"I think it does since you're using my body."

"Fuck you!" she yells, and then the intercom cuts off.

She won't answer my next buzz, so I sit down on the steps to wait. I don't know what I'm going to say to Scott, but don't have time to figure it out because his car pulls in. He comes up the walk looking confused. He's carrying a bouquet of daffodils, my favorites.

"Hey! Weren't you just at the gym?"

"Uh-huh," I say, still not sure what to do.

"What are you doing here?"

"I live here. Well, I used to live here. I should live here, but everything's really messed up."

"Oh," he says, and stops in front of me. I'm crying now, big snot-filled sobs. Scott doesn't know what to do. He stares at me. I can't stop crying, and Scott looks around hoping to see someone else to help.

"Well, I need to go inside. Are you going to be okay?" he asks. He is flushed and impatient.

"I don't think you should sleep with her," I say without looking up.

"What?" he asks, shocked.

"I don't think you should sleep with her," I repeat.

"I heard what you said and I don't think it's any of your business."

"It's completely my business," I say as I get up. "She's not who you think she is."

"You don't even know who I'm here to see."

"I know exactly who you're here to see and I think you should be careful. She's not the same person you used to know."

"How do you know?" he sputters. I can tell he's curious. He knows something's not quite right with Leann.

I take a deep breath. What do I say? He'll never believe me. But I'm tired of pretending. I am not Leann. I don't want to be who she is. I'm not sure I want to be who Carin was, but I know I'm not Leann. I stand up.

"Do you remember the day Carin first got hurt?"

"Yes," he says, and now we're looking at each other eye to eye because I'm standing a step above him.

"I came to your house."

"I remember. You wanted to come in."

"I told you I was Carin."

He doesn't know what to say, but I can see he's wrestling with this logic.

"I told you that because I am Carin. Scott, something happened when that Valentine's display heart hit my head. Somehow I ended up inside the body of the cashier, Leann. And somehow she ended up inside my body."

He's shaking his head. I can see he doesn't want to believe this. But, just like Trevor, I know he's suspected that something is amiss. He shakes his head and says, "That's impossible. You're messing with my mind. You can't be her. Maybe you want to be her, but you aren't. This is fucked up."

"It's completely fucked up."

He's shaking now, but he steps past me to go inside. He has a keycard that lets him in. I gave it to him. I watch him go inside. I know he believes me. He doesn't want to, but he does. I can't do anything else and I've got to get to work, so I leave.

Later, looking at myself in the bathroom at the Shop N Save, I shudder. My hair is still pulled back in multiple tiny pony tails, my workout look. Luckily, my smock covers the sweat stains on my back. I'm shaky from all the crying and from hunger. I never ate my lunch. I usually eat on the bus ride from the gym. My lunch is stowed in my locker at the gym. It'll smell real nice by tomorrow. Oh shit! Tomorrow the gym is closed for the long holiday weekend. Lovely. The whole locker room will be ripe with the smell of my moldy cheese sandwich by Monday. But I suppose that's okay since Monday will be my last day.

Trevor and I are leaving Monday. I don't know where we're going, but after I finish at the gym and get my last paycheck, we're off. I can't wait anymore for the right moment. I've just got to make it the right moment. We're getting paid on Monday since the gym will be closed Friday. Adding that to the $686 I have in my locker should give us enough money for bus fare to somewhere far away. I have a bus schedule in my locker. I'm going to let Trevor pick where we go. Maybe somewhere warm.

I'm deep in thought, imagining San Diego, California, when I feel someone grab my ass from behind. I turn around quickly to see Franklin grinning at me.

"You're looking better every day, babe. You losing all that weight for me?" I turn to go, and he slides past me and blocks my way.

"Hey, you know you want me as much as I want you."

I hold up a hand. "Franklin, listen carefully. I will never have sex with you. I have no interest in you whatsoever except when I need you to take someone's groceries to their car. I'm sure some women find you attractive, God help them, but I'm not one of those women." For a second, he looks hurt, but then his face cracks open in a sleazy smile. He leans close to my face and licks his lips before he walks past me chuckling.

Franklin is another reason to get out of this place. I want to believe Jimmy when he says not to take him seriously, but something about Franklin's arrogance and the hungry look in his eyes makes me uneasy. He does frighten me, almost as much as he disgusts me.

Jimmy doesn't have his jukebox tonight at dinner, so I guess that was a onetime special event. We're sitting on the crates just inside the storage room doors. It's raining. Jimmy finishes before me and lights up a cigarette. He's blowing perfect smoke rings and we watch them disappear in the darkness. "Jimmy, if you could go anywhere in the country, where would you go?"

He takes a drag of his cigarette and thinks. I love that he doesn't ask why I want to know.

"I think I might go to Iowa."

"Iowa? Why Iowa?"

"I don't know. It's the first place that came into my head. I always like to go with my first thought. I think your first thought is your heart's answer, but then your head gets in on the thought and changes it all around to what makes the most sense. I should say something like Hollywood or New York City or Disney World, right? That's what most people would say. Nope, Iowa. That's where I'd go."

"Iowa." I mull the idea over in my head. I've never really thought about Iowa. I think they have a lot of cows. Probably a lot of farms and white people. I don't think I know the name of a single city in Iowa.

"Where would you go?" he asks. I try to let my heart speak, but my head has already been thinking about this question.

"I'd go somewhere the sun shines a lot. Somewhere you can see all the stars."

"The sun shines in Iowa," he says simply. "I bet they have a lot of stars too."

I smile, but don't say anything. I watch as he begins blowing smoke rings again.

chapter 27

ᨆ ᨆ

On Good Friday morning, Trevor sleeps in. I can't. I'm wired. I'm so anxious, it feels like a hummingbird has taken up residence in my stomach. We're leaving in three days. I have to figure out what I'm going to tell Trevor by then. I have to convince him that leaving his dad is the best thing. But how can any six-year-old ever understand that? Even a six-year-old as smart and insightful as Trevor. He might never forgive me.

Trevor and Mr. Giovanni sit on the couch watching a baseball game. Mr. G is explaining the finer points of each batter's stance to Trevor. With each strike, Trevor yells, "Steeeerike one!" and whenever anyone strikes out, he and Mr. G yell together, "You're out" and throw their thumbs over their shoulders. It's adorable. I shuttle back and forth between our apartment and Mr. G's, doing laundry.

At lunchtime, it starts raining here and wherever the baseball game is being played, so Mr. G takes Trevor to his apartment to look through his pictures from his days of playing baseball.

At 2:00 p.m., I leave for work. Even though it's raining, I walk to the store. I'm worried three days without the gym will slow down my weight loss. I've lost so much weight now that I know we will have to go to the Goodwill tomorrow. I need traveling clothes. It will be difficult to find an apartment and a job wearing stretch pants and Disco Fever T-shirts.

When I arrive at the Shop N Save, I'm drenched. The umbrella didn't do much good because the rain was coming down sideways. My pants cling to me and I'm grateful for the smock that covers my wet shirt, which is embedded between the creases of my fat rolls. Not a pretty sight. It's just my luck that Franklin is in the break room when I arrive. His rude comments are cut short when the deli ladies arrive. Even a sleazeball like Franklin can't talk trash in front of a grandma. I pull on my smock and escape to my register.

At 5:00, I remind Vernon that I need to leave early tonight and he nods from his desk where he is drowning beneath register tapes, order forms, and his own incompetence. If it weren't for Peggy, our bookkeeper, he would be lost. She handles the computer work for Vernon. Peggy could be robbing the store blind and no one would be the wiser, but she seems like an honest sort. She keeps her glasses on a leash and her hair frozen in an unnatural position by massive quantities of hairspray. She smokes constantly. A sign in the hallway just outside her office reads, *No Smoking.*

Since I'm leaving at seven, I don't get a dinner break. Jimmy makes one of his rare appearances at the front of the store and hands me a small shoe box with a bow. I'm embarrassed and don't know how to respond. The box is heavy. "It's nothing special, I just want you to have it," he says. Then he turns quickly and leaves. Phyllis shoots me a knowing smile and the customer who has been waiting during this exchange sighs loudly. He doesn't care about what's in the box, he'd like me to focus on his groceries. I put the box under the register.

At 6:25, Scott enters the store. I know exactly what time he enters because I have been watching the clock above the entrance, willing it to move faster. He makes a beeline for my register. I have a line, so I ignore him, concentrating on the items swimming up my conveyor belt and making bland conversation with the woman waiting for me to bag her groceries. Scott is next in line, but he doesn't have anything in his cart. I eye Vernon up in the Eagle's Nest. He's on the phone and turning red in the face. Two employees wait for his attention.

I don't know what to say to Scott, so I say nothing and busy myself cleaning off the conveyor belt. I want to ask what happened.

I want to ask if he slept with her. I want to ask if he believes me. I want to ask if he's still my friend. But nothing seems appropriate.

"How late are you working?" he says calmly. Another customer comes up behind him, so he grabs a few packs of gum and I ring them up.

"Can I talk to you?" he asks as he grabs some magazines, several lighters, and a convenience pack of hand sanitizers.

"I'm finished at seven, but I have to get right home."

"Can I give you a ride?"

I bag up his stuff and run his credit card. I can't tell what he wants from his tone. I scrutinize his face. He looks tired. The circles are deep under his sad eyes.

"Okay," I say. "Wait for me out front."

He doesn't say anymore. He doesn't even smile. What the hell is he thinking? I used to be able to read him like a book.

At seven, I take Jimmy's gift out from under the register, clock out, and pick up my paycheck. Vernon says, "Have a nice holiday," in a strangled voice. I doubt he will have a nice holiday. Franklin is gathering carts in the parking lot when I walk out. Scott pulls up to the curb immediately. Franklin is watching us.

"Go, please," I say as I get in. Scott waits for me to put on my seatbelt before he hits the gas. Some things don't change. Franklin turns to watch us leave the parking lot.

We drive a few minutes and then Scott says, "Can we stop somewhere and talk?"

"I need to get home."

"Where's home?"

I give him the address. "That's not a nice neighborhood."

"That's where I live." I can't help but be annoyed. No sense pretending here. I still don't know if he believes me or not, but he wouldn't be here if he didn't believe me a little. He pulls over at an old gas station that's been closed for years. Weeds snake up through the concrete surrounding the pumps. The sign is falling down, but still reads *$1.79 a gallon*. I stare at the spider web of cracks in the glass enclosing the attendant's station and will myself not to cry.

"Look, I don't know if I understand what's going on. All I know is Carin is not herself. She's not the person I know. At first I thought it was the head injury. She'd get back to normal. Her doctor says she's fine physically, but she's still not the person I know. She's rude and mean and ugly."

My head turns at the word ugly. Scott has always told me I'm beautiful. The most beautiful girl he's ever known. He called me his Beauty Queen.

He tries to explain. "I try to talk to her. I try to be patient, but she won't have anything to do with me. She doesn't even talk like herself. It's like she's forgotten how to speak correct English. She talks like she grew up in the projects."

"She talks like that because she did grow up in the projects."

Scott looks at me. "How is this possible?" he asks. His voice cracks and I swear he's going to cry. But I'm not. This time, I'm not.

"I don't know. Believe me, if I knew how this happened, I'd fix it. Scott, this is me in here. Ask me anything and I can tell you. Ask me how we met; ask me about the first time we slept together. Ask me about your toenail issue." He smiles at this. He loves painted toenails. He used to love to paint my toenails and even asked me to put clear polish on his.

"God, Carin, I've missed you," he says, turning to face me. He can't bring himself to embrace my bulk. I know that, but he wants to touch me. I don't know that I want to be touched yet. "What are you going to do?"

"I'm going to leave and start over somewhere. It's too hard here. Leann's husband, who I guess is my husband, is a real loser. I don't even know what he does, but he's gone all week. He comes home on the weekends and wants all the money I've made. He smokes dope and I think he's sleeping with the fifteen-year-old babysitter. And he's horrible with Trevor."

"Who's Trevor?"

"My son, well . . . Leann's son."

Scott shakes his head and smiles.

"I know, I know. Me with a kid? But he's amazing. He's smart and sweet and so innocent. And he deserves better than the crummy parents he's got. I have to get him out of this place."

"Come to my house," he says. For a second, I consider this. But it's not the answer. This situation is so much more complicated than a simple white knight rescue. Besides, I don't love Scott. I mean, I love Scott as my dear friend, but I don't love him in any other way. And now I realize how much he does love me. But I don't know, and he doesn't know, if he can love me as Leann. I can't do this to him. It wouldn't be fair.

"I appreciate that, but I'm going to handle this."

"Does your mom know?"

"No. I tried to tell her, but she didn't believe me. And you know what, it's okay. I think she knows she lost me, but I don't think I could ever fix things. I don't know, maybe someday I'll try. But she has always been more into the idea of me than the actual me, so I don't think she could handle this."

"She might surprise you," he says. "She's pretty upset. Right now she's giving Carin, I mean Leann, the silent treatment. She told me she won't speak to her until she apologizes for the rude things she's said."

I smile. Mom. She's a classic. "Maybe by the time I'm ready to apologize, she'll be ready to hear me."

Scott smiles. "Carin, you don't have to do this alone."

It feels so good to hear someone say my name. I close my eyes. "Thanks," I whisper.

Scott drives me to the apartment. He offers to walk me up, but I assure him I'll be alright. I hear his automatic locks as he pulls away.

Lucky for me, Leroy has not yet made an appearance. I retrieve Trevor from Mr. Giovanni's. He's not happy about this. A game is about to start, and Mr. G has promised popcorn. I need this weekend to go smoothly. Leroy would not be pleased to find his son in Mr. Giovanni's apartment. So we trudge back to our place, Trevor complaining the whole way.

I stash Jimmy's present under a pile of dirty clothes. Trevor plops down in front of his computer. He's angry with me.

"Trevor, I know you're mad. I'm sorry."

"Why can't I stay with Mr. G? We were gonna watch the game. We had hot dogs and nacho chips for dinner just like at the ball park. We even had peanuts."

"I know, sweetie. I'm sorry about that. I'd like to let you stay, but I know your dad will want to see you too."

"He will not," he says, leaning back against the couch and crossing his arms. I don't know what to say here. Somehow I have to convince him to keep Mr. G's involvement quiet. I don't want Leroy going after him once we leave.

"Honey, here's the thing. For some reason, your daddy doesn't like Mr. G." Trevor's eyes open wide and he turns to look at me.

"Why?"

"I don't know, but he has his reasons and we need to respect that. So it's really important that you not tell him that you spent the day with Mr. Giovanni."

"But Mr. G is my friend."

"I know he's your friend, but you can't let your daddy know that, for now. Maybe someday we can tell him, but not this week-end. Okay?"

Trevor doesn't say anything. He's thinking this over. Maybe he's realizing that adults don't make sense. I tell him not to lie, but then ask him to. Twice.

"Trevor? I need your word that you won't tell your daddy about Mr. G."

"Can I ever tell him?"

"I'll let you know when it's okay to tell him."

"Does that mean I can't watch the game with Mr. G tomorrow?"

"Yeah, it does buddy. I'm sorry. Maybe your dad will want to watch the game here."

"Nah, he hates baseball."

"How do you know that?"

"Duh, Mama, he always says so. He never wants to watch baseball. He says it's for sissies."

"Do you think it's for sissies?"

"No! Baseball players are the most intelligent athletes in the world. Mr. G says so. And he knows 'cause he's a baseball player. Well, he was. Did you know he played in California?"

"I didn't know that."

He nods.

"So, are we clear on this—no mention of Mr. G to Daddy?"

"Yeah. But I think it's stupid."

"It is," I agree. "Now, how about we make some popcorn ourselves? You can even turn on the game until your dad gets here."

"Really?" Trevor jumps up.

"Really," I say.

"We have popcorn?"

"I think so." I remember a bag of popcorn in one of the milk crates. It looks pretty old, but with enough salt it'll do. I measure some oil in a pan and Trevor watches with wonder as I drop the "test kernels" in. We both jump when one pops. Trevor laughs and wants to pour in the rest. I'm afraid the hot oil will burn him so I do it instead. We wait, and once the popcorn starts pelting the lid of the pan, Trevor is jubilant. He's dancing around yelling "Pop! Pop! Pop!" when Leroy barges through the door. He throws his bag on the table and yells at Trevor to shut the hell up. I take the popcorn off the stove and glance over at the TV where the game is just beginning. Trevor quickly turns it off.

"Why you watching that sissy game, boy? Ain't I told you I don't want that crap on in my house?" Leroy asks. He looks disheveled. He has the beginnings of a beard and his pants are torn and covered in mud. He glares at me as he walks to the bathroom.

"What the hell you lookin' at?" he says.

I put the popcorn in a bowl and give it to Trevor. I tell him to take it outside to eat on the steps. I wipe the table and sink just to have something to do to calm my nerves. When I hear the shower turn off, I purposely turn to the sink and scrub. I do not want to see Leroy's naked body parading through the dining room. He has a penchant for walking around naked. He comes in wearing nothing, not even a towel, retrieves his bag, and then goes to the bedroom. He doesn't say anything to me, but I pretend I don't see him and wash the popcorn pan again.

I hear Leroy in the bedroom talking on his cell phone. He doesn't sound happy. Trevor comes in and quietly begins playing with his computer. I pull out my library book and sit down on the couch to read. Except for Leroy's occasionally raised voice, it's quiet. I'm glad that Trevor is wearing a headset when Leroy comes back into the living room. He looks strangely different.

I'm not sure what it is. Maybe nervous? That's it. He looks nervous, and I've never seen him look nervous. I don't know how to respond to this.

He starts slamming things around in the kitchen. He finds his Twizzlers and pulls a bottle of whiskey out of his bag. He upends the bottle and drinks three long swallows. If I did something like that I would burn my throat right out of my body. He looks like he's guzzling water. Then he sits down at the table and pulls out a handgun. My heart just about jumps out of my chest. I've never even been in the same room as a gun. I glance over at Trevor. He is transfixed by his game. I try to concentrate on my book. Probably this isn't a big deal for this family. Dad guzzling whiskey and cleaning a gun. Normal Friday night, right?

Leroy hasn't even asked for my paycheck or complained about the lack of food in the house. He looks up and catches me looking at him. He holds the gun up and aims it at me. My mouth drops open and I freeze. Then he puts the gun down and laughs. He mumbles, "Such a stupid bitch. How'd I get stuck with such a stupid bitch?" He finishes with the gun and tucks it back in his bag. He bites off another piece of Twizzler and stares at Trevor.

"He plays on that damn machine too much."

I don't say anything. I'm terrified that I'll say the wrong thing and set him off. I can't get the image of the gun pointed at me out of my head.

"Ya hear me? How come you let him play that damn computer so much? It's not good for him."

I nod in agreement, still not able to find my voice. "What, cat got your tongue?" Leroy laughs to himself. "Such a stupid bitch. You used to be good for one thing, but now you ain't even good for that." He gets up and walks over to Trevor. He towers over him. Trevor doesn't look up. I'm not sure if he's so wrapped up in his game that he doesn't notice him or if he's afraid to look up. Leroy reaches down and yanks the headphones off. "Hey, can't you even say hello to your old man?" Trevor gets up and stiffly hugs Leroy around the waist.

"That's better. Now, turn that damn thing off. It's not good for you."

"But I'm playing," Trevor says, and I know that's a mistake. Leroy is dangerously drunk and unsteadied by something other than alcohol.

"Oh, you're playing?" he says in a mocking tone. Then he picks up the computer, tearing the cord from the wall. He walks to the window, struggling to open it while holding the computer. He can't, so instead he flings the computer against the far wall. It leaves a jagged gouge in the wall, but falls to the floor, mostly intact.

"Daddy!" yells Trevor. I grab him before he can run to the computer.

"What? You love this computer more than me?" Leroy is screaming now in a voice I've never heard before. Should I call the police? I hold Trevor tightly. I will protect this child. I glare at Leroy, willing him to stop.

"That's right, you protect the little sissy. He's turning into a wuss right before my eyes because of you and this stupid piece of crap!" He walks to the computer and kicks at the monitor. It takes several tries before his boot finally shatters the screen. Trevor screams and I hold him tighter. Trevor's terror seems to ignite something in Leroy. He continues to kick the computer and when he's done all the damage he can, he kicks the wall.

"Leroy! Stop!" I hear myself yelling. "Stop! What are you doing?" He doesn't hear me in his blind rage. He puts several holes in the wall and then turns to the table. He picks up his bag

and then flips the table over. I'm screaming and Trevor is sob-
bing. Leroy looks at us. It is a black look. One that is pure hatred.
But it can't be us that he hates. Something more consumes him.
He picks up a chair and flings it at us. It hits the coffee table and is
deflected. And just when I think it's about to get worse, he leaves.
He doesn't even close the door behind him.

I hold Trevor and stare at the yawning door. After a while,
Trevor stops crying and looks up at me.

"Why was Daddy so mad?" he asks.

I shake my head. "I don't know. I really don't know." I set
Trevor on the couch next to me. "Trevor, your daddy has a problem that we can't help him with. He needs to get help, but we can't
help him. Do you understand that?"

He nods and quiet tears slip down his cheeks.

"I'm going to get us out of here real soon."

He nods again. I leave him on the couch while I gather up
some clothes and put them in a bag, tucking in Jimmy's gift too.
I pick my paycheck off the floor where it landed when Leroy
flipped the table. Then I take Trevor's hand and we walk out.
Trevor looks longingly at Mr. G's door when we pass, but I hold
his hand tighter to tell him no.

Once we get down to the street, the warm night air hits me.
Finally, the weather has turned to spring. I don't know where to
go. I consider going to Scott's, but that would be too confusing for
Trevor, and now that Scott knows the truth I can't bear for him to
pretend that I'm Leann. We walk to the bus station. It feels late,
but it's only 9:30. I go to the only place I know I will feel safe.

Jimmy opens the door on the second knock. He's wearing a
torn T-shirt and frayed jeans, and his trademark ball cap is turned
inside out and backwards.

"What's with the cap?" I ask.

"Rally cap."

I look at him questioningly and he says, "Trevor can explain
it." He steps back and holds the door open to let us enter. Trevor
can hear the ballgame and runs for the TV.

"You want a beer?" Jimmy asks. He holds up his bottle.

"A beer would be great," I say and then I start crying.

"Whoa, whoa," Jimmy holds up his hands. "That looks like more than a beer." He glances over at Trevor and then motions for me to stay where I am. He returns with my beer and two lawn chairs. I follow him back outside and he walks around to the side of the building where the sidewalk widens. He sets up the chairs. When I sit down, I realize that I'm squeezed in so tightly the chair may be permanently attached. But luckily it holds my weight. I sip my beer and watch as Jimmy lights a cigarette. We sit in silence for a long time. He's not going to pry. It's not his style. So finally, I start talking. I tell him about Leroy trashing the computer and flipping the table and throwing the chair. He doesn't react to this except for his hand that has been resting on the arm of his chair becomes a fist. When I'm finished, he's quiet. He lights another cigarette and offers me one. I shake my head. I think I've finally helped Leann quit that habit. He takes a few drags, then he looks at me. His eyes are ripe with my pain.

"Does he hit you?"

"No, not really."

"Either he does or he doesn't. Sometimes you can hit someone without using your fist."

I nod and he shakes his head.

"You can stay here." He offers.

"We can't. I have to get Trevor far away from here."

"I meant for tonight."

"Thanks," I say and finally let my breath out. I feel like I have been holding it since Leroy first walked in the door.

That night, Trevor and I sleep in Jimmy's room and he sleeps on the couch. I tried to argue with him, but he dismissed me. I lay awake watching Trevor sleep for hours. What kind of life will he have? Can I really be a mother to him? I know he knows I'm not Leann. But he doesn't ask about her. Maybe when I take him away from Leroy, it won't be as bad as I think it will be. Maybe he wants to escape this life too. But what will he be escaping to? How can I provide for him? Shit, I don't even know what I want to be when I grow up. My life was never this serious. Never this important. I've never mattered so much to anyone.

I sit up and pull Jimmy's gift out of the bag. It's wrapped carefully in pink and silver paper. The kindness of his efforts makes my heart ache. I wipe away a tear and pull at the paper. Inside is a small pink and silver box decorated with tiny daffodils. When I open it, music begins to play. I recognize the tune immediately. It's Patsy Cline's "Crazy." I hold the box to my chest and let the tears come.

chapter 28

In the morning, I wake to the smell of coffee. I'm still clutching the music box and Trevor is gone. I can hear Jimmy humming in the kitchen. It's an old tune I remember my dad humming years ago.

I catch my reflection in the mirror of Jimmy's bathroom. God, I look awful. My eyes are puffy and my acne is back. I climb in the shower. The warm water feels wonderful. I lean against the wall and let it rush over me. I look down at this body that is becoming familiar. My belly is still encapsulated in rolls of flesh and my thighs have dimple upon dimple of cellulite. Even my toes seem pudgy. But I'm still me in here. I have to remember that.

I get dressed and make the bed. When I make my way to the kitchen, it's empty. I spot Jimmy sitting on his balcony, coffee cup in one hand, newspaper in the other. He's watching Trevor, who is down at the stream playing with his dam.

"Hi," I say as I open the door.

"Hey. Did you sleep alright?"

I shrug. "Coffee?"

"It's in the pot," he says and points behind me. "There are donuts on the counter, too."

I pour my coffee and forego the donuts, grabbing a banana from the basket on the table. What kind of guy has a fruit basket of real fruit? Jimmy surprises me constantly. I sit next to him on the balcony. He hands me part of the paper. We both ignore the paper and watch Trevor. He's much more interesting than the news.

"Crazy?" I ask, looking at him intently.

He shrugs. "It seemed to fit." His cheeks look red and this makes me smile.

"Thanks," is all I can say, because I don't want to cry in front of him again. We sip our coffee and the silence feels heavy. There is so much unsaid. And so much I'm afraid to hope for.

"We'll get out of your hair soon," I say.

"You don't have to," Jimmy replies.

"I'm sure you have things to do."

"A few."

He doesn't offer his plans. I know we have to go back to the apartment. We can't leave town until I get my money out of my locker, and the gym is closed until Monday. Besides, if I keep Trevor away, Leroy will come looking.

"Trevor! We gotta go!" I call down to him. He looks up and shakes his head.

"He can stay here if you've got things to do," Jimmy offers.

"I can't expect you to babysit."

"It's not babysitting. Trevor's cool. I like hanging out with him." Jimmy smiles as if it's settled.

The idea of leaving him here is tempting. It would keep him safe from Leroy. But the long-term way to keep him safe from Leroy is to do this carefully. This means not doing anything to arouse Leroy's suspicions. Still, for right now, for this morning I need to keep Trevor safe. So I leave Trevor with Jimmy, promising to be back in the afternoon. Jimmy offers to drive me, but I want to walk. I need the exercise and the time to think.

It's further than I thought from Jimmy's place to the apartment. It takes me almost two hours. My feet hurt, but I feel good. Emptied. I needed the walk. Leroy isn't home when I arrive and it doesn't look like he ever came back. I put the table back on its feet and take the computer down to the trash. I sweep up the pieces as best I can. Nothing can be done about the holes in the wall. Maybe it will be good for Leroy to see what he's done. I'm not sure he was in his right mind last night. If he has a right mind. I spend what remains of the morning sorting Trevor's clothes into piles. What we will take and what we won't. I make a list of the things I need to buy and head to the Goodwill. I won't need to do the grocery shopping for the week, so I can spend money on the things we need.

I get lucky at Goodwill and find a suitcase, a nice pair of shoes that fit me, and a couple of dresses that will do. I've gone down two sizes since the last time I tried on clothes here. After I pay for everything, I set my bags down on the sidewalk and repack the clothes and shoes in the suitcase. I still need a swimsuit for Trevor. I don't know where he's going to swim, I just know when I was a kid that was the most important thing you did when it was warm. And where we're going it will be warm. Walmart is a short bus ride away. Only one other person is waiting for the bus. It's an older lady. She stares at me. Finally she says, "Leann? Is that you?"

I try to pretend I don't hear her and look longingly up the street for the bus.

"It is! Why, you've lost a lot of weight! I hardly recognized you."

I turn and smile. What do I say? I have no idea who this woman is.

"And how is your mother these days?"

"She's fine," I say and turn to look for the bus again.

"She's such a devoted member. My husband says he can't start his sermon until he looks out and sees her in her pew." She laughs and looks expectantly at me. So she must be the pastor's wife. Great. Just what I need. Someone who'll go blabbing to Leann's mother and send her back on the war path. "But we haven't seen you in some time. Is anything wrong?"

"Nope. I just started a job on Sundays. We needed the money."

"Oh," she says and frowns. "I guess that happens. I'll pray for you. I'll pray that your schedule changes so that you can let the Lord back into your life." She seems proud of this plan, and luckily the bus pulls up right at this moment so I don't say what I'm thinking—*Keep your damn prayers.*

The greeter at Walmart offers me a smiley face sticker. I start to decline, but then thank her and stick it to the front of my

T-shirt. Put on a happy face. That was always one of my favorite camp songs.

I pick out two swimsuits for Trevor. One is red and the other has Sponge Bob on it. Then I look through the women's clothing and find several sun dresses that are generous and comfortable. In the food section, I buy some trail mix and granola bars. They will be good snacks for traveling. I select a new coloring book for Trevor and a fresh box of crayons. After I pay for everything, I put my new purchases in my suitcase. I catch the bus back to the apartment and knock on Mr. G's door.

"Leann! Are you alright? I heard all that commotion last night and then you were gone. Where's Trevor? What did that no-good jerk do?"

"We're fine. Trevor is staying with a friend. I need to leave these things here with you for now. Is that alright?"

"Of course, whatever you need. I almost called the cops last night, but I didn't want to make trouble for you."

"I'm glad you didn't. We're fine. Leroy just tore up the apartment a little."

I guess Mr. Giovanni is used to this. He sighs and shakes his head.

"Thanks Mr. G. I gotta go deal with this. I'll be back for this stuff on Monday."

"It'll be here."

I open the apartment door slowly. I don't hear anything except the shower running and then Leroy starts singing. I can't quite make out the tune until he belts out the chorus, "Roxanne!" I'd be embarrassed for him except for the fact that I have no respect left for him. I fill a glass with water, sit on the couch, and wait. I'm tempted to turn on the baseball game, knowing that's what Jimmy and Trevor are watching. But that's just inviting a fight, so I settle for a cooking show. I get so wrapped up in the process of making a crepe with a newfangled crepe maker that I don't hear the water cut off.

"Well, look who decided to show up." Leroy is standing naked in the doorway between the living room and the bedroom, combing his hair.

I say, "Hey. Where'd you go last night?" as if last night were just a regular occurrence. The best defense is a good offense.

"None of your business. I do whatever I want to do." He turns and heads into the bedroom. I consider leaving. I feel jumpy and scared. I still don't know what I'm going to tell him when he asks about Trevor. I try to focus on the cooking show again, but I can't. I drink the entire glass of water and go to get another. When I turn off the tap, Leroy is standing in the kitchen entrance.

"Where's Trevor?"

"He's at a friend's." I try to sound nonchalant, but my voice is shaking. I'm shaking.

"You know I don't like him going to other people's houses. You don't know what goes on there." I consider laughing in his face. He's safer just about anywhere but here. It's ironic that Leroy worries about what could happen at a friend's house.

"He's fine. He's been bugging me to go to his friend's for weeks. He's going to play in a stream. I think it's good for him to be out in nature."

"He could drown in a damn stream. Go get him right now."

I glare at him. He steps aside to let me leave, but doesn't say anything else.

It's a quick bus ride to Jimmy's. When I arrive, he and Trevor are parked on the couch watching the game. Trevor is wearing one of Jimmy's hats. They're eating popcorn and drinking root beer. Trevor grins when he sees me.

"We gotta go, buddy. Your daddy wants you home."

"Now? It's only the fourth inning!" whines Trevor.

"Does he really have to go now? Why don't you stay and watch the game with us?" Jimmy holds out his bag of popcorn to me. Suddenly, I realize how hungry I am. I take the bag and sit down on the chair by the sliding door.

"You can't see the game," Jimmy says. "Come sit on the couch." He scoots closer to Trevor and waves me over. I hesitate.

I take up a lot of room on a couch. If I squeeze in I'll practically be in Jimmy's lap. He's waiting and I don't want to offend him so I get up and sit gingerly on the couch. Our thighs are touching and it sends electricity through my body. I feel a little dizzy suddenly. This is silly. It's just low blood sugar, but the warm feeling working its way through my body doesn't subside, no matter how much popcorn I eat. When I finish the bag, Jimmy gets up and makes more. In his absence, Trevor scoots over near me and I pull him onto my lap.

At the seventh inning stretch I realize I'd better get Trevor home before Leroy gets any angrier. I thank Jimmy, who keeps telling me we don't have to go. I tell him I wish we could stay, because I really do wish we could stay. And not just for Trevor's sake, but for my own. I tell him I'll see him on Monday, knowing that I won't. I have a tremendous urge to touch him. I'm afraid I'll never see him again.

Jimmy is the one person who has been kind to me throughout this whole mess. He hasn't asked the questions he has every right to ask. He's taken me just as I am. And he is my friend. A real friend. Not because of the way I look on the outside. He likes who I am. And that counts for something. I don't know if I ever realized that before. I've always considered a person's appearance before anything else. I thought it was critical to being liked, admired, successful. Jimmy has helped me see that's not the case at all. Or at least it shouldn't be. And real people aren't fooled by what you look like. I know I'll miss him. He seems to see who I am despite who I am.

I can't seem to find words for what I want to say to him. I watch him say goodbye to Trevor—giving him a high five and telling him to keep the hat. I lean against the doorframe and look at him, unable to walk away. He matches my gaze but doesn't say anything either. This is the part in the romantic comedy when he should take me in his arms and kiss me. Only this isn't a romantic comedy and I'm not certain he would want to take me in his arms. I can't read his eyes. They are waiting. Finally, I say, "I appreciate everything you've done for us. You're a good person. Thank you, Jimmy."

He shrugs. "I like helping you. Besides, I didn't do much."

"No, you did more than you'll ever know and I'm grateful."

He looks up at me and searches my face. After what seems like hours, he says, "Are you going somewhere?"

I wish I could tell him. With every fiber of my being I wish I could tell him. But I can't. So I say, "Just home."

When we get back to the apartment, Leroy is lying on the couch. He's drinking beer and watching WWE.

"Hey buddy!" he calls. "Come watch some real men fight!"

Trevor runs to the couch and climbs up next to Leroy. Leroy scowls at me. "Where'd you have to go to get him? Alaska?"

"The bus was late," I say and head for the bedroom.

"Hey, woman—go get us some pizza. I'm hungry. You hungry, Trevor?"

"No, I had some popcorn at Jimmy's."

"Jimmy? That your friend's name?"

Trevor nods. "He works with Mama," he says and turns back to the TV.

I freeze and wait.

"Is that so?" says Leroy, and I hear him set down his beer. Quickly, I pick up my purse and head for the door. "Pepperoni, okay?" I call. Leroy gets to the door before me. He grabs my arm roughly and pushes me against the wall.

"Who's Jimmy?"

"He's a guy I work with."

"I got that. What was Trevor doing at his house?"

I try to think quickly. I don't want to draw Jimmy into this.

Leroy squeezes my arm tighter, and I wince.

"He's not weird or anything like you're thinking. He offered to watch him while I was running some errands. Trevor likes to play in the stream."

"So he's been there before?"

Oops. The most important detail about lying is not to provide details.

"Once."

Leroy glares at me. "I don't want you leaving Trevor with some nutcase just so you can run around on the town."

As if I would ever run around anywhere. "I wouldn't leave him with just anyone." I wrench my arm away and open the door. I don't look back.

When I come back with the pizza, Trevor is tearing out pictures from the magazines Leroy brought home. The magazines Leroy brings home are stolen from trucker lounges, so the selection isn't great. Sometimes, I find Trevor staring at the ads for X-rated movies and condoms. I'm fairly certain he doesn't understand what he's seeing, but he senses something thrilling. It's obvious in the rapturous faces of the models. I try not to fuss about it, thinking if I make a big deal about it he'll want to look even more. At least that's how I was as a kid. Once I discovered my dad's *Playboy* stash I went searching for more titillating stuff. It was a thrill even if I didn't know why.

Leroy is on the phone and looks angry. I only hear his side of the conversation, but it's enough to know things aren't going his way. He looks up as I set down a slice of pizza on the coffee table. He flings it onto the floor.

He flips his phone closed and glares at me. "Make yourself useful. Get me a damn beer. Trevor! Get over here and eat some pizza."

After about an hour, Leroy's phone rings again. Trevor and I are reading in the bedroom. We hear Leroy talking low and then I hear his phone hit the wall. His keys rattle and the door slams. He's gone.

I take a deep breath and start to read again. When we finish our chapter, Trevor asks, "Why does Daddy get so mad?"

"I don't know." Maybe if I did, I'd have some idea of what's going on here.

"Sometimes, I think . . ." Trevor begins. He rubs his eye. I can tell he's trying not to cry. I wait. He says, "Sometimes it seems like he don't like us very much."

I don't know what to say to this. He's right. Leroy doesn't seem to like us much.

"Trevor, I think your daddy is different from most people. I don't think he knows how to show his love. And sometimes I think he gets busy with his own life and he doesn't have room for us." I don't know if Trevor understands. But I need to help him see why we have to leave.

"When he gets like this, he's dangerous. We have to be careful."

He looks at me. He wipes away a tear that's making its way down his cheek. Then he whispers, "Sometimes he scares me."

"Me too," I say and pull him into a hug.

～～

leann

The whole thing with Scott didn't go so good. I got all done up—makeup, red lipstick, and a waitress outfit I ordered off the Internet with fishnet stockings and a shorty dress cut real low with a push-up bra that made it look like I got real boobs. I even bought some red high heels like them special ones Leroy bought.

I was workin' on a real good beer buzz when that damn Carin showed up. She couldn't get in the building. She was just tryin' to make me feel bad about sleeping with Scott. Jealous, I guess. I told her to fuck off, but she ruined my mood. Then I didn't know what to do when Scott showed up a few minutes later. I wasn't so sure about my plan.

He was all weirded out, but I could tell my costume turned him on. I tried all the moves I seen Victoria use on Edgar, but Scott couldn't really relax and get into it. He kept pouring vodka and drinking it like it was water.

"Hey, Scotto," I said. "Maybe we could get me outta this thing?" I was teetering on the new red heels, and the garters were really cutting in to me. If we were gonna do this, I wanted to get it over with. It was starting to feel really sleazy and I was thinking it weren't such a great idea after all. Plus, my stomach wasn't liking all the vodka.

He sat down on the couch. I sat next to him, but he didn't touch me. I swear he acted like he was someplace else.

"I think I better go," he said, but he didn't move. He just set his head on the back of the couch. I left him there staring at the ceiling and went to take a shower. I wanted to wipe off all the god-damn makeup I'd put on for the occasion. When I got out, he was gone.

I think I'm tired of pretending to be somebody I'm not. Sounds crazy from someone who is right now living in the body of someone she is not. Maybe all this craziness ain't about my wishing I was someone else. Maybe it's more about being who I am.

I don't know if Carin's gonna let me have Trevor back, but I want him back. Somehow I need to get him away from Leroy and all that meanness.

Today when I got up, I cleaned this damn place. I started reading a book on bein' a good parent. I went to the corner market with Esperanza and I bought some healthy food. I even ordered a bed just for Trevor—one with baseball players on the blanket. And then I started makin' phone calls. Funny how you can find just about anybody on the Internet. I Googled Leroy again. And then I Googled some of the places where we used to live. And I Googled some of the people he used to have "business meetings" with. And I contacted them, told them I was sorry we left in such a hurry and I gave them Leroy's cell number and his address. Somebody's bound to give Leroy his due, or at least lock him up.

chapter 29

～ ～

Leroy doesn't come home at all. I wonder if it's the last I will see of him. I'm glad, though, because I wasn't sure how he'd handle the concept of the Easter Bunny. Before I go to bed, I hide eggs filled with chocolate all over the apartment. It's hard to find good hiding places, but that's okay because Trevor won't have any competition. I was never good at finding Easter eggs when I was a kid. I hated all the hunts my mother dragged me to. The aggressive kids would push and shove and I was always too slow. I'd spot an egg, but by the time I reached it another kid had already swooped in and scooped it up. I'd be the kid with just two eggs in her basket. Other mothers would admonish their kids and force them to share some of their eggs with me. They only ever gave me the eggs with stickers inside, keeping all the candy for themselves. Mom always seemed disappointed in me. Some years she even shouted out directions to the eggs' locations. But this would only confuse me more and I'd stop, turn to wherever she was and yell, "Where?" Then she would be too embarrassed to tell me and she'd just wave me on.

The Easter Bunny never hid any eggs at our house. I don't know if my mother didn't want to get up early or if the idea of filling plastic eggs would be too hard on her nails. I asked about it once and she looked at me and said, "I think you've gotten plenty of eggs on the six egg hunts we've gone to this week. Do you really think you need another?"

On Easter morning, I would wake to my beautiful pink Easter basket that always contained one hollow chocolate bunny, one pack of sidewalk chalk, and new tights for church. I always said that if I ever had kids they'd get a solid one. The tights matched the ridiculously frilly church dress and hat my mother always bought for me. It was one of the only days we ever went to church. Otherwise, Sunday was for sleeping in. But on Easter I got up early, always hoping the Bunny would have hidden some eggs. Never happened.

After hiding the eggs, I set Trevor's baseball-themed basket filled with goodies on the table. This is a good way to leave this place. I can hardly sleep. I don't want to miss the expression on Trevor's face when he discovers the eggs. He hasn't mentioned the Easter Bunny all day. He isn't expecting anything.

When I wake, Trevor is standing beside the bed, holding a blue plastic egg. His eyes are big.

"Mama, I found this on the couch. Can I keep it?"

I laugh. "Of course you can. It must be from the Easter Bunny. Did he leave you anything else?"

"I don't know!" he shouts and runs back to the living room. I crawl out of the bed that is just as uncomfortable as it was the first night I slept in it, and pull on a sweatshirt. It's cold in the apartment, even if it is Easter. Leroy turned the heat off at the end of March. He told me I had enough fat to keep me warm. Trevor is bounding all over the apartment, shouting so loud someone below us starts thumping on the ceiling. I thump back and watch Trevor. This is happiness. I don't know if I've ever felt happy like this. It's a rich kind of happy. He sits down on the floor with his eggs and opens each one. Even though most of them have the same thing, he announces each find: "A chocolate chick!" "Jelly beans!" "More jelly beans!" "Another chocolate chick!" It's a good morning. When he's finished, he closes them all back up, loads his basket, and runs to Mr. Giovanni's apartment to show him.

Trevor and I eat breakfast with Mr. Giovanni and he recaps the game from the night before, complete with cheering and screaming about umpires. What is it about boys and baseball?

It's early and the day stretches out in front of us. I feel edgy and nervous and just wish it would be tomorrow. I'm ready to go and don't want to risk another episode with Leroy. I'm just about to suggest we go to the park when an insistent knock on the door interrupts our fun. Trevor rushes to answer, but I pull him back and open the door myself. It could be one of Leroy's people. But it's not. It's Leann's people. Her mother, to be exact. She brushes past me and then turns to look at us.

"Church starts in thirty minutes. You can't go like that!" I look down at myself. I'm wearing sweatpants and a Woody Wood-pecker T-shirt. Trevor is in his Yankees jersey and blue jeans.

"Why not?" I ask, completely sidestepping the question of whether we are even going.

"It's disrespectful," she snorts and heads to the bedroom. "Trevor, come with me." I don't really want to follow, but can't help myself. She begins digging through my neat piles of clothes and pulls out some khaki pants and a button-up shirt—the nicest outfit I had in my "take with us" pile. "Here, put these on," she says and thrusts them at Trevor. He looks to me for help, but I shrug my shoulders. Not much I can do with this.

Leann's mom turns on me next. "And you! Don't you have a decent dress you can wear? I'm sick of you showing up in church wearing those skin-tight pants. Men don't need that," she says as she begins to pick through the boxes of clothes that no longer fit.

It's hard for me to picture men being turned on, even dis-tracted, by the sight of Leann in skin-tight pants. I pick up a dress she flings on the bed. It's covered in giant red flowers. I pull it over my head and it is quite literally a tent on me. But I smile, pull off my sweatpants and say, "Okay, I'm ready." Let's get this over with. I take Trevor's hand and we follow his grandmother out of the room. We're almost to the door when she turns and scrutinizes us, finally fixating on our feet. Trevor's sneakers are covered with dried mud from yesterday. Mine aren't a whole lot better. They're worn out from all the walking I've been doing. I gave up on tying them back when it was so hard to reach my feet, so the laces are tied in hard double knots sticking out of the top holes. This makes them basically slip-ons. It does not necessarily make them very attractive.

"Shoes!" she says. So we troop back to the bedroom. Is she hoping our fairy godmother miraculously created some clean shoes appropriate for church? She finds Trevor's slippers, which look like moccasins, but I have to agree seem more appropriate for church. He puts them on and whines, "I can't wear my slippers to church!"

"I don't know what the hell happened to the good loafers I gave you for Christmas. Did you sell those too, Leann?"

I look up from where I'm pretending to be rummaging through boxes for some shoes. "How could I sell them?" I'm astounded. What mother would sell their own kid's shoes? Trevor looks at me and I realize Leann would. "I don't know where they are."

I turn back to the boxes, but I know where Leann's other shoes are. I've buried them at the bottom of the boxes. I open the box containing the pair of red pumps both Leroy and Leann have insinuated are made for one purpose. I can't put them on. I swear I cannot. Not knowing where they have been and what they have seen.

"Those will have to do," says Leann's mother, looking over my shoulder. "They look like a prostitute's shoes, but you can't wear sneakers to church. C'mon, we're going to be late." She marches out of the room, taking Trevor by the hand. He looks back at me with a pleading look. I stare at the shoes. How can I do this? But I do. I slip off my sneakers and socks and pull on the pumps. They are tight and cut my heels. I can barely balance on them. I take a few tentative steps. I will kill myself wearing these. I pick up my sneakers, tuck them in my purse, and wobble out to the car. It's not easy negotiating the stairs. This task is made even more stressful by the constant blaring of her car horn. We ride in silence to the church. Leann's mother, whose name I finally discover is Gertie (she puts on her church name tag when I get in the car), smokes nonstop. Trevor is in the backseat and I mime to him to open his window, which he does, but Gertie screams that the wind will ruin her "do."

When we arrive, the service has started. Gertie is furious when the ushers won't let us enter until a hymn. She paces back and forth and I know she's jonesing for a cigarette. I sit on a bench and slip off my shoes for a few moments. This is a mistake because my feet swell in the interim and when I pull them back on they feel like sausages stuffed into casings that are several sizes too small. We make our way down the aisle to a pew near the front, which is apparently Gertie's pew. She stands and waits while a young couple, who apparently didn't know better, scoot out and find other seats. We are almost seated when my heel snags on the carpet and I'm pitched head first on top of an elderly man who has the misfortune to share Gertie's pew. I land sprawled half on the pew and half in his lap. I slip to the floor and look up, reaching around for some way of hoisting myself up. I'm staring at his Jesus Saves belt buckle and he is leaning back in his pew with his hands held up to his armpits, looking at me in horror. I have no choice but to grip his knees as I haul myself up off of him. I try to apologize, but Gertie mutters, "Jesus Christ, Leann, you are such a damn oaf! In church, no less."

The hymn ends just as I say, "Jesus Christ, yourself. You're the one that wanted us to come!" Complete silence envelops the church. Gertie turns bright red and shoots me her nastiest look yet. Trevor giggles and I clamp a hand over his mouth. The pastor looks pointedly at us and smiles.

"Welcome to South Street Baptist Church." He launches into the announcements and finishes with a request for additional money. "I know that you all are as committed as I in our belief that we must share the gospel of Jesus Christ. I invite you to show me just how committed you are now with the gift of your tithe." The organ gets going again and several men in suits come forward holding small wicker baskets. When the man next to me passes me the basket, I quickly hand it to Trevor, who hands it to Gertie, who hands it back to Trevor and points to it as she glares at me. She expects me to put money in it? No way. But she is a stubborn woman and more people are staring, so I reach in my purse and pull out two dollars. That seems sufficient, so Gertie allows

Trevor to hand her the basket. I need those two dollars a lot more than this fancy church does.

I'm not sure I've ever been this miserable. My feet are throbbing. The pastor begins his sermon. He has just a few points to make about how bad we are and how much we need Jesus. After his ninth point, I can't take it any longer. I slip off my shoes and quietly drop my sneakers out of my purse. Putting my feet in them feels heavenly. I kick the shoes back under the pew. Maybe they'll get saved.

The pastor finishes his sermon and steps out from behind his altar. He's holding his hands up and inviting us to come and repent. Several women rush forward and throw themselves at his feet. He cups their heads with his hands and exhorts them to begin a new life. I'm mesmerized by grown adults behaving like this. I can't take my eyes off them. A line of people who wish to kneel in front of this man has formed. I'm captivated by the power he holds over them. Before I realize it, Gertie is standing and tugging at my arm. I'm bigger than she is so I pull my arm away and shake my head. She steps over Trevor, who curls up on the pew and covers his eyes. She takes a hold of my arm again and digs her long, sharp red nails in my flesh. It hurts, and I gasp. I have no choice but to allow her to lead me up front. She grimaces as I step out of the pew and she spots my sneakers. I think maybe this will get me off the hook, but it seems to motivate her even more and she shoves me in front of her.

When I reach the pastor, I realize I'm just as tall as him. He seemed much bigger from the pew. I look him in the eye. He smiles expectantly at me, like Santa might smile at a child about to climb in his lap. I have an incredible urge to cry. Not because I'm sorry for my sins or because I want Jesus to save me, but because all of this does no good. It doesn't change anything. It doesn't make Leroy a good father. It doesn't make me Trevor's real mother. It doesn't make what I have to do tomorrow any easier on Trevor. I could kneel here all day and nothing would change.

I'm still staring at the pastor and confusion begins to flicker at the edges of his eyes. Before he can graduate to real panic,

Gertie pokes me in the back with the edge of her purse and growls, "Kneel." I do. I kneel at this man's feet. I wait for something to happen. I feel his hands on my head as he prays for me to repent and follow Jesus. I begin to cry. Gertie is pleased. And I don't just cry, I sob. I sob so hard that I can't stay on my knees anymore and roll over onto my side. Now Gertie's pleasure turns to embarrassment. She whispers, "Leann, get your ass up." I watch as she smiles at the pastor and turns and looks tightly at the congregation. Then she says loudly, "Leann, honey doll, it'll be okay. You know Jesus can forgive you. Let's get you back up to your seat now." She reaches for my arm, but I snatch it away. I curl up in a ball. I just want to stay here forever. I never want to move again. I don't want to deal with Gertie or Leroy or any of this shit. But then the one thing I do want to deal with crawls up next to me and lays his head down next to mine. He looks in my eyes and says, "Mama? Are you alright?"

I smile and nod that I am.

Then he whispers, "Why are you laying here?" and I whisper back, "Because I feel like it." He smiles and looks up at Gertie. "Grandma, we're just going to stay here with Jesus, okay?" The whole congregation laughs at this and Gertie forces herself to laugh too. The pastor directs her to sit back down and then he motions to the choir to begin singing. Trevor and I listen to the choir. Their voices make the rafters rattle. The floor vibrates from the organ like a mini-masseuse. I feel like I could lay here forever. But when the pastor begins his final prayer and it seems to be unending, I motion to Trevor to follow me and we crawl out the side door unnoticed. We end up in a stairwell that leads us down some stairs and out to the back parking lot.

"We're free!" I yell, and we both run across the parking lot to the street. I don't know which way it is to a bus stop, but I know we have to keep moving. I can't take any more of Gertie. We walk as fast as we can until we reach a McDonald's. This seems like as good a place as any to hide out, so we go inside. I buy us both Happy Meals with the few dollars I have left. Trevor says he could live on French fries and I tell him he'd get scurvy. After a long discussion about scurvy, pirates, and taking your vitamins, we venture back outside. We walk a few more blocks and come to a gas station. I go inside to ask the attendant where to find the nearest bus stop.

A bell rings as I push the door open. Trevor is right behind me, already eyeing up the candy display. A grimy looking young guy with mangy black hair flowing out from under a John Deere ball cap looks up, registers my enormous red-flowered self, and looks back at the grimy piece of metal he's working at with an equally grimy toothbrush.

"Excuse me?"

"Uh-huh?" he replies without looking up.

I lean on the counter and my excess dress trails over the display of car air fresheners and caramel Cow Tails. "Can you tell me where the nearest bus stop is?" When I straighten back up, several air fresheners stick to my dress.

He watches with disgust as I pick them off, then says, "Two blocks or so."

"Two blocks or so in which direction?" I ask, simultaneously shaking my head at Trevor who is holding up a Milky Way bar for my approval like Vanna White and her letters on *Wheel of Fortune*.

"That way," he mumbles and looks back over his shoulder. I'm still not completely clear on this, so I ask again.

"Two blocks up which street?"

"Jesus Christ, what are you, stupid? Up Crocker Street," he says and cleans his toothbrush on his oil-coated jeans.

"Thanks for your help," I say through gritted teeth. I take the chocolate bars that Trevor is still clutching and fling them in the basket of air fresheners, grab Trevor's hand, and drag him out. I should be getting used to this kind of treatment, but I'm not. No one should have to.

We find the bus station and wait for our bus. We're on the bus for twenty minutes before I realize we should have gotten off already and caught a different bus, so we end up backtracking and riding three buses total before we reach home. I'm exhausted. When we reach the top of the stairs we can hear Mr. Giovanni's

TV blaring the ballgame. Trevor looks at me hopefully and I nod. He sprints for Mr. G.'s door. As I'm entering our apartment, I hear Mr. G say, "Trevor! You got here just in time. You gotta see this play."

The apartment is empty. I can tell Leroy is not coming back. The whole place seems to be breathing easier. I collapse on the couch and click on the TV. I don't know how long I sleep, but when I wake up it's almost dark. I panic for a minute when I realize Trevor isn't here. I pull myself up and change out of the awful red flower dress. Then I pad over to Mr. G's in my socks. My feet still haven't recovered.

He and Trevor are watching yet another game. They inform me it's a West Coast game. They're eating hot dogs and baked beans. Mr. G's specialty. He's good at pretty much anything you can make in a microwave. It's hard knowing that Trevor probably won't see Mr. G again. I feel guilty and sad, but excited. My stomach is in knots. We stay for the entire game. I can't bring myself to make Trevor say goodbye. This man means so much to him. He means so much to me.

chapter 30

In the morning, after Trevor leaves for school, I knock on Mr. Giovanni's door. I don't have much time, but I want to get the suitcase now so I can pack before I go to the gym. He opens the door and I guess my face is an open book, because he just turns and pulls the suitcase out of his closet.

"He's really going to miss you," I say.

Mr. Giovanni's eyes are misty. "I'm gonna miss him."

We look at each other for a minute. Then I reach out and hug him. His frame is just bones and he feels fragile. "I'm sorry," I say.

"You don't have anything to be sorry about. You have to take care of your boy. You have to get him out of here."

I nod. I'm sad for me, but more sad for Trevor. I think Mr. G might be his first real friend and now I'm going to take him away. What if I'm wrong? Or what if tomorrow I wake up and I'm no longer Leann. Where will that leave Trevor?

"Someday, I hope you'll let me know you're okay," says Mr. Giovanni quietly.

"I will. I promise. But maybe not for a while."

He nods. He understands. Then he steps back to let me out and I wave as I leave. In the apartment, I pack up all of Trevor's things that Gertie scattered in her mad rush to find church clothes. I even pack his church outfit that is covered with baked bean stains and ketchup. It's the only nice thing he has. I'll wash it somewhere.

I'm jittery all morning at the Kiddie Korner. I need to keep moving, keep busy, so I start cleaning toys. I spray them with the disinfectant spray that is probably much worse for the children than the germs it's killing. I line up all the blocks by size and sort the Legos. Finally, it's time for me to go. I get my final paycheck from Denise and feel like I'm walking across a stage as I make my way down the hallway to the locker room. I look at other employees and smile, knowing that I have this big secret. My heart is practically thumping out of my chest. When I get to my locker, I have to sit down on the bench for a minute. I take a deep breath. Just for chuckles, I decide to weigh myself one last time. It takes me a minute to find the scale. The whole locker room has been rearranged and repainted. I look around and notice the spotless carpet, the shining lockers, even the mirrors are clear. I look back at the scale and reconfigure the weights. Seems crazy, but I've lost another six pounds! I've been so preoccupied with my plan that food hasn't had such a grip on me. Until I was Leann, I never knew it could be so distracting. It's weird to think about food so much. It all comes down to survival. Leann's body was trying to tell me how it survives, but then I realized our survival depended on me getting us out of here. So surviving Leroy trumped surviving food.

My locker is now pink. It used to be blue. For a moment, I consider how difficult it would be to paint all the vents and avoid the latches, but then panic strikes. I fumble with the lock. It takes me several tries to open the locker. My things are in a pile at the bottom of the locker. The fresh paint was not just on the outside. They must have opened all the lockers to paint inside. My dinner that should have been here molding is gone. I dig through the clothes trying to find the plastic Ziploc baggie in my extra shoes. No bag. I pull everything out and dump it on the bench behind me.

"No!" I yell. "This cannot be happening!" But it is. It's gone.

An hour later, Bruce is telling me that every effort will be made to recover my money.

"But I don't understand why you had that much cash in your locker, Leann. Doesn't seem smart. Why wasn't it in a bank?"

I look up at him and I have no words. In my head I'm screaming, *Because, you moron, I don't exist. How can I open a bank account?*

I don't have a phone! I'm not even certain of my social security number. I'm just making this up as I go along! Because I'm the moron and I didn't think. But I just shake my head.

I walk to Shop N Save and punch in. Jimmy is nowhere to be found. I shouldn't be here. I was supposed to leave. What do I do now? I make so many mistakes on register, Vernon tells me to go straighten shelves. We aren't busy. Nobody shops on Monday nights. I'm aimlessly lining up the tuna cans when Jimmy appears. He seems surprised to see me.

"Hey!" he says and stops with the pallet he is dragging.

I look at him and I want to cry. "Hey," I say back.

"I didn't expect to see you here," he says.

"Why wouldn't I be here? I don't have any place else to go," I say.

"I don't know. Just got the feeling you might be moving on."

I look at him, taking in his cheerful face, his crooked ball cap, his black socks and white sneakers, his kindness. I want to tell him everything. I want to cry on his broad shoulders. I want him to fix all this the way he fixes old jukeboxes, but I don't say anything and turn back to the tuna.

"Well, I'm glad you're still here," he says and drags his pallet up the aisle away from me.

I stay in my own fog for most of my shift. Several times, customers have to repeat their questions. They sound like they're under water and I struggle to truly care whether they actually had requested paper, not plastic bags, because in the scheme of things who really gives a shit? The me that used to be concerned about whether the earth would be here for the next generation is gone. I'm not sure this new me has time to care about the plethora of plastic that is suffocating our planet. I'm just so tired. This morning, I felt like my life was about to begin, and now I just want to go to sleep and never get up.

Sooner or later, I know my perennially positive outlook will return. But it may take some time. I've always liked to have something to look forward to, whether it's a vacation, a new recipe, a change of routine, even a good book. Now I have nothing to look forward to. Just another couple months of trying to save enough money to escape this hell. Another couple months of trying not to make Leroy too angry, of keeping Trevor safe, of helping this body drop the wet suit of fat it's wearing, and of staying marginally sane.

When it's time for my break, I'm not hungry, which is good because I spent the grocery money for the week and didn't pack dinner since I wasn't supposed to be here. I ask one of the deli ladies for a cigarette and then bang on the soda machine until a Diet Coke pops out, like I've seen Franklin do. I'm taking my first drag when Jimmy appears. He's carrying his metal lunch box and two crates. He looks at me carefully and then sets down a crate for me to sit on. I watch him settle on his crate and pop open his lunch pail. He has a sandwich as usual, and I can see a bag of Fritos and an apple tucked in underneath it. He's pretty predictable. I'd get tired of eating the same thing for dinner every night.

I flick my cigarette ash and then sit down on the crate. I turn to Jimmy, who is still watching me, and ask, "How can you eat the same thing night after night after goddamn night?"

Jimmy raises his eyebrows in mock hurt and then spits his mouthful out in a fit of laughter. When he finally recovers, he says, "What's up your ass?"

"Nothing." I take a drag of my cigarette and then blow it out forcefully and say, "Everything."

"Hmm," says Jimmy as he chews on his sandwich. "Can I help you with that?"

I want to cry, but I don't think I have tears for this. It's all so stupid and crazy and wrong. As much as I think Jimmy is the one person I could trust with this, I know I can't tell him. So I shake my head and drink my soda. We sit silently for another fifteen minutes and then I get up and go inside. I don't even say goodbye. I already did that.

When I get to the apartment, Mr. G is there. I'd forgotten Jillian is on spring break until tomorrow. He doesn't ask, just gives my arm a squeeze and makes his way back to his apartment.

chapter 31

In the morning, after Trevor leaves, I unpack my suitcase and take it back over to Mr. Giovanni's.

"Didn't work out like I planned," I say to his curious look.

At the gym, Bruce pulls me aside and hands me fifty bucks. He feels awful about what happened and knows I need every penny I can get. I don't want to take it, but I'm past the point of embarrassment anyway. I thank him and he waves me off. I'm in a foul mood and grumble at the kids in the Kiddie Korner. Denise must have heard about my money because she's incredibly patient and, instead of reprimanding me for growling at the children, she assigns me to the baby room. Rocking the babies calms me some. I don't know how I can continue this life, but if we leave with no money, Trevor and I will end up in a shelter somewhere.

I wasn't going to work out today; I'm tired from not eating. But when I leave the Kiddie Korner, Scott is standing right outside waiting.

"Hey, I thought we could bike together," he says, smiling and looking everywhere but directly at me. He's freaked out by this. He wants to still like me even at size 18, but it goes against his nature.

"I'm kind of tired," I say.

"C'mon, you'll get over it." He turns to lead me to the bikes. I'm glad he does because exercise is what I need. I crank the resistance up on the bike until I'm panting and sweating and can't talk, which is okay because Scott is doing all the talking. I want to

ask him what happened the day he went to see Leann and I followed him, but I'm afraid. I don't need to because he volunteers.

"Remember that day you came to your apartment and I
showed up to see you, I mean, the you I thought was you?"

I nod and keep panting and pedaling.

"I didn't believe you, you know. I thought you were a nutjob.
But you knew so much; it was weird. When I got inside, Carin,
I mean Leann, was wasted. She could barely walk. I was really
confused. I wanted her, I did. I mean she's all I had been thinking
about for months. I missed her, I mean you, so badly. We were
friends, you know?" He stops pedaling and turns to me. "I guess
I wanted us to be more, but bottom line was you were my best
friend and I was, I am, incredibly lonely. I had a couple drinks
and watched her smoke. She smokes, you know? She wanted me
to make love to her."

I raise my eyebrows, but don't say anything.

He looks sheepish. "I couldn't do it." He looks around.
There's hardly anyone in the gym; it's such a beautiful day. "I
knew she wasn't you." Here he pauses and shakes his head. "But
that isn't possible. It's crazy."

I say nothing. Scott takes a breath and keeps talking. "Being
with her is nothing like being with you. I think I knew all along
that she wasn't you, but I didn't want to believe it. It couldn't be
happening. I started to think *I* was nuts."

"After I left, I started thinking about what she'd said and how
she'd acted and then about you and the day you showed up at my
apartment and you knew all those things about me." He looks at
me with fresh tears in his eyes. "I knew you were actually Carin,
not her. And I had to see you."

"But it's weird, isn't it?" I venture. "You want to like me like
you used to like me, but I'm in this strange, fat body." He just
looks at me for a while and then almost imperceptibly, he nods.

We pedal along together for a few more minutes, but I'm
spent and I need to get away from him. Not one soul in this world
knows who I am and loves me anyway.

I take a long shower and get on the scale to confirm that I really have lost more weight. Much of yesterday is hard to believe. I stop in the juice bar and have a protein shake. I feel jittery and figure it's got something to do with the fact that I haven't eaten anything in twenty-four hours. Julia, the manager of the juice bar, is tight with Bruce and heard my sad story, so she won't let me pay. I thank her and, feeling much better, decide to save the bus fare and walk to the store.

I'm about to clock in when Franklin rounds the corner.

"Leann, I've been thinkin'."

"Good for you," I say. I'm in no mood for his shit. I push him aside and walk forcefully out the door. It's good that we're busy today. Big 10 for $10 sale. It's a relief to have no time to think.

I can't get away from Scott. Early in the evening, he shows up to do his grocery shopping, but I know he's here to see me. He waits patiently in my line with his box of cereal and can of coffee. When he's my last customer, I turn off my light. It's about time for my break anyway. I really don't want anyone overhearing our conversation.

"Hey," I say when he places his things on the conveyor belt.

"What time are you finished here? Could we maybe go somewhere and talk?"

"Nope. I have to get home. I've got a kid, remember? The babysitter can't stay late," I lie, knowing Jillian has no curfew. No one cares where she is.

"Oh," he says, disappointed. "Maybe tomorrow? I could buy you lunch?"

Jimmy appears next to me. It's rare to see him in the front of the store. Two appearances in one month must be a record for him. He leans into my register space, ignores Scott like he's any other customer and says, "Hey, you want to go get a frozen yogurt? It's hot as hell out back."

"Okay," I sputter. "I have to go clock out."

"I already clocked you out," he says and waits for me to finish with Scott.

Scott doesn't say anything. When I hand him his change and groceries, he actually looks hurt.

"I'll see you tomorrow at the gym," I offer.

Jimmy and I walk to the ice cream shop. I've never liked frozen yogurt, but as we walk he explains why frozen yogurt is better for you than ice cream.

"It's got all the good bacteria," he concludes.

"So you're telling me I should eat it because it's got bacteria?" I ask, smiling a real smile for the first time in what feels like ages.

"*Good* bacteria," he says again, with emphasis.

"Where'd you learn all this?"

"It was on *Good Morning America*."

"You watch *Good Morning America*?" I ask, starting to laugh.

"That's not funny. They have real news." When I don't stop laughing, he says, "I watch it while I work on the jukes."

"At least you're informed. I never watch the news."

"Why not?"

"Don't have time."

"How can you not have time to watch thirty minutes of news?"

"As soon as Trevor leaves, I go to work at the gym, and then I go directly to the store, and by the time I get home it's too late."

"You could watch the late news."

"I'd really rather sleep than be informed. Besides, that's what I have you for, right?" I smack him on the arm playfully.

"Yup. You got me, what else could you need?"

chapter 32

~ ~

On Wednesday morning, Trevor has a fever. I'm frantic. Should I find a doctor? I'm overcome with the realization that I'm not really a mom and I don't know what to do. I pace the apartment, trying to calm down and think. I'm afraid to leave him here alone to go get medicine. What if it's something horrible like appendicitis or cancer? I bang on Mr. Giovanni's door. He doesn't answer, and I'm about to break down in tears when he appears behind me holding his morning paper.

"Leann, what's the matter?" he asks.

"Oh God! Trevor's sick and I don't know what to do. I don't have any medicine and I don't know any kid doctors. And I don't know what the hell I'm doing."

"Calm down. Kids get sick. What's the matter?"

"He's really hot and he says his tummy and head hurt."

"Sounds like a bug to me. Not much you can do about that."

He seems so calm I want to smack him.

"What do you mean, there's not much I can do?"

He looks at me like I've got two heads. "Hasn't he ever had a virus before?"

"I don't know!" I practically shout. He looks at me again, leaning towards me and looking in my eyes. He must think I'm on drugs. He shakes his head and gets out the key to his apartment.

"Give me ten minutes, I'll be over."

I rush back to my apartment and find that Trevor has fallen asleep. I'm supposed to be at work in thirty minutes. I can't lose this job. By the time Mr. Giovanni appears in our doorway I've worked myself up into a state again.

"I don't know what to do. I've got to get to work, but he's so hot. He's sleeping now. Do you think it's okay to let him sleep?"

"Let him sleep. Best thing for him. You go on to work. I'll take care of him."

This stops me in my tracks. "Really?" I practically screech.

"Really," he says, and he sits down at the table and opens his paper.

"But what if he needs a doctor?"

"I doubt he needs a doctor, but if he does I'll take him."

"Really?" I say again. I'm amazed at how calm he is.

"You better get going."

I'm still in my pajamas. I race to the bedroom and find some clothes as quietly as I can. Changing in our tiny bathroom is a bit of a challenge. I lose my balance pulling on my stretch pants and end up sitting in the bathtub, which is thankfully dry since I've spent the morning freaking out about Trevor instead of taking my shower. I thank Mr. G profusely and look in on Trevor one last time. He's still asleep, and I have to put my hand on his chest to be sure he's alive. He's incredibly hot.

"He seems even hotter," I inform Mr. Giovanni.

"When he wakes up, I'll put on some onions," he says without looking up from his sports section.

"Onions?" I ask incredulously. He waves at me to leave. I want to stay. I hope I'm doing the right thing, but I don't have time to be sure. I have to trust Mr. Giovanni. So I thank him again and hurry to the gym.

The time at the Kiddie Korner crawls by. I've told everyone who'll listen about Trevor. One older woman who works in here part-time told me she's used onions to bring down a fever too. "Smells god-awful, but it works," she says. I feel better, but the moment my shift is done I catch a bus back to the apartment.

When I walk in, Trevor and Mr. Giovanni are watching a soap opera. Mr. G is filling Trevor in on the story he apparently

280 i'm not her

follows on a regular basis. Trevor is sipping soup and the whole apartment smells like onions.

"Everything alright?" I ask cautiously. They both look up and Trevor says, "Shhhh!"

I make myself lunch and join them on the couch. Mr. G has been watching the same soaps for over fifteen years. On my way to work at the Shop N Save, I picture my life as a soap opera. It would be a good one. Franklin and Leroy would be the bad guys and Scott would be the guy who never wins. Mr. Giovanni would be the wise patriarch. Who would Jimmy be in my soap opera? The hero that gets the girl?

I'm feeling much better about Trevor until Phyllis tells me that fevers usually spike at night. This gets me frantic again. Jillian won't know what to do. Jillian probably won't even notice that Trevor is sick. I know that I've got to get home so I close my register and knock on Vernon's door.

"Come in," he says. He doesn't look up when I enter.

"Mr. Slick, my son is sick."

He looks up. "Oh, Leann, sorry to hear that." He looks at me expectantly.

"I need to go home to take care of him."

"Is that necessary? Can't his father take care of him?"

"No, his father can't," I say, even though I really want to say, *His father is a drugged-out asshole.*

"Oh," he says and begins striking the eraser of his pencil on his chin as if he's in deep thought.

"I need to go home immediately. We're not very busy. I'm sorry to leave you in a lurch." At this, he puts down his pen.

"You can't leave in the middle of a shift. That would be irresponsible."

"No, it would be irresponsible not to take care of my sick child," I say and glare at him. He thinks about this. "Well, don't expect to get paid for this time," he says, dismissing me with a wave and turning back to his desk.

I don't have time to tell Jimmy why I'm leaving. I head for the bus station. I'm feeling panicked at this point. I actually run, with all my loose parts jiggling about, from the bus stop to the apartment, but after the first flight of stairs, I have to slow down because I can't breathe. I'm sweaty and panting when I open the door. The apartment is empty. Now I'm sure I'm going to have a heart attack. I start yelling for Trevor. I'm frantic. Is he at the hospital? I left the phone number for the Shop N Save for Mr. Giovanni when I left, but they were so enmeshed in their soap opera maybe he didn't notice. I decide to go to the hospital, but before I get halfway down the stairs, I hear Mr. G call, "Leann! He's in here!" I fumble back up the stairs and follow Mr. G to his apartment. Trevor is happily sitting on the floor playing cards and sucking on a Popsicle. He smiles when he sees me. I burst into tears.

After I've calmed down, Mr. G explains that he decided to bring Trevor to his place so he could cook him dinner. His temperature has come down (thanks to the onions?) and he is feeling better. Before I can ask about Jillian, Mr. G says he left her a note and twenty dollars saying she wasn't needed tonight. I can't imagine what Jillian made of that, but hopefully she was happy for the money and the free time.

I take Trevor home and put him in bed. No sleeping bag on the floor tonight. I lay next to him, reading to him from a storybook his teacher gave us. Soon, he is sleeping. I turn off the light and lay down next to him. I put my hand on his back. I need to know that he is okay. I'm exhausted from worry. I've never in my life been so completely consumed by another person's welfare. And I've never felt so completely inept and over my head. Who do I think I am that I can be his mother? I'm an imposter. Looking the part doesn't make me real.

chapter 33

I'm reluctant to send Trevor to school today, but he insists he feels fine. Mr. Giovanni arrived first thing with a fresh bag of onions, but thankfully they weren't needed. We both watch as Trevor practically skips down the hall.

"Kids are so resilient," Mr. G says and smiles.

"I don't know how to thank you," I tell him. "You truly saved me yesterday. I don't know what I would have done without you."

He smiles and pats his bag of onions. "I was happy to be useful."

When I arrive at the gym, Bruce pulls me into the owner's office.

"Good news, Leann! We found your money!"

"Really?" I'm dumbstruck. Bruce hands me the Ziploc bag filled with my money. I stare at it. Then I turn to Bruce and hug him.

"The supervisor found one of the temps counting it after his shift here. He didn't know it wasn't his. The guy gave him some song and dance about it being his babysitting money, but lucky for you the supervisor didn't believe him. He called yesterday, but you had already left and we don't have a phone number for you." He's smiling but leaning away from me, maybe afraid I might hug him again.

"Thank you, Bruce! You don't know how happy this makes me!"

"Well, I can understand. Just don't leave cash in your locker anymore, okay?"

"I won't," I say and stuff it in my pocket. My mind is spinning with plans. We can leave tomorrow!

At the Shop N Save, even Franklin can't spoil my mood with his obscene noises and gestures each time he walks by my register. Every so often, I touch the bag in my pocket just to be sure it's still there. I counted it at the gym, $686 dollars, minus the fifty I insisted Bruce take back. In my other pocket is the bus schedule I picked up on my way to the Shop N Save. On break, I'm too excited to eat, so I pull out the schedule and read it.

"Where ya going?" asks Jimmy as he slides his crate next to mine.

I look at him and smile. "I don't know."

"Huh," is all he says as he opens his dinner.

"Have you ever been to Columbus?" I ask.

"Nope," he says with his mouth full.

"How about Chicago?"

He swallows and looks at me. "Why would you want to go to Chicago? It's crowded as hell."

"That's presuming that hell is crowded," I retort.

He laughs. "I'm fairly certain hell is crowded."

"When you leaving?" he asks. He seems nervous. I know he likes me and Trevor, but I can't imagine he won't get over us.

"Soon," is all I can say.

He continues to eat and when I get up to leave, he asks, "Why?"

"Why what?" I ask and sit back down.

"Why would you leave?" He looks away, and then continues, "I mean, I know you gotta get out of that apartment and all, but you don't have to move away, do you?"

I sigh. I'm not sure how to answer that. I suppose if anyone deserves some explanation, it's Jimmy.

"It's no good here for Trevor. We need a clean start. Somewhere I can be me and where Trevor is safe."

"Why can't you be you here?"

"Because I'm not me."

"Sure you are."

"No, Jimmy, I'm not."

We sit quietly. I'm getting used to his silences. I might even miss them. I'm the kind of person that always has to fill up the quiet, but these last few months have taught me that sometimes it's better to keep your mouth shut. You can learn a lot more.

When I get home, Jillian questions me.

"Where the hell did you take Trevor last night?" she asks.

"None of your business," I say and walk past her. For once, she doesn't race out.

"You coulda at least let me know before I hauled my ass all the way over here."

"I'm sorry; I don't have a phone number for you. Oh, and I forgot, I don't have a phone," I say in the sweetest voice I can muster. I smile at her and wait.

"Well, I left Leroy a message. Told him I thought you might'a run off with his kid."

My heart stops. "What did he say?" I ask, trying to act like I'm not completely freaked out by this information.

"Nothin' yet. He ain't called back."

"Do you know where he is?"

She sits down at the table and starts playing with her iPod.

"He don't tell me where he goes. I think he's in South Carolina. Said he had a new run to make."

"He's not hauling flower foam," I say.

"Don't act surprised. You know what he's into. He's working on something."

"What?"

"You're his wife! Why don't you ask him? It ain't my fault if he don't tell you."

I try a new tack. "Jillian, I would truly appreciate it if you could tell me what Leroy is working on."

She looks up at me, skeptical. Then she lets out a long breath. "Shit, Leann, he's trying to put together some serious money. He owes his bookie, plus he's got to split town before that court date. You know they'll lock his ass away for transporting drugs across state lines. He told the lawyer he didn't know it was in the truck, but that don't matter 'cause someone's gotta pay. It sure as hell ain't gonna be his boss. They'd lock him up now if they knew he was still makin' runs. He's supposed to be stayin' in town according to his bail agreement. His boss knows that, but he's still drivin', ain't he? So you see how much shit he gives about Leroy."

I'm dumbstruck. "How much money does he owe?"

"I don't know. It's a lot. But so far, his bookie don't know where he's at. He placed the bet over the phone and used one of your old addresses."

"What would happen if his bookie found him?"

"Before he comes up with the money?"

I hesitate. This feels like a made-for-TV movie. "Yeah, what would he do to him?"

"You don't skip out on your bookie. Leroy knows that. He's tryin' to pay him back double. That's why he's been doing all these extra runs."

"But what would happen?"

"How would I know? Leroy thinks they might kill him."

I guess Leann would have known this. I knew he wasn't a legitimate trucker, but I didn't know where the money was going.

"If Leroy makes drug runs, why are we living in this dump?" I ask.

Jillian looks at me again, trying to gauge my intentions.

"It's not like he really lives here. You live here. Besides, Leroy's got plans. He's savin' his money. He says he's gonna move to the Islands. Take me and Trevor." She watches me for a reaction. Maybe she thinks I'll be jealous. "But don't think just 'cause you're losin' all that weight and tryin' to win him back, it's gonna work. He's just waitin' for me to be eighteen."

"He didn't wait for me to be eighteen," I say.

"That's 'cause you got knocked up. He wouldn't be with you at all if it weren't for Trevor."

"I guess that's true," I say calmly. Jillian has filled in so many blanks for me and even though she's still a nasty, mean, ridiculous teenager, I suddenly feel grateful to her.

"I gotta split," she says and gets up from the table. "I'll tell Leroy everything's okay if he calls."

"Thanks," I say and I mean it. I watch her leave. Of course, everything is not okay. That much I know.

chapter 34

It's still dark when I hear someone pounding on the door. I look at the clock; it says 3:30 a.m. Even Gertie doesn't show up this early. Leroy would have a key. Who could possibly be banging on my door like this at 3:30 in the morning? Trevor doesn't wake, so I crawl over him and pull on my robe. The banging doesn't cease. I'm almost to the door when it smashes open and two men barge in. It happens so fast, I can't react. The first one in the door, a tall man with dark curly hair, hits me across the face with such force that I fall against the table. Then another man, fat and sweaty with a scar around his neck like someone tried to hang him, grabs me by the arm and shoves me against the wall. He twists my arm behind me and turns me around to face the tall man.

The only light comes from the outside hallway and it is gone as soon as the first man slams the door. I hear a noise in the bedroom and I know that Trevor is awake. I try to send him mental messages, begging him to hide.

"Where's Leroy?"

"What?" I stammer.

"C'mon ya fat whore, you know!" the man yells and thumps me against the wall for good measure.

"I don't know!" My eyes are blurry from tears and my cheek is throbbing. The tall man comes over and smacks me across the face again, but not as hard this time. I feel like I'm in a movie, a really bad movie.

"Look, bitch, Leroy owes me. You're gonna tell us where he is, even if I have to mess you up."

I'm stunned. The man who has me by the arms reeks of liquor and the crazy one screaming at me has eyes so red they practically glow in the dark. I have no idea why they want Leroy. Or why they think he'd be here. I look at my baggie of cash still on the counter where I left it. The tall man follows my stare and snatches it up. I watch as he counts it on the table. "This ain't shit." He stuffs it in his pocket and walks over to me, leaning close to my face. His breath smells like an ashtray filled with rotten vegetables. I fight the impulse to gag.

"I don't know where Leroy is! He doesn't tell me where he goes!"

The tall man looks right through me and says calmly, "Oh, you know where he is, it's just a matter of us asking the right way." He fingers my face and looks down at my chest.

My mind races. I need to get to Trevor. My cheek is swelling and I taste blood in my mouth.

"I really don't know," I squeak, at the same time there is a noise in the bedroom.

"Sounds like we got company."

I watch, helpless, as he goes in the bedroom. "Trevor!" I scream.

The tall man comes out, shoving Trevor in front of him. Trevor races to me. I want with all my heart to pick him up, but my arms are pinned behind me.

The tall man walks calmly over and reaches for Trevor's hand, "You better start talking or I'm gonna start taking off fingers."

A shiver goes through me, but something else fills me too. I will not let them hurt this boy. They will have to kill me first. I wrench one arm free and smack the man's hand away. I stretch my hand down to Trevor's shoulder and pull him to me.

"You ain't in charge here, bitch. You need to start talking."

I have to do something, say something. I try to think of something to tell them that will make them leave, but my mind is frozen with fear.

"Please, I don't know where he is. I don't. He doesn't tell us."

The tall man yanks Trevor away from me. He shoves him across the dining room table and pulls out a knife. Trevor's eyes are huge, but he is silent. He looks to me. He expects me to do something, but for the life of me I don't know what.

"Trevor," I say, "Do you know where Daddy is?" Maybe he knows.

He shakes his head quickly and then closes his eyes. I don't know what to do. How can I convince these men that I don't know anything? Then it dawns on me! Maybe Leann knows where Leroy is.

"Do you have a cell phone?" I ask the fat guy since he seems like the nicer man. His eyes looked almost as scared as Trevor's when the tall man threatened to dismember Trevor. He looks to his accomplice, who is calling the shots, then says, "Why?"

"I think I know someone who might know where he is." He hands me his phone and lets go of me. I walk to the couch and sit down. It takes two tries to dial my number because my hands are shaking. I pray that Leann will answer. She does.

"It's me," I say.

"What the hell do you want? Do you know what time it is?"

Panic threatens to engulf me so I focus on Trevor. He is sitting at the table now with his hands shoved in his armpits, holding his fingers close so they won't be cut off.

"Leann, there are two men here who say if they can't find Leroy, they're going to hurt Trevor."

"Hurt Trevor? That's shit. You're just playin' with me."

"No, I'm not. Here, listen," I say and hold the phone out to the fat guy since he's closest. "Ask her," I say. The tall guy is standing near the kitchen, his eyes on Trevor.

"Who is that? You didn't call the police did you?" he asks. Why didn't I think of that? These guys must be as dumb as Leroy.

"It's someone who might know where he is," I say.

The fat man grabs the phone, "Where's he at?" I can't hear Leann's response. I reach for Trevor and pull him close. Leann must be telling the fat guy something because he looks from me to Trevor and back again.

"She says she'll tell us, but she wants to talk to the kid first." The man with the awful breath nods and the fat guy takes the phone to Trevor, who stands up slowly like an old person and reaches for the phone. I pull him away from the awful men and we sit on the couch together.

"Hi," he says.

"I know," he says and looks at me with tears in his eyes. "It's okay." He listens a little longer and then says, "I will." Then he holds the phone out towards me. The tall guy tries to grab it, but Trevor is quicker and pulls the phone to him.

"She wants to talk to her," he says. All I hear is the word *her*. He doesn't call me Mama. It's like a knife cutting through this whole charade. I take the phone, my eyes never leaving his.

"What?" I ask Leann.

"Don't let them hurt him."

"I won't."

"I don't know where Leroy's at, but I know what they're looking for. I'll be there as quick as I can. Tell them to sit tight."

When I hang up the phone, the men are angry that they have to wait. The fat one keeps looking at his watch and shaking his head.

"I don't like this. She could be calling the cops!"

I don't know what Leann is up to, but I'm hoping she's calling the police.

"This ain't good," says the tall guy. "I think we should wait outside. I ain't gonna stay here like no sitting duck." He turns to me. "You call the cops and I'll be back for the little guy!"

I nod. I'm shaking and holding onto Trevor tight. They turn to go, but there are footsteps in the hall. Leann couldn't possibly have gotten here already. Both men jump up, and the fat one wrenches Trevor away from me and holds him under the armpit with a knife aimed at him.

The footsteps reach the doorway and Leroy appears.

"Leroy!" I gasp.

The tall one pulls out a gun and aims it at Leroy.

"What the hell you doin' here? I told you this bitch don't know nothing."

Leroy steps in but holds his hands up, keeping his eyes on the tall guy.

"I told you I'd get you what you're looking for. You just gotta be patient."

"We're done being patient, Leroy. I need the money now."

Leroy looks at me. "Alright, Leann, get the man what he wants."

I stare at him. I have no idea what he's talking about. I'm still trying to formulate my answer when I hear footsteps on the stairs. Leann appears in the open doorway.

"Who the hell is this?" yells the tall one.

"It's me," she says.

Leroy looks confused. Trevor breaks away from the fat guy and runs to Leann. The tall one doesn't know who to aim the gun at, so he waves it around frantically.

"What is this, a fucking family reunion? Get me the money, Leroy!"

"Go on, Leann," he says nodding at me. Trevor clings to Leann, who is crying.

"I'm not her," I say quietly.

"What the hell are you talkin' about?" He walks towards me.

"I'm not her, I'm not Leann," I say again.

The tall guy has had enough of his heist gone wrong and strides towards me. He grabs my arm and shoves me towards the bedroom. "You heard your ole man, go on and get it!" I'm frozen. So he shoves me harder, and as I stumble forward I trip over the computer cords for Trevor's game system that are still lying on the floor where the computer used to be and I crash forward. I see the corner of the table coming towards my head, and then everything goes black.

~ ~

leann

The phone ringing in the middle of the night is never a good thing.

"What?" I yell.

"It's me," she says. Damn her, always callin' me. I want out of this situation as bad as she does but I ain't buggin' her about it in the middle of the night. First I got to get Leroy out of the picture. Why can't she be patient?

She tells me that there are two guys there looking for Leroy and they're gonna hurt Trevor if she don't tell 'em where he is. Oh Christ, is this my fault? I only gave up his cell phone. I'm the one gave up his cell phone and address.

"You're just playin' with me," I tell her, but she hands the phone to some guy who wants to know where Leroy's at. He owes them money. I'm sure he does. He owes everyone something. I have no idea where he is, but I know where he keeps his money at. He keeps all kinds of stuff there too. Stuff he's waiting to fence and stuff he's going to cash in when the time is right. It's in a special locker in the nice part of town. The key is hidden in the apartment. Leroy's always been paranoid about someone breaking in and takin' it. He made a special compartment for it in a pair of shoes he gave me. Like a real James Bond. Whenever I put on them shoes he got all excited, but I wasn't allowed to wear them out of the house.

I tell the guy I'll be there and I can take them to the money, but I need to talk to Trevor first. I don't give a shit about Leroy and his stash, but I want my boy back. They can't have him.

Trevor gets on the phone and it's like the sun coming out. I start cryin' and I tell him how much I love him and that I'll be there in a few minutes and then everything will be okay. Ain't no one gonna hurt him once I get there.

Then I tell him to let me talk to Carin again. I tell her I know what they're looking for and I'll be there quick as I can. I tell her she better not let them hurt Trevor. She promises she won't and I can tell she means it.

I find the keys to the car and grab a jacket. I still ain't driven the thing, but I know which one it is because every other car in the lot has moved. Hers is covered in dust and bird shit. It starts right up. I knock into the car next to me backing out, but other than that I make it to the apartment in one piece.

When I open the door to the apartment, the first thing I see is Leroy's back. I don't know what he's doin' here. He has no idea who I am, but Trevor does. He runs to me. Leroy is screamin' at Carin to get the key and she's staring at him like she don't know what he's talking about, 'cause she don't know what he's talkin' about. One of the other men grabs at her and shoves her toward the bedroom where Leroy is pointing, but she trips over Trevor's computer cables that are in a tangle on the floor, even though I don't see his computer nowhere. Carin falls towards the coffee table and hits it smack on the corner with her head. There is a big flash of light and my head hurts as if I'm the one who clocked the table. And then everything goes dark.

chapter 35

When I wake up, I'm clutching Trevor. Leann is lying in a pool of blood on the floor. Only she's really Leann. I'm not her. Everyone just stares at her and she doesn't move. I let go of Trevor, grab a towel from the kitchen, and run to her. She's not dead, but she isn't conscious either.

"Call 911!" I yell.

"Like hell," says the tall one. "This don't change nothing, Leroy!" But it obviously does, because he's looking around frantically and hysteria is hovering moments away. Leroy seems to be struck dumb by all that's happening. It's as if his brain is trying to connect the dots, but the dots are just too far apart for him to grasp. Finally, he walks towards the bedroom with the tall guy following him, gun in hand.

Through the open doorway, I can see movement on the stairs. I see a badge flash and in moments they're all over the apartment. The first policeman in the door yells at the tall guy to put the gun down, and defying all odds, he does. Three more race into the apartment and tackle Leroy and the other man as they come out of the bedroom. Another officer rushes over to Leann and radios for help. Mr. Giovanni sheepishly stands in the hallway. I get up and go to him.

"Hey, is Leann going to be alright?" he asks.

"I think so," I tell him. "You called the police, didn't you?"

"The door was standing open, and I heard what was going on. I didn't want anything to happen to Trevor or Leann."

"Thank you," I say and shake his hand. He looks at me and there is a glimmer of recognition in his eyes, but then Trevor spots him and rushes him. They hug and Trevor says, "My momma's back." And with that we all see Leann sit up, holding her head.

Later at the police station, after we've both given our statements, Leann tells me that Leroy wanted me to get the red shoes. Apparently he keeps a key in the hollowed-out heel of one of the shoes. Maybe that's why they felt so rickety. The key is to a storage unit where Leroy keeps the money and stolen goods he's been gathering. I don't say anything about where the shoes are, that way Leann honestly doesn't know what happened to them. There's no way the police can connect her to the money or the stolen property, at least for now. When Leroy mutters something about the shoes, everyone assumes he's high on something. It sounds like he and his two buddies have a long series of court appearances ahead. I'm just glad that Trevor and Leann are safe. They don't let go of each other. Every now and then I see Trevor watching me.

A social worker comes to interview Trevor. While we wait, Leann and I go to the ladies' room to try to clean up her head.

"Your face is pretty busted up," I say. She reaches up and touches her face. I look in the mirror at her reflection. A huge bruise is blooming purple on her cheek and the eye above it is swelling.

"I thought someday, Leroy and Trevor and me, we'd be good together. I didn't think no one else would want me and maybe when we took that money and moved away together things would be better. Stupid, huh?"

I watch her but don't say anything.

"I know he weren't gonna take me now. But back then I was just getting by, ya know? I didn't think it could ever be different. I didn't see what he was doin' to Trevor." And then quietly she adds, "And me."

I nod.

"When he was gone, I used to pretend he weren't comin' back. That it'd just be me and Trevor. But on Fridays I was glad to see him. I didn't like being alone. I still don't." She glances around, catches her image in the mirror, shakes her head. "And he took care of things. I ain't never had to take care of things before. Things like paying the rent or gettin' the cable hooked up." She takes a deep breath and pinches her nose. "But now I know I gotta. I have to do it for Trevor. And I've been learning stuff." At this she looks up at me and smiles. "I've been readin' some books. I used to love to read. I forgot that. Leroy'd get mad if I brought home books so I just stopped. He said it was a waste of money. But you got so many damn books at your place." She smiles at me and shakes her head. "And Esperanza downstairs, you know, Mike's old lady? She's been a good friend to me and she's teaching me how to cook healthy things. She don't speak English, but she don't need to. I understand what she's teaching me. I know I gotta do better. Being you wasn't what I thought it'd be. It don't mean nothing without Trevor. Here it was, I got to be the person I always wanted to be, but without Trevor, it kind of sucked. "

She's crying now as she looks at me. I nod. I know life would suck without Trevor. And without warning, I'm crying too.

"You kept callin' me and I didn't know what to say. And your mom, she never shut up. Never. I know she's your mom and all, but man, some days she just gets on my nerves." I smile at this. Poor Mom.

"I was goin' crazy, ya know? I was afraid to go out because someone might figure out I wasn't you and I was alone there, 'cept for my soaps and Esperanza. And I'm sorry about Scott. I didn't know what to do with him. I don't know why he kept comin' around." She pauses, then looks at me, "Was Scott really your boyfriend?"

I laugh. "Sort of."

Leann makes a face and wipes at her eyes, using her sleeve to wipe her nose. "Why did this happen?" She looks at me expectantly and I try to answer.

"I don't know, Leann. At first I thought it was a test and when I passed it would be over and everything would go back to the way it was. But that's not what it was. Maybe being you was something

I needed to do so that I could learn to be me. I think I've been playing at life, pretending to be all the things that I thought would make me happy. But I don't think I was really happy. And I don't think I was a very good person. I don't know if I'm either of those things now, but I think I'm closer.

"Trevor's a great kid. I'm gonna really miss him." I have to stop here for a moment because the idea of never seeing Trevor again makes it hard to breathe. "Do you think you could let me see him, or at least know how he is from time to time?"

"I could do that," Leann says through her tears. She reaches over and takes my hand. "Thank you, Carin."

I let go of her hand and stand up.

"What'll you do now?" she asks.

"I don't know," I say and I really don't know.

It's midday by the time they release us. We collect Trevor and a police officer drives us to my apartment. When we get inside I say, "I want you and Trevor to stay here."

"We can't do that."

"Yes, you can. Isn't there a whole bucket load of money coming in from the store? I don't want it. I don't think I want any of this. Besides, you can't take Trevor back to that awful apartment. He needs a fresh start." I wander aimlessly. I pick through my old makeup, marveling at the sheer quantity. I'm continually surprised by my reflection in the multiple mirrors in my old bedroom. Did I really need that much confirmation that I was beautiful? Maybe that's the greatest gift Leann has given me. For the first time in my life, I don't need a mirror to prove to me that I'm beautiful. I could feel my beauty when I looked in the eyes of Trevor or Jimmy. No mirror could ever give me that and no mirror will ever take it away.

I need to say goodbye to Trevor, but I don't know how. How do you say goodbye to a piece of your heart? He isn't mine to keep, as much as my soul will never really let go of him. I don't know how often Leann will let me see him, but I hope it's a lot. I kneel in front of him and he melts into my arms.

"I love you," I say into his curls.

"I know," he says back. "I love you, too."

"Thanks for letting me be your mom for a while." I hold him tightly. I don't ever want to let go, but finally I relax my grip and he looks up at me.

"You were a good mom. I like the way you read." A tear slips down his face too and I realize I have to pull it together. "Are you gonna marry Jimmy?"

I laugh.

"Will I still get to see Mr. G?" Trevor asks.

I look over his head at Leann. "I'll bet if you tell your mom about Mr. G, she'll take you to see him." Leann looks confused, but nods. I hug Trevor again. I want to memorize this feeling. Loving someone so much they're a part of you.

"You be a good boy for your mom. And you keep reading. Some day that bag of dreams just might come true," I say as I stand up, fighting back the tears and losing. I hold his hands and look him the eye and say, "Trevor, you are an amazing person. Stay who you are."

He smiles up at me, looking concerned. "I will. I'll stay me. You stay you, okay?"

I let go of his hand. "I will."

I don't know how to say goodbye to Leann. I'm not sure I can hug her. But before I can decide, she holds up her hands and asks me to wait. She disappears into the bedroom. When she returns, she has one of my best Coach handbags.

"It's just some cash and some lipstick." She smiles and hands it to me.

I smile too. She knows me. "Thanks," I say and turn to leave. I feel her hand on my arm. I turn. She has tears in her eyes.

"Thank you for looking out for Trevor," she pauses, then reaches out and wraps me in a hug. "And for me," she says softly.

As I walk down the sidewalk towards the rest of my life, I'm not sure which way to go. A thought crosses my heart, so I change directions and head to the Shop N Save. I'm in the store entrance where the extra carts are stashed and the bulletin board spills over with notices about complete bedroom sets and lost dogs. I stare

at the gaping automatic door and feel the whoosh of supermar-
ket air. It smells of disinfectant and overripe fruit. I breathe it in
deeply.

It seems like the first real breath I've had since this craziness
began. Who are we really? Am I the person everyone sees or the
person only I can see? Maybe this is a gift, this knowledge that
it's the heart that counts. The outside is just wallpaper—easily
changed.

I turn around and leave. I don't want anything in that store.
I walk around back to the loading dock. Sure enough, Jimmy is
there. He's always early for his shift. He's always exactly where I
need him to be.

As I approach, he looks at me questioningly. He doesn't know
who I am, but he sees me, smiles, and hops down off the dock.
Such a friendly soul.

"Can I help you?" he offers.

"I think so," I tell him. I jump up on the edge of the loading dock, dangling my feet and pat the spot next to me. He looks
confused.

"Do I know you?"

I smile and nod.

acknowledgments

Thanks to Angelique Zolomij and Conor Butler, the very first readers of this tale, whose enthusiasm for it gave me the courage to not only finish the story, but throw it out there in the world.

Thanks also to Lisa Weigard and Margot Tillitson who are always my most faithful readers. You overwhelm me with your generosity of time and feedback—lucky, lucky me.

Thanks also to Patricia Hazlebeck and Margie Geasler, serious bookaholics who read and loved the story and whose validation made me feel like a real writer. Yes, Margie, your book club can read it now!

I'm exceedingly grateful to Lou Aronica for plucking my manuscript from the multitudes that came his way and for his expert hand at making *I'm Not Her* a reality. Thanks also to the unknown eyeballs, hands, and hearts at Story Plant who shepherded this story through the high hills of publishing.

Thanks also to Tina Schwartz, of the Purcell Agency, for signing me right when I was about to throw in the towel and then showering me with her positive energy.

Thanks to my three favorite kiddos—Brady, Adelaide, and Ian, who challenge and inspire me in equal measure and are doing a great job of turning me into a better person.

Most of all, thanks to my incredible husband Nicholas, who lets me talk about my characters like they are friends of ours. He gets me—what more could a girl ask for? I am blessed.

FIC ACHTERBERG

Achterberg, Cara Sue.

I'm not her

AUG 2 0 2015

about the author

~ ~

Cara Sue Achterberg is a freelance writer and blogger who lives on a hillside in South Central, Pennsylvania with her remarkable children, adoring husband, quasi-obedient horses, completely non-obedient dog, occasional foster dogs, three perfect kitties, and a frequently changing number of chickens.

Her essays and articles have been published in numerous anthologies, national magazines, websites, and blogs. You can find links to her blogs, news about upcoming publications, and inspiration for teen writers at her website CaraWrites.com.